A Counterfeit Suitor

Darcie Wilde is the author of:

A Counterfeit Suitor

A Lady Compromised

And Dangerous to Know

A Purely Private Matter

A Useful Woman

A Counterfeit Suitor

DARCIE WILDE

KENSINGTON
PUBLISHING CORP.

www.kensingtonbooks.com

KENSINGTON BOOKS are published by

Kensington Publishing Corp.
119 West 40th Street
New York, NY 10018

All Kensington titles, imprints, and distributed lines are available at special quantity discounts for bulk purchases for sales promotion, premiums, fund-raising, educational, or institutional use. Special book excerpts or customized printings can also be created to fit specific needs. For details, write or phone the office of the Kensington Special Sales Manager: Attn. Special Sales Department. Kensington Publishing Corp, 119 West 40th Street, New York, NY 10018. Phone: 1-800-221-2647.

Library of Congress Card Catalogue Number: 2021940074

The K logo is a trademark of Kensington Publishing Corp.

ISBN: 978-1-4967-2088-7
First Kensington Hardcover Edition: December 2021

ISBN: 978-1-4967-2094-8 (e-book)

10 9 8 7 6 5 4 3 2 1

Printed in the United States of America

A Counterfeit Suitor

PROLOGUE

*Every trace of a gentleman is becoming effaced
from his nature; he who was once, they say, one
of the best dressed and most fashionable men
about town!*

Catherine Gore, *The Debutante*

Bath, December 1819

Sir Reginald Thorne's head ached. The scents of the coal
fire in the hearth and the burning candles on the table beside his desk wormed their way into his throat. It left him
parched. He tried to focus on the half-written letter in front
of him, but his vision would not stay steady. He knuckled his
eyes and blinked hard, but it was no good.

"Get me my drink," snapped Sir Reginald to the liveried
servant seated beside the hearth.

"You've had your drink, sir," replied the man without
glancing up from the book he was reading.

"Well, bring me another. There's plenty in this house, I
know it."

"I can bring, sir, a cup of tea, or chocolate, or coffee if he
prefers, although at this time of night I would not recommend it."

"If I'd wanted coffee, I would have asked for it. I said bring me a drink!"

The man sighed and turned a page of his book. He was a tall, raw-boned fellow dressed in good livery with a well-kept wig perched on his head. From the look of him, a person might assume this was the personal servant of an indulgent master. They would have been wrong.

A proper servant would have remained standing in a gentleman's presence, no matter how late it grew. A proper servant would not remain insolently at leisure in a room when his master desires him heartily to be gone.

This man was a guard and he knew it, and Sir Reginald knew it. He was there not on Sir Reginald's sufferance, but at his daughter's orders. Those orders were to make sure Sir Reginald remained a captive.

Sir Reginald buried his head in his hands. It was hopeless. It had always been hopeless. Ever since his daughter Charlotte had brought him to this house and given him over to these men. His favorite child. The one person in the world he had believed would never betray him. He'd shared all the wonders of the world with her, depended absolutely on her companionship, and this is what she did to him. Turned whore and locked him up in this miserable little house in Bath, of all places! He who was welcomed at the tables of kings! Now he couldn't even walk down the street on his own.

I never should have trusted her. I should have taken Rosalind with me instead.

No. Not her.

He still remembered what happened the last time he saw her. Did she open her arms and her heart to him as a grateful child should? Did her eyes shine with joyful tears to see her father had at last returned? Not she! Instead, she'd stood on the staircase, her face sick and white and so uncomely he could not in that moment believe they shared any blood at all. She did not lift a finger as her minions—her so-called godfather!—turned him away.

Damn, but he wanted that drink.

He glanced at the guard but gave it up as a bad business. The man would not see reason, as Sir Reginald knew from a hundred nights of trying to persuade, cajole, or, once—wretched memory!—even pleading. He could not be made to understand that when a gentleman had been through so many disappointments and betrayals, he should be allowed a gentleman's solace. But no, the she-wolves Sir Reginald had sired were determined to withhold even that much from him.

"Daughters," Sir Reginald sneered at his guard. "Leprosy would be less of a curse than daughters."

"I'm sure you're right, sir," replied the guard placidly

"Haven't any yourself, have you?"

"Not that I'm aware of."

Sir Reginald felt his mouth twist into a bitter smile.

"Ready for bed, sir?" inquired the guard.

Truth was, he was tired, but Sir Reginald was in no humor to make things easy on his guard.

"I have this letter to finish. I'll thank you not to disturb me."

"Very good, sir," he said calmly.

He picked up his pen, dipped it carefully in the ink, and addressed himself again to the letter he'd been writing. *I'm not forgotten yet*, he assured himself. Not yet. *Even the she-wolves cannot get to all my friends.*

He read the last line over:

> *I daresay you wonder at not having heard from me in so long, but I have been much abroad recently, recouping my health after having suffered from a bout of*

Sir Reginald rubbed his forehead. What had it been? What could he say? He had indeed been ill, he knew that. Gravely ill. That was what caused these sweats and blurred his vision.

And still his guards kept away the wine and brandy that would strengthen him. This deprivation was, of course, the she-wolf's doing. She wanted to keep him weak and confused. Unnatural being that she was.

illness, he wrote. *However, I am now returned to England, and finding myself lodged at Bath, I*

"What the devil?" muttered the guard.

Sir Reginald jerked himself around. He'd been so focused on the task of writing, he hadn't noticed anything else. The guard was on his feet, the book tossed aside. He hurried to the window and pushed back the drapes. The light that entered now was strangely orange and flickering.

There shouldn't have been any light outside at all. It was well past ten o'clock.

The guard struggled with the window latch and threw the sash up. At once, a wave of heat and the acrid smoke blew into the room.

"Fire!" The shout rang up from the street. "Fire!"

The guard at once bolted for the door. "Reynolds!" he shouted. "Morgan! Get to the pump! There's a fire!"

"Fire!" came the shout outside again. "Fire!"

The guard ran down the stairs, leaving the door open behind him.

Sir Reginald laid his pen down. His heart was beating rapidly, but not from fear. The roar and crackle of the flames intensified. He stole softly to the window. The street outside was filling rapidly with people, some carrying buckets and others blankets. The smell of smoke grated on the back of his throat.

But here he stood in his little jail cell of a room, quite alone, with the door opened wide.

He listened. Below there was clattering and men's voices shouting. It was hard to tell which of the noises came from inside and which from outside. His mouth had gone dry. His ears rang.

He was in his shirt sleeves and slippers, but he did not dare take time to dress. He ran for the boudoir and grabbed a jacket and pair of boots from the wardrobe.

What of money? Sir Reginald shook his head. He'd worry about that later. He still had his watch, the chain, his signet ring. He could raise money enough on those to get him started.

A drink. A ticket for the mail coach to London. Humiliating way to travel, but needs must . . .

Sir Reginald clutched boots and jacket to his chest and tiptoed to the door. He listened, straining his ears with all his might. His hand trembled. He clutched his bundle harder.

Nothing. That noise is all outside. Hurry!

As softly as he might, he stole down the stairs. Surely his guards had gone out the back way. Surely the foyer would be empty. Fate would be kind, this once.

A trickle of sweat ran down his temple, but he didn't dare lift a hand to wipe it away. His throat was dry as dust.

Never mind. Never mind. A drink first. Then a ticket to London. My friends will remember me. The she-wolves will soon regret their treatment of their father.

There was the door.

His slipper toe caught the edge of the foyer carpet, sending him stumbling forward. He slammed up against the central table. The china vase tipped over, spilling water everywhere. He caught the vase before it crashed to the tiles, but dropped his jacket and boots. He stayed there in that ridiculous posture, holding vase and table, trembling and terrified.

No sound other came from inside the house. The racket remained safely outside.

Sir Reginald sucked in a breath. He released the vase and bent down to gather up his jacket and boots. Then, he bolted out the front door.

The cobbles were slick under his slippers and he stumbled.

He was able to right himself but fumbled his boots and jacket.

Won't do. Must remember who I am. A gentleman remains a gentleman. No matter what the circumstance.

Sir Reginald straightened his shoulders and lifted his chin. In this confident attitude, he started down the street. He had no idea where he was going, but he'd get his bearings soon. He was not exactly a stranger to Bath, after all. He'd find a public house soon, and there, after he got that drink, he'd get directions to the post house, and maybe even be able to find a buyer for his watch.

"Sir Reginald?"

The hail stopped Sir Reginald in his tracks. Panic filled him, and for a moment, he considered running.

Never. A gentleman is always a gentleman.

He turned. He fixed the importunate stranger with a withering glower.

"Do I know you, sir?"

The stranger was gray haired with pale skin and pale eyes. He was well dressed in high-crowned hat, caped coat, leather gloves, and top boots. He carried a silver-handled walking stick. It was, however, his easy and confident bearing that told Sir Reginald this was a man of some standing.

"We have met, a long time ago," said the stranger. "My name is Fullerton."

He presented a credible bow. Sir Reginald nodded warily. At the same time he racked his brains. *Fullerton, Fullerton? Where have I met a Fullerton?*

Nothing came. Thirst and the urgency of getting out of sight of the house clogged his mind.

But the man did not seem to notice Sir Reginald's hesitation.

"I was hoping you might agree to join me for a drink, sir," Fullerton went on pleasantly.

"My carriage"—he pointed his stick toward an enclosed vehicle pulled by a pair of dark horses—"stands ready to take us back to my establishment, where the surroundings are quieter and the port is, if I do say so myself, very good."

A drink.

And one for which he would not have to go through the humiliation of selling his watch, or the risk of seeing what he could raise in a card game.

His face does look familiar. Perhaps we met in Paris. Yes. Surely it was Paris.

"Thank you, Mr. Fullerton." Sir Reginald moistened his lips. "It has been far too long since I have been able to accept a friendly drink in civilized company."

"Well, we must remedy that directly." Fullerton smiled. "I am entirely at your disposal, Sir Reginald."

He bowed again and gestured. His coachman was clearly as superior as his master. That man jumped down from the box at once to open the carriage door.

Sir Reginald nodded with dignity and crossed to the vehicle. The coachman held out his hands for Sir Reginald's things. He surrendered them and climbed in. The inside was well upholstered, and the vehicle felt well sprung. Sir Reginald felt himself relax at once.

It occurred to him to wonder about this man appearing at such an hour, just at the time when Sir Reginald happened to be walking into the street. Well, it was no matter. Once he'd had that drink to steady nerve and mind, he'd be able to question the man more closely. If there was aught amiss, he'd ferret it out soon enough.

Fullerton also climbed in and arranged himself on the seat opposite. The coachman secured the door and climbed up on the box.

"I cannot tell you how pleased I am at this opportunity to renew our acquaintance." Fullerton rapped the handle of his cane on the ceiling. "I've had to delay that pleasure much longer than I would have liked. But you understand how business affairs may come to occupy a man's time."

"Oh yes, of course," replied Sir Reginald. Why were they still standing here? Could not that stupid coachman get these nags to move? The alarm would be raised soon. The coach would be stopped. He'd be dragged back to that pestilent little house, confined, humiliated, dry . . .

"Walk on!" the coachman called to the team. The harness jingled, the horses' hoofs clattered against stone, and the carriage began to move.

Sir Reginald moistened his lips again. He wiped the sweat from his temple.

"You must excuse me for the state you find me in," he said, belatedly. "The truth is . . ."

"The truth is sometimes a gentleman must avail himself of opportunity the moment it arrives," said Fullerton. "I only hope this is the first of many opportunities you and I may share. Right after we share that drink."

Sir Reginald smiled and settled back. It was full dark outside, but suddenly the world seemed brighter to him than it had in some time.

CHAPTER 1

An Unexpected Caller

The vast extension of society in London . . . has necessitated a degree of caution in the formation of intimacy.

Catherine Gore, *The Banker's Wife*

London, December 1819

"He says yes!"

Alice's shout jolted Rosalind from contemplation of her latest piece of correspondence. So did the fact that her friend leapt to her feet and began dancing about the small parlor, waving a piece of paper over her head.

"He said yes! He said yes!"

"Is that a letter from Mr. Colburn?" asked Rosalind mildly. Alice Littlefield supported herself as a writer, a translator, and gossip columnist. Last year, however, Alice had received an invitation from the publisher, Henry Colburn, to submit a novel manuscript.

"And he said yes!" Alice thrust the letter at Rosalind and recommended her exuberant dance.

Rosalind read:

Dear Miss Littlefield:

I trust this letter finds you in the very best of health. I am writing to inform you that I have finished reading the manuscript for Eversward, *which you were so good as to submit for my consideration. I found the novel delightful in its entirety and I have no doubt the reading public will as well.*

I should very much like to request the honor of calling on you at your earliest convenience to discuss matters relating to publication, so that we may put your excellent tale before the waiting world as soon as possible.

Your Obedient Servant,
Henry Colburn

"Alice, this is wonderful!" Rosalind got to her feet and embraced her friend. The two women were a study in contrasts. Alice was tiny, quick, and dark, whereas Rosalind was tall, pale, and statuesque with darkly golden hair and a pair of steady blue eyes.

"Of course, I knew he would accept," Alice said loftily. "Being such an excellent judge of literary merit."

"Of course," Rosalind answered with perfect sobriety. The pair of them stared at each other for a full ten seconds before bursting into laughter. The fact was that in the month since she'd taken Mr. Colburn her manuscript, Alice had been scarcely able to sit still for five minutes altogether. It was something of a trial on their friendship, because at that same time, Alice had also moved into Rosalind's house in Little Russell Street.

Alice fell back into her chair by the window. Rosalind's small parlor had been made even more cramped by the addition of a table that was perpetually piled with Alice's books and papers, not to mention her portable writing desk and assorted ink pots. Rosalind kept her desk with its neat stacks of correspondence and account and visiting books beside the hearth.

"Oh, I can't wait to see the look on my dear brother's face when I tell him!" Alice crowed. "He was so set against the idea for so long."

"You cannot entirely blame him," said Rosalind. "It was a risky proposition. Your editor at the *Chronicle* could have taken offense."

"Never. The Major was thrilled when I told him. The possibility that his gossip column might now be written by a 'celebrated novelist' has him counting new sales in his sleep." Alice grinned broadly. "We must celebrate, Rosalind! Where shall we go? What should we do?"

"I'm so sorry, Alice, I can't tonight. I must keep my appointment with Mrs. Walford to attend the opera."

"Oh! It's the season opening! This letter from Mr. Colburn drove it right out of my head. Have you heard from Sanderson yet?"

"This is his letter here." She held up the piece of correspondence. "He reports that he was entirely successful in his errand and will meet me in the salon tonight."

Like Alice, Rosalind lived in what was frequently termed "distressed circumstances." Her life had begun promisingly enough. She was the younger daughter of a charming baronet who was prized as a party guest by all the best hostesses. Her mother had charted her course through London's social networks with a skill that got her into the visiting books of some of the city's most prominent ladies. Rosalind had even attracted the attention of Devon Winterbourne, the younger son of the Duke of Casselmaine.

Then it had all gone wrong. Rosalind's charming and delightful father had fallen into debt. Sir Reginald has always gambled, but debt tempted him deeper into gaming and speculation. When none of this was enough, and his friends began to turn away his begging letters, he turned to forging letters of credit.

At last, unable to find his way out of the morass he made, her father fled. He left behind nothing but the ashes of burnt dunning notices and a letter assuring his wife and youngest daughter of his eternal love.

His oldest daughter, Charlotte, he took with him.

It had been too much for Rosalind's mother. She had supported Sir Reginald with every ounce of her energy, and he had abandoned her. Her nerves snapped. When she died, Rosalind was left to make her own way.

With help from her mother's friends, Rosalind learned to apply her talent for organization and her understanding of London's social world to help these ladies of the *haut ton* manage their households and their seasons. Gradually, she developed a reputation for being a useful woman for the ambitious hostess to know, and cultivate. This allowed her a genteel, if frugal, living and kept her at least on the periphery of the world in which she was raised.

Two years ago, however, Rosalind's world had changed again. A murder had occurred at the most improbable location—the ballroom at the famous Almack's Assembly Rooms. Rosalind was engaged to make sure no taint of scandal became attached to the assembly rooms, or to its famous patronesses. In the end, Rosalind had done this and discovered the murderer as well.

Now, Rosalind continued her life as a "useful" woman, but the requests for help with particularly delicate matters became more frequent. She found herself consulted by a number of powerful families of London who wanted, or needed, to be preserved from scandal, and even prison.

It was in this capacity she was engaged to attend the opera this evening.

"You know, Rosalind, I've been on the verge of becoming annoyed with you about this current business of yours," Alice said. "You have been more than usually secretive about it."

"I'm sorry, Alice. The truth is, I've been rather uncertain about it all."

Alice detected the change in Rosalind's tone and the light in her eye. "Well, perhaps if you'd tell me what it is . . ."

Rosalind smiled. "I will, and right now, because I'm going to need your help. You see, about a month ago I was approached by a Mrs. Walford, on the recommendation of Mrs. Gregory. Mrs. Walford said she wanted to give a charity ball to raise money for the widows and orphans of the late wars, before the *ton* scatters for Christmas."

"But what Mrs. Walford really wanted . . ." Alice leaned forward eagerly.

"Was for someone to look into the background of a young man her daughter had met," said Rosalind. "Mr. Horatio Salter."

"Oh wait, this was the man we came upon so conveniently at Mrs. Holding's private concert last month? The concert you suggested that George and Hannah and I should attend with you?"

"It was also where George was so enormously helpful in getting Mr. Salter talking about all his school chums."

"And you immediately set about seeing which of the sisters and mothers of those school chums you were acquainted with, so you could start asking leading questions about Mr. Salter?"

"Exactly," said Rosalind. "Miss Augustina Walford is an heiress, not on the heroic scale, but respectable. The family is from Manchester, so they do not have the connections among the London *ton* to thoroughly inquire into a suitor's background for themselves. This leaves them vulnerable to fortune hunters."

"Not to mention the fact that the London *ton* will surely look down their very long noses at any Manchester soap manufacturer seeking advice."

"Gingham," Rosalind corrected her. "And yes. Despite the fact that Mrs. Walford was raised in London, the family has received all the usual snubs. That is part of what the charity ball is meant to assist with. In the meantime, I have been able to unearth a number of salient facts about the man who wishes to ensnare Miss Augustina Walford."

Rosalind pulled a stack of letters out of her desk. Alice took them and scanned the pages quickly. "Oh, Rosalind! I mean, I expected debt, but . . . he was part of the 1814 stock fraud?" The fraud had been a major scandal. It started with a rumor in a coffeehouse saying Napoleon was dead. That rumor had spread and mushroomed into a stock-buying spree that had cost the public millions of pounds, ruined whole families, and nearly crashed the entire market.

"A minor player, but yes, he was instrumental in spreading those initial rumors."

"Well, that seems all very straightforward." Alice leafed through the letters. "He's a fraudulent fortune hunter, and mother's instincts have saved the day. What is it that's made you uncertain?"

"I don't know," Rosalind sighed. "It's something about Miss Walford herself. She shows all the signs of being attached to Mr. Salter, but there's a way she looks at him, and at me sometimes, like she's suspicious."

"Could she have guessed that you're checking up on her fiancé? If my mother did any such thing, I would have been furious!"

"I know. I just wish I felt more certain. There's something at my fingertips, but I can't quite get hold of it."

"Well, you will," said Alice. "You always do. Perhaps it will happen tonight."

"Yes, it very well might. The plan is that Sanderson Faulks

and I will be creating a small scene at the opera, one that will involve Mr. Salter. I hope A.E. Littlefield will write up the incident and include mention of some shocking information"—Rosalind tapped the letters in Alice's hands—"that has come to his attention."

"Well, as delighted as I'm sure the Major would be to unearth a member of such a notorious fraud, shouldn't this go to Bow Street? Or even Parliament?"

"Unfortunately, what we have is rumor—repeated rumor, but rumor all the same. Coupled with what has been confirmed about Mr. Salter's debts and gaming habits, I'm sure it is true, but I don't have definite proof yet. I'm hoping that will come next."

"I'll get these to George right away," said Alice. Like Alice, George wrote for the *Chronicle*, but was generally assigned to what Alice referred to as the "richer" stories. "He can write the main article. It will be a change from writing about Bonapartists."

"Bonapartists?"

"Yes, it seems England and France are both absolutely riddled with secret societies of Bonapartists. All with terribly dramatic names—the *Carbonari*, the Friends of This, the Society of That, The Congregation . . . oh no, wait, those are supporters of the Bourbons . . . anyway, the country is full of such societies, half of them are dining at Holland House and trying to get motions passed in Parliament. The other half is sending money to his brother in Philadelphia, or is it Mexico now?"

"Whose brother?"

"Napoleon's! His brother Louis is settled in America, working on fomenting revolution and setting his brother up a new empire just as soon as all these secret societies manage to get him off St. Helena. There was talk of a hot-air balloon, but that seems to have gone nowhere. The submarine is apparently rather more promising. Although, if I were to place a bet, I'd favor the corsairs who are being outfitted in Argentina. Honestly, Rosalind, don't you read the papers?"

Rosalind could not tell from her friend's face whether Alice was serious about any of this. "Forgive me," she said blandly. "I'm afraid I've been rather busy of late." Since summer, she had been answering an increasing number of pleas from ladies who wanted her help. The benefit to their household budget was measurable, but it was taking a great toll on Rosalind's reserves of energy and concentration.

"Yes, of course," said Alice. "Well, as I say, I will get these to George, and I'm sure he'll appreciate the change. Not a secret society in the bunch." She waved the letters like a fan, but then some motion outside the window caught her eye. "Rosalind, were you expecting any calls today?"

"No, no one."

"Well, there's a lady hurrying up to your, that is, our door."

Rosalind came to her friend's side and looked out the window. A slender woman in a plain, dark coat and a broad, concealing bonnet with plenty of lace trimming was walking up the street, and mounted the steps to Rosalind's door.

It was impossible to see her face from this angle, but Rosalind's breath grew short anyway.

Why would she come here?

A moment later, the new housemaid, Amelia, came into the parlor. "A lady to see you, Miss Thorne. She sent this in." She held out a card. "She said you would know her."

Rosalind took the card without reading it. "Yes, I know her."

"Rosalind?" began Alice, but Rosalind shook her head. Alice would see soon enough who their visitor was. Right now, she could not trust herself to speak.

The parlor door opened and the maid stood back to let their visitor enter. Rosalind rose slowly to her feet. Alice openly gaped.

The woman was a bit older than Rosalind, and thoroughly out of breath. Her dress was plain, but its blue woolen fabric and cream trim were of the highest quality. Its skirt was fuller, and its waist was lower than current fashion, hinting that changes in the mode were soon to come. Her honey-gold hair was simply but stunningly arranged. Her face was a perfect, pale oval, and she was tall enough to look Rosalind directly in the eye. But where Rosalind's form was generously curved, this new arrival was slim as a willow wand.

Her clear blue eyes, though, were strikingly similar to Rosalind's own.

"Hello, Charlotte," said Rosalind to her sister.

"Hello, Rosalind," replied Charlotte. "Hello, Alice."

"Charlotte." Alice swallowed. "This is . . . a surprise."

"Yes, I'm sorry. But something . . . it's very urgent." She hesitated. "Rosalind, I think we had best speak in private."

"There's nothing you can say that Alice can't hear," said Rosalind. Her sister's cheeks were pale, and there were dark rings under her eyes. Rosalind felt her chest tighten with sudden fear. "What's happened?"

"It's father," Charlotte said. "He's escaped me."

CHAPTER 2

The Past Made All Too Present

*You might dressed elegant as the most elegant
lady in London . . . and you would have servants
of your own, and a carriage of your own, and
nothing to do day long but take your pleasure.
And, after all, what is asked of you?—only to
make a person happy.*

Maria Edgeworth, *The Dun*

Escaped. Rosalind felt her knees tremble.

Alice was at her side at once. "Sit down, Rosalind, you've gone quite pale."

"Yes." Rosalind let her friend steer her toward her desk chair. She sat. She smoothed her skirts reflexively. But as she tried to force her thoughts past Charlotte's abrupt revelation, they would not move.

"You sit as well, Charlotte," directed Alice. She threw open the parlor door. The housemaid was already there, looking startled and guilty. "Coffee, Amelia," said Alice sharply. She also closed the door.

"Mrs. Kendricks is no longer with you?" murmured Charlotte absently. Despite Alice's offer of a chair, Charlotte remained on her feet, pacing back and forth in the limited space the parlor afforded.

The sight of her agitation was another blow. Charlotte was a highly successful courtesan. Her particular skills included being able to maintain a calm and cheerful façade, no matter what the provocation.

"Charlotte, how did this happen?" asked Rosalind.

"I don't know." Charlotte yanked on her bonnet ribbon and pulled it off, revealing how very pinched and white her face had become. She looked around for somewhere to put her hat. Rosalind rose and took it from her. Alice shoved aside a pile of books to create a small, clear space.

This done, Charlotte perched on the very edge of the canebottomed chair, her back ramrod straight. Fear and frustration filled her eyes. In her dark cloak, she looked far too young and too frail to be the worldly woman Rosalind knew her to be.

It was this sight that forced Rosalind's thoughts back into motion.

"Tell me what you do know," she said.

Charlotte nodded once. "I received a letter from Drummond, one of the men I've hired to care for Father since we returned to England. He told me that a fire broke out in an alley near the house. Father took advantage of the distraction to flee.

"At first, Drummond was not truly concerned. He expected to find Father in some nearby drinking establishment. Father is kept on a strict ration of spirits," she added. "It is enough to keep him quiet, but not enough to, well, completely satisfy him.

"It was only when Drummond failed to find him in the pubs that he became alarmed and wrote to me."

"When was this?" asked Rosalind.

"Four days ago," said Charlotte.

"Four days!" cried Alice. "And you waited this long to come tell us?"

Charlotte drew herself up. "I have had the sole management of my father for quite some time. You will forgive me if my first impulse was not to come running to the sister with whom I have barely spoken for nearly seven years."

Alice looked ready to give a sharp retort, which would not be at all helpful.

"Did you go to Bath?" Rosalind asked quickly.

Charlotte's face tightened.

"I did. We were able to find a man who said he saw father climbing into an enclosed carriage, but that was all. It is as if he's vanished into thin air." Charlotte's voice shook.

"Could he have hired a carriage?" asked Rosalind.

"No, he was not allowed any money."

Rosalind considered. "Some friend, then?"

"But who?" Charlotte spread her hands. "Since we returned to England, he has not been able to send any letter that my man has not read. There have been no visitors to the house. When he ventures out, he is strictly supervised."

"Could he have bribed one of the day servants to carry a letter for him?"

"With what?" Charlotte demanded. "I told you, he has no money."

"Jewelry," said Alice promptly. "A watch, a snuff box, a stick pin. A pretty promise."

Charlotte hesitated. "I did question the servants, but I was in such a hurry . . . I suppose it is possible."

She was not able to add anything, because at that moment, Amelia entered the parlor carrying Rosalind's massive silver coffee tray.

"Good heavens," murmured Charlotte. "Of all the things we had, you kept *that*?"

The elaborate setting dwarfed the side table Amelia set it on.

"Well, it is the family plate," murmured Rosalind.

"That's no excuse."

Amelia stood back, blushing, and Rosalind sent her from the room. As soon as the door closed, Alice moved the tray to her much sturdier writing table.

Rosalind got up to pour out the coffee and hand around the cups. "Sugar?" she asked her sister.

"Yes, please," answered Charlotte. There was no mistaking the relief in her voice. Rosalind found herself wondering when it was Charlotte last ate.

Rosalind hoped the homey act of pouring and serving the coffee and passing the biscuits (slightly burned at the edges) would help steady her. It was a vain hope. Too many memories forced themselves to the surface of her mind. She remembered all the long, sleepless nights after Father and Charlotte ran away. She had laid awake constructing endless reasons, or at least excuses, to explain what he'd done. She'd found a thousand ways to blame her mother and her sister instead. She'd even blamed herself.

She remembered the last time she'd seen Sir Reginald. She'd been living with her godparents, and he'd forced his way into the house. He was drunk and railing at the heavens, and at her. Her father, whom she still loved in the deep corners of her heart, was demanding money and accusing her of the vilest possible behavior—dishonesty, disloyalty, and even prostitution, although that was not the word he used.

Rosalind remembered staring down at him from the stairway while he heaped abuse on her and her godparents. She remembered the shame that flooded her.

And now he is free again. To go where? To do what? Rosalind added several biscuits to Charlotte's plate and held out the cup and saucer for her. Charlotte accepted them wordlessly and drank.

Alice waved Rosalind back from the coffee set and served herself.

"Where do you think he's gone?" Alice asked Charlotte.

Charlotte nibbled at one of the biscuits. "I am assuming he would come to London."

"To this house?" asked Rosalind.

Charlotte swallowed and set the dry biscuit down. "Possibly. Or it may be he turns up on the doorstep of some old friend. Although I cannot imagine who would take him in. He certainly won't try to find me, except perhaps to exact some form of revenge." Her voice shook again.

"After all the years you cared for and supported him," said Rosalind.

Charlotte looked down into her coffee. Rosalind wondered what memories had risen in her mind. They might be on speaking terms again, but Charlotte had not yet told her anything of her years of exile in Paris, nor of how she'd begun her career as part of the *demimonde*.

"To Father's way of thinking, it makes no difference what support I might have given him in the past," said Charlotte. "I couldn't give him what he really wanted—the restoration of fortune and reputation." Her words all had ragged edges, as if they were torn from some deep place. "Therefore, eventually, I was added to his list of enemies."

"You could have abandoned him."

Charlotte met Rosalind's gaze directly. "And you could have abandoned our mother."

Which was, of course, nothing but the truth. *But what good does it do either of us?* Rosalind tried to regain a grip on her renegade thoughts. Memory, pride, and recriminations could all be indulged in later. She must deal with what was before her. She could not see where her father was, or what he was doing, but Charlotte was here in this room. She had come here pale and shaken beyond anything Rosalind had ever seen. She spoke of revenge, and her calm voice trembled. These were facts, and she must pay attention to this as well.

"Has something else happened, Charlotte?"

Charlotte looked up at her, and for the first time since they were girls together, Rosalind saw the sheen of tears in her sister's eyes.

"I am . . . I was . . . to be married."

CHAPTER 3

A Change of Circumstance

*In this marriage . . . I secure a place in the world,
which I flatter myself I shall be able to fill with
effect at all events.*

Theodore Edward Hook, *Cousin William*, or
The Fatal Attachment

"Whh . . ." began Rosalind, at the same time Alice
said, "But . . ."

"But I'm a notorious courtesan. What man would agree to
take me as his wife?" snapped Charlotte.

"Yes," said Alice flatly and without shame.

The look Charlotte turned on her was filled as much with
contempt as pity. "And you have made your living with the
gossip of London's ballrooms for how many years now? You
know very well that if a man is rich enough, he may marry
whom he chooses. Well, I have been chosen."

It seemed to Rosalind the best thing to do was shift the
subject. "And this man—your intended—does not know
about Father?" said Rosalind.

"He thinks Father is ill and taking the waters under a doc-
tor's care. I did not . . . I could not hazard the whole truth.

Rosalind, if he . . . my fiancé finds out, he will drop me entirely. I know that he will."

Rosalind felt herself frown. She had only recently come back into acquaintance with her sister, but up until this moment, Charlotte had seemed perfectly comfortable with her role in the *demimonde*. She had even expressed a preference for her situation over the protected, but much confined, role of wife. *What has changed?*

One immediate possibility occurred to her.

"Charlotte, are you with child?"

Charlotte's hand stole to her abdomen, and that was answer enough.

"And your fiancé has agreed to acknowledge the child?"

"It is one thing if I decide to dare the world's opinion for how I live," said Charlotte. "I am not prepared to make that decision for a child of mine."

Rosalind nodded. Above and beyond the social stigma of bastardy, there were a number of laws that placed limitations on any child born out of wedlock. If that child was a boy, there were schools and professions he could not enter. Any right of inheritance could be easily and legally denied him, even if he was the eldest child. If the child was a daughter, well, it did not matter how well connected the father was, the opportunities for a good marriage would instantly vanish.

"How has your fiancé taken the news?" Rosalind asked.

Charlotte's mouth twitched, like she was trying to smile but could not quite remember how. "He's thrilled. He has no other children and finds the idea of becoming a father at his age rather . . . charming."

"I'm glad for you," said Rosalind.

Charlotte looked at her and saw she meant it. "Thank you."

"Can you not find some way to explain the truth about our father?"

"It is one thing for a man to make his mistress his wife," said Charlotte. "It is another to take on responsibility for a forger, a debtor, a drunkard—" She bit the words off and began again. "It is my own fault. I lied to him. How could I have known it would ever matter? But now, if I am caught out in this lie, what else will he begin to doubt?" Her fingers flexed. "I should have known my situation would become insupportable. I should have taken steps while I had the chance."

The soft anger in those words sent a shiver up Rosalind's spine. "What more could you have done?"

Charlotte did not answer, which only deepened Rosalind's sudden chill.

"We must find our father," said Charlotte. "Before he has the chance to destroy us both."

She was right, of course. Rosalind's position, if anything, was more delicate than Charlotte's. As a woman alone, Rosalind maintained her social standing only as long as she maintained her reputation for gentility and respectability. The revelation of a criminal connection could cause the ladies she depended on to desert her in droves.

The answer was obvious. Rosalind wished it wasn't.

She set down her coffee cup. "Charlotte, have you any money?"

"Some. Yes."

"Very well. This is beyond what we will be able to do ourselves. We must hire one of the Bow Street runners to search for him. The fee will be high, but we have no time for anything else. The longer our father is free, the greater the risks." Even just talking about the actions they could take heartened Rosalind. Anything was better than letting memory and fear roll over her in their chilling waves.

"Rosalind," said Alice. "You can't mean to enlist Adam Harkness?"

Adam Harkness was a principal officer of the Bow Street police station. He and Rosalind had met while she was trying to unravel the scandal at Almack's Assembly Rooms. Since then, he had helped her through a number of difficult, and violent, situations. Rosalind knew him to be honest, diligent, intelligent, and kind.

She felt Alice watching her, and resolutely refused to blush. Because Adam Harkness made no secret of the fact that he harbored feelings for Rosalind. That she returned those feelings was something Rosalind had only been able to acknowledge carefully, and briefly. At least, so far.

But her personal regard for Mr. Harkness was not something she chose to discuss at this time. She ignored Alice and kept her focus on her sister.

"I will only contact him if you agree, Charlotte," Rosalind said. "We can trust him to be discreet."

It was a long time before Charlotte spoke again. "Do you know what is so ridiculous?" she murmured. "Even now, after all Father has done and destroyed, all I can think is how humiliating it would be for him to be brought before the court. What does that say about me?"

"As much as it says about me," said Rosalind. "Because I'm thinking the same thing."

Charlotte rose to her feet again. She paced the length of the room, once, twice, three times. Alice stared out the window, her face set in a frown. Rosalind knew her friend was holding back a great deal.

I'll thank her later.

"It's the decision I never wanted to make," she said. "Whatever he's done, he remains my, our, father."

"I know," said Rosalind. "But has he left us any choice?"

"No good ones," muttered Charlotte. "Very well, hire your Mr. Harkness. I will pay the fees. I will also write Drummond again and ask him to press the day servants, in case you're right about the bribery, Alice."

"I rather hope I am," she admitted.

"Pride?" Charlotte tried to force some drawing-room cynicism into the word.

"Not a bit," replied Alice tartly. "But it would mean he found his own way out, which would be preferable to the other immediate possibility."

"That someone came to fetch him for their own reasons?" asked Rosalind.

"Yes," said Alice.

Charlotte pressed her gloved hand against her mouth, her eyes wide. Rosalind wanted to go to her, to offer some comfort. But before she could get to her feet, Charlotte had shifted her whole attitude, becoming at once an aloof and dignified beauty, poised as if to enter a ballroom.

It was like watching her put on her armor. *Perhaps that's what it is.*

"Thank you for your offer of help, Rosalind," Charlotte said. "I'm afraid I must go. I'm expected elsewhere."

"I will see you out."

Rosalind handed Charlotte her bonnet and walked with her into the foyer. Fortunately, Amelia was nowhere in evidence.

Charlotte faced her. "I am sorry about this, you know. I kept him as best I could."

A hundred memories and a dozen regrets flooded Rosalind. She'd always felt that Charlotte was the cannier of the two of them. When she'd gone with their glamorous father, Rosalind had envied her, missed her, and felt sorely betrayed by her. Now she longed for nothing so much as some way to simply have her sister back.

But that could never happen. They had both been changed too much. Whatever came next for them, it would have to be some new kind of relationship.

If anything can come after this.

Despite her doubts, Rosalind reached out and pressed her

sister's hand. "We will find him," she said firmly. "Our father is many things, but subtle and careful are not among
them."

The sound Charlotte made might almost have been called
a snort. "No. That's true enough." She paused and then covered Rosalind's hand where it rested on her own. "Rosalind,
will you take care? I'm afraid Alice might be right. There
might be something driving this disaster besides our father's
desire for freedom."

Despite their danger and the years and doubts that separated them, Rosalind felt a thread of warmth slip through her
uneasy heart. "I don't mean to simply engage Mr. Harkness.
I'll be opening other inquiries of my own, and I'll write the
minute I have any word."

Charlotte raised one elegant brow.

"You must trust me, Charlotte. I do have some small
expertise in this area. If, as you suspect, there is something more to this business, the sooner we can discover it,
the better."

"I daresay you are right, as you are the one with experience." She tried to make a joke of it, but the words were
forced. "Rosalind . . . since you and Alice are sharing rooms,
may I take it that you've made your decision concerning
Lord Casselmaine?"

Rosalind tried not to wince at the change of subject. "I am
not going to marry him, if that's what you mean. I will continue as I am at present."

"I suspect that some outsider might find our shifted situations ironic."

"I suspect they might," agreed Rosalind.

Charlotte smiled, and this time, Rosalind saw a hint of the
girl she used to be—the one who whispered and giggled in
the schoolroom. The one who sat beside Rosalind in cold
and frightened silence as they listened to the angry quarrels

that no one in the house would ever speak of. The one who could sum up any occupant of a drawing room with a single tart phrase and conquer the heart of any man she turned her attentions toward.

Charlotte turned away without another word. Her coat hems rippled in the stiff autumnal breeze as she hurried up the street to where a plain, enclosed carriage was waiting.

All Rosalind could do was stand and watch.

CHAPTER 4

Urgent Correspondence

On the hint of scandal thus afforded, it was not difficult . . . to embroider with ingenuity.

Catherine Gore, *The Debutante*

The instant Rosalind returned to the parlor, she collided with Alice, who wrapped her in a warm embrace.

"Oh, Rosalind! How awful! What will you do?"

"Exactly what I said." Rosalind hugged her friend, once, hard. Then she moved aside to her desk. "I will write to Mr. Harkness at once, and after that I'll start inquiries. Sanderson Faulks will be able to assist."

"Yes, of course." Alice stepped back to give Rosalind room to return to her desk. "And perhaps it will come to nothing. Perhaps your father will choose to return to Paris rather than London."

"It is possible, but wherever he has gone, we must know." Rosalind brought out a fresh sheet of writing paper and unstoppered her ink bottle.

"And you're really going to bring Mr. Harkness into this?"

"I have no choice." Rosalind sat heavily in the chair by the hearth. Old anger pressed hard against her, leaving no room for more thought, or feeling.

"But you haven't seen him since you got back from the country."

"That is no one's fault. He was injured, and then he was sent to Dover to help discover a smuggling ring. We've corresponded since."

Alice stared, her face blank. "You've corresponded with Mr. Harkness? Since you got back from Cassell House?"

"I have written his mother." It was not proper for an unmarried woman, even one of Rosalind's age, to write directly to an unmarried man. Rosalind found she could not bring herself to violate that ingrained rule, not even for Mr. Harkness. Perhaps especially for Mr. Harkness. She needed the restraint of knowing that some third party could easily see what she wrote. Otherwise, she might grow careless and say more than she should to the man who had saved her life, and nearly kissed her.

"You wrote his mother," said Alice. "And?"

"And he has added some lines to her replies."

In truth, they were whole pages. Rosalind had carefully preserved them in her bedside table, tied in red ribbon. Alice, however, did not need to know that.

"Well. You might have told me!"

"Alice." Rosalind's sigh contained what might have been a touch of impatience. "I have just had some very bad news, and I do not have time to discuss your opinions of my relationship with Mr. Harkness."

"I know, and I'm being unfair, and I'm sorry." Alice wrapped her arms around herself. "I suppose it's easier for me to worry about you and Mr. Harkness than it is to worry about you and . . ." Alice bit her lip and did not finish the sentence. "Rosalind, I take it you did notice that Charlotte did not name her fiancé?"

"Yes, I noticed."

"You don't find that strange?"

Rosalind sighed. Alice's brain was a very busy place, and once she seized on an idea, she would not easily let it go. "No, in truth, I don't. She's frightened, and she's angry, and she does not like the fact that she has to trust me at all. Therefore, she is not telling me any more than she has to."

"You're not afraid she's lying?"

"I think if Charlotte meant to deceive us, she would not pick something so obvious."

"Or she doesn't want you making inquiries around any name she gives."

Rosalind felt her brows knit. "Why would she worry about that?"

"Because inquiries are what you do, and because he might not exist."

Now it was Rosalind's turn to stare. "What would the point of inventing a fiancé be?"

"To gain your sympathy and ensure you will help her recover your father."

"She knows I would help."

"Does she?"

"Alice, what are you implying?"

Alice clearly heard her change in tone, but she only leaned forward. "Two things." She began ticking the points off on her fingers. "First, she doesn't know for certain what you will do, any more than you know for certain what she will do. Second, she's a courtesan, Rosalind. No, don't look at me like that, I'm not being missish. But it is part of her living to lie and to flatter. She is used to saying what she has to to get what she wants."

Rosalind could not deny either of these points, but there was something else. "Alice, part of your living is to report the gossip of the first families. You do realize that she may not have said his name so it wouldn't show up in A.E. Littlefield's column."

Alice turned a remarkable shade of pink. "No, I confess I had not thought of it."

"Charlotte knows you far less well than she knows me, and she knows me hardly at all now. You could not blame her for being cautious."

"Yes, I suppose that is the case. I'm sorry, Rosalind. I'm probably not thinking straight."

Rosalind nodded. Alice had also had her life overturned by her father's ruin. The difference was, her father had determined death was better than disgrace.

"You know that whatever you need, George and I will be there for you," said Alice.

"I do know." Rosalind touched her friend's arm. "And I am grateful for you both." She let those words settle between them for a moment before she picked up her pen. "Right now, however, I need to write Mr. Harkness and then go to Mrs. Walford. I must postpone our business for a few days at least, and that is better done in person."

"And I'll write to George." Alice opened her writing desk. "We'll need him before too much longer."

Rosalind wanted to argue, but she could not. Alice and her brother might not live together anymore, but they still worked hand in glove. Any business that involved her must also involve him.

And Rosalind had the distinct feeling she would need every one of her friends before much longer.

I must not think about that now. She addressed herself to the sheet of paper in front of her and began to write:

> *Dear Mr. Harkness,*
> *I know you will be surprised to hear from me directly, but I am writing on a matter of urgent business. My sister and I require your professional assistance. Our father, Sir Reginald Thorne, has gone missing from*

his home in Bath. Thus far, we have no indication where
he has gone or what company he keeps.
  It is vital that we trace his whereabouts immediately.
Please let me know as soon as possible if you are able to
assist.
  Yours in haste,
  Rosalind Thorne

It was an unsatisfactory letter. Over the past few months,
the correspondence they had exchanged had been dense with
detail, humor, confidences. On sleepless nights, she would select one of Mr. Harkness's letters to read, just so she could
hear his voice inside her mind.

He would help if he could. He would not judge her. He
would know how much she put into his hands.

She was sure of all these things. There was no reason for
her hand to shake as she sealed the letter and wrote the direction.

Ignoring Alice's concerned glances, Rosalind left the parlor
to fetch her cloak, bag, and bonnet and tried not to feel like
she was running away.

In this, she was unsuccessful.

CHAPTER 5

A Mother's Fear

Indeed, I never employ such artifices with my
friends: to them, and to you in particular, my dear,
I always speak with perfect frankness and
candour.

Maria Edgeworth, *Manoevering*

Given the urgency of the matter—as well as the slush and muck that fouled London's December streets—Rosalind decided to hire a cab to carry her to the Walfords' residence.

The family had taken a house in the fashionable neighborhood surrounding Grosvenor Square. When Rosalind inquired if Mrs. Walford was at home, the liveried footman conducted her to the rose-pink morning room. A cheerful fire crackled in the hearth. Mrs. Walford sat at a small table, sorting through a stack of correspondence.

When Rosalind was announced, Mrs. Walford got to her feet at once.

"Miss Thorne! Do come in. I thought we would not meet before tonight."

Mrs. Valentina Walford was a striking woman. She was as tall as Rosalind, with a queenly figure and a presence to match.

Her thick black hair was streaked with gray, but her blue eyes remained clear. Age had lent her face a distinctive character and added gravity and grace to her manner. Were it not for the *ton*'s prejudice against fortunes made from manufacturing, she would have easily become one of the most popular hostesses in town. As it was, society had decided to hold the source of her late husband's money very much against her. Added to this was the matter of her French heritage. Even though Mrs. Walford had spent most of her life in England, there were still those who looked at every French émigré with suspicion. The sentiment lingered even now that the Bourbons had been restored to the throne.

This combination of circumstances left Mrs. Walford and her children socially isolated, and therefore especially vulnerable to schemers such as Mr. Horatio Salter.

"Will you sit?" Mrs. Walford gestured to the tapestried sofa. "Do you know, I'm becoming quite confident our charity ball will be a great success. I've had three more acceptances to our invitations just this morning and four requests for tickets." Then she saw the expression on Rosalind's face. "I hope nothing is wrong? Not . . ." She lowered her voice. "It's nothing to do with Augustina?"

"No, no." Rosalind smoothed her skirts, hoping the gesture would help settle her nerves. She did not like to speak of her private life, especially as it related to her father. "Indeed, as far as Mr. Salter is concerned, there has been a great deal of progress."

But before Rosalind could get any further, there was a staccato rapping at the door. Mrs. Walford looked up sharply, angrily. The door flew open and Augustina Walford breezed into the room, followed more languidly by her oldest brother, Louis.

"Oh, I beg your pardon, Mother!" cried Augustina. "I didn't realize you were engaged. Miss Thorne, how do you do today?"

"Very well, thank you, Miss Walford."

To Rosalind's experienced eye, Augustina Walford seemed perfectly fashioned for the whirl of London society. She had inherited her mother's striking looks. Her hair was a thick, glossy black that took easily to the latest fashion in ringlets. Private amusement glimmered in her blue eyes. She danced and bantered with equal ease and always seemed to be enjoying herself. She wore her forest-green woolen dress with its trimmings of lace and fox fur gracefully.

It was something of a surprise to Rosalind that such a girl would attach herself to an unknown entity like Horatio Salter, especially during her first Season. Even when their families were not among the first circles, belles such as Augustina usually had their minds either on great conquests or on maintaining their freedom as long as possible so they could continue to enjoy themselves. A fortune tended to buy one time.

Perhaps that's what worries me. Why should she be in such a rush?

Rosalind thought of Charlotte, so pale and distressed. Could Augustina have a similar reason for wanting to be married as quickly as possible? She discarded this idea. Augustina was many things, but in distress was not one of them.

Her brother was of a similar cheerful and teasing disposition. He strolled up to Rosalind and took her hand to bow over it.

"And how does the lovely Miss Thorne today?"

Louis Walford was the oldest of the two brothers. Like his sister, he had a head of jet-black hair and startling blue eyes. Added to this he was tall and lean and wore the current fashions in breeches and coats with an easy confidence. Had he smiled at her coming out, Rosalind had no doubt her heart would have fluttered more than once or twice.

But as matters stood, it was clear he thought he was doing Rosalind a favor by flirting with her.

Augustina laughed.

"Oh, Louis, leave off! You are disconcerting poor Miss Thorne. She can hardly be used to such attentions."

"I am sure Miss Thorne has received much more attention than I could offer."

Flirtation and mockery danced in his eyes. There was no question but that the young man meant to raise a blush from a woman he regarded as an aging spinster. But there was something else as well. There was a veiled insult in Louis's smooth voice, as there was in the way he kept hold of her fingertips.

Rosalind covered her concern with a look of thorough indifference. She also withdrew her hand.

"Ahem!" Mrs. Walford coughed sharply. "I'm sure that neither of you came here to address Miss Thorne."

"Oh no, Mother!" said Augustina. "Louis is taking me shopping." Like the rest of her family, Augustina used the French pronunciation for her brother's name. "We were wondering if you had any errands for us."

"Oh. Oh. No. Not right now. But remember to be back in time for supper. We are attending the opera tonight."

"Oh, but, Mother—" began Augustina.

Mrs. Walford cut her off. "Have you forgotten, Mr. Salter promised to be there?"

Augustina looked at her blankly for a moment and then covered her mouth with her fingertips. "Oh goodness! What a numbskull I am! I do remember now. She's right, Louis, we mustn't be late."

Louis's face fell. "Well, as much as I hate to admit it, Augustina's not the only numbskull among your offspring, Mother! I'd clean forgotten as well, and now I'm going to have to beg off."

"I need you there, Louis. So does Augustina."

Louis's bright blue gaze flickered sideways toward Rosalind. Calculations flickered behind his eyes. "Impossible, I'm afraid," he announced. "There's a board meeting. At the club. About the finances, you know. I have to be there. After all the work to get me in, it would look very bad if I was not. You understand, I'm sure?"

Rosalind suppressed the urge to frown. *What would he say if I were not here?*

Mrs. Walford threw up her hands in motherly resignation. "Well, I suppose since you say so, it cannot be helped. But you will come as soon as you can?"

"Absolutely. And you'll have Etienne with you, you know. I'll remind him. Miss Thorne." He bowed to her, but this time the flirtatious smile was completely absent. When he took himself out the door, it seemed to Rosalind he moved a little too hastily.

"I'm so sorry about that interruption," said Mrs. Walford as soon as the door closed.

Rosalind kept her face placid. "It is of no matter at all." Inside, however, her discomfort was growing. Something had just happened, but she had no idea what. There was no mistaking the undercurrent of unspoken words between the family members.

"Now, you said there was some progress on our private business?" Mrs. Walford prompted her.

"Yes." Rosalind forced her thoughts back to the matter at hand. "It happens that I have some connection to several families who know, or knew, Mr. Salter. A number were quite reluctant to speak about him directly, but there were enough hints that I decided to call upon an acquaintance involved in private banking. He, in turn, spoke with several of his colleagues at the Exchange. It seems Mr. Salter was involved in the collapse of the markets in '14."

Mrs. Walford had an expressive countenance. Rosalind could see the exact moment she recalled the details of that disaster. Perhaps she and her husband had even been touched by it. Business people were generally investors. The Walfords may have lost money in the crash.

"The . . . but wasn't that caused by someone spreading rumors that Napoleon had died?"

Rosalind nodded. "Mr. Salter helped bandy those rumors about the coffeehouses. He was paid to go from one to the other. In each, he let slip the supposed 'news,' along with suggestions as to which stocks a smart man should buy. This drove up the price of the shares his paymasters just happened to own."

As Rosalind spoke, the color slowly drained from Mrs. Walford's face.

"To use the death of such a one . . ." she croaked. "For the sake of money!"

It was an odd reaction, but Rosalind could not remark on it now. "Mr. Salter is a gambler," she said. "And such men are frequently in debt. Sometimes far enough that they will do anything to try to redeem themselves."

"I am familiar with the type." Mrs. Walford spoke softly, but that did nothing to mask her deep resentment. "Well, I suppose it is some small mercy that we will be able to treat this one exactly as he deserves." She paused, and in the look she leveled on Rosalind, Rosalind felt the full, startling force of her determination. "That is what you are come to tell me, is it not?"

"Yes, and soon." Rosalind lowered her gaze. "I had hoped it would be tonight, as you know. I regret to say, however, a personal matter has arisen. I am afraid we must postpone our plans for a few days."

Mrs. Walford drew back. Her hand went to the collar of her flowered morning dress, as if it were suddenly too tight. "But you led me to believe everything was in place."

"It is, Mrs. Walford." *I hope.* "Miss Walford will hear the truth about her suitor, in a way that she will find difficult to ignore. Indeed, think it probable that Mr. Salter will choose to remove himself from the neighborhood once the news becomes public. My private matters will not require more than a week's attention, perhaps less."

Mrs. Walford started to her feet and strode to the hearth. Her long, pale fingers tugged restlessly at her lace collar.

"No," she said, her voice low and hoarse. "It will not do. Especially with what you've just told me. We must proceed. The danger grows every minute."

"If this were still the Season, with its constant parties and gatherings, I would agree," Rosalind said. "There would be too many chances for Mr. Salter to converse with Miss Walford and win her more firmly to his suit. But now in December, the social schedule is greatly curtailed. Between today and Wednesday se'en night, there will be next to no opportunities for her to see Mr. Salter. And from what I have seen, matters there have not advanced to the point where your daughter's heart is fully engaged."

At this, Mrs. Walford chin shot up and she turned swiftly, heedless of how close her skirts came to the fire. "But they have, Miss Thorne."

Rosalind blinked. "I'm sorry?"

Mrs. Walford returned to her own chair and leaned forward. "I'm afraid—I'm very much afraid—that Augustina is preparing to elope."

Rosalind struggled to keep her expression cool.

"I have seen no indication of that. I admit, I have not had much time with your daughter, but I've watched her and Mr. Salter closely—"

Mrs. Walford cut her off. "Yes, yes, as have I. But I promise you, Miss Thorne, something new is in the works. You see, I'd . . ." She seemed to be searching for words. "I'd discounted the way in which Mr. Salter has taken my sons into his confidence, and his company."

Rosalind frowned. There had been no hint of this. She'd deliberately used her position as private assistant to their mother to move freely about the house, which led her to overhear scraps of casual conversation. The young men had never mentioned Salter's name, nor had she seen him come to the house when she was there, except to call on Mrs. Walford, and by extension Augustina.

"They have felt as left out of London social doings as I have," said Mrs. Walford. "They are young men. They wish to have their share of the clubs and so forth. Salter knows enough of the right people that they are taken round and introduced. You heard Louis make mention of it just now. And, of course, they are welcomed everywhere because they have deep pockets and can always stand their friends to a round." She paused again and knotted her fingers together. "I have perhaps been overly indulgent."

Rosalind said nothing.

"But as a result of this, Mr. Salter has got them completely on his side. They say that he is a capital fellow and have been highly supportive of his courting Augustina. Their mother"— she bowed her head—"is too old-fashioned and stuffy to understand. They've been carrying notes between the two of them, and I believe they may be inclined to assist in an elopement, just for the lark." Her proud head drooped, and her normally straight shoulders hunched in on themselves. "I have failed all my children. London has proved too much for us, Miss Thorne."

"I wish you'd said something to me earlier." Her voice sounded too plaintive and too faint. *Collect yourself, Rosalind. This will not do.*

"I know, I was foolish. I wanted—" Mrs. Walford hesitated again. "I wanted to preserve some shred of my dignity, and I truly thought you already knew enough. I was sure tonight would be the end." Mrs. Walford dropped her gaze and twisted her fingers, suddenly the picture of helplessness. "But if this . . . person . . . has another week, who knows what he will be able to convince Augustina of? Or her brothers?"

Rosalind forced herself to be calm and to consider what

she heard. Mrs. Walford was a sensible woman, a careful manager, and kept good order in her household. Rosalind could not discount her worries as those of a woman simply overwhelmed by the force of London society. If she said she felt a change in her daughter and sons, that must be taken seriously.

So must this display of defeat. It nagged at Rosalind. It was wholly in the character of a distracted mother worried for her daughter, and yet, unlike the anger and the determination she had seen earlier, it seemed out of character for her hostess.

Rosalind wanted to remind Mrs. Walford that her daughter really was a sensible person and she would not casually risk her relationship with her family. Yes, Augustina was witty, in the careless way of someone who was young and well-off, but Rosalind had long sensed that at bottom, there was more to the girl. She was intelligent, and observant, and, despite all her teasing banter, remarkably levelheaded.

But there was that undercurrent of unspoken words between Louis and his sister just now. Could that have something to do with Mr. Salter? Indeed, if Salter was getting desperate enough to use subterfuge to gain Augustina's affections, and if her brothers were engaged as friends to help him, shopping could be the furthest thing from Miss Walford's real plans for the afternoon.

A disquieting idea crept into Rosalind's thoughts. It was possible that someone had noticed her inquiries into Salter's past affairs. After all, she had been talking to old school friends, and men talked as much in their clubs as women did in their drawing rooms.

The looks Augustina had flashed to her, the casually disrespectful way she and Louis had spoken to her. It was possible they knew what Rosalind's true purpose in the household was.

Rosalind thought of Mr. Salter's history as a fraudster. Was it possible he had found a way to involve Louis and Etienne in his schemes? Perhaps even compromised them? There were dozens of ways it might be done, especially with young men who were inexperienced in London ways.

Rosalind suppressed a sigh of frustration. She needed information she did not have, and now she had no time to acquire it.

There was a simple way to circumvent the problem. She could assure Mrs. Walford that the plans would move forward. Then, as soon as she returned home, she could send a message to Sanderson Faulks and tell him not to approach her at the opera. She would find some excuse to give Mrs. Walford. A thousand accidents great and small could befall a carriage in London traffic.

But where would that leave me?

She would have failed in her promise to Mrs. Walford to help unknot the tangle of her daughter's affections, and she would have done nothing at all to prevent Charlotte from losing her future security, and that of her child.

It is one night, and then my part in the business is done. The articles Alice and George write will accomplish the rest. Beginning tomorrow, I will be able to focus all my energies on finding Father and curtailing whatever his plans might be.

"Very well, Mrs. Walford," Rosalind told her hostess. "We will proceed."

It is one night, Rosalind told herself. *Just one.*

CHAPTER 6

The Best-Laid Plans

People went to the opera to talk, and to
exhibitions to show themselves.

Catherine Gore, *The Debutante*

Normally, Rosalind loved a chance to visit the opera. All of London's theaters vied to outshine one another in terms of luxury and opulence. However, The King's Opera stood head and shoulders above the rest with its rose silk hangings and profusion of gilt ornaments. Most magnificent of all was the grand chandelier. Recently fitted for gaslight, this splendid creation provided brilliant illumination to show off the audience.

This was the first performance of the new theater season (not to be confused with the social Season, which would not begin until Easter), and much of fashionable London had turned out, ready to be entertained. With the hunting season over and Christmas still weeks away, those who could return to London did. They came to see and be seen, to prepare for the New Year, and, of course, to shop. Even Rosalind had a new dress, or at least one that was new to her. There were distinct advantages to George Littlefield having married a dressmaker. The new Mrs. Littlefield had taken Rosalind's relatively plain Clarence blue gown and performed absolute miracles with silver velvet trim to lengthen sleeves and hem, additional lace and beaded netting to conceal the new seams. Extra netting had been gathered up behind to make a large bow and a brief train. With her mother's pearls, and a silver lace fan borrowed from Alice, Rosalind felt quite regal.

But she also felt very much on edge. As of yet, she had received no answer from her letter to Mr. Harkness. She began to fear he had been called out of the city. If that was the case, she might not hear from him again for days, which would give her father plenty of time to work whatever mischief he had planned.

Wherever he has gone.

The mystery of her father's whereabouts was not the only one that nagged at her. As the day had stretched on, she grew increasingly certain that there was some unspoken secret playing out between the members of the Walford family. Neither could she get past the feeling she had been discovered. Which meant that her whole carefully orchestrated scheme might be about to fall apart.

Then what will I do?

Something hard poked her in the ribs. It was Alice's fan. Rosalind blinked and saw the red velvet stage curtain was descending. Around her the audience was applauding politely and getting to their feet to go in search of refreshments.

"Good heavens, Rosalind!" Alice whispered as she reclaimed her shawl.

It was, of course, not possible for Rosalind to arrive at the opera unaccompanied. Even when she held a ticket, a single woman might well be refused admittance on moral grounds. Fortunately, Alice's "Society Notes" column required her to attend the opening as well. Alice wore a dress of bronze bro-

cade trimmed with a beautiful copper-colored velvet that
Hannah had altered for her. Bronze and copper ribbons glimmered in her dark hair.

"I'm sorry, Alice." Rosalind got hastily to her own feet,
gathering up fan, reticule, and wrap. "This day had left me
unmoored."

"I know it's been upsetting. But even if tonight does not
work out as you hope, you'll think of something else."

"But will there be time?" murmured Rosalind. "If Augustina suspects her suitor is being maligned, she'll only
draw closer to him."

"It's not like you to go borrowing trouble, Rosalind."

"I know," she sighed. "It's Charlotte's news. I'm jumping
at shadows."

"How about a glass of champagne?" suggested Alice. "It
will steady your nerves."

"And cloud my head," returned Rosalind. "I can't take the
risk. I had best stick to lemonade."

Impeded by the crush, Rosalind and Alice eventually filed
into the grandly decorated salon. Waiters bearing covered
trays for those dining in their boxes edged their way through
the colorful and tightly packed throng. Even Rosalind had to
stand on her toes to see anything.

"I've spied the Walfords." Rosalind dropped down onto
flat feet and leaned in to speak directly into Alice's ear. "I
have to go."

"All right, but wave to me from the box to let me
know you're all right," Alice shouted back. "I'm worried
about you."

"I will be fine," said Rosalind. "Truly." She mustered a
confident smile. Alice, in answer, just narrowed her eyes.

Rosalind ignored her friend's silent suspicion. Instead, she
fixed a pleasant expression on her face and edged her way
through the crowd to where the Walfords clustered together.

Etienne and Augustina stood beside their mother, with Mr. Horatio Salter stationed at Augustina's shoulder.

Rosalind did not acknowledge them immediately, but simply paused within their line of sight, as if searching for someone entirely different.

Mrs. Walford hailed her. "Miss Thorne!"

Rosalind turned as if she had just seen Mrs. Walford, and smiled in acknowledgment. Mrs. Walford waved her fan, inviting Rosalind to join the family, and Rosalind waded over.

"Miss Thorne! I thought that must be you." Mrs. Walford wore a sumptuous gown of striped chocolate brocade and wine-colored velvet. A matching turban with ostrich plumes emphasized her height, and a pearl and topaz necklace adorned her throat. "Mr. Salter, have you met Miss Thorne?"

"Only briefly." The man in question favored Rosalind with a polished bow and a teasing smile.

Mr. Horatio Salter was very much the fashion in beaus and he knew it. He was tall and slender. His black hair fell in waves to brush his high collar. Dark eyes sparkled with lively interest in a long, pale face. His cravat was elaborate yet immaculate, his black coat was perfectly cut to show off his broad shoulders, and his white silk breeches and stockings were fitted to show off his legs. The gold and garnet buckles at his knees matched the ones on his shoes and were becomingly enhanced by the gold signet ring on his hand and the garnet pin in the middle of his cravat.

Augustina was clearly proud to have such a fine man at her side. She herself looked very well in a gown of rose and cream velvet trimmed with antique lace. Pearl pins and more lace decorated her black hair. Mr. Salter carried her cashmere shawl.

Poor Etienne Walford faded into the background beside the dazzling couple. He had the family's good looks, but on him they seemed flat, as if worn one too many times. He wore the gentleman's uniform of black coat and white breeches with an air of habit rather than distinction. All in all, he gave Rosalind the impression of someone who was waiting to be told what they should do.

"But surely you're not alone?" Mrs. Walford was saying to Rosalind.

"Oh no," she answered quickly. "But I'm afraid I am leaving. My friend has developed a sick headache and needs to return home."

"Oh, that is too bad. And it is such a charming performance." Augustina's sigh was a just little overexaggerated.

"Well, perhaps you'd care to join us?" said Mrs. Walford. At her shoulder, Augustina's expression tightened suspiciously.

I was right. She knows I am here for more than planning a charity ball. Now what do I do?

Fortunately, years of practice in polite society allowed Rosalind to keep all trace of private consternation out of her expression.

"You are very kind, but . . ."

Mrs. Walford waved away the rest of Rosalind's words. "There is plenty of room for you in our box, and we shall be glad to have you."

Rosalind hesitated. This had been the plan. She would join the Walfords. Mr. Faulks would arrive shortly to create the scene between him and Mr. Salter. But Mr. Faulks knew none of the Walfords, so Rosalind had to be there to function as a sort of sign post. She would also help with the aftermath, both assisting with consoling Augustina and mentioning certain other rumors about Mr. Salter.

But now that she was certain Augustina's suspicions had been roused, she should perhaps instead put an end to things.

No. Better to follow it through and find out what she knows. With an effort, Rosalind kept her gaze from shifting to Mr. Salter. *What they know. And how they found me out. Then we'll be able to form a new plan.*

"Thank you, Mrs. Walford," said Rosalind. "I shall be glad to accept. Only let me go and make sure of my friend."

"Of course." Mrs. Walford smiled.

Rosalind had arranged to meet Alice at the head of one of the grand staircases. Alice had beaten her there. She had also acquired a glass of champagne.

"You have established your connection with the Walfords?" She nodded toward their little cluster.

"Yes, that's done." Rosalind longed to tell her what she'd discovered already, but there was no time. "Have you seen Mr. Faulks anywhere?"

"Not yet, but don't let that worry you. You know the dandy set is never on time for any performance."

Which was certainly true but did nothing to soothe Rosalind's agitated nerves. "Will you be able to see yourself home all right?"

"Of course. I've found Margaret and Lady Shilling. They've invited me to join them, and I think they've got news for me, or at least for A.E."

"Good luck, then," said Rosalind.

Alice raised her glass. "And you."

Rosalind squeezed her friend's hand and made her way back to the Walfords.

"Excellent," said Mrs. Walford as she rejoined their little grouping. "Now, Etienne, you must—" But as she turned, someone else in the shifting crowd caught her eye. "Oh! Is that not Lady Holland?"

Rosalind followed Mrs. Walford's eager gaze to the tall, stout, elegantly dressed lady, very clearly holding court amid a select circle. "Yes, I believe so."

"I must go and pay my respects." Mrs. Walford gathered her hems. "I won't be a moment."

Without waiting, she plunged into the crowd.

"I did not know Mrs. Walford was acquainted with Lady Holland," remarked Rosalind.

"They've corresponded," said Etienne blandly. "Once or twice, I believe."

"I don't know that they've met more times than that," said Augustina. "But then I am not a political person."

Etienne looked down at his sister with an expression that could have been disbelief, or simple contempt. Rosalind wondered at it.

"And Lady Holland, I understand, is little else but political," said Mr. Salter. "Well, when a woman's children are grown, I expect she must find some way to keep busy."

"I expect Mrs. Walford hopes to claim her for the ball," mused Rosalind. "It would be an excellent addition to her guest list."

"Ah, yes. The ball. I do keep forgetting about it." Augustina tilted her head toward Rosalind and regarded her knowingly. "Are you enjoying the performance, Miss Thorne?" she asked suddenly.

"Yes. Do tell us what you think of the . . . players," added Salter. Etienne looked bored.

Rosalind considered her next words carefully. "I think the spectacle is more glittering than it is enlightening."

"Oh-ho!" laughed Mr. Salter. "Our Miss Thorne is a critic!"

"It is her famous eye for detail," added Augustina.

"But, Miss Walford, what would lead you to believe my eyes are at all famous?" shot back Rosalind.

"Oh, you are too modest, Miss Thorne," put in Mr. Salter. "You have developed quite the reputation about the town. I can't help but wonder if Mrs. Walford knew that when you were recommended to her as someone who could assist her."

Rosalind did not answer. The couple smiled at her, their expressions remarkably similar.

They knew. They had at least some inkling of the extent of her work with other women of the *ton*, and they knew, or they suspected, that she was acting in that capacity for Mrs. Walford.

But their particular mockery made something else plain. However much or little they might know about her, they were not at all concerned. They believed they had stolen a march on her, and that she had failed to notice the truth behind their sly comments.

Well and good.

"Do you know, Miss Augustina," Rosalind said pleasantly, but in a tone that made it plain she was changing the subject. "I don't believe I've ever heard the story of how you and Mr. Salter were introduced."

Miss Walford smiled shyly. "Oh, it was nothing very remarkable. It was at a dinner party you know, during the Season."

A gleam lit Mr. Salter's eyes. "Now, my dear Miss Walford, you must not sport with our Miss Thorne's intelligence. She's asked a simple question. She should hear the truth."

Augustina arched her neatly shaped brows. "Well, the truth, Mr. Salter, is a little shocking."

"Oh, our Miss Thorne is made of stern stuff." Mr. Salter winked conspiratorially at Rosalind. "She will not be so easily shocked."

"Yes, but Etienne might," countered Augustina. "He has not heard it, either, you know."

"No, but now he very much wants to." Etienne folded his arms. "Do go on, sister dear. I'm fascinated."

Augustina hesitated, but for no more than a heartbeat.

"You tell it, Salter." She turned a sparkling smile on her beau. "You know I get so muddled."

Salter chuckled modestly. "Well, it was, as Miss Walford says, at a supper party. I was only there because a friend was doing a favor to the hostess, bringing me to balance out the table at the last minute, you see. Well, we were all gathered in the hall, waiting to be ushered into supper. That was when I saw her, and my heart stopped. She was quite unaware of me, of course, but I could not leave off looking at her. But to my consternation, I had no one from whom I could beg an introduction. Imagine! There I was, just a few feet from the loveliest, liveliest creature I'd ever seen, and I could not even speak to her."

"And what did you do?" asked Rosalind.

He leaned in. "I told the hostess we were old acquaintances and bribed her to let me escort Miss Walford into dinner."

"He didn't even know my name!" added Augustina. "It was the most shocking thing. He's paired with me, and I'm sputtering because I haven't even heard *his* name, and he takes my arm and says, 'Do please go along, otherwise I shall die of boredom and fall facedown in the soup.' Wasn't it awful?" Augustina laughed. "Perhaps I shouldn't have been flattered, but I was. No one had ever taken such pains to get close to me." She let her gaze drop demurely.

Etienne turned his head and muttered something.

Augustina's head snapped up. "What was that, brother?"

Etienne sighed. "I said, ridiculous ritual. Why shouldn't you just sit where you please?"

Augustina rolled her eyes. "You must excuse my brother, Miss Thorne. Like Lady Holland, he is endlessly political."

"You see politics in dinner seating, Mr. Walford?" inquired Rosalind.

"I see the ludicrous interference of a system that values a man's birth above his merit."

"Or a woman's," added Rosalind.

He looked shrewdly at her. "Yes, or a woman's."

Augustina gasped and held up her fan to cover her mouth. "Oh dear, Miss Thorne, don't tell me you're also a radical? Now I'm beginning to wonder if you might shock me!"

Etienne laughed. "Serve you right if Miss Thorne proved to be horribly conventional and went straight to mother with your little story!"

For the first time, Augustina looked genuinely discomforted. Mr. Salter noticed as well and gave her arm a gentle pat. "I'm sure we have nothing to fear on that score, do we, Miss Thorne?"

"Oh, you may rely on me entirely," said Rosalind as pleasantly as she could manage. Inside, though, she felt not only cool, but cold. Yes, it was just a little mischievous banter, but to Rosalind, the exchange spoke volumes.

Mr. Salter had lied about that first meeting, and not only did Miss Walford know he lied, she helped him along. The entire thing happened so smoothly and naturally, it would have been easy to miss.

But Rosalind did see it, and a chill ran up her spine. Mrs. Walford was right. Her daughter's heart, her mind, and much else was already engaged. In fact, Augustina had already entered into partnership with Mr. Salter.

But to what end?

And how on earth am I to tell her mother?

CHAPTER 7

The Scene

It is a melancholy and distressing sight to observe, not infrequently, a man of a noble and ingenuous disposition . . . gradually sinking under the pressure of his circumstances, making his excuses at first with a blush of conscious shame, afraid to see the faces of his friends from whom he may have borrowed money . . .

Maria Edgeworth, *The Dun*

Fortunately for Rosalind, Mrs. Walford was shouldering her way through the crush. She looked flushed from the heat, but also excitement.

"Such a charming woman!" she gushed. "So very kind. We are invited to call, Augustina!"

"Oh, how nice," replied her daughter.

Mrs. Walford did not seem to notice the disappointment in her daughter's voice, or the way Mr. Salter patted her arm again. Instead, Mrs. Walford craned her neck to see around the crowd.

"Well, I suppose we had better make our way back," she

said. "Unless you've spotted anyone else we know?" She looked directly at Rosalind, the worry plain in her eyes.

Where is this scene you promised?

"No one here," said Mr. Salter promptly. "I'll try to snare a waiter, though. Have a bottle brought to the box, eh?"

Rosalind suppressed a frown. *Where on earth are you, Sanderson?* She remembered how she'd considered inventing a carriage accident as an excuse for him. Now, though, she began to wonder if he'd truly met with some trouble. Despite his careless and cynical affectations, he had never failed her when she needed him.

Rosalind opened her mouth to say something innocuous but was interrupted.

"Ah, Miss Thorne," said a woman's languid and highly cultured voice. "I was certain that was you. I had no idea you were in attendance this evening."

The whole party turned as one. All the Walfords, and Mr. Salter, stared.

The woman who greeted Rosalind was tall, dark, and queenly. She dressed in an elaborately beaded gown of ruby-red velvet with a collar of pearls and diamonds around her neck and a towering arrangement of ostrich feathers in her dark hair. Her fan was gold lace, as was her shawl. Another woman would have looked hopelessly overdressed, but she wore it all as lightly and as easily as a summer frock.

"Your grace." Rosalind made the deep curtsy etiquette required. This was the Countess Dorothea Lieven, and she was one of the most powerful women in the city. Her long list of titles and accomplishments included being a patroness on the governing board of the exclusive Almack's Assembly Rooms. It was she who introduced the waltz to London society. In addition to these accomplishments, she was the wife of the Russian ambassador, Christoph von Lieven.

The man on the countess's arm, however, was not her husband.

"Have you met my dear Lord Palmerston?" Countess Lieven smiled winningly at the smaller, portly man on her arm. "Lord Palmerston, this is my good friend Miss Rosalind Thorne."

Lord Palmerston bowed. He was not a handsome man, but Rosalind saw a sardonic twinkle in his eye that spoke of intelligence and a capacity for good humor. He was immaculately dressed in black and white, but eschewed the extra ornamentation that Mr. Salter affected. He also seemed perfectly at ease in his surroundings and prepared to enjoy himself. It was no surprise that such a man could attract a woman like the countess, especially if he was well connected. Indeed, Rosalind knew, Lord Palmerston was a member of the cabinet and intimate of the royal family.

"How do you do, my lord?" murmured Rosalind. "Sir, ma'am, may I present my friends, Mrs. Walford, her son Etienne Walford, her daughter, Miss Augustine Walford, and Mr. Horatio Salter?"

The countess nodded regally to them all.

"How is it you come to know our delightful Miss Thorne, Mrs. Walford?" she asked.

"Miss Thorne has been good enough to assist me in the planning of my charity ball, for the relief of the widows and orphans of our noble soldiers and sailors," said Mrs. Walford, obviously a little flustered at being addressed by a woman whose comings and goings were regularly noted in the papers. Her eyes avidly drank in every detail of the countess's dress and adornment. Rosalind suppressed a smile. Even a serious matron could be dazzled by the countess.

She was also very aware that Mr. Salter was watching her, not the countess. *What do you see, Mr. Salter?*

Etienne was watching her, too, but with rather less curiosity and more contempt.

"Well, your business is in excellent hands." Countess Lieven was smiling lazily at Mrs. Walford. "Even our dearest Lady Jersey has consulted Miss Thorne on . . . complex social affairs. Now, I must bid you all adieu. We have a few complex affairs of our own to attend to, do we not, Palmerston? Miss Thorne, I am at home this Thursday and I should be very glad to receive you then. It has been far too long since we've had a chance to talk."

"Thank you, your grace," replied Rosalind. "I shall certainly call."

"Excellent. Come along, Palmerston. It's back to work for you and I. Mrs. Walford, Mr. Walford, Miss Walford, Mr. Salter." The countess swept his lordship away, which in this crowded room was no simple feat.

"Well!" Mrs. Walford snapped open her fan and used it vigorously. "How very unexpected."

"Yes, indeed." Mr. Salter eyed Rosalind with a great deal more close speculation than he had previously. Rosalind felt her pulse quicken. Before this, he had been all smooth mockery. But his attitude had changed. Even without him speaking a word, she could feel that he now regarded her with a deeper seriousness.

That could be dangerous.

Mr. Faulks, I need you here now.

As if summoned by her impatient thought, Rosalind saw a familiar elegant figure among the sea of operagoers.

Sanderson Faulks was a fair-haired, fine-boned man. He eschewed black. The coat he wore was a deep plum velvet with statin cuffs, and his waistcoat was embroidered with bronze and gold. In all the years she had known him, Rosalind had never seen him hurry. He did not hurry now. Nor did he force his way through the crowd. Despite the fact that the patrons stood shoulder to shoulder, Sanderson simply strolled forward, making a graceful and wandering path between the audience members without seeming to exert any effort at all.

"Well, now." Sanderson stopped in front of Mr. Salter and planted his walking stick between them. "There you are!" Sanderson's gaze flickered up and down, taking in the details of the man in front of him with the air of a tailor picking out all the flaws in a competitor's garment.

He ignored Rosalind as completely as if she'd been a potted plant.

Mr. Salter removed his arm from Miss Augustina's and thrust out his chest. "Do I know you, sir?"

"Ha! Very good. If that's the game you wish to play. Do forgive the intrusion." Mr. Faulks bowed elaborately to Salter. "Sanderson Faulks at your service, as indeed his purse has been these past six months."

"I do not understand you, sir." But Rosalind saw the first flicker of fear in Salter's eyes. Etienne straightened up, getting ready in case a second was needed. But his mother gently touched his shoulder with her fan and shook her head. Etienne shot a glance of sharp inquiry at her, but he did subside.

Augustina saw none of this. Her attention was all fixed on Salter and Mr. Faulks.

"Come, come, Mr. Salter, let us cease this pretense," said Mr. Faulks. "My representatives have called round to your rooms, but they tell me you are never to be found at home. It's been most frustrating and has led to some uncomfortable suspicions. There's even been some speculation that you might be attempting to avoid paying back what you borrowed. But now, of course, that I see your charming companion." Mr. Faulks smiled broadly at Augustina. "I understand perfectly why you might be choosing to spend your time elsewhere than in your rooms."

Augustina's hand tightened around her fan. Her cheeks had gone distinctly pale.

She's frightened, thought Rosalind. *And more than she should be.*

"You are insolent, sir!" Salter barked.

"Merely running out of patience," Mr. Faulks corrected him. "When may I expect my payment?"

"What is this man talking about, Salter?" breathed Augustina.

Salter's eyes flickered from side to side, as if he were already seeking his escape route. "I have no idea, my dear, I promise you."

"I trust you do not," said Mrs. Walford, color rising in her cheeks. "It would be a great shame to find you were in difficulties."

"I promise you!" Salter's voice broke. "I have never met this man before!"

The heads of those nearest were beginning to turn. Voices around them were starting to whisper. Even the countess was looking on, slightly bored and even more slightly amused.

"Are you calling me a liar, sir?" inquired Sanderson calmly. "I am quite prepared to prove what I say." He reached into his pocket. "A note, sir, with your signature. To be paid upon demand." He held it out. "You may interpret this as my demand."

Mr. Salter looked into Augustina's anxious and ever-so-slightly suspicious eyes. He swallowed. "This is hardly a fit conversation to have in front of the ladies," he said, attempting to muster some bonhomie. "Why don't you and I go get a drink, Mr., erm, Faulks? We can talk this over. I'm sure it's a simple misunderstanding," he added, more to the Walfords than to Mr. Faulks.

Augustina's eyes were attempting to bore into his. The fear Rosalind had seen was fast being replaced by anger.

Where was a young girl's bewilderment? What did Augustina think she was seeing?

"I don't suppose you'd mind me coming along?" said Etienne suddenly. He might appear bored, and uncertain, but clearly he felt himself to be the man in this situation, whatever it might be.

"I've certainly no objection," Mr. Faulks announced. "I assure you that all I want is what I am owed." He tucked the note safely into his pocket.

Augustina, on the other hand, looked like she did mind. Badly. Salter noticed as well.

"No, no, Etienne, you stay and attend the ladies," said Salter. But Rosalind couldn't help noticing how he had begun to go green about the gills.

Mr. Faulks stepped aside and gestured with his stick, indicating that Salter should go first.

"Salter?" blurted out Augustina. "It is a mistake, is it not?"

Salter squared his shoulders, but his color got no better. He did smile, though. It was a real smile, filled with bravado and affection. Rosalind felt the warmth in it, and it startled her.

"Of course it is a mistake," he said. "You'll see. I'll join you in the box before the end of the third act."

Rosalind held her fan to her face, struggling to muster the appropriate expression of shock and concern as all three men moved away.

"What can that have been about?" murmured Mrs. Walford. "Augustina? Do you know?"

"No, of course not." But Augustina didn't take her eyes off the two men, even though they had all been swallowed up by the crowd. "It must be a mistake, as Salter says." But the next breath she took sounded suspiciously like a sob.

Rosalind moved to her side and pulled a handkerchief from her sleeve. She held it out to Augustina.

A clammy hand yanked her backward and spun her around.

"*You!*" bellowed the man behind her. "I knew it! It is *you*."

The man was portly, hollow-eyed, and pale. His unkempt gray hair hung lank around his puffy face, and his coat and waistcoat gaped and strained to cover his paunch.

But Rosalind knew him. She would always know him.

"Father."

CHAPTER 8

There is no person so insignificant, but some advantage may be made by them.

Maria Edgeworth, *Almeria*

"Here now, fellow!" barked Etienne. "You forget yourself!"

"Oh no." Sir Reginald's words grated between his clenched teeth. He was grinning, broad and triumphant. "And my girl hasn't forgotten me, either. Have you, Rosalind, my dear?"

"No," breathed Rosalind. The room was spinning. There was no air. "My God," she whispered again. "How is it you found me here?"

Mrs. Walford took a step back and drew her daughter away with her. Surprise and disgust froze her features.

"That's it?" Sir Reginald grinned. "That's all you have to say? Where are your manners, Rosalind? Aren't you going to introduce me to your . . . friends?" He turned and bowed unsteadily. "You really must forgive my daughter, Mr. . . . Mrs. . . . Missish," he concluded. "Her mother spoiled her shockingly and even now, even now she has no idea of respect or mannerses."

He was drunk. Of course he was. How could he not be?

Rosalind's mind whirled. And another thought struck her. *I'm watched.*

Years of training took hold of her limbs. Her back straightened of its own accord. Her hands lowered themselves, her chin rose.

"My apologies, Father," Rosalind murmured. "You startled me. I had no idea you were in town."

Inside, Rosalind wept, and she screamed. But that could not be seen. Not here. Not ever. So, she smiled.

Her father's answer was a leering grin.

"No," he drawled. "I rather imagine this is a bit of a surprise for you, eh? Thought you were rid of me, did you?"

"Oh, never! I'm so glad you came, Father." She quickly slipped her arm through his. "Come, let's go and talk. I know there's a great deal you have to say. You must excuse me," she added to Mrs. Walford.

But Sir Reginald reared back and tossed his daughter's arm from him. "Oh no, miss! I'll not slink into corners with you! You will hear what I have to say in front of the whole world! They will all know your crimes!"

Rosalind reeled backward. They were now the center of attention. The entire crowd stared—eyes wide and mouths open, where they were not hidden behind fans or gloves. Rosalind felt herself shrinking and shriveling.

Her father stretched out his arm, pointing directly at her. "Everyone is going to know what you really are!" he cried. "You ungrateful, scheming b . . ."

Someone was applauding. Slowly, deliberately. Heads turned. The crowd parted. Slowly, Countess Lieven sauntered up the aisle made for her, clapping her velvet-gloved hands together as she went. A muscular footman followed like a silent shadow.

"Oh, bravo, Sir Reginald!" she laughed. "My dear, sir.

You really must stick to port if this is what champagne does to you."

Sir Reginald drew himself up. "I don't know you."

"Ah, but I know you." The countess smiled. "You are Sir Reginald Thorne, and I have so longed to meet you. Now, you are clearly in want of another drink. My man has procured a bottle for us. You will join us, sir, will you not?"

Just as she issued this smooth invitation, the gongs had sounded, and back in the auditorium the orchestra began to play. The audience began to stream back toward their seats and boxes—at least some of them did. Others seemed to believe the most interesting show was happening right in front of them.

Sir Reginald wavered. "I'm not, I'm not ready. . . ."

"But of course you are," said the countess. "And we do not wish the bottle to get warm. Alexi, you will show Sir Reginald the way."

The footman bowed. He was a tall man. His gold-laced jacket strained at the shoulders, and a puckered red scar ran along the side of his neck.

"If you will come with me, sir." His accent was heavily German.

Sir Reginald swayed on his feet.

"The drink is getting warm, sir," the footman prompted.

"Yes, of course. How . . . how kind." He leaned forward and stumbled. Alexi caught his arm, as if it was nothing at all, and steered him away.

Wherever they were going, it was not to a private box. Rosalind turned to face Countess Lieven.

"Th . . . thank you," stammered Rosalind. The countess met Rosalind's gaze for one moment, but then laughed and leaned forward to press her hand.

"Look to your left, at the bar," murmured the countess. "He brought your father here." Then she raised her voice.

"And that, my dear, is how you deal with a drunkard. I will expect you Thursday." She sailed off.

Feeling as if she was in a nightmare, Rosalind turned and looked. A man was shoving his way through the crowd, hurrying after Alexi and Sir Reginald.

It was Russell Fullerton.

CHAPTER 9

*His conscience was not entirely callous to
reproach, nor was his heart insensible to compas-
sion, but he was in a fair way to get rid of all
troublesome feelings and principles.*

Maria Edgeworth, *The Dun*

"I'm so sorry," murmured Rosalind, but she did not wait
to see if the Walfords heard. Instead, she dove straight
into the crowd.

Rosalind shouldered, slid, and finally simply barged through
the tide of bodies, all the while trying to keep Alexi in view.
The footman bobbed through the crowd, heading out of the
main salon and into the broad, curving corridor that skirted
the auditorium.

The stairway, she realized.

She broke through the ragged edge of the crowd, coming
out onto the landing. Alexi and Sir Reginald stood at the top
of the rose-marble stairs. Alexi was directing Sir Reginald to
descend. Her father was trying to understand what was happening. Rosalind did understand. Alexi meant to pitch Sir
Reginald right out into the street. Rosalind gathered up her
hems to dart forward. She had to be first to reach them.

She was too late.

Russell Fullerton also breached the crowd. His long legs carried him forward far faster than Rosalind, encumbered by her evening gown, could manage. He strode directly up to Sir Reginald, but he addressed himself to Alexi. Rosalind was too far away to hear, but she could easily interpret what he said. He was apologizing for his friend's behavior. He would take charge of him now. The countess would not be inconvenienced again.

Alexi hesitated, clearly caught between his mistress's instructions and the reassurances of this gentleman. Sir Reginald straightened himself up as much as he was able and assumed a swaggering air.

In the end, Alexi took the path of least resistance. He stepped back from Sir Reginald, bowed, and headed away toward the salon and, presumably, to Countess Lieven's private box.

With every fiber of her being, Rosalind wanted to turn and run, to hide away and pretend this choice was never hers. She felt how alone she was. She felt all the fear, anger, and loss of the girl she had been.

But she could not run. She straightened herself. She set her features into an expression of gentle concern that was the furthest thing from what she actually felt. Free of the crowd, she was able to move smoothly forward. There would be no more scenes.

Of course the two men saw her. She had nowhere left to hide. Fullerton turned first. Then her father.

"Ah! She returns!" Sir Reginald tugged at his jacket lapels. "The youngest of my poisonous brood!"

Rosalind bit the inside of her cheek, hard. She reached deep into her mind and her heart for a fund of old memories she had believed she would never need again.

She remembered when she loved this man without reservation and believed that he loved her. She remembered that once she—like her mother, like her sister—believed that being a part of his world was a special stroke of good fortune, and they would do anything to support him.

She let all those memories shine in her wide eyes.

"Father," she breathed. "Father, please."

Fullerton stepped directly into her path.

As ever, Fullerton played the part of the confirmed dandy. His coat was deep green and his waistcoat patterned gold and cream. His spotless cravat cascaded down his chest in an elaborate waterfall of crisp folds. His iron-gray hair had been tousled into a riot of fashionable curls. Gold rings glinted on both hands. Gold buckles decorated his shoes, and his hand rested on a gold-headed walking stick.

She had heard him compared to a snake, or a hawk. She thought this was unfair to predators in general. They only did as nature dictated. Fullerton acted from the delight of destruction, and a malicious joy that came from knowing when another person was wholly in his power.

The first time Rosalind had heard of Russell Fullerton, it was from a newly married young woman, Mrs. Devery. She had only come recently to London and discovered a taste for card playing. But she played too deep, and rather than tell her husband she had outspent her income, she accepted a loan from a sympathetic gentleman.

What followed was commonly known as blackmail. The young woman had come to Rosalind to recover the evidence of her folly.

Since then, Rosalind had found out that Fullerton made an excellent income from similar loans and similar incidents of extortion. Nothing illegal, of course. There was no law against using what one knew to extract private money, or private favors, from private individuals, especially should the individual be a woman who had behaved foolishly.

Fullerton knew her reputation and her work as well as she knew his. She had offended him gravely by interfering with the course of his regular business. He had threatened her. He had even tried to bribe Alice to turn against her.

Rosalind had since then made it her concern to find out as much as she could about this man. It was not easy. She seemed to be forever chasing shadows. But some of his victims had talked to her, as had some of his rivals. She had some pertinent letters in a private box at the bank, and she had hoped to accumulate more.

Now came this.

Behind him, Sir Reginald grabbed the elaborate stair railing. Rosalind snatched up her hems and swiftly dodged past Fullerton.

"Father! You are not well."

Sir Reginald looked up at her, his eyes blurred by wine. For a moment, his expression was blank, as if he could not remember who on earth she was.

She saw the moment of recognition, and for a single heartbeat, she thought she saw regret, and her heart shuddered. But in an eyeblink, contempt washed that wine-bred regret away. He jerked his hand out of hers as he straightened up.

"I do not require your interfr . . . inderfrance, ma'am."

Rosalind stretched out one trembling hand toward her father, and whispered, "I'm so sorry, Father."

"Sorry, you say!" snorted Sir Reginald.

"Forgive me, Father, please. I was so startled to see you . . . but now I'm so glad. I've been looking for you everywhere."

"So you say!" he repeated, but this time his voice quavered.

"Let me take you home," Rosalind pleaded. "Let me explain what has happened, and when I'm done, I hope—I pray—you will grant me your forgiveness."

It was not easy to force tears into one's eyes, but time in the ballrooms and salons of London had taught Rosalind a few theatrical arts. She used them now. She even managed to raise a blush.

Her father leaned unsteadily forward. He had always swung from belligerence to sentimentality when he was drinking.

"Do you mean it?"

"I do, Father." Rosalind clasped his hand in both of hers. "Please, come home with me. Do not be a stranger any longer."

He covered her hands. Drunken tears shone in his eyes. "My own . . ."

Rosalind was so intent on keeping her words and her earnest expressions focused on Sir Reginald while suppressing her true feelings that she didn't see Fullerton had moved. He was behind her now and speaking into her ear.

"One more word, Miss Thorne, and I will go straight to your friend Mrs. Walford and ask if she knows she has been entertaining the sister of one of the most notorious courtesans in London."

Rosalind whirled around. Fullerton was too close. She drew herself up immediately, ready to demand apology for the insult of his presence.

Fullerton smiled.

"Now, now. Your airs hold no terror for me. I have heard all of your secrets, you know." He nodded toward her father.

"Father?" breathed Rosalind.

"Ah, yes." Sir Reginald smoothed his coat down. "My good friend . . . my very good . . . You have been introduced, of course?"

"Yes," admitted Rosalind bitterly. "We have been introduced."

"Good, good. I . . . forgive me." He fumbled for his handkerchief. "It is the heat."

"Of course," said Fullerton smoothly. "What you need is a cool glass of champagne. Shall we return to my box?"

"Yes, yes. Excellent. I appreciate a man who understands generosity."

"You daughter is of course welcome to join us as soon she has taken her leave of her friends." He bowed politely toward Rosalind.

Rosalind found her ability to dissemble had melted quite away.

"What do you want from me?"

"Nothing at all," replied Fullerton calmly. "And that is exactly what I expect you to return."

Rosalind made no reply.

"I see I am too obscure. Very well." Fullerton rested both hands on his walking stick. "You will no longer interfere with my business, Miss Thorne. Nor with my pleasures."

"Sir, you forget . . ."

"But as you continue your little affairs, you will consult with me about any matter you think I might hold an interest in. Of course, I will also inform you if your business and mine seem likely to intersect. While I have the greatest respect for your intelligence, I do not expect omnipotence." He grinned. "In return, you may rely on me to treat your father as my special guest, and you may be sure I will keep him in a much better style than your sister ever did."

"A mere short-term necess . . . need," mumbled Sir Reginald. "As soon as I am . . . have reminded certain friends . . . obligations of the past . . . established . . ." His cheeks flushed as his mind struggled to get past the fog of the wine. "You should not speak of my daughter in public, sir."

"No, of course not," said Fullerton. "This way."

Fullerton slipped his arm through Sir Reginald's and steered him to the auditorium doors. Rosalind watched, aware of her rising tide of anger and fear.

She had to get out of here. She was going to drown. She was going to collapse on the floor and beat on the carpet, and that could not be seen. She could not give in to this blow she'd been dealt. She would not. Later, perhaps. When it was finished, when she had dealt with Fullerton, recovered her father, done all that must be done. Then she could collapse. Not now.

Rosalind turned swiftly around and crashed straight into Adam Harkness.

CHAPTER 10

The Complications of Family Connections

*Why am I so anxious, if it is not from love
to you?*

Maria Edgeworth, *Manoevering*

Rosalind reeled backward. Hands caught her gently, but firmly, and did not hold on a second longer than it took for her to regain her footing.

"I came as soon as I could." Mr. Harkness bowed.

He wore his day clothes—a dark, caped great coat hung open to show worn buff breeches, a plain white shirt, and the scarlet waistcoat that marked him as a "Robin Redbreast," a Bow Street officer.

Rosalind had seen Mr. Harkness in evening clothes exactly once. They were borrowed and fit badly, and it was one of the few times she had seen him ill at ease. Today he had not bothered with appearances, and she was grateful for it.

"Thank you," she murmured in acknowledgment of both his presence and her feelings.

"I thought you might need rescue."

"I do." As usual, his presence robbed her of her ability to formulate any polite fiction. Rosalind was not used to needing another person. She had friends, yes, but in certain fundamental ways, she had always relied on herself alone. The melting gratitude she felt that Mr. Harkness was beside her now, offering a physical shelter that could not be shaken, was unfamiliar and even frightening. It was also very real, but she could not let herself think about that now.

"Was that Russell Fullerton leaving there?" Mr. Harkness nodded toward the auditorium doors.

"I'm afraid it was."

"Is there cause for me to fetch him out?"

Of course he'd put it that way. He was here in his official capacity. She could see his staff of office tucked into his inner coat pocket.

"No," she admitted. "Not yet, at any rate. Did you . . . did you see Alice as you came in? Or Sanderson Faulks?"

He didn't ask her what happened. He clearly wanted to know, but he could wait, and he would wait as long as it took. That was his nature. "I did. Let me take you to them."

He paused, however, to pick up the shining high-crowned hat that had fallen to the floor at some point.

"Your mother told me you'd gotten a new hat." For as long as she had known him, Adam Harkness had worn an ancient tricorn cap.

"Yes, it seems the old one was finally past repair."

"I'm sorry that I should be responsible for the loss of such an old friend," she said with studied lightness.

Adam's old hat had been ruined when he engaged a band of brigands attacking the carriage Rosalind and her former housekeeper, Mrs. Kendricks, were riding in. That he had very nearly lost his life at the same time was not something Rosalind could think about with any sort of detachment. There was a crease in his cheek and a missing piece to his earlobe that had not been there before. When she saw them, responsibility burned painfully inside her.

"Do not worry yourself." He could have been answering her internal feelings, as well as her light banter. In fact, he might have been. Mr. Harkness had a knack for being able to understand much of what Rosalind did not say.

"How did you find me?" she asked him.

"Your new housemaid told me. She was very well informed. Seemed to know exactly who I was."

Rosalind resisted the urge to groan. "She listens at doors. I am going to have to write the agency. Again."

Alice and Mr. Faulks were not exactly difficult to find. They stood together in the middle of the almost-deserted salon. Servants and waiters in livery and maids in black and white scurried to and fro on their errands, and ignored their little grouping. A pair of ladies whispered together on the far side of the room. Possibly about the pair of gentlemen getting determinedly foxed at the bar.

"He got away?" asked Alice as soon as Mr. Harkness and Rosalind reached them.

"Yes."

"Blast," muttered Alice. "How on earth—"

"Not here, please." Rosalind's head was spinning. Too much had happened too quickly. She needed the safety of her own crowded home, and space to think. "What happened to Mr. Salter?"

"I'm ashamed to admit I lost sight of the fellow," said Mr. Faulks. "I think he's done a runner."

Rosalind suppressed a groan of frustration. *You must stay focused*, she admonished herself.

Salter's whereabouts were important, but more important was the fact that her father had fallen in with Russell Fullerton, a man who had sworn to destroy her, and who now had the means to bring that threat to pass. Part of her wanted to collapse in terror. Part of her raged at the threat to all she had made for herself.

Neither of them could be seen in the harsh light of the opera's salon.

"I can see you home, if you wish," said Adam.

"I am ready to perform that office," put in Sanderson. "My carriage is quite at Miss Thorne's disposal."

"Thank you, Mr. Faulks," said Rosalind. "But I wanted to ask you to keep an eye on the Walfords' box. I need to know if they stay for the performance, or if anyone comes or goes."

Mr. Faulks bowed. "You'll have word from me first thing tomorrow."

"Thank you."

Alice slipped her arm through Rosalind's. "Let's get you home, Rosalind. You've gone a very bad color. Mr. Harkness, I believe we'll take you up on that kind offer."

While Mr. Harkness handled the business of arranging a hired carriage, as well as reclaiming his horse from the nearby carriage house, Alice and Rosalind stood in the foyer. A few other women waited with them, along with some bored dandies, rowdies, and ballroom brilliants who had seen enough of opera-land and were ready to be off to the next entertainment. One of these was a "gentleman of the press," whom Rosalind remembered Alice introducing her to. The sight of him brought yet another horror to the fore. Every single paper would include an account of the opera's opening. Prominent people would be mentioned, and their costumes described, and all the current gossip about them would be repeated.

Any entertaining scenes were sure to be detailed, and speculated about.

Alice reached up and straightened Rosalind's bonnet.

"You can stop worrying, Rosalind."

"Why?" she asked wearily.

"Well, all right, probably you can't, but at least you don't have to worry about the papers tomorrow." Rosalind blinked, feeling uncharacteristically thick.

"Was it that obvious?"

"It was to me," replied Alice. "However, all anyone is talking about is how a drunkard accosted the Countess Lieven and she fended him off with her usual combination of boldness and excellent *ton*. At least, that's how A.E. Littlefield will be wording it. No one even noticed you."

"And there's for my vanity." Rosalind felt the tiniest smile form.

Alice shrugged. "That's what you get for being too good at what you do. You've maintained such a sterling and modest reputation, I'm afraid from a society standpoint, you're simply not that interesting."

"We must thank heaven for small mercies," murmured Rosalind.

"Miss Thorne and Miss Littlefield!" called a footman in the theater's livery. "Carriage for Miss Thorne and Miss Littlefield!"

Rosalind and Alice hurried out the doors and down the steps to where Mr. Harkness waited beside a hired cab. He helped bundle Alice and Rosalind inside. Once they were snug, he swung himself up onto a savvy, city-worn chestnut gelding and took the lead of the carriage.

It was not until they were in motion, and all possibility of being overheard had passed, that Alice turned to Rosalind.

"Did Fullerton catch you?"

"Yes," said Rosalind. "He . . . my father is staying with him, and he fully intends to keep him."

"But how could Fullerton have even found him?"

Rosalind shook her head. "How did Fullerton even know that Father could be dangerous to me? There's no one left who knows what he's done, except for Charlotte and me."

"And the men whose credit he tried to use without permission," said Alice quietly.

"Yes, and them." Rosalind bit her lip.

"Should I ask what you're going to do?"

Rosalind looked out the carriage window. The street outside was filled with the noisy shadows of passing carriages. "I am *not* going to let either of them destroy me, or Charlotte."

Alice paused, then said carefully, "Do you know how to stop him?"

"Yes." Rosalind didn't look at her. "I've known for quite some time."

All in all, it might have been faster to walk back to Little Russell Street. Between the winter muck and the traffic, their carriage's progress was agonizingly slow. Alice and Rosalind took turns poking at each other to keep themselves awake. It was an old amusement, from when they were schoolgirls, but this time failed to bring the usual smiles and giggles.

But finally, they reached their modest doorway. Rosalind felt a rush of relief.

Adam had the driver hold his horse's reins while he placed the carriage step and helped Alice down. Then he reached up for Rosalind.

"Will you call tomorrow at noon?" she murmured to him. He nodded. He did not so much as glance in Alice's direction.

There was a lamp lit at the door and another in the parlor. Amelia was sprawled in the chair by the partially banked fire, snoring.

Alice rolled her eyes and gave the housemaid a shake. She scrambled at once to her feet, blushing furiously and struggling to straighten her cap and curtsy at the same time.

"Thank you, Amelia," said Alice. "You can go to bed now."

"Yes, miss. Thank you, miss."

Alice shut the door and turned the key in the lock. She poked up the fire and turned up the lamp.

"Now, Rosalind," she said.

Slowly, Rosalind crumpled into the chair Amelia had abandoned. Her shoulders slumped, and she buried her burning face in her palms.

Last of all came all the long-delayed tears.

CHAPTER 11

Some Polite Breakfast Table Conversation

*Reduced to the meanest tricks and subterfuges to
delay or avoid the payment of his just debts, till,
ultimately grown familiar with falsehood, and at
enmity with the world, he loses the grace and dignity of man.*

Maria Edgeworth, *The Dun*

Russell Fullerton sat in his luxurious breakfast room, with
his coffee, papers, and the morning's correspondence.
Like the Prince Regent, he believed that a man should sur-
round himself with comfort and beauty—fine fabrics, fine
art, fine clothing. Therefore, his breakfast room was hung
with rich brocades of red and gold. More gold brocade covered the breakfast table. The coffee service was silver-gilt, im-
ported from Paris at enormous expense, and not a little risk.
An opulent, life-size painting of Venus rising from the waves
hung over the fireplace. The room, Fullerton felt, was a perfect, jeweled miniature of the world he had built for himself.

The world that Sir Reginald would now help him not just
maintain, but expand.

Important to remember that. Fullerton looked sourly at the empty chair across the table from him. Because the truth of the matter was, Sir Reginald was proving to be a considerable irritant. Indeed, if Fullerton had known how much work and trouble the man was going to be, he never would have started down this road.

Fullerton's mood was in no way improved by the entirely unsatisfactory nature of the morning gossip columns. The usual tattlers prattled on about the "enlivening incident" at the opera, but the "that most glamorous, foreign lady, Countess L—n," was the only named participant.

Interfering creature.

If she'd kept her distance, the columnists might have printed the names of Rosalind Thorne and the Walfords instead.

It was beyond frustrating. For two years now, he'd tried to find the chink in the Thorne woman's armor. She had plenty of weaknesses that should have been most amenable to attack—family disgrace, personal poverty, dubious friendships with all manner of riffraff, including writers, librarians, and policing officers. Her sister was a courtesan, for God's sake! Yet, somehow she managed to bob across the vicious sea of London's gossip like a cork. Her luck was unbelievable. Everyone seemed to know so much about her, but no one had any proof.

But then, it wasn't just luck, was it? The woman was incredibly calculating.

As little as he liked to admit it, Fullerton felt forced to concede he might have let his desire for profit override his natural caution. He had decided he could depend on the damage Sir Reginald could do. He should have prepared the means to shore those efforts up in advance.

Rumor alone might be enough to destroy a woman without protection. But in making herself useful, the Thorne woman had also made powerful friends among the gossiping classes. Lieven's intervention was not a coincidence. She was a patroness of Almack's, and that little crew had reasons to shelter Miss Thorne from most casual slights.

Protected as she was, Fullerton could not bring her down with a quiet word here and there. Not helping matters was the fact that she had no husband to be outraged by a rumor or three, no matter how scandalous. He needed stronger proofs. He needed ink on paper. But no matter how many avenues Fullerton pursued, he had not been able to find one single letter that betrayed her. He had not been able to track down any loan, or written promise, or other document that he could dangle in front of those who held the power to stoke rumor's fire.

Sparkes presented himself at tableside. Sparkes was his valet and general factotum. Fullerton truly trusted no one, but he came closest with Sparkes. As the longest-employed servant in the house, Sparkes looked the part of trustworthy manservant—white haired, lean, dignified to the point of desiccation, and rigid as a corpse. But he had a nimble brain and understood to a nicety how profitable serving his master's interests could be. He had, Fullerton happened to know, made himself quite the tidy nest egg from perquisites and tips, and yes, out-and-out bribes, over the years.

"What is it, Sparkes?" Fullerton asked.

"I am informed that Sir Reginald has finished dressing and will be joining you shortly."

"Excellent. Is the champagne ready?"

"Yes, sir."

"Very good."

Sparkes withdrew to the corner of the room beside the marble-topped buffet. One of the liveried footmen kept his post there also, silent and waiting. Fullerton's servants were all well disciplined and chosen for the uniformity of their look and manner. They were, after all, part of the domestic scene. He could not employ anyone who might create a jarring impression.

Sparkes had barely resumed his place when Sir Reginald entered the breakfast room.

Sir Reginald looked better than Fullerton expected. His puffy face was only a little paler than it had been, and the rings under his eyes not appreciably deeper.

The truth was, Fullerton found himself beginning to feel some small respect for Charlotte Thorne. He had only had possession of this man for a week, and he was beginning to profoundly regret his decision. She'd had to keep charge of this rascal for years. The man drank like a fish, complained incessantly. When he wasn't actually unconscious, he rattled around the house telling long, ludicrous stories of his supposed adventures.

"Good morning, Fullerton." Sir Reginald bowed.

"Good morning, Sir Reginald." Fullerton assumed an air of languid good humor, as if he welcomed a good friend. "Please, do sit down."

Sir Reginald took the offered chair. The footman stepped up to pour coffee and present a fresh rack of toast.

"What is your pleasure this morning?" Fullerton asked. "My cook makes an excellent omelette. Quite in the French style."

Sir Reginald turned only slightly green. "Thank you, but I seldom dine at this hour."

"Perhaps some champagne? I find there's nothing more refreshing after a late night."

"With pleasure. Your health, sir," he added as Sparkes filled his glass. He drank quickly. Fullerton sighed to himself. This month was going to be a drain on his cellar.

Sir Reginald lowered his empty glass. "The finest, most civilized tonic for the stomach," he announced.

"Now, sir, perhaps I can tempt you to that omelette?" Fullerton suggested.

"Well, perhaps I will indulge, this once." He eyed the champagne remaining in his glass and took another swallow.

Fullerton signaled to Sparkes, who bowed and sent the footman to relay the order to the cook.

"Now, as to last night," said Sir Reginald. "I feel I owe you some word of explanation. I must admit, I did not expect to see certain parties there. I fear I may have overreacted somewhat."

"Not at all, not at all." Fullerton waved the apology away. Indeed, he found himself surprised the man remembered what happened. He'd expected to have to provide a summary of the events. "Sparkes, some more champagne for Sir Reginald." Fullerton settled back in his chair and took up a cup of black coffee. "Your shock was only to be expected after the treatment you have been subjected to."

"Just so!" Sir Reginald drained the second glass as quickly as he drained the first. His pasty face began to take on some extra color, especially high in the cheekbones. "How rightly did the Bard declaim, ''tis sharper than a serpent's tooth to have a thankless child!' And I have two, sir! Two!"

"It is more than a shame," prompted Fullerton "It is unnatural."

"Unnatural." Sir Reginald savored the word as if it had been another swallow of champagne. "Yes, that's it exactly! Did I not bring them into this world? Do they not owe me their unconditional support and obedience? Instead, I am abandoned, I am *imprisoned* . . ." His voice rose to a shriek.

Fullerton leaned forward. "It is a story the world should know."

"I don't understand you."

"Let me introduce you to some friends," said Fullerton.

"Men of excellent social standing. Once they hear how you have been treated by your daughters, you may be sure they will be moved to do whatever they can to assist you."

Sir Reginald flushed like a schoolgirl. "Erm, yes, well." He coughed and fidgeted with his champagne glass. *Trying to find a lie I might believe.* Fullerton could not help but be impressed by the gall of the man.

"A gentleman should not . . . that is to say . . ." Sir Reginald hesitated. "You understand, sir, I am speaking of personal matters here."

Fullerton spread his hands. "Thorne, I assure you, anything you say to me will be held in complete confidence."

"Yes, well. It may be that some steps I took, years ago now, to try to preserve my wife's reputation and to protect my family are open to being misconstrued. Letters and . . . other documents were drafted. Perhaps it would be best if some discretion were maintained about how I came to be in such tiresome circumstances, just for now, you understand."

"Ah. Of course." Fullerton nodded sagely. *Neatly worded, you sad, drunken rogue.*

The footman reentered, bearing a tray of covered dishes. Sparkes set them down on the table and removed the covers to reveal on each a perfect golden omelette garnished with cheese sauce and herbs.

Despite his earlier protestations, Sir Reginald attacked the offering with gusto. Sparkes refilled his champagne glass, and he drank.

"If I could but find some way to *quietly* reestablish myself," said Sir Reginald between bites. "Just for a grace period as it were, while I set my private affairs to rights. Then, sir, then I would be able to serve up to those women their just desserts!"

"Well, you may say so." Fullerton took his own bite of omelette. Watching Sir Reginald's gluttony was quite de-

stroying his own appetite. "But I expect a father's fond heart
would shrink from taking open revenge, no matter how richly
deserved. After all, disgracing any woman in public is something a true gentleman must shrink from. How much more
quickly would one turn away when it is one's own daughters!"

Sir Reginald swallowed his latest gulp of champagne and
flushed red. "You mistake me, sir! It is not desire for revenge
that moves me! It is a father's love! If I do not offer my
daughters correction, who will? No. Once I have my own establishment, and have cleared up a few trifling unfinished
matters—ones, I freely admit, I've left for too long!—then
they will be made to understand how badly they have trans-
gressed. Afterwards, if they humble their hearts, and sincerely beg my pardon, of course, I will forgive them and take
them back in an instant." Sir Reginald paused and looked
Fullerton as directly in the eye as he was able. His face
was quite red by now. "It is an establishment I need, sir. A
cornerstone on which I might build my return."

"Well, if that's all that's needed, Sir Reginald, you are welcome to stay here as long as you require."

"Your generosity does you credit, Fullerton, but I would
never choose to burden a fellow gentleman. But if I had but
one true friend willing to make a small, and quite tempo-
rary—"

"Do you know, Sir Reginald. Something has just occurred
to me."

Sir Reginald stopped. Belatedly, he realized his mouth was
hanging open, and he closed it.

"What might that be?"

"We both know of your daughters' perfidy, and how cru-
elly they neglected and abused you. What is needed is some
proof that could be put before the world, without your good
self being seen as the instigator. Motives as generous as a fa-

ther's firm and guiding love can so easily be misunderstood by the rabble."

"Yes, of course," agreed Sir Reginald. "And when I have reestablished—"

"If only there were letters," Fullerton went on.

Sir Reginald frowned. "Letters?"

"It's astonishing what a woman will reveal in a letter. In company, she may appear to be the most proper of individuals, but in private, and on paper, quite another side may be revealed."

Sir Reginald did not answer at once. He set his knife and fork down and leaned back in his chair. His eyes narrowed. The unnaturally high color in his cheeks dimmed a little.

Interesting. Perhaps there is a mind at work in there after all.

"You speak like a man of experience." Sir Reginald chose his words with care.

Fullerton shrugged. "Sir Reginald, you and I know the world is a hard place. We must all protect ourselves. If a man comes across certain documents that may relate to a matter of business or that could affect his reputation, well, it is only prudent that he preserve them. Strictly as a precaution, of course."

"Of course," said Sir Reginald. "Who could be blamed for taking care in such a fashion?"

"If I had two wayward daughters whom I loved—although they may have forfeited all proper claim to a father's love!" Fullerton went on. "And if I had letters that provided proof of their ignominious conduct, I would keep them. Such letters, handled correctly, could very well prove to be an effective instrument of correction. They could be shown to the daughters. It might be intimated that their contents could easily become public. Thus could the wayward children be warned to change their ways, before it was too late." Fullerton paused. Sir Reginald was watching him like a snake. "With such letters in hand, it would not even be necessary for the man to tell even his most intimate friends of the letters' contents. Women in general are very aware of their precarious position in the world. The mere existence of such letters would be enough to bring them to heel. That, of course, would be much better for the whole of the family than a public scandal."

"Yes," said Sir Reginald slowly. "I can very well see how such letters—if there were such letters—might indeed be a strong preventative. If the daughters could be induced to see reason." He steepled his fingers. "Perhaps by a third, entirely disinterested party."

"Yes." Fullerton nodded. "A disinterested third party might indeed be helpful. Of course, one could understand why a man might hesitate before revealing the existence of such a store of letters. After all, the family bond is sacred. He might even forebear to tell anyone that he had them, at least for a while."

"Yes. Just so," agreed Sir Reginald.

"Now." Fullerton dropped his napkin on the table and pushed his chair away from the table. "As delightful as our conversation has been, I must excuse myself. Some trifling matters of business claim the rest of my day." He stood and swept his hand out to indicate the whole house. "Please make yourself entirely at home. Sparkes is under orders to see to all you might require."

"Thank you, Fullerton. I have been in ill health, as you know, but I am certain that after a few days of your most excellent hospitality, I shall quite recover my strength, and then I will be able to recover, shall we say, portions of my life that I may have left behind when I was forced to flee in such ignominy."

Fullerton smiled and left him there.

Excellent.

The seeds of action were now firmly planted in the old sot's mind. But there was that moment when Sir Reginald watched him with narrowed eyes. His gaze had been unclouded by the champagne. It reminded Fullerton that the man was not without nerve, or a certain share of low cunning.

Sir Reginald could still be dangerous. He would bear watching.

Well, there is no reward without risk, and this time the reward will be worth any risk at all.

CHAPTER 12

The Scope of the Problem

But he was so easily led, or rather so easily
excited by his companions, and his companions
were now of such a sort, that it was probable he
would soon become vicious.

Maria Edgeworth, *Belinda*

Rosalind slept in far later the next morning than she'd meant to. Since Alice had sent Amelia to bed, they each helped each other out of their evening things. Rosalind was so tired she barely had breath to blow out the candle before she fell asleep.

By the time she got herself dressed and downstairs, Alice had evidently already been awake for some time. There was a pot of tea on the table, and Alice was engaged in that homely and improper pastime of toasting a slice of crumpet over the fire.

"You always were the best at that," said Rosalind, remembering all the times they filched stale muffins from the kitchens at school.

"The benefits of long practice." Alice carefully thumbed

the hot crumpet onto a plate and handed it to her. "There's butter and some excellent jam. She may have her faults, but Amelia does an excellent job with the marketing."

Rosalind looked guiltily at her informal breakfast. Alice pointed the fork at her.

"If you are thinking of apologizing for last night, you needn't bother. You have absolutely nothing to apologize for. But what you will do is eat." She stabbed the fork at the toasted crumpet. "Because I'm not speaking until you do."

Rosalind smiled. "Yes, miss." She smeared her crumpet with a thick layer of butter and raspberry jam, and poured out a cup of Amelia's ridiculously strong, dark tea.

The combination proved to be exactly what she needed.

Alice concentrated on spearing another crumpet half on her fork and finding the proper angle to hold it over the fire.

"Alice . . ." Rosalind began.

Alice held up her hand, without taking her eyes off the fire. "Not until you've finished all that crumpet."

"Is this how you treated George?"

"Every morning of our lives." Alice lowered the crumpet minutely closer to the flames. "Now you're about to say it's no wonder he left me to get married."

Rosalind smiled. "I never would say such a thing."

"Liar."

Rosalind smiled again. She also followed instructions and ate all her crumpet and drank the entire cup of tea. By the time she finished, Alice had claimed her own breakfast and was munching with gusto.

"Can I talk now?" Rosalind poured herself another cup of tea.

Alice gave permission with a wave of her crumpet.

Rosalind picked up the toasting fork and carefully speared a new slice of pastry. "My problem is I can't believe that this incident is all Fullerton had planned."

"Why wouldn't it be? What he wanted was to show you that Sir Reginald was in his power. He did that. Handily. The swine."

"Yes, but how did he know where to find me?" Rosalind held the crumpet slice over the fire. "It wasn't exactly advertised that I'd be attending the opera yesterday."

For the first time that morning, Alice looked uneasy. "Do you think he's having you watched?"

"He must."

"I don't suppose it would do any good to go draw the curtains?"

"I don't mean I think that anybody's lurking. It's more likely he had someone talk to—" She nodded toward the door. Alice's brows shot up.

Amelia? she mouthed.

Rosalind nodded.

"I don't believe it," Alice breathed. "She's a bit skittish, but she's not one to go talking to strangers."

"She told Mr. Harkness where to find us."

"When he showed up in all his glory as a Bow Street runner," Alice pointed out. "Besides, she may have heard you mention his name once or twice."

"Yes, she might. And she might be proud of how much she knows. Or simply in need of extra money."

"Oh dear," murmured Alice, obviously deflated. She also got up, opened the parlor door. Thankfully, the foyer was empty. She closed the door and sat back down, obviously disconcerted.

Rosalind frowned at the fire, lost in thought. She'd never considered that she might become one of those women who couldn't trust their servants. Mrs. Kendricks had spoiled her. If Amelia was selling information to Fullerton, or his agents, how was she to find out? She was not ready to dismiss the girl on simple suspicion. When a servant was turned her away without a reference, it was nearly impossible for them to find a new position. The results could be a short slide into poverty and ruin.

Alice took the toast fork from her hand. Rosalind didn't object.

"What I can't understand is what's changed?" Rosalind said. "Why is Fullerton doing this now?"

"Well, it's not as if he's just started, is it?" Alice reminded her. "He's been threatening you for over a year."

"Threatening yes, but this is fundamentally different." Rosalind held out her plate for the fresh crumpet slice. "This is taking effort and outlay, probably a fair amount of both, and Fullerton is a fundamentally lazy man."

"How could you know that?"

"Gamblers are lazy." Rosalind spread fresh butter and jam across her crumpet. "And they have a need to convince themselves they are smarter than the men who work for what they gain. This means they'll always look for a way around whatever's in their way, rather than trying to re-move the obstacle."

Alice speared the last crumpet slice. "So when a lazy man makes an effort, there must be an object in view."

Rosalind nodded. "In this case, either I have done some-thing that affects his plans or I am about to."

Alice turned the crumpet just a little. "Unless it isn't about you."

"I'm sorry?"

"This could be about Charlotte, and her upcoming mar-riage."

Rosalind had to admit she hadn't thought about that. "It could also be about her child."

"Yes, there might be someone who will be disappointed to find her fiancé is getting married and about to have an heir. That person could perhaps make trouble."

"That person could be a wife," said Rosalind.

"Possibly, although I respect Charlotte enough to assume

she's checked for all the obvious problems before accepting this proposal."

Rosalind had to agree. "But if Charlotte is Fullerton's target, why am I the one he exposed Father to?"

"Because you're not only more vulnerable, you're more dangerous," said Alice. "You're the one who keeps frustrating his plans. After all, what did Charlotte do when she realized the extent of the trouble? She came straight to you."

"Then, the plan could be to cut us off from each other so Charlotte is without assistance."

"Or to use a threat against you to apply pressure to Charlotte," said Alice. "If he frightens you badly enough, you might urge your sister to go along with whatever he asks."

"And thus he gains control of us both."

"And Charlotte's would-be husband in the bargain." Alice flopped backward in her chair, somehow managing to do so without her crumpet sliding into her lap. "As a scheme, you must admit, it's very neat."

"If that's what's happening," Rosalind added.

Alice looked miffed. "You said yourself, something must have changed."

"Yes, but that doesn't necessarily mean we've seen what it is yet." She sipped at her tea again. "It might have something to do with the Walfords."

"The Walfords? They're not even from London."

"That doesn't mean they all sprang fully formed from the head of Zeus," Rosalind reminded her. "Everyone has a past. Mrs. Walford might have indiscretions she'd rather were not made public, especially while she's attempting to establish her children in their lives. She's also from a French émigré family. That's been known to create special entanglements." Even as she said it, Rosalind remembered Augustina's and Salter's little comments about Lady Holland's politics.

Mrs. Walford must have some acquaintance with Lady Holland, or she wouldn't have gone to speak to her in such a public setting, not without an introduction. But if she had an acquaintance she could presume on, why didn't she apply to Lady Holland when she came to London? She'd always protested to Rosalind that she knew absolutely no one in town.

Why would she lie about that?

"What about Mr. Salter?" put in Alice.

"Yes, what about him?" murmured Rosalind. "There's definitely more between him and Augustina than I initially thought. I don't know what their relationship is, but it's very different from what it seemed."

"Then perhaps Augustina is the one Fullerton is after," Alice suggested. "If she's gone further afield with a sharp character than a genteel girl should . . ."

Rosalind considered this. "That's possible, but that sort of blackmail is Fullerton's daily bread. He wouldn't need to go through the trouble of threatening me to get to Augustina Walford." She shook herself, then drank the last of her tea. "But sitting here won't untangle this mess. Alice, I need you to take a message to Charlotte. She needs to know what's happened, and I'm afraid we have to assume the house, and the post, are being watched."

"I should think so." Alice paused, turning this little problem over in her quick mind. "I know. I'll go to the *Chronicle* offices. I'll hand the note off to George, and he can take it the rest of the way."

"Yes, that will do perfectly."

It would also get her out of the way for the requisite amount of time. Alice was her dearest friend, but what she must do next, she did not wish even Alice to see.

Rosalind went to her writing desk and dashed off a quick and ambiguous note.

I have found him. Meet me at Clements's Circulating Library at three o'clock. Send any message only by

*trusted hand. Commit nothing to the post. Do not come
to the house.*
   R.

Any other day she would have laughed at herself for being
alarmist, but not now. Fullerton was relentless, and he had a
great deal of practice at what he did. She would not underestimate him.

Rosalind folded and sealed the letter, then wrote *Cynthia
Sharps,* her sister's *nom d'amour,* across the front. Alice took
the letter and stowed it in her reticule.

"I have to deliver my notes on the opera, anyway," she
mumbled around a last bite of crumpet. "By the way, I've
saved you some time and read the papers." She patted the
stack of morning newspapers piled on her writing table. "It's
as I predicted. The Countess Lieven eclipsed everything else.
Do you think she knows she saved you?"

"I'm sure of it. She asked me to call. She needs something."

Alice laid one hand on her shoulder. "Do be careful, Rosalind. That woman intrigues on a far different level from the
rest of us mere mortals."

Rosalind squeezed her hand. "Believe me, Alice, I shall
handle her as if one of us were made of glass."

That seemed to reassure her friend, and Alice took up her
reticule and her gloves. "Well, I am off. I don't suppose I can
persuade you to stay inside today and recoup yourself from
last night?"

"I wish I could, but if nothing else, I have to go see Mrs.
Walford and explain, at least as much as I can."

Alice sighed. "I was afraid of that. Well, perhaps by
tonight we'll have hit on a solution to this mess."

I hope so, thought Rosalind as her friend headed out into
the foyer, calling for Amelia.

Because there was another possibility, one that she was certainly not ready to talk about out loud, even with Alice. It almost did not bear thinking about. Rosalind swallowed against the tightness in her throat.

It was possible that Fullerton had already gotten to Charlotte. If that was true, it was possible that Charlotte had allowed or even aided Sir Reginald's apparent escape.

Because if Rosalind could be used against her sister, wasn't it also possible that Charlotte could be used against her?

CHAPTER 13

Domestic Complications

*Perhaps there is nothing in the report—I really
only repeat what I hear everybody say.*

Maria Edgeworth, *Almeria*

After Alice left, Rosalind tried to keep herself busy with
her correspondence and her account books—anything
she could find to help her ignore the slow ticking of the mantel clock.

The bells outside rang the quarter hour, then the half, and
Rosalind felt like the intervals between were only slowing
down.

*Why did I say Mr. Harkness should come at noon? I
should have asked him to be here at first light*, she thought irritably.

Finally, Amelia poked her head into the parlor. "May I
take the breakfast things, miss?"

"Yes, Amelia, thank you."

Rosalind refolded a letter from an old family friend and
placed it on the stack of correspondence that needed answering. Amelia moved about the little parlor, picking up the cups

and plates, rattling everything as she strained to be quiet. She looked pale, too. Unnerved.

Or is that just me jumping at shadows? Rosalind sighed. At the same time, she could not deny that Amelia was a problem, or at least a question, that had to be addressed.

Better to do it now.

She had never missed her former housekeeper Mrs. Kendricks so much as she did now. Rosalind could trust Mrs. Kendricks as family, and more than once she had been able to provide Rosalind with invaluable information gleaned from belowstairs.

But Mrs. Kendricks's dream for Rosalind had been that she—they—might regain the life that had been lost. She had stayed on through thick and thin so that she might shepherd Rosalind to a good marriage, and thus a secure future.

Rosalind had chosen a different and much less certain path—a path that did not even have a proper name. The choice required more than Mrs. Kendricks was able to give, and they both knew it. It had also meant that Rosalind was by no means certain to be able to fill that one final obligation of a mistress to a faithful servant—a comfortable retirement. Because of this, Rosalind had made no objection when Mrs. Kendricks had decided to go live with her sister and her family. Rosalind enjoyed her gossiping letters and kept her own as light as possible.

She would be lying, however, if she said that Mrs. Kendricks's absence was not part of why she had felt so unmoored of late. Or that her departure had not created a servant problem with more than the usual number of angles.

"Amelia? I need to speak with you a minute."

The housemaid straightened up, the toasting fork in her hand. She had gone paper white.

"Miss?" she whispered.

"About the gentleman you spoke with yesterday."

Amelia lowered the fork. "He came here?"

"You know he did."

Amelia looked toward the window. "He said he would." She gripped the toasting fork until her knuckles turned as white as her cheeks. "Well, he can say what he likes. I know I didn't do nothing wrong. It was just a bun and a cuppa and some laughs, wasn't it? No matter what *he* might say."

It occurred to Rosalind that the girl was talking about somebody other than Adam Harkness. She carefully schooled the surprise out of her features.

"Perhaps you should tell me your side of the story."

Amelia's own expression said she most decidedly did not want to tell it, but that she was going to, come what may.

"It was just three weeks ago, wasn't it? My half day, an' I been over to see my cousin. She's a nursemaid in Camden, and we've got the same day. I was walking through the market on my way back, and, well, there was this gentleman and we got to talking and before you say it, miss, yes, I know as good as any what that can mean, but he was a young 'un and, well, there's no harm in talking. And like I said, I let him buy me a bun and a cuppa, and I came home. Alone as ever.

"Next week he was there again, and we talked some more. Just talk, a bit of a laugh. I'm careful. I know which end is up."

"I believe you," Rosalind told her.

"Next week he gets into it. Says I'm too pretty for my work. *Uh-oh*, I thinks. *Now you're for it, Amelia Riggs.* Says he don't want nothin' from me hisself, but he says there's this other gent who'll pay, and pay handsome, for . . ." She paused.

"For?" Rosalind prompted.

"For word about you, miss. And Miss Alice. Anything I can bring about your business, and where you're going and who you're seeing, and what letters come to the house, and all that."

"What did you tell him?"

Amelia's raw hands knotted tight. "What I told him you couldn't print in papers. I also told him what he could do with both his buns, and you couldn't put that in the papers, neither." She stuck out her chin, waiting for Rosalind to chastise her for this immodest behavior.

"And his response?"

Amelia's defiance wavered. "That's the trouble. I thought he'd go off, but he didn't. He said not so fast. Said I'd better be nice, or he'd be showing up at the front door here, saying I was a bad girl, that it was me that made up to him and . . ." She swallowed. "That it was me that offered to tell what goes on in the house, and that you'd be sure to believe him, and I'd be out in the street. And now he's done it." The final word came out as a harsh croak. "Well, you can do what you like. I've told the truth and I will swear to it before God and all. So help me."

She stood there squarely, clutching the toasting fork like she might have to use it to fend off attack. But the color had returned to her cheeks, and the nervousness that had been so evident when she came into the parlor was entirely gone.

Rosalind considered her next question carefully. "Is that why you've been listening at doors? You wanted to hear if Miss Littlefield and I were talking about you?"

"Yes, miss," she croaked.

"And what would you have done if I hadn't spoken to you today?"

Amelia hesitated. She looked at the toasting fork and then laid it carefully on the tray with the rest of the breakfast things.

"I don't know," she said. "I laid awake about it for two nights, and I still don't know."

It was the uncertainty of this answer that convinced Rosalind the girl was telling the truth. She nodded and watched some of the fear drain from Amelia's eyes.

"This gentleman, the one who tried to get you to spy on me, can you describe him?"

Amelia's eyes narrowed. "He was a gentleman, no mistake. His clothes were quality, cut to fit. Not spanking new, but new enough. Dark hair, some color to his skin like he spends a bit of time out of doors, but not too much. Clean shaved, no side whiskers. Long sort of chin. Young, like I said, not much older'n me. That's why I talked to him at all. He seemed kind of awkward, at least before he turned on me, didn't he? I remember thinking, *This one's a bit of a boy, really.*"

Amelia, it seemed, had more than a little talent at observation. "What name did he give?"

"Parker. John Parker. I expect that's a fiddle."

"I expect it is," murmured Rosalind. Inwardly, she sighed. She had been wondering if she was being watched, and now she knew. She felt that cold fact crawl across her skin. At the same time it was perversely reassuring, because it brought a level of certainty.

Amelia's gent first approached her three weeks ago. That was before Father was taken. She bit her lip. Fullerton had been planning this for some time.

Unless . . . She frowned. *Unless it's someone else.*

Rosalind shook herself. This was no good. She could turn it all over later. Right now, she had to finish with Amelia.

The maid was standing as straight and determined as ever.

"Am I to go at once, miss?" she asked with the air of someone trying to get the worst over all at once.

"No, Amelia, you are not to go at all, unless you want to."

Amelia's jaw dropped open.

"I believe you," Rosalind went on. "And I appreciate your honesty. You may actually have helped me." She folded her hands. "However, since you've been honest with me, I need to be honest with you. This house may be about to fall into grave trouble and scandal. If you choose to leave now, you will have your wages and a good reference."

Amelia's mouth moved silently. She looked toward the door, and the window, and the toasting fork. Rosalind found herself wondering if the girl was getting ready to escape or fend off attack, and found she liked Amelia better for considering both possibilities.

"No thank you, miss," said Amelia finally. "I'll stay, if it's all the same to you."

"Very well. I'm going to have a caller at noon, and after that I must leave on some errands. It may be that some persons will come to the door, front or back, and try to engage you in conversation. It may even be that your gentleman is one of them. They may create some pretext to be let in, and they may offer you . . . inducements."

Amelia drew herself up. Her dark eyes flashed with sudden and entirely unexpected fire. "Well, they can just as well save themselves the trouble, miss. I'll send any such on their way, no fear!"

It might have been the bravado of a young woman hearing the prospect of adventure, but the hard light in Amelia's eyes told Rosalind there was a story behind her words. She only wished she had time to draw it out.

"Thank you, Amelia. I can't say how long I'll be, but I hope to be back before dinner."

"Don't you worry, Miss Thorne. I'll have your supper hot, and you'll find all in order."

Amelia took up the tray and bustled out with such energy that all the breakfast things rattled, leaving Rosalind with some concern for her few good pieces of china. She found herself staring at the closed parlor door with knitted brows. She was very aware that she'd been lucky. It was pure chance that her new housemaid was made from stuff stern enough to keep from being intimidated, or to succumbing to bribery. At least so far. How long would such luck last?

How far has it been stretched without my even knowing it?

Rosalind shuddered. She found herself wishing she hadn't sent Alice away. The fact that there had been a plot brewing for so long left her feeling terribly alone.

But, of course, she wasn't alone. The bells and the clock were striking noon. For better or for worse, Adam Harkness was now in view, striding up Little Russell Street.

Rosalind smoothed back her hair and her skirts and tried to put some kind of smile on her face. It was not easy.

CHAPTER 14

Threats and Promises

*A promise is in the nature of a verbal covenant,
and wants nothing but the solemnity of writing
and feeling to make it absolutely the same.*

John Impey of the Inner Temple, *The Modern Pleader*

"Good morning, Mr. Harkness," said Rosalind. Mr. Harkness always seemed a little too large for her crowded parlor, or perhaps it was simply that being so close to him had an unusually intense effect on Rosalind's senses. It didn't help that this was the first time that they had been alone together since the both of them had returned to London.

That she had spent so many of those days, and nights, poring over his letters like an infatuated schoolgirl did not make this reunion any easier.

Rosalind immediately took refuge in the rituals of courtesy. "Please sit down. Will you have some coffee or tea?"

"Thank you." Mr. Harkness sat in the slat-backed chair. "But no coffee for me, I'm afraid I do not have much time this morning. Will you tell me what happened last night?"

That calm question brought Rosalind fully back to herself. Softer feelings, she reminded herself, could wait.

Will have to wait. Might have to be done with altogether.

"I barely know what happened," she admitted. "That's part of the reason I needed to see you. I can tell you that this chain of events did not begin last night. Yesterday, my sister, Charlotte, came to see me. Have I told you she had taken charge of my father?"

"You have mentioned it." Sir Reginald had always been a delicate point between them. Rosalind suspected Mr. Harkness knew of her father's crimes, although neither of them had ever spoken of them openly.

Yet.

"Father was lodged in Bath, but he . . . escaped her. She came to warn me. When I wrote that letter to you, I thought I would be asking you to help find him. Instead, he found me at the opera. Which was when I learned he had help in making his escape."

"Fullerton."

"How much do you know about him?"

"I know his reputation." Rosalind sensed an extra level of care in those words. "So far, he has been careful to remain outside of Bow Street's range of authority."

"This does not surprise me," said Rosalind. "He is cautious in that way." She paused, marshaling her nerves, and her words. "Fullerton brought my father to the opera last night specifically to be shown to me. The display was followed by a threat."

When Adam was startled, or upset, he went very still. He was very still now. "What was this threat?"

"Mr. Fullerton said that unless I swore to refrain from interfering with his activities for good and all, and accept . . .

certain other restraints, he would let my father loose upon society to create what scandal he could. That would very likely mean ruin for me, and for Charlotte."

"Why would he do such a thing now?"

"I asked myself that question this morning, and I have no answer yet. As far as I know, the lady I am currently employed in assisting has no connection to him. It is possible there is a connection between him and the man who is courting the daughter of the family."

"And the suitor is?"

"Horatio Salter. He's a gambler and has heavy debts, and it's known, or at least rumored, he was involved in a scheme to commit fraud upon the stock markets."

"Not the man I'd choose to marry my daughter," Adam remarked.

"No," agreed Rosalind. "I have no proof he and Fullerton are connected, but the only reason that I can think of for Fullerton moving against me at this time is that he doesn't want me interfering with Salter's relations with the Walford family. I hope, however, I will be able to find out more shortly."

Adam nodded. "What can I do to help?"

She looked up at him. *Be here with me*, she wanted to say. *Give me shelter. Tell me that even if the rest of the world falls away, you'll still be there.*

But she couldn't. Not yet. Perhaps not ever.

"I cannot allow my father to run mad through London," said Rosalind. "Neither can I allow Fullerton to keep him as a caged bear to let loose upon me and Charlotte when he chooses. I need . . . I need you to retrieve him."

"I will do all I can." It was an absolute promise. She could see that much in his eyes. She knew she would see much more there, but she could not stand to look that long.

"I have arranged to meet with my sister this afternoon. It may be she knows more about Fullerton's haunts than we do."

"Likely," Adam agreed. "I can make some inquiries. If he's been involved in fraud before, he's sure to be known to someone at Bow Street."

Rosalind smoothed her skirts. The fabric was too thin and too smooth under her palms. She felt shabby, coarse, overused. She knew none of these things was true, but the feelings would not leave her.

"I want . . . you should know that this is not a favor," she said, speaking to her hands and her skirts. "Your fees will be paid."

"At the risk of being offensive, can you afford it?"

Rosalind smiled, just a little, and found she was able to lift her gaze, at least for a moment. "Charlotte can."

"Ah." Mr. Harkness nodded once.

He did not say, *I would have done what you asked anyway.* He did not have to. She heard it clearly in his voice, and he knew that she did. Rosalind's heart was a brittle thing, but just then it felt full and whole.

It did not make what she had to do next any easier, but it did make it possible.

"There's something else."

Rosalind kept the bottom drawer of her desk locked. She brought out her ring of keys, opened that drawer, and took out an iron box. She used a second key on this. She moved aside various legal documents and pulled out a packet of notes bound in black ribbon.

She stared at them a moment, hesitating. She could still turn back. She did not have to do this. Not yet.

No. I will not deceive myself.

She tried to tell herself that empowering Mr. Harkness and

Bow Street to formally arrest Father would cause Fullerton to make good on all his threats. He would become relentless in his pursuit of her ruin. Rumors would attack her from every side. Some of them would even be true.

It was her own destruction she held in her hands.

Is it really better to bring that all crashing down than to try to hold it off just a little longer?

Yes, Rosalind answered herself. *Fullerton has one play. If I can weather this, he is no longer any threat to me. Us.*

But can I weather this?

Rosalind grit her teeth, turned, and held the letters out to Mr. Harkness.

He took the slim packet. "What are these?"

"Promissory notes," said Rosalind "My father forged them and then sold them off to raise money when he was in distress."

The stillness of Mr. Harkness's expression told Rosalind he understood exactly what she handed him. There were many crimes that could take members of the lower classes to the gallows, but forgery was one of the few that could put a noose around a gentleman's neck. The forgery of promissory notes or banker's drafts interfered with the delicate net of trust and credit that kept the system of British banking and economy together.

It was quite possible Rosalind had handed Mr. Harkness her father's death warrant.

He took the packet. "Can I ask where you got these?"

Of course he would need to know that. And I knew I would have to say. Her hesitation was just one more absurdity heaped onto this entire conversation.

"The last time I saw my father, I was still living with my godparents," Rosalind said. "He forced his way into the house, drunk, and demanded money, and, well, me."

Mr. Harkness said nothing. His silence wrapped around her, but this once, it provided no warmth, no steadiness.

"After that, I vowed to myself that I would not be given back into my father's custody. I am of age, of course, but I was not then. And, of course, I was and am unmarried. If my father took it into his head to go to court"—*especially with Fullerton to help pay his legal fees*—"he could easily gain a share of my income. Indeed, according to the solicitors I have consulted, it is likely that he could gain full control over all my monies, including any future earnings simply because he is my nearest male relative. The law, you see, does not look kindly on a woman who tries to live alone, and a jury would be inclined to believe that if I had any natural feeling, I would want to support and care for my father.

"Knowing that, I tracked down some of the men against whom my father had forged promises. I found three who had kept the notes and were willing to give them to me. That way, if my father returned and made demands, I could . . ." She gestured toward the letters and Mr. Harkness.

"You could protect yourself," he said.

"Yes." Rosalind did not look at him. She did not want to see him understanding at last how very cold her heart was. Protecting herself meant being ready to send her father to his death. She had known that when she sought out these letters. She had known that every day she kept them. Even before she had the excuse of protecting Charlotte and her baby, she had known she would use them, just as she did now. She was cold. She was selfish. Unfeminine. Proud. Ambitious. Calculating.

"Rosalind," said Adam.

Rosalind lifted her gaze reflexively. His eyes were gentle, honest, and filled with feeling. There was so much she wanted to say. They were alone. There was nothing to stop her, except herself, and she was still afraid.

Adam reached across the space between them and took her hand.

"It is no shame to want to live your own life, and it is not wrong to fight against someone who would take it from you," he said. "But surely, surely there is another way?"

"What way?" she demanded. "The law is all on his side. No matter what he has done to me, he remains my father. I am inferior to him, and I am ungrateful and unnatural because I will not give him all I have without complaint. I have no husband behind whom I can hide, or to whom I owe a greater duty in the eyes of the law." She met his steady gaze. "Tell me that I'm wrong," she begged. "Please. Tell me that law and custom leave me another way to save myself and my sister from him."

His skin was rough against hers. He never had to pretend to be protected from his own life. She closed her fingers around his, savoring the warmth of them, the strength of this simple touch.

But she had to let go. She always had to let go. That fact had never made her as angry as it did now.

But Adam would not let her draw back so easily. He caught her hand gently, turned it over, and laid the letters in her palm.

"Keep these," he said. "Let me find him first. Then we can decide. There may yet be another way."

"What other way?"

The corner of Mr. Harkness's mouth twitched. "Well, as he is keeping company with Russell Fullerton, it may be he is involved in some other activity which we can bring to the attention of the magistrates, without recourse to those." He touched the letters again.

"And that keeps my hands clean," murmured Rosalind.

"I am more concerned about your heart," answered Mr. Harkness. "And your memory."

Rosalind's throat felt raw from the pressure of everything she held inside. She wanted to scream that there was no way. How could there be any other way?

And yet, wasn't that how she had lived all this time? By finding the other way, even when it could not be clearly seen? What she did for others, Mr. Harkness was now offering to do for her.

All she had to do was trust him for a little while. It was just that simple, and that complex.

Rosalind laid the letters back in their box.

"Thank you," she breathed. "I'm sorry to have to come to you in distress, yet again."

Mr. Harkness stood, and he bowed. "As often as you need, I will be there."

He meant it. He had not turned away. He would not. Her heart had felt full before. Now it overflowed.

She stood. She would face him on equal ground while she said what came next, as inadequate as it might be.

"When this is finished, Mr. Harkness, I very much hope we will see more of each other."

The moment the words left her, Rosalind wished them back. The time was entirely inappropriate. What woman would in the middle of such a disaster speak so boldly to such a man as this. Could she even be sure—

Adam smiled and Rosalind's galloping thoughts came to an abrupt halt.

The first day she met him, Rosalind noted that Adam Harkness was a handsome man, with a smile that was positively unfair. He smiled now, and for a moment she felt herself turn quite weak in the knees.

"In that case, Miss Thorne," he said, "I will make sure it is finished very soon."

They said their farewells and he left her, and Rosalind collapsed back in her chair. A woman her age and in such straits
should not feel giddy. She should not feel hope.

But she did, and more than that. She felt renewed.

We will make sure this is finished very soon, she thought
toward the place where Mr. Harkness had stood. *Together.*

CHAPTER 15

Missed

Winter is generally admitted to be an unsociable moment in London.

Catherine Gore, *The Banker's Wife*

Unfortunately, Rosalind's optimistic mood was destined to be short-lived.

"Miss Thorne!" exclaimed Mr. Clement from his station behind the library desk. "How very good to see you!"

"I am glad to see you as well, Mr. Clements, and your fire." Rosalind stripped off her damp gloves. Mindful of her budget, and the uncertainty of the days ahead, Rosalind had elected to walk from Little Russell Street to Clement's Circulating Library. A decision she regretted as soon as the slow winter rain began to fall. "I'm quite raw."

"Then you must have a seat at once!" Mr. Clement rounded his desk and conducted her to the table beside the fire. "What can I bring you? Tea, perhaps? A biscuit?"

"Both, thank you," replied Rosalind. "And a copy of *La Belle Assembleé.*"

"At once." Mr. Clementss bowed and then signaled for his assistant.

The reading room of Clements's Circulating Library was a well-appointed, parlor-like chamber with reading tables and comfortable chairs. Its arrangements were altogether pleasant and relaxing. If one wanted to read in solitude, it was easy enough to find a little nook at the edge of the room. If one wanted to be found by friends and acquaintances, one might choose to be at the center or by the windows.

Mr. Clement's given name was Ernesto Javier Garcia Mendoza y Clemente. Rosalind knew he originally hailed from Argentina. He did not, however, speak much of his past. The straight red scar that showed through his thinning hair suggested it had not been entirely sedentary. He had risen through the ranks of a printer's establishment before turning to books, then bookselling, and finally the office of librarian. In this, he had prospered so much that he now had two assistants, and his establishment could provide its patrons with light refreshment, as well as the latest books and papers.

A broad desk separated the bookshelves from the reading room. Sometimes, Rosalind thought it would be delightful to sneak behind the desk and roam about those aisles where the books were stored. That, however, was not the way things were done. A library patron requested books or magazines from Mr. Clements or his assistants, who would then go and fetch them. One might read in the library or take the books home, provided one had paid the guinea subscription fee.

Today, the library was almost empty. Aside from Mr. Clements, Rosalind's only company was a dowager pouring over a thick book of poetry and a comfortable-looking gentleman reading *The London Times*.

Charlotte was nowhere to be seen.

As Mr. Clements and his assistant brought her the requested journal and the cup of tea, respectively, the bells outside began to toll three o'clock. The little carriage clock on the mantel added its dainty chime. Rosalind glanced toward the door and the windows overlooking the high street. But if Charlotte was in the crowd, Rosalind couldn't pick her out.

Mr. Clements noticed Rosalind's distraction and shooed his boy away. "I will leave you to your reading," he said to Rosalind. "Do not hesitate to ask for anything you might need." He bowed again.

Rosalind thanked him, sipped her tea gratefully, and opened *La Belle Assembleé.* She soon realized, however, she was not going to be able to concentrate on the pages in front of her. Her gaze kept darting toward the door, and the windows, looking for Charlotte.

A quarter hour passed and then a half. Rosalind sat in her comfortable chair, occasionally turning an unread page. She drank her cooling tea, but the cup seemed to grow increasingly bitter as Rosalind grew increasingly restless. She wanted to pace, but she could not. She wanted to stare out the window, but that was also to draw attention to herself. It was bad enough that Mr. Clements was watching her with increasing concern. Worse, every time the doors opened, it sent a jolt through her. The few strangers present were beginning to glance sideways. Probably, they suspected her of waiting for a highly inconsiderate beau.

What do I do?

She had hoped to be able to go from here to call on Mrs. Walford. She needed to offer her some kind of explanation for the scene from yesterday evening and to pass on what little she had learned.

Including that I'm being watched.

When Rosalind had heard Amelia's description of her "gent," she realized that man could well have been Horatio Salter. If Salter had been digging for information about Rosalind, who else might he be after?

I have to let Mrs. Walford know.

But the time of day during which it was acceptable to call

was rapidly drawing to a close, and Charlotte had still not arrived.

Could the message have gone astray? Rosalind stared determinedly at her journal. No. Alice and George would not have permitted it. *But then what could be keeping her?*

There was one answer that came immediately, and easily.

Fullerton, having threatened Rosalind so blatantly, might have set out to do the same to Charlotte. Now, Charlotte was too ashamed, or too afraid, to meet with her.

But the idea of Charlotte afraid and ashamed did not sit right. Her sister had nerve and resources of her own. Fullerton would have had to do something worse than threaten her.

But it isn't just her anymore. Rosalind's heart thumped heavily.

Fullerton was ruthless. Even Sanderson Faulks, who could himself be a dangerous man, was wary of the extent of Fullerton's reach.

Rosalind leapt to her feet before she'd realized she'd moved. The other patrons frowned. Papers rattled. Faces were pointedly averted. Rosalind pretended not to notice and made her way to the desk.

"Mr. Clements, I do need your help after all."

"I am entirely at your service." He spread his hands. "What can I do?"

"I need a note taken to a Mrs. Walford. I also need a cab."

"Of course." He crooked his fingers to his assistant. The young man bustled forward.

"And," Rosalind added, blushing, but only a little, "I'm afraid I must trouble you for pen and ink."

Mr. Clements, of course, had both to hand and had them brought to her table. Rosalind dipped the quill into the ink pot and wrote:

Mrs. Walford:
I trust this letter finds you well.

*I must apologize most profoundly for being unable
to keep our appointment today. If you would please let
me know when I may call, I will be able to present you
with the explanation for my neglect, and also let you
know what I have since learned about Mr. Salter and
Miss Walford.*

   Yours Sincerely,

However much Rosalind wanted to with Mrs. Walford,
that lady was in no immediate danger. Charlotte very well
might be.

Rosalind signed and folded the letter. She tried to ignore
the way her hands shook. She had not always been able to
bring her ladies' business to a successful conclusion. Sometimes she had been asked to answer questions that might
have been better left alone. But never had she had this sense
that events were galloping so quickly out of control.

There was nothing to do but run on behind and pray she
kept her feet.

Rosalind spent the cab ride to Charlotte's house torn between extremes. With each passing moment she grew more
afraid that something really had happened to her. But when
she tried to tell herself to be sensible, that nothing could possibly have happened, she grew angry. If nothing dire had happened, why did Charlotte neglect their meeting, without even
sending a note? It was Charlotte who had come to Rosalind,
just yesterday. She knew exactly what they were in the middle of. She had as much to lose as Rosalind, if not more.

Which meant something must have happened to keep her
away.

Charlotte's neighborhood was one of the newest in Mayfair. Her house stood on one side of a pretty little square enclosed by a freshly painted iron railing. At this time of day,
the street in the early evening was almost empty of traffic.

Only a few carriages waited in readiness to carry their owners to an early supper or late appointment.

The air of peace grated against Rosalind's raw nerves. She asked her driver to wait and all but ran up Charlotte's front steps to knock. She stood back, her heart in her mouth. She tried to tell herself that the house would not appear so calm if something was really wrong. This only created another surge of anger.

The door was opened by a slender parlor maid with a smooth, calm face and intelligent, dark eyes.

"Good afternoon, Miss Thorne," the maid said. "We were not expecting you. Will you step in?"

Rosalind would and did. Charlotte's marble foyer was as cool and calm and entirely empty as her doorstep had been. "Is your mistress home, Jane?" she asked.

"I'm sorry," replied the maid. "She is not."

Rosalind knew Jane would not volunteer one scrap of information beyond what the question called for. Rosalind had known London dowagers who would envy this girl's impenetrable shell.

"Where is she?"

"I couldn't say, miss."

"When is she expected back?"

"I couldn't say, miss."

"Did she leave any messages for me?"

"No, miss. I'm sorry. Would you care to leave one yourself?"

What she wanted to do was scream. But that would accomplish exactly nothing.

"Jane, I have to find my sister at once. I am, and she is, in trouble. You know I would not say that if it were not true."

The briefest ripple of concern crossed the maid's placid face.

"I am sorry, miss, but I cannot tell you where she has gone. She did not leave any directions, or instructions."

I am going to throttle her, thought Rosalind in a wave of peevish despair. She couldn't even tell if she meant Jane or Charlotte.

"Did she leave voluntarily?"

"Miss?"

Rosalind throttled a sigh. "Did she receive any unexpected message or caller before she left? Was there any indication she was concerned, or in a hurry?"

"I could not say, miss."

She thought again about Amelia and her "gent." "Jane, has anyone been trying to find out information about this house? Or about Charlotte? Perhaps they've been trying to talk to you on your off days?"

"No, Miss Thorne." This time she spoke firmly. "The mistress has warned us all about that, but no one here has ever been approached that I'm aware of."

"I see," Rosalind breathed, unsure whether to be relieved or disappointed. "Well, I had best leave that note."

"This way please, miss."

Jane showed Rosalind into a little parlor all decorated in shades of blue. She brought ink, pen, and paper, and stood by the door while Rosalind dashed off her note. It was quite short.

> C.
> *We must speak at once. Send word of where and when by trusted hand. We are watched.*

She folded it. Thankfully, Jane had also provided some wafers so she could seal the letter.

"As soon as your mistress returns, or sends you word of where she is, give her this." Rosalind handed the maid her note. "Tell her I was here. Repeat to her that I must see her."

Jane looked at the missive in her hand. "Is something . . . very wrong?"

"Yes, Jane."

She nodded and tucked the letter into her apron pocket. "I'll see to it, miss." Her voice grew firm. "You may rely on me."

"Thank you." Rosalind stood and collected her things. "And, Jane?"

"Yes, miss?"

"If . . . if you get the sense that something has happened, will you send for me? I'm worried about your mistress. She might need help."

Jane nodded and curtsied, and Rosalind took her leave.

Outside, the bells were striking the hour. Rosalind paused beside her cab and counted the ragged tolling. Five o'clock. The sun was already setting and the chill wind cut straight through her wool coat. It was time for the polite world to dress to go out for the evening's engagements. It would be unforgiveable to call on Mrs. Walford at this hour.

Where are you, Charlotte? What are you doing?

But no answer came, just another gust of cold wind. Rosalind signaled to the driver that he should climb down and let her into the cab.

There was nothing to do but go home, write her letters, search for her answers, and wait.

And pray that Charlotte really was all right.

CHAPTER 16

Yet One More Blow

Then they are come thither . . . upon the oath of
them, shall inquire in this manner, that is, to wit,
1. If they know where the person was slain . . .
and who was there.

John Impey of the Inner Temple, *The Practice of the Office*
of Coroner

"Adam! Adam!"

At the sound of his name, Adam came swiftly and silently awake. He also squinted. His mother stood beside his bed, a shawl over her nightdress and a lamp in her hand.

"There's a boy downstairs, from the station."

Adam started to curse, but stopped when he saw the seriousness of his mother's face. "I'll be down as soon as may be."

Adam did not bother with a light. He was used to dressing in the dark, and kept his clothing and boots where he could easily reach them. He made his way down the stairs, ducking reflexively so as not to hit his head on the ceiling beams. No one else in the house stirred. Life in the center of London made for a clan of sound sleepers.

The Harkness house was a tall, half-timbered building on a narrow, crowded, lively street. The traffic that passed by the window was as likely to include geese and pigs as it was people and pushcarts. His sister had married a sailor who was seldom in port, so she lived with them, along with his younger brothers. His widowed mother ruled them all, no matter how old or how married, and none of them would have it any other way.

The "boy" from the station was a rangy young man with a flannel muffler around his neck and stout gloves on his hands. He stood in the chimney corner. Steam rolled off his damp coat.

"Perkins," Adam greeted the youth through a jaw-cracking yawn. "What's to do?"

"It's Captain Goutier, sir. Says you're to come at once. There's been a murder."

That final word cleared sleep's remaining fog from Adam's thoughts. "Where?"

"Kensington Park, sir," Perkins answered. "At the house of a man named Russell Fullerton."

Perkins had not been able to bring an extra horse for Adam. Collins, who ran the carriage house on the end of the street, was not pleased to be roused from his bed. The horse Collins saddled for Adam was even less pleased than the man was.

Fog hung low and yellow in the streets. The icy drizzle did nothing to clear the air. The combination made for a long, slow ride, with horses and riders both making their way more by instinct than by sight.

But there was no mistaking when they'd arrived at the right house. Despite the wretched hour, a crowd gathered around the stoop, barely kept at bay by members of the night patrol.

"All right, all right, make room!" Perkins shoved his scrawny self into the crowd with surprising force. "Bow Street! Make room!"

The crowd shifted reluctantly, making a stingy lane for Adams and Perkins.

The house was an elegant one—broad and terraced and brand new from the look of it. The foyer was tiled with marble and paneled with carved wood. Gold leaf sparkled on the ceiling trim. A crystal chandelier glimmered above a marquetry table and a bowl filled with drooping hothouse flowers.

Captain Goutier waited for them by those fading flowers. Sampson Goutier, a captain of the night patrol, was an imposing figure of a man—far taller than average, with midnight-black skin. He was also one of the best and most levelheaded officers Adam had ever worked with.

"What's happened here?" Adam asked Goutier.

"I was passing in the next street with my patrol when some of that crowd out there came running and shouting blue murder." Sampson spoke with a faint French accent, inherited from his parents, who'd made their way from Barbados to Paris and then across to London. "We pushed in and, well, you can come and see for yourself." Goutier beckoned Adam toward the doorway on the right.

Lamplight, heat, and a lingering smell of smoke all drifted out from the chamber. When they got up to the threshold, Adam saw the door was splintered around the jamb.

"It was locked when we got here," Goutier told him. "There was a commotion inside, and we had to force it."

The room was book lined and luxurious, but it also reeked of smoke, oil, and brandy. The fire looked dead, but Adam heard a faint crackling, indicating it still burned inside the heap of ash. Adam took up the poker and stirred through the ashes, spreading them out, letting the trapped smoke and heat escape before the whole lot flared up again.

He straightened. A pair of paintings hung over the fireplace, in the spot usually reserved for family portraits. The first was an oil painting of a voluptuous nude woman sprawled across a red velvet lounge. She held up a mirror to admire her own face. Next to that was the portrait of Russell Fullerton himself. He wore a sky-blue silk coat and held a gold-handled cane. He'd been posed beside a table loaded with papers, books, and deeds that gave the impression of a man of business or law. One had to look hard to see the deck of cards tucked among the papers.

Adam turned away from the paintings. A crystal decanter had been overturned onto the patterned Turkey carpet. So had a painted lamp. A black burnt patch spread out next to the dead man.

He lay faceup. He was portly, gray haired, and aging badly. Death's pallor had not dimmed the pattern of threadlike veins spreading across his nose, cheeks, and jowls that marked him as a heavy drinker. His silken dressing gown had come loose. Dark blood stained his linen shirt and the carpet.

"That's not Fullerton," said Adam. "Who is he? What was he doing here?"

Goutier's face twisted. "Fullerton said his name was Marcus Gill, and that he was a friend come up from the country to stay for a few days. But have a look at that signet ring on his hand."

Adam crouched down and lifted the dead man's hand so he could see it more clearly. As he did, he noticed the hand was cold but had only just begun to stiffen. The ring itself was heavy, carved gold set with onyx. The golden letters RT glimmered in the center of the black stone.

"Not what you'd expect to see on the hand of a man

whose initials are supposed to be M.G.," Goutier remarked blandly.

"No," murmured Adam. He lowered the dead man's hand. His mouth had gone dry. He could not stop from staring at the slack face. R.T.

Reginald Thorne.

"Dear God," breathed Adam.

"What is it?" asked Goutier.

"This man . . . this is Sir Reginald Thorne. Rosalind Thorne's father."

Goutier's right hand moved, making a swift sign of the cross. Captain Goutier had known and helped Rosalind in the past and, like the rest at Bow Street who knew her, had been impressed with her intelligence, and her steadiness.

"This is bad," he said. "But it explains the letter."

Adam shot to his feet. "What letter?"

"On the desk here."

The desk was as luxurious as everything else in the room, with a marble top and enameled pulls for the drawers. It was also a mess of writing paper and used quills. An inkwell had been knocked over, but the liquid had leached into the polished marble before it reached the completed letter lying the middle of the chaos.

Adam picked the letter up it. Goutier held up one of the lamps so Adam could read, or try to read.

The handwriting was graceful and looked to Adam to be a woman's work.

Dearest Rosalind, it began. *How much to tell you!*

What followed was the description of an amorous encounter that was graphic to the point of obscenity. The letter's author elaborated on the charms of her young paramour at length, and then laughed about leaving him in the early morning to go home and refresh herself in time for a much

briefer and less satisfying interlude with her wealthy protector.

*. . . the poor old fool! Were it not for all the money he lav-
ishes upon me, I should never waste my time. But you understand how it is. After all, you told me that your man . . .*

Adam felt the unfamiliar sensation of blush rising in his
cheeks. He turned the page over and skimmed down to the
bottom to see the signature.

Your Loving Sister,
Charlotte

Adam felt his whole self go very still. This was an ugly,
compromising letter. Rosalind's father, dead at his feet, was a
known forger. Fullerton had vowed to destroy Rosalind, and
Rosalind believed he was using Sir Reginald to do it.

Adam felt Goutier watching him as he folded the letter and
put it in the inner pocket of his coat. When he could be sure
of himself, he'd turn around. But not yet.

Rosalind had just this morning told him she was threatened by Fullerton, with this man's seeming cooperation. She
had given him proof of his criminality.

And now he was suddenly, violently dead with a deeply
compromising letter on a desk where he might reasonably
have been working. Adam felt a sharp twist of anger in his
guts.

"What was the state of things when you came in?" he
asked Goutier.

"Quite the crowd, inside and out. All the neighbors turned
up, plus some passing idlers. The manservant—a fellow
named Sparkes—was on the stairs shouting at them all to get
out. Didn't do him any good, but I had our lads start clearing
the place out right away. Then, I heard noise behind the door
here, but it was locked and no one answered our shout.
Sparkes was yelling at us to get out with the rest, but we

broke it in anyhow. Your man there"—he gestured toward the corpse—"was as you see him, and the master of the house was standing over him, covered in blood, and was tossing enough papers into the fire to make a three-volume novel."

"Covered?" Now Adam did turn around. "You're sure about that?"

Goutier nodded. "Hands, shirt front, breeches, shoes, the lot."

But the blood was dried here now, and the body was cooling. So, Fullerton had been in the room when the murder was freshly done.

Adam looked toward the broken doorjamb. Fullerton had not raised the alarm himself, or he wouldn't have locked the door. But if Fullerton did not cry murder, how had the murder come to be discovered by the neighborhood? Someone else must have come in here after the deed was done. Someone unexpected. But who? And what had their purpose been?

A knife, not large but serviceable, lay on the carpet beside the body. It, too, was covered in blood. It had a plain wooden handle, and the blade was pitted. This was a tool that had seen hard use. It looked entirely out of place in this gilded room.

Adam pulled his handkerchief from his pocket, wrapped the knife in it, and tucked the grim object into his great coat pocket.

He let his gaze travel along the corpse, taking in the details. The robe and breeches fit him badly. *Borrowed?* He also saw that bruises had formed around the signet ring.

Like someone tried to pull it off? He frowned and set the man's hand down. *Was it a try at robbery? Or someone trying to hide something?*

Then, because this was Rosalind's father, he gently closed the dead man's eyes.

Adam climbed once more to his feet. His gaze swept the
room, at the same time a chill crept up his spine. While the
scene of a murder never left one calm, something in this
room's luxuriant atmosphere sank through his skin and left
him more uneasy than he should be.

"Where's Fullerton now?" Adam asked. "And this Sparkes
fellow?"

"Both upstairs in the drawing room."

"Is anyone else in the house?"

Goutier shook his head. "Sparkes is the only one who
sleeps in. The rest of the servants are just here days."

"What has Fullerton to say for himself?"

"Precious little." Goutier folded his arms. "Closed up like
an oyster when I told him I was with the night patrol."

Adam muttered a highly spiced opinion of this behavior
under his breath. "I'll see if I can loosen him a bit," he said
out loud. "Have the men take the body over to The Brown
Bear. We'll send for the coroner as soon as the sun's up." The
Brown Bear was a public house that stood directly across
from the famous Bow Street police station. Down the years,
the pub had become a sort of annex to the business of the
station and its magistrate's court. Prisoners and witnesses
were both held there, as was the occasional corpse.

Adam could as easily had Sir Reginald taken to the great
city morgue, but Rosalind would have to come claim her father eventually, and he wanted to spare her the grim walk
past the rows of London's dead.

This is all bad enough, and it will get worse.

"Make sure you show the coroner this." Adam handed
Goutier the linen-wrapped knife. "And get one of the lads to
sweep up those ashes. I want to see if we can find some hint
as to what our Mr. Fullerton was burning." Fullerton had destroyed a considerable quantity of paper, but the salacious
letter from Charlotte to Rosalind had been left out in plain
sight.

Now, why would that be?

"Harkness." Goutier's soft voice cut across his thoughts. "If Miss Thorne should need any help . . ."

"Thank you, Captain," said Adam. "I hope it won't come to that."

He left Captain Goutier and the bloody scene without looking back.

CHAPTER 17

A Few Trifling Questions

*If the party be slain and the felon is not known,
they . . . shall bind over the first finder of the body
to the next gaol delivery, and return his
examinations.*

John Impey of the Inner Temple, *The Practice of the Office
of Coroner*

Adam did not bother to knock.

This room was as opulent as the one he'd just left, but instead of books, it was fully dedicated to art. Paintings hung on the walls, and more were perched on easels. Small bronze figurines stood on plinths arranged along the walls.

The favored theme was women in various degrees of nakedness. Plump white-and-rose figures were getting dressed, or being dressed, or had just undressed. They lounged about on various pieces of furniture, or stepped fresh from their baths. Occasionally they lay on riverbanks with satyrs squatting nearby.

Russell Fullerton himself sat in a deep velvet armchair, cradling a glass of brandy in both hands. He gazed coolly at the nearest painting—a nymph emerging from a rushing river, while a satyr played his pipes to welcome her. Fullerton wore a quilted silk dressing gown. His milk-white face was stubbled, but freshly washed. His iron-gray hair had been slicked back against his skull. The eyes fixed on the nude were unusually pale, almost colorless. His hands, which cupped the brandy decanter, were as white and bloodless as his face.

This was a man who lived his life indoors and in darkness.

Fullerton's manservant—presumably the watchful Sparkes—stood beside the drinks cabinet, awaiting his orders. He was an older man, nearly as tall as Sampson Goutier, and lean to the point of emaciation. Notwithstanding this, his face and form were still strong and distinctly chiseled.

Fullerton might be pretending to ignore Adam, but Sparkes openly watched his every move.

"Mr. Russell Fullerton," Adam said.

"Mr. Adam Harkness," replied Fullerton dryly. "I thought it might be you who was summoned here."

Fullerton clearly meant to surprise him with this token of recognition. Adam himself had only recently become aware of Fullerton's existence. Most of the crimes Adam was called upon to resolve involved stolen money or goods. Fullerton, as far as Adam knew, had never stolen physical property. His business was threatening the individual destruction of men and women for personal gain, and the law considered that purely private business.

But Fullerton had threatened Rosalind, and that made him Adam's business. Since Rosalind had first mentioned him several months ago, Adam had talked confidentially with his fellow officers. In his spare time, he'd followed up on this rumor and that one to learn what he could.

Mostly, he'd learned that the man he'd recently helped send to the gallows for stealing a jeweler's strong box was a worthier human being than the elegant, bloodless gentleman sitting in front of him now.

"What do you have to say about this business, sir?" Adam asked.

"That I had been out for the evening." Fullerton spoke in the slow, cultivated drawl of the society dandy. "That I returned, and as I approached my door, two men ran out of my house and nearly knocked me down. Before I could demand to know their business, one of them shouted, 'Murder! Murder!'"

"And what happened to these two men?"

"I have no idea. As you can imagine, upon hearing such a cry, I rushed into my house, only one step ahead of the gathering mob. There, I found the gentleman bleeding out the last of his life on my carpet. I bent over him to see if he might be saved. Indeed, he might have been, but the mob burst in and I was forced to lock the study door to protect myself from being overrun. This meant there was no way to summon a surgeon before he expired."

"Was he a friend of yours?"

Fullerton took a slow sip of brandy. "A business associate. He was staying with me for a few days."

"You gave his name to Captain Goutier as Marcus Gill."

"I did."

"This despite the fact that you know him to be Sir Reginald Thorne."

Fullerton's brows lifted, ever so slightly. "Sir Reginald Thorne?" He spoke the name carefully, as if this was the first time he'd heard it. "Is he? How extraordinary. I can't see how I would have been expected to know that."

"What business did you have with Sir Reginald?"

Fullerton's smile narrowed his cold, pale eyes. "My own."

"Did it involve his daughters?"

"He had daughters?" Fullerton raised his brows again. "I had no idea."

"But he was staying with you."

"We were dealing in business matters," Fullerton reminded him. "Not personal ones."

"Captain Goutier says when he entered the house, you were dressed for the evening and covered in blood."

"I told you, I had just returned home. I got the blood on me while I was trying to see if he yet lived."

"He also says you were engaged in throwing papers into the fire."

Fullerton shrugged. His attention wandered back to his paintings. "Surely what I do with my papers is my affair." He sipped his brandy, bored and unconcerned.

Adam turned to his servant, who had not moved an inch or uttered a single sound.

"May I ask where you were during all this, Mr. Sparkes . . . ?"

Sparkes's dark eyes flickered toward Fullerton. "Mister . . . Gill had told me I could retire. He . . ." Sparkes hesitated. His gaze flickered toward Fullerton again. "He had said it was my master's instructions. I did not believe him. Mr. Gill"— he spoke the name with more confidence the second time— "could be rather free with his declarations, especially if he had been drinking. But I did withdraw to my room at the top of the house."

"And you were there the entire time?"

Again, that flicker of the eyes. Sparkes was not going to say a word that was not approved of by his employer.

"I was."

"You heard nothing?"

"Nothing at all."

Adam considered his next question carefully. "What about these two men your employer spoke of?"

Sparkes's eyes flickered again. Fullerton looked into his brandy glass. Sparkes immediately picked up the decanter from the table and poured a neat measure into Fullerton's glass. He returned the brandy to its place, and himself to his, so that all was in order before he spoke.

"It was nearly three, I believe, although I may be mistaken about the exact time." He paused. Fullerton sipped. "I did hear some noise and descended the stairs. Two men ran from the study and out the front door. The cry of murder went up shortly afterwards and my master rushed into the house. The mob broke in immediately afterwards." He spoke the word *mob* with profound distaste.

"Could you describe these men?"

Fullerton sipped. Sparkes paused, judging his words. "The lamps had all been extinguished, so it was difficult to see. I believe they both wore great coats."

"And then what did you do?"

Sparkes's silence stretched out. "I did nothing," he said. "I had no time, and Mr. Fullerton had already closed the study door."

"Did you try to follow him into the study?"

Sparkes drew himself up even straighter. "I did not. If I was needed, I would be called for. In any case, the mob was everywhere, and I could not have fit myself into the foyer even if I wanted to."

It was a convenient story, to say the least. It was also a lie, in whole or in part.

Adam had been fairly sure when he walked in that neither man would tell him the truth. But now he had the dimensions of their lie, and more importantly, he now knew that nothing Sparkes said could be trusted.

There was a knock at the door. Goutier leaned in. "A word, Mr. Harkness?"

Adam followed the captain out into the hallway, far enough from the door that they were unlikely to be over-heard.

"We're finished here," he said. "The body's on a cart and

headed to The Brown Bear. The street's been cleared of the idly curious, or at least mostly so."

"Did you have your men question the crowd?"

"I did, sir. Got little enough. Nothing that's likely to be of any use, I'm afraid."

Adam sighed. "Well, Fullerton and his man say two men were in the house, that they raced out the front door, and they were the ones who put up the cry of murder. Anyone you talk to say anything like that?"

Goutier shook his head. "But I'll tell you this, to my mind, and despite the spilled lamp, that room was uncommonly neat and tidy for a place where a man had been overpowered by two strangers. You'd think there'd be some piece of furniture overturned, or that the blood would be smeared further about."

"Fullerton might have tidied it up," suggested Adam.

"But left that lamp spilled out on the floor? While he was burning those papers?"

Adam nodded. Goutier had come to Bow Street from the Thames River police. If there was anyone at Bow Street who had seen more murder done than Adam, Goutier was the man.

"So what would be your guess about what happened?" Adam asked.

"That Sir Reginald was killed by someone he knew," Goutier replied. "Someone who could get right up close without him wondering what it was all about. That's a wicked sharp knife we found. Sir Reginald might have died before he knew anything was wrong."

That cold disquiet Adam had felt earlier returned. Something was wrong with all of this.

Or maybe it's just that it's Rosalind's father in there, and Rosalind's name on that letter in my pocket.

"All right, Captain," said Adam, to shut out those thoughts. "We'll want at least two men to keep guard on the door, and yourself and one other to stand ready. The papers are going to have this soon, if they don't already. I expect by morning we'll have another mob scene on our hands."

"Too right we will. I'll see to it." Goutier touched his hat brim.

Adam went back into the drawing room. Fullerton glanced at him with the mildest curiosity. Sparkes, though, shot him a look of pure, distilled poison. Adam locked his gaze on the servant. The poison vanished, replaced by a wall of stoicism it would take a cannonball to smash through.

Fullerton made no immediate remark. He sat calmly drinking his brandy surrounded by his painted mistresses. He might not have done it, Adam reflected. It could have been as he said—that he came home to discover the criminal he had been sheltering had been killed by person or persons unknown. Sir Reginald had been seen by that great crowd at the opera. One of the men he had wronged might have been in the crowd and decided to get their revenge.

But Fullerton was lying, and his man was lying for him. Adam would have bet his new hat on it. He was equally sure that if he left this man alone, his next move would be to flee London. *Make a run to Scotland or France, or even further afield.*

Fullerton swallowed his latest mouthful of brandy. "I trust you're finished here, Mr. Harkness?"

Adam's answer was to drop his hand onto Fullerton's shoulder.

"Mr. Russell Fullerton, I am arresting you in the King's name, on the charge of murder most foul."

CHAPTER 18

A Sense of Obligation

Her smoothly polished exterior prevented all possibility of obtaining any hold over her.

Maria Edgeworth, *Almeria*

"Any word?" asked Alice.

Rosalind tossed her letters down. Amelia had brought the morning post into the parlor as soon as it arrived, and Rosalind had all but snatched it from the maid's hands. But while there was a letter from Sanderson Faulks, there was nothing from Charlotte or Mrs. Walford.

"What will you do?" asked Alice.

"I don't know." Rosalind eyed her mantel clock. It was only just past nine. The next post was not due until noon at the earliest, and by then she must be away to call on Countess Lieven.

"Alice, do you know who Charlotte's protector, that is, her fiancé, is? Since she is not at her house, she may be at his." Wealthy men seldom bothered to hide their mistresses. A lovely and costly woman on one's arm was as much a mark of one's stature as a fine carriage or an elegant house. Alice's work for the *Chronicle* frequently involved writing arch hints about exactly who was parading about with whom, and unlike some gossip columnists, Alice usually knew what she was talking about.

But this time, Alice just shook her head. "I'm afraid not. Not that that means much. I'd only have heard about him if he was on visiting terms with the *haut ton*. That leaves a lot out. He could be a nabob back from India, or a shipping merchant, or a Manchester gingham manufacturer."

"Could you find out?" asked Rosalind. "It might be she went to him and got delayed, or lost track of time." Even as she said it, it did not sound plausible, but it was all she had.

Alice considered. "Yes, I think I could. I certainly know where to start asking."

"I did not want to violate her privacy, or her confidence, but I'm worried."

"So am I," said Alice. There was a bitter undertone to her voice that made Rosalind wonder what exactly Alice was worried about. "I have to take my column to the Major this morning. I'll call round some friends of mine after that."

"Thank you," said Rosalind. "I can't believe Charlotte would come tell me about Father and then vanish without reason."

"You may not like the reason when you find it," said Alice.

"Yes, I know," answered Rosalind. "Nonetheless, I need to know what it is."

"I wish I could disagree." Alice sighed. "I take it there's nothing from La Walford, either?"

"Nothing. Just a note from Sanderson."

"Well, you read that while I get my things together. It looks to be another lovely winter's day in London." Alice glanced sourly toward the gray fog lowering itself into the street outside.

Rosalind broke the seal on Mr. Faulks's note. She read:

My dear Miss Thorne:

I am writing to report that Mr. Salter did not return to the Walford box for the remainder of the opera. Miss Walford herself did leave once. I was able to follow her to the salon and then down to the lobby. She lingered there awhile, behind one of the pillars. Quite probably a prearranged meeting spot of some variety. She was, however, quite disappointed. No message, or confidant, arrived, and she returned to her box.

I am sorry I could not be of more assistance. Today, I shall make a round of a few likely clubs and see if I am able to hear any word of the man.

Yours, faithfully, etc.

"Well, that's something I suppose." Alice closed her leather folio. "If there's anyone can sniff out a scent in clubland, it's Sanderson." She took up her warm gloves. "Will you be all right?"

"Yes, yes," Rosalind lied. "I've a great deal to keep me busy. And who knows? Charlotte may yet send word. There's plenty of time still."

Alice gave her a long, skeptical look, but evidently decided to leave this alone. She walked out of the parlor, calling for Amelia, and her warm bonnet and an extra shawl, if there was one.

Summoning her resolve, Rosalind turned toward her correspondence. But without Alice to distract her, she found her mind straying constantly back to Charlotte's silence.

Rosalind had thought she was used to waiting. But not like this. She was waiting for Adam to find Fullerton, and her father, for Alice to find Charlotte, for Mr. Faulks to find Salter. For Mrs. Walford to answer her letter.

Unable to sit still a minute longer, she found herself roaming about the house like an aimless ghost, staring out the windows, looking for the postman, or a messenger, or anyone at all.

Rosalind was grateful beyond words when the time came to put on her best walking costume and warmest coat. Then, she instructed Amelia that if Charlotte arrived, she was to be kept in the house until Rosalind returned.

"You may lock her in the attic if necessary," she added, frustration and worry stretching her to the breaking point. The light that gleamed in Amelia's eager eyes probably should have concerned her, but Rosalind had too much to worry about as it was.

Rosalind had visited Countess Lieven's house on two previous occasions. Once for an afternoon garden party, and again for a fancy dress ball. Countess Lieven had appeared as the Byzantine Empress Theodora in flowing silk robes and a king's ransom in freshwater pearls. Both invitations had been a mark of interest and acknowledgment, but of a distant sort. Rosalind understood the countess wanted to keep her as a possible source for some later favor or errand. She did not, however, want Rosalind getting notions of intimacy.

Until now, she had certainly never invited Rosalind to call.

Rosalind alighted from the hackney cab in St. James's Square. The Lievens' residence was a new house of terraced brickwork with grand wrought iron gates surmounted by the Russian double-headed eagle. The footmen who opened the doors wore full livery in scarlet and gold, complete with powdered wigs and white gloves. Maids dressed in gray silk with perfectly starched white lawn aprons and caps with lace ruffles and ribbons helped Rosalind with her coat and bonnet.

The front hall was an enormous expanse of oak paneling with a floor mosaicked after the Greco-Roman style. A grand marble staircase swept up to the first floor and the countess's receiving rooms.

The rooms were large and airy. The walls had been painted a pale green and hung with a selection of magnificent landscape paintings. The furniture possessed more gilding, curlicues, and elaborate tapestry than Rosalind would have found comfortable, but she recognized it was all in excellent and elevated taste. A number of the chairs and the little sofas were occupied by a cluster of women, like her, come to pay their morning calls.

"Ah, Miss Thorne," Countess Lieven drawled as soon as the footman announced Rosalind. "I believe you know everyone here?"

Rosalind curtsied, and the ladies returned polite nods. Their looks were filled with a disturbing level of curiosity. The sensation at the opera was clearly a subject of talk today.

"It is very kind of you to call," Countess Lieven went on. "It has been so long since we've had a chance to talk, but I know you are always so busy. How does our friend Lady Kirklands?"

It was plain what the countess was doing. Any one of these ladies might have been in the salon when matters erupted. Countess Lieven was letting it be publicly known that she had not struck Rosalind from her visiting list.

That was why she insisted Rosalind call, rather than arranging a private interview. This way Rosalind would be seen in the open, with no hint there could be anything surreptitious or shameful about her visit.

Rosalind wanted to feel simply grateful, but she knew the countess too well.

Now that the opening pleasantries had been exchanged, the etiquette of social calls required that all the other ladies announce that they were so sorry, but they must leave. They thanked the countess in order of precedence and did, in fact, take their leave. This they did with practiced efficiency, despite the extraneous sideways glances they gave Rosalind. She returned an air of perfect insouciance. This was hardly Rosalind's first experience with personal scandal. She knew how to carry herself within the necessary balance of pride and awareness of her proper place.

But it had been a long time since it was this hard.

"Roberts," said Countess Lieven to her footman. "I am not at home to anyone at this time. Now, come sit by me, Miss Thorne, so that we may talk frankly, you and I."

Rosalind did as she was instructed and settled herself onto the tapestry chair at the countess's right hand. Another footman came forward with a fresh cup and saucer, but the countess waved him away.

"No, no, none of your English tea. My guest requires something stronger. A glass of sherry for Miss Thorne. And you will try some of the salmon on our Russian blini." With a practiced gesture, the countess directed her maid to arrange a plate from the dainties spread out on the carved sideboard. "You are quite pale."

It was no surprise that the countess's staff was exceedingly efficient. No sooner was Rosalind settled into her designated place than the sherry and salmon were given to her. She sipped, and she ate. The blini proved to be hearty little cakes heaped high with thin layers of cold salmon and a dollop of rich cream. It was strange, yet delicious, and by the time she had finished all three portions, she had to admit she felt better.

Or she would have, if she had not been so very aware of the countess watching her with a knowing and slightly amused air.

Rosalind set down her plate.

"Your grace, I must thank you for your intervention at the opera. I am . . ."

Countess Lieven waved her words away, assuming a world-weary air. "I am always glad to be of service to a friend, especially one being forced into an unjust scandal. And we are friends, you know," she said, and the fact seemed to amuse her more than anything. "You are a rare creature for an Englishwoman, Miss Thorne. Most of your countrywomen are helpless, vaporous creatures. You, however, have a practical turn of mind that is almost Russian."

This was probably meant to be a compliment, but Rosalind had no idea how to reply to it, so she merely dropped her gaze in acknowledgment.

"Do you know where your father is now?" The countess asked.

"I do not, but I have asked a friend of mine to make inquiries."

"Very good. Now, tell me, what is your father's connection with the Fullerton creature?" Poison oozed from the countess's voice as she spoke the name.

"It is not my father who is connected to Fullerton," said Rosalind. "At least, I don't believe he is. Fullerton said to me that the reason he has taken my father into his . . ." she faltered. "I don't even know what the correct term would be."

"Keeping, perhaps?" Countess Lieven suggested.

"Perhaps." Rosalind paused to try, yet again, to regain her full composure. "In any case, he says he intends to maintain his hold over my father in order to keep me from interfering with his business."

"The implication being that if you do not behave as Fullerton would wish, he will unleash your father onto the polite world."

"It was not implied. It was stated quite directly."

The countess arched one perfectly shaped brow. "That is interesting."

"In what way, ma'am?"

"If he wants you destroyed, why delay? He has the means. Why not simply proceed to the grand event?"

Rosalind concentrated on her hands for a moment. It was

important they stay neatly folded, that they not clench, or fidget. "I have considered this. But nothing about any of my current affairs has brought me in any way close to him." *That I know of.* Rosalind now concentrated on her features. She must not frown.

Because the truth was, she knew Horatio Salter was a fraudster and a gambler. Such activities could very well have taken him into Fullerton's orbit.

And Salter had known that she was doing more than helping Mrs. Walford with the charity ball. Had he found that out from Fullerton? Or had Fullerton perhaps told him? *But why would he? And where is Mr. Salter now? What is he doing?* Rosalind did not dare hope he had simply fled London.

Without answers to these questions, Rosalind did not want to bring Salter's name up to the countess. Certainly she did not wish to speak freely before she knew for certain why she had been brought here.

"I think we may safely say what Fullerton wants is to be certain you will leave him to scheme undisturbed." The countess cocked her head thoughtfully toward Rosalind. "This suggests that he has some plan currently in motion. Also, that he fears that his power over you is not as strong as it first appears."

"Or that he thinks once he has me cowed, he might make use of me in the future."

"Yes, we must also admit that is a possibility." Her brow knitted. She was not looking at Rosalind, however, but at some thought passing through her mind.

"May I ask, ma'am," said Rosalind. "How is it you know Mr. Fullerton?"

"By reputation," the countess replied. Her tone was one of casual dismissal, and Rosalind did not trust it. "But, Miss Thorne, are you absolutely certain there is no past acquaintance or connection between Fullerton and your father?"

Rosalind took another small sip of the sherry, using the time to choose her words with care. The countess would recognize the barest hint of a falsehood. She must tell the truth, but she could choose how to tell it.

"I am not entirely certain," she admitted. "My father left us when I was very young and went to live in Paris."

"Left you?" prompted the countess.

Rosalind looked her hostess directly in the eye. "My father was heavily in debt. He fled to France, taking my sister with him."

It felt like a violation to say it all out loud to a relative stranger. At the same time, she had a feeling she was not telling the countess anything she had not already heard.

"And your sister," said the countess. "She stayed with him in his exile?"

"She did. And she looked after him in his decline."

"A devoted daughter, and an excellent sister."

"More than I appreciated at the time," admitted Rosalind.

The countess made a small, sympathetic noise. "I should like to meet her. Can you introduce us?"

There it was. That was the favor. The countess not only wanted news of Fullerton, she wanted to meet Charlotte.

Why Charlotte? What is it you know?

The countess must know, or suspect something, or she would not make such a request.

But Charlotte was missing. Rosalind tried to search the countess's expression for any hint. Of course, there was nothing.

Rosalind's only option was to demur. She certainly could not tell the countess Charlotte was missing.

"There are complications," Rosalind said. "But I will certainly do all that I can."

"It may be as private as you wish, but it must be soon."

"I understand, your grace."

The air of perpetual languor that surrounded the countess

chilled, just a little. "I would be most intrigued to know what you understand."

Rosalind sipped her wine again and set the glass down. *How much do I tell her?*

"Ma'am, you are the wife of the Russian ambassador to the Court of St. James." *And mistress to Lord Palmerston, and possibly others.* "Mr. Fullerton is in the habit of collecting compromising correspondence and gossip. I do not expect ordinary scandal to trouble you. You told me once that the life of Russia's nobility is more orderly than it is for England's. You have only to be seen as the best servant of the czar. There is very little that could happen to you or your husband that would discomfort you, unless Fullerton had somehow stumbled across information relating to affairs of state."

Rosalind had the very warm satisfaction of seeing her hostess openly surprised. Then, Countess Lieven laughed once, a loud, hard, triumphant sound.

"There! I knew I was right about you! Oh, truly, Miss Thorne, you are wasted on the English. You should have been born Russian. But from now on, you shall be my treasure! Yes, you are correct. Mr. Fullerton has sought to insert himself into affairs of state, and more to the point, he is seeking to aid and abet the Bonapartists."

Bonapartists? It was all Rosalind could do to stop herself from sputtering.

"But, surely, no one takes the Bonapartists seriously," she said. "Their emperor is imprisoned. The Bourbons are restored to the throne."

"Their emperor is alive." Countess Lieven's tone said she considered this to be a most ridiculous oversight. "As are members of his family. One brother is in Philadelphia. Another is in Rome. Their admirers and supporters are . . . everywhere. They plot and they plan, and they do so here in London as they do in all the capitals of Europe from Paris to

Krakow. Neither is the man himself as isolated as might be believed. Ships are landing all the time at St. Helena. The captains, the passengers, and even the crew are permitted to visit him in his exile."

Rosalind remembered Alice going on about secret societies. George had been writing about them. She hadn't assigned it much importance. She'd just thought it was another entertaining story for the papers.

"You think Fullerton a . . . a secret Bonapartist?" The countess was a woman of sharp intelligence, and she must know a great deal about the intricacies of state craft. But Rosalind simply could not picture Fullerton the role of believing Bonapartist, or even of abetting such people. He moved against vulnerable women and foolish men for personal gain. That his activities might rise to the level of espionage . . . it was not a possibility that had ever occurred to her.

"I do not believe men such as Fullerton have principles or politics," said Countess Lieven. "I think he consorts with Bonapartists because they pay him."

Rosalind longed to ask what this had to do with her father, or her sister, but she held her tongue. She might say too much. She might accidentally betray Charlotte, or herself, more than she already had.

Instead, she readied some platitudes about how all such matters were quite beyond her. But when Rosalind lifted her gaze and saw how closely the countess observed her, she decided that would never do.

"I will certainly speak to my sister as soon as I can," she said. "But I must tell you that we have not been close for many years. I cannot answer for her willingness to agree to your invitation."

"But you will do your best to persuade her?" pressed the countess.

"I will, yes."

"Excellent. Write me as soon as you are able."

This was a dismissal. Rosalind rose and made her curtsy. "Thank you, your grace."

"I look forward to hearing from you, Miss Thorne."

The liveried footman led Rosalind down the stairs. Two of the efficient, silent maids helped her into her coat and bonnet. She performed the necessary actions without feeling them. Her mind felt distanced from her body.

She had believed that her scandal was private and personal, and that her quarrel with Fullerton was something that she must solve with her own powers. Now, it seemed, she was incorrect. Fullerton was in some way seeking to interfere with affairs of state.

Rosalind did not claim any particular grasp of politics. Her expertise lay in drawing rooms and salons. However, it did not require any particular genius to understand that the Czar of All Russias might prefer France to be governed by the *ancien régime* rather than the heirs of the self-styled emperor whose invasion had so recently worked such destruction on those same Russians.

Rosalind suddenly felt very aware of the fact that it was not only Fullerton and her father who were out of their depth.

CHAPTER 19

A Thorough Examination

*If any person be slain or murdered in the day
and the murderer escape untaken . . . the coroner
have authority to inquire thereof upon view of
the body.*

John Impey of the Inner Temple, *The Practice of the Office
of Coroner*

The clock on the patrol room wall was striking ten.
Rosalind will be well awake by this time. Adam rubbed
his eyes. He had paper, pen, and ink in front of him, ready to
write his report on last night's doings. All of them remained
untouched.

Adam did not consider himself a coward, but he was acting the part now. The business of rousing the sheriff and
committing Fullerton to his charge, and from there to the
Clerkenwell jail, had taken some hours. Captain Goutier had
already gone home to his breakfast, his wife, and his bed.

Adam could have gone to Rosalind as soon as Fullerton
was in the sheriff's hands, but instead he'd returned to the
Bow Street station house to stare at this blank page and try to

make sense of what he'd seen in the house where her father
had been killed. The salacious letter signed with Charlotte
Thorne's name felt heavy in his pocket.

His excuse for staying away was that he did not want to
go to Rosalind with partial answers. He did not want to
watch her try to resolve events for herself, which she would.
He did not want to see her try to hold herself together until
he left so she could cry. Because she would never cry in front
of him. Perhaps one day she would trust him that far. But
not yet.

She's skittish as a new kitten, that one, his mother had said
after they'd first met. *You'll need all your patience with her.*

She's none for me, Adam had said. *I've no business with her.*

His mother had smiled. His sister had laughed. And here
he was, months later, still being patient, still living to see another smile, hear another tart comment, to watch her sort
through the problems of the world with grace and good
sense.

Still imagining walking with her, taking her hand, kissing
her, coming home to her. Looking up to see her come home
to him.

He didn't know how these things could be made to happen, but he wanted them more than he wanted to keep
breathing.

The patrol room at the Bow Street Police Station was an
unadorned, workaday room.

Bound volumes of newspaper clippings filled the shelves.
The walls were hung with maps of London and Westminster
and the network of roads and turnpikes that surrounded
them. Recent newspapers from all around England, Wales,
and Scotland hung on racks or were stacked on the tables, including Bow Street's own publication, *Hue & Cry*. This
broadsheet circulated among the policing offices, and its

pages were given over to descriptions of crimes and crimi-
nals, as well as descriptions of stolen property that either was
still missing or had been discovered in the pawn shops, or
other similarly inappropriate places.

A long, scarred, ink-spattered table stretched down the
center of the room. Adam and his unused writing implements
sat at one end.

"Hear you had a long night, Harkness."

Samuel Tauton strolled in from the ward room. Tauton
was a grizzled veteran among Bow Street's principal officers.
He was shrewd as any fox and possessed a memory for faces
that was second to none. He dropped into the chair across
from Adam and folded his hands across his protruding belly.
"Bad one?"

"Bad enough," Adam admitted. "Sir Reginald Thorne, father of Rosalind Thorne, was found done to death in the wee
hours."

Tauton whistled. "You sure you should be here? Shouldn't
you be breaking the news, before the papers get to her?"

"I should," admitted Adam. "But I wanted at least to wait
for Sir David to do his work." Sir David Royce was the coroner for Middlesex County. He was over at The Brown Bear
with the body now.

"Well, you or your Miss Thorne need any help, lad, you let
me know."

Adam smiled briefly and didn't even argue with the idea
that Rosalind was his Miss Thorne. "You can tell me how to
sort through a bag of ashes."

"How's that?"

The sack of ashes from Fullerton's fireplace squatted in the
corner beside the wooden filing cabinets. Adam regarded it
accusingly, as if it were deliberately withholding its secrets
from him.

"Even though his guest had just been stabbed, Russell Fullerton, the owner of the house where Sir Reginald was found, decided it was more important to burn a lot of papers instead of raising the watch. I thought the ashes might hold some hint of what he was trying so hard to hide." Adam smiled wryly. "But didn't stop to think how I'd find it out without taking a year and making an unholy mess."

Tauton chuckled. "That's because you've never done a lick of honest work in your young days. What were you thinking, galavanting off with the horse patrol just as soon as you were breeched? Leave your ashes with me. Go hear what Sir David has to say. Not doing anything here, are ye?" He leaned forward and tapped the blank page.

"No, I suppose I'm not." Adam got to his feet. "Thank you, Tauton."

Tauton waved one weathered hand, and Adam, still feeling too much like a coward, left him there.

For the most part, The Brown Bear was no different from any other public house to be found across the length and breadth of London. What made it special was that it stood so close to the famous police station. Down the years, The Brown Bear had come to play a leading part in the business of the station, and its magistrate's court. Prisoners were held there, questioned there, and even searched for stolen property there. A man might think he'd been invited for a drink, only to find he was being singled out by some witness sitting in the back of the barroom.

Adam took off his new high-crowned hat so it wouldn't knock against the roof beams as he descended the stairs to the cellar. Normally, a gloomy twilight filled the warren of storerooms stocked with barrels and crates. Today, however, four blazing oil lamps lit up the space around a makeshift trestle table that held the pale body of Sir Reginald Thorne, facedown.

Sir David Royce stood beside the table and its sorry burden. A delicate knife gleamed his hand. He must have heard Adam's boots on the stairs because he looked up from his work.

"Mr. Harkness," Sir David greeted him. "Captain Goutier told me you'd be here."

"Thank you for taking this on yourself," said Adam. Sir David shrugged this away. The two men had worked closely together in the past.

"What can you tell me?" Adam asked him.

"Well, our man here"—Sir David pointed his scalpel at Sir Reginald's back—"died of a stabbing, as suspected. We've two wounds. One in the back, here." He gestured for Adam to come closer and see for himself.

The wound was little more than a dark line in the middle of the corpse, with a bit of pale bruising around it. Whoever struck him meant business, that much was certain. Those bruises most likely came from the knife hilt.

"Then there's another on the front, almost identical. Here, help me turn him."

Adam, fortunately, had experience with the unwieldy weight of a dead body, and between them they rolled the corpse over. As Sir David had said, there was a matching wound in Sir Reginald's belly, just as dark and ugly as the one on his back.

What in the name of heaven did you get yourself into? he wondered toward the corpse. "Do you know what happened?"

Sir David wiped his hands on the scrap of towel slung over his shoulder. "Well, it wasn't a fight. There's no bruises or any other sign that he defended himself." Adam nodded.

That sorted with Captain Goutier's idea that he'd known the attacker.

"If I had to guess," Sir David went on, "I'd say he was stabbed from behind first, and then the assailant turned him over, or he turned himself, and they delivered the second blow to his guts. Either from haste or because they knew what they were doing."

"How so?"

"Most people aim for the heart, naturally enough, but that's a risky business. You could hit a rib and turn the knife and have to go in for another blow. Going for the guts is much safer. Even if your man survives the initial attack, a gut wound always turns septic. Nature can be relied on to finish what you started."

"Could it have been two persons?" Adam asked.

Sir David pursed his lips. "It could. They could have got him between them and struck together. It would be a nasty business, but very quick and very clean."

So that a servant in his room all the way at the top of the house would not have heard a thing.

Adam did not want to ask his next question, but he could not neglect it. "Could a woman have done it?"

The coroner considered this. "If she took him by surprise, perhaps slipped the blade in from behind first. It's a good, sharp knife, so it would not have taken a deal of strength. She'd need a steady hand, to be sure, but anger and resolution can furnish that. So, I'd say, yes. It's entirely possible for a woman to have done this." Sir David crossed to the basin and ewer set on top of a pair of barrels and started washing his hands with a cake of harsh yellow soap. "Do we have a name for this poor fellow?"

"Sir Reginald Thorne."

"Thorne?" Sir David turned, his brows raised. "As in Miss Rosalind Thorne?"

"Her father." Like Captain Goutier, Sir David had come to know Rosalind when they worked together on a matter that involved one of the most influential families in the kingdom. Like Goutier, Sir David had been most impressed by Miss Thorne's steadiness and intellect.

"I'll have to send her my condolences. It's an ugly business, this. Goutier said they found him at home?"

"He was the guest of a man named Russell Fullerton. A gentleman with some very unsavory habits, including extortion and moneylending."

"Marvelous," muttered Sir David. "Well, I shall have to convene an inquest, but there's no question that Sir Reginald was murdered. Have you someone you suspect?"

"I've arrested Fullerton, but that's mostly to keep him where I can see him."

"You don't like him." Sir David polished his scalpel and laid it carefully back in its case.

"I don't," admitted Adam. "And it could well be he's up to his neck in this, even if his hand didn't strike the blow."

Sir David closed the velvet box and tucked it back into his bag. "What's he have to say for himself?"

"That he wasn't in the house at all that evening, and that when he did get home, he was near knocked flat by two men running out of his house and crying bloody murder."

"Which is why you asked me if it could have been two men."

Adam nodded. "His manservant backs up the story, but he's lying."

Sir David's sigh pushed out his cheeks.

"Well, if you like, we can put the inquest off at least a day or two while evidence is gathered."

"I'd take it as a favor."

Sir David waved this away. "You've earned more and

larger favors than this from me, Harkness. I'll tell Townsend to put you on it, and my office will pay the fees." John Townsend was the officer in charge at Bow Street. Technically, he and Adam were equals, but in all ways that mattered, Townsend was his commander, and Townsend did not take well to his officers working without receiving their fees.

"Thank you," said Adam. "Stay for a drink?" he added.

"Not this time. I've got to be getting on." Sir David snapped the catch on his bag. "When you see Miss Thorne, be sure to tell her if there's anything she needs, she only has to ask."

"I will," Adam agreed. *When I've worked up the nerve to see her.*

The men shook hands and Adam followed Sir David back up to the barroom. Sir David collected hat and coat and took his leave, but Adam lingered there awhile, taking a beer and talking with the landlord and the other men he knew. At last, he turned up his coat collar and stepped out into the December chill. He thrust his hands in his pockets and started walking with a steady, easy stride. He dodged traffic, frozen mud holes, and the crowds of passersby as an only experienced Londoner could.

He should be headed across to the station. Townsend would be impatient for his report, but Adam still had no idea exactly what to tell him. Sir David had failed to provide what he so desperately wanted—proof positive that Fullerton had killed Sir Reginald. Or, failing that, assurance that only two men could have killed him.

But Sir David had not said it. At least, not so that other, unwanted possibilities were excluded.

Steady. You don't know anything at all yet, Adam reminded himself. *You've not even begun to ask your questions.*

But this did not reassure him, because just now he found himself staring at two obvious and ugly possibilities as to who was responsible for the death of Sir Reginald Thorne. The first was that Charlotte Thorne, whose name adorned the forged letter Adam still carried in his pocket, had killed her reprobate father.

The second was that the blows had been dealt by her sister, Rosalind.

CHAPTER 20

An Unexpected Encounter

*And there was an air of vast circumspection and
mystery about her . . .*

Maria Edgeworth, *Almeria*

As it turned out, Alice had gotten home to Russell Street before Rosalind.

"Finally!" Alice ran into the foyer the minute Rosalind opened the door, arriving just two steps behind Amelia. "What happened? What did the countess say?"

"I'm not entirely sure," Rosalind admitted as she handed her bonnet and coat to Amelia and went into the parlor. She waited until Alice had closed the door behind them to say anything else. "Did you find any trace of Charlotte?"

"I'm sorry, but not yet. My best chance is an actress friend, and she was in rehearsals. I've left her a message saying I'll call. Now." Alice favored Rosalind with a steely glower. "What happened at the countess's?"

Rosalind swallowed her disappointment at Alice's news and forced her mind to other subjects. "Alice, do you remember you telling me that George had been writing about," she paused, scarcely able to believe she was about to speak these words in all seriousness, "secret societies of Bonapart-ists?"

"Of course I do." Alice dropped into the chair at her writing table. "The Major loves them. They hint at dastardly intrigue, and they sell papers without risking running afoul of the censorship laws. But what have Bonapartists to do with the Countess Lieven?"

Rosalind took her own chair beside the fire. "The countess seems to believe they have something to do with Mr. Fullerton."

Alice sat up very straight. "You're joking!"

"I'm not, and she certainly wasn't." Rosalind remembered the façade of laziness the countess exhibited as she spoke. Very like a cat at the mousehole, waiting for the creature within to make the smallest mistake.

"The man's a loathsome creature," said Alice. "And we know he'll stick at nothing to enrich himself, but . . . to support the return of the emperor? That means flirting with espionage and treason. It seems a bit much even for him."

"Yes," agreed Rosalind. "And that's just what I would have thought, until today."

Alice clicked her tongue against her teeth. "But didn't you tell me Fullerton is fundamentally lazy? Spycraft is not work for a lazy man."

"Her grace suggested that he wasn't himself a Bonapartist but was being paid by someone who is."

"Or extorting someone who is," added Alice. "That I could readily believe. Bonapartist sympathies would be excellent fodder for blackmail."

"But would they?" asked Rosalind. "Many prominent people openly express sympathy for that cause. Lord Holland is just one example." Lord Holland, in fact, went so far as to make speeches decrying the British treatment of the exiled emperor in Parliament.

"Expressing sympathy is one thing, but George says there

have been genuine attempts to get the little man off St. He-lena. Active involvement in such a scheme might be a trifle more difficult for the Crown to tolerate."

"Yes." The word came out hoarse and uncertain.

"What is it?" asked Alice.

"Something I'd much rather not have to think about," Rosalind admitted. "My father and Charlotte lived in Paris for several years."

Alice blinked as she realized what Rosalind was actually saying. "Oh, Rosalind, you can't really think your father got mixed up with some Bonapartists while he was abroad? What would be the point?" She saw Rosalind's expression and made a dismissive gesture. "Yes, of course, the money, but who with a single grain of sense would trust your father with any sort of important commission?"

Again, Rosalind had to agree, but unfortunately, there was another possibility. "They wouldn't trust him, no."

Alice opened her mouth and closed it again. "Charlotte?" she breathed finally.

Rosalind folded her hands neatly in her lap. She wished she'd thought to ask Amelia for some tea. She needed something she could fuss with. Sitting still felt intolerable just now. "As a courtesan, she has an unusual amount of freedom to move among the *haut ton*, at least the male precincts. She could meet with any man of any standing freely, and alone. Even if she was seen, it would be assumed they were her new paramour."

Rosalind had never allowed herself to inquire why Char-lotte had brought their father back to England. She had let herself believe it was to escape the extended uncertainties of life in Paris. It was true that Rosalind seldom paid close attention to politics. Despite Alice's doubts, however, she did read the newspapers, and of course, Alice and George kept her au courant. It was common knowledge that the English were not exactly beloved by the people of Paris.

They were, after all, members of the Holy Alliance that defeated Napoleon, and were exacting a heavy war debt from the French nation. To add to the unwelcoming atmosphere, the new French king, Charles X, had many allies who were determined to take revenge on those who had supported the Revolution, or who might still exhibit some loyalty to the old emperor.

Rosalind's throat closed tight and she had to swallow hard to clear it.

Alice sighed sharply. "Rosalind, I know what I've said about Charlotte being less than truthful, and I know you still have misgivings about what Charlotte does to earn her keeping. I do assure you, however, there's a difference between being willing to share a bed with whoever can pay for the privilege and being willing to turn traitor."

Rosalind felt herself blushing uncomfortably. "Thank you, Alice. I am aware of that. But Charlotte has been in straits, and keeping our father must be expensive. It may be that there came an opportunity she could not refuse." Alice looked like she wanted to argue, but Rosalind did not give her time. "If she took money to deliver a message, or to find out some information from one of her protectors, and if Father knew about it, or if Fullerton thought Father knew about it, that would explain what he's done."

"But not why he'd throw it all out in front of you."

She was right. If Fullerton wanted to extort Charlotte, he had no reason to display their father to Rosalind.

Unless, of course, he wanted to keep Rosalind at bay until he'd concluded his business with, or against, Charlotte.

Confusion and anger surged inside her. To cover these unwelcome emotions, Rosalind took up the stack of fresh letters on her desk and sorted through them, looking for some trace of Charlotte's hand. But there was nothing, and she dropped them all back down.

"Looking for something from Charlotte?"

"Yes." Rosalind ran her hand across her brow. "But there's still nothing."

As if summoned by these disappointed words, Amelia entered the parlor, carrying a tray with a letter on it.

"If you please, miss. A messenger's come." She held out the tray. Hope flooded Rosalind as she picked the note up. She barely noticed how Amelia's gaze slid from her to Alice and back again.

"Thank you, Amelia," said Alice firmly. "Really, Rosalind, we have to do something about that girl."

"We can trust her," Rosalind murmured. She flipped the letter over so she could see the back. Her heart plummeted. The seal was not Charlotte's elaborate script C. This one belonged to Valentina Walford.

"How can you be so sure?" asked Alice, but Rosalind didn't answer. Instead, she broke the seal and read:

> Miss Thorne:
> I have received your communication regarding that unpleasantness at the opera. You will be so good as to meet me at Upton's Assembly Rooms as soon as you have received this note, so that we may discuss the matter further. I am most disturbed by these events and am not at all certain I am prepared to continue our present association.
> Sincerely,
> Mrs. Valentina Walford

Alice came up behind Rosalind to read over her shoulder. Rosalind did not bother to remark on this.

"Well. That's some dreadful timing, isn't it?" Alice remarked. "But I suppose you'd better go."

"I suppose." Rosalind folded the letter closed and tapped it against her palm.

"I thought you'd been waiting to hear from her?"

"I had. And I do need to go. It's this talk with the countess and the thought that . . . Charlotte might be involved in something dangerous. It's making me far too nervous for anyone's good." She gestured with the paper.

"Do you want me to come with you?"

"Yes, I think that I do." She paused. "Amelia as well."

Alice frowned. "Are you sure?"

"I am." Rosalind told Alice about the conversation she'd had with Amelia earlier, how the maid had come forward and admitted to being approached by persons seeking information.

Alice drew back, clearly surprised. "Well, that's far more spine than I would have expected of the girl. But I tell you, Rosalind, she watches us both too closely. Especially . . ." Then she stopped.

"What is it?" asked Rosalind.

"Nothing," Alice said. "At least, nothing I'm ready to talk about yet. However, you trust her and I trust you, so let her come along. This day is rapidly becoming a complicated one. An extra pair of eyes might well prove useful."

Only the grandest houses in London had their own ballrooms, and only the very pinnacle of those had rooms large enough to accommodate the true "crush" that could number as many as eight hundred guests. Those who wished to entertain on the grand scale, or who wished to raise money for their charitable cause, needed to turn to public assembly rooms. Such rooms provided comfortable and more-or-less commodious space for dancing, cards, and dining. There were additional advantages, besides spacing and staff, such as a strong room where any monies brought in during the charity event from sale or auction of items could be securely held until they could be taken to the bank or distributed to the appropriate persons. A trusted master of ceremonies might be had as well, to help with the duties of host and to take charge of the staff hired on for the event.

The most famous of all such public rooms was Almack's, with its highly exclusive Wednesday night balls. To hold an event at Almack's, however, required approval from a board of patronesses, who jealously guarded access to their establishment. Fortunately for London's aspiring hostesses, the city and its environs boasted over a score of other establishments that were at least as lavish, and much less ready to turn away paying customers.

Upton's was a relatively new set of rooms and just outside the most fashionable of districts. But Rosalind had had dealings with the manager, Mr. Hodges, as well as his wife and their three daughters, who all helped run the establishment. They knew their business well, and Rosalind was able to assure Mrs. Walford she would have as grand an affair as she could wish and not have to worry about the bills being padded out unduly.

"Good afternoon, Piper," Rosalind said to the plump, young porter who had the bad luck to be assigned to the door on such a raw day. "I think we're expected?"

"Just so, Miss Thorne." He bowed and pushed the doors open. "Up in the card room. Good to see you again, Miss Littlefield." He touched his hat to Alice.

Once inside the soaring foyer, Rosalind shot her friend a knowing glance. Alice responded with a shrug.

"You'd be amazed what sorts of useful things a porter can tell one."

"Was it your money you spent to ensure his good will, or the Major's?"

Alice lifted her chin. "That, Rosalind Thorne, is not any of your business." She turned to Amelia, who had followed them in, a few steps behind.

"Amelia," she said softly. "Rosalind told me about your

gent, and you know, it might be he's watching more than the house. Do you think you could go about belowstairs and try to learn if anybody's been hanging about here, asking questions they shouldn't?"

Amelia looked mulish for a moment, but then Alice smiled at her. "It could be of very great help to me," she murmured. "And Miss Thorne."

Somewhat to Rosalind's surprise, Amelia blushed. Not any delicate pink tint, but a truly impressive shade of scarlet.

"I'll do my best, miss," Amelia said hoarsely. She bobbed a curtsy and hurried away. Rosalind had the distinct feeling the girl wanted to run.

She looked inquiringly at Alice, but Alice was looking after Amelia, her face suddenly quiet and thoughtful.

The card room waited at the top of the grand staircase. It was decorated to resemble a tasteful gentleman's club, with dark paneling and green painted walls that had been hung with landscapes and hunting scenes. The playing tables had all been draped in white muslin to protect them from the dust and sunlight. There was a fire in the hearth nearest the door, for which Rosalind was deeply grateful, and the velvet curtains had been thrown back to let in what little sunlight the day afforded.

But when Rosalind saw who was standing in front of those windows, she froze in her tracks.

It was not Mrs. Walford who stood at the windows looking out over the busy streets. It was Augustina. She stood silhouetted in the gray winter daylight, her face drawn tight, her entire posture on alert. Tension rolled from her in waves, as palpable as the heat from the fireplace.

Augustina must have heard the door, because she turned. When she saw Alice, she drew herself up in an excellent imitation of her mother at her most dignified.

"Who is this?" she demanded of Rosalind.

"Miss Littlefield is a friend of mine." Rosalind crossed to

the fire and pulled her gloves off so she could warm her hands. "I was concerned something might be wrong and so I brought her along. The tone of the message I received was not quite like your mother."

Augustina's cheeks flushed. She dropped her gaze. Her fingers knotted in the fine woolen cloth of her skirt. "I was afraid of that," she murmured.

"Did you write the letter?" asked Rosalind. Augustina nodded. "Why?"

Augustina looked again at Alice. Her restless hands gathered up more fabric, knotting themselves in the fine burgundy wool. "I needed to see you," she said. "But . . . privately. It was the only way I could think of. I wasn't sure you'd come if you knew the message was from me."

Because I am working for your mother's interest. You showed me you knew as much at the opera. But knowing that, why aren't you afraid I might tell her about this meeting?

Rosalind kept her features calm. She did touch Alice's shoulder. Alice nodded. She took herself over to the sofa nearest the fire, where she could sit with her back to the windows and Augustina. She pulled a small book out of her reticule and pointedly held it up in front of her face, making a great show of not listening.

Augustina hardly looked reassured. Which spoke to the girl's intelligence. Alice's sense of hearing, developed by long years of listening for stray remarks in crowded ballrooms, was exquisitely acute.

Rosalind crossed the room to stand in front of the girl. Now that she was closer, she could see that Augustina's eyes were red, with tears perhaps, or exhaustion.

"Where is your mother, Miss Walford?" Rosalind asked.

Augustina touched the corner of her eye, as if holding back an unruly tear. But her other hand remained knotted tightly in her skirt. "She's at home. Etienne brought me. He thinks I'm at a dress fitting."

"Do you know why she didn't answer my letter of yesterday?"

"I have no idea." Augustina seemed to realize she was crumpling her skirt and hastily brushed it down. "That's not the sort of thing she'd tell me."

She's lying, thought Rosalind. And she was making a very good job of it. If Rosalind hadn't already seen how artfully she exchanged her banter with Mr. Salter, she might not have caught it.

"Well, perhaps you can tell me why you wanted to talk to me so badly," said Rosalind.

Augustina looked at her in surprise. "Because you're my mother's—" She stopped, perhaps realizing there was no way to finish the sentence without giving offense. "I know Mother brought you to our house to find out about Salter. I know that person who presented him with the note at the opera was some acquaintance of yours. It was part of your plan, and Mother's plan, to separate us." Her fingers twisted another knot in her skirt. "Well, now I want you to work for me."

CHAPTER 21

An Unseemly Offer

*In London, people are accepted as what they
pretend to be.*

Catherine Gore, *The Debutante*

Rosalind found she could not make herself understand what Augustina had said. "I'm sorry?"

"I want you to work for me instead of my mother," Augustina said. "Whatever recompense she's promised you, I can match it, and surpass it." She strode over to the table where she'd laid her gloves and reticule, and pulled out a folded note. She laid it on the muslin-covered table. "This is a bank draft for fifty pounds, if you will help me."

Finally, Augustina's meaning blossomed fully in Rosalind's reluctant comprehension. On reflex, she glanced toward Alice. Her friend still sat unmoving on the sofa, the book open in front of her face. Rosalind doubted she'd turned a single page.

Slowly, outrage flickered to life inside Rosalind. The appearance of that bank draft was a direct indictment against Rosalind's character. A true gentlewoman did not trade her time or skills for money. As absurd as Rosalind sometimes found it, she was unable to openly discuss compensation with the ladies to whom she made herself useful. What came to her was in the nature of a gift, frequently something that could be sold, or that would be helpful for her expenses, such as an account at a shop or a milliner to be extended for a season, or even a year. When there was money exchanged, it was offered surreptitiously, and according to the rules of propriety, not flung about in a card room.

Rosalind could have dealt equably with the violation of that façade. Augustina's offer, however, said that she thought Rosalind could be bribed to break her word.

With an effort, Rosalind tried to see herself from Augustina's point of view. Augustina knew very little of Rosalind Thorne. She did know that Rosalind was a woman who had been brought into the house to pry into her private relationship with Horatio Salter.

As jolting as it might be to Rosalind's dignity, it was not so surprising that Augustina would believe she could be bribed to change course.

I made a mistake, she acknowledged silently to Augustina. *I should have taken the time to know you better, to gain your trust.*

Why didn't I?

She looked again at the young woman in front of her. *Only a few years younger than me.* Augustina Walford was stranger to London and caught up in . . . what, exactly?

What was it that drove Augustina toward such a man as Horatio Salter?

Rosalind marshaled all her practiced calm and asked, "What is it you would want from me?"

But Augustina shook her head. "No, I won't tell you until you promise me you will . . . act in my interests." She pushed the bank draft a little closer.

Rosalind found herself marveling at Miss Walford. Where

did a girl who had just turned twenty learn to comport herself like this? Rosalind would have expected the usual tools—tears and pleading, possibly fainting. Not naked bribery and an open attempt to extract serious promises.

And where did she acquire a bank draft for fifty pounds? According to Mrs. Walford, Augustina did not come into her own money until she was twenty-five. Rosalind could not imagine a mother, however generous, giving her daughter a full fifty pounds for pin money. That was at least three times what Amelia would make in a full year of service.

Rosalind felt her head swimming. She had thought her association with the Walfords would be a simple thing. A matter of a few letters, a few conversations. But now she was thrown into this strange world of fraudsters, bribes, accusations, and threats.

And my father's returned and my sister is missing, and I am forced to consider the doings of Bonapartists. Rosalind pressed her hand to her mouth, lest a hysterical laugh escape.

"I need your answer, Miss Thorne," said Augustina.

And I need to compose myself. Rosalind lowered her hand.

"Miss Walford, you are an intelligent young woman," she said, and she meant it. "You've surely considered that I might simply tell your mother about this meeting."

But Augustina shook her head. "You won't do that."

"Why won't I?"

The look Augustina returned her held a trace of smugness. It reminded Rosalind abruptly of the knowing, mischievous glances she'd exchanged with Mr. Salter. "Because while my mother may not trust what I say, I have two brothers who still believe me, and she, for her part, believes them. Between us, we can accomplish a great deal, if we try."

Rosalind made herself remain quiet. Inside, she was reeling from the turn this meeting had taken, but she could not allow herself the luxury of confusion. A single misstep on her part and Miss Walford would leave. If she did, and if she made good her threats to enlist her brothers against Rosalind, it would take all the Walfords out of Rosalind's reach. She could not afford that. Not only because of the damage it might do to her reputation, but because of the possibility that Salter or one or more of the Walfords were caught up in Russell Fullerton's machinations.

"Before I make you any promises," said Rosalind. "I have one question."

"What is that?"

"How did you really meet Mr. Salter?"

Augustina thrust her chin out belligerently, and for a moment, Rosalind thought she might refuse to answer. At last, however, she gave a one-shouldered shrug.

"We met at a gaming club, during the Season. It was their ladies' night. I badgered Louis into taking me. I was so bored. You have no idea what it is to be marooned as the orphaned daughter of a Manchester gingham manufacturer in London. We know no one except some of mother's émigré and political people. Most nights I was left kicking my heels and wishing desperately for a fortune hunter to come and sweep me off my feet.

"I wanted to go simply for a lark. Louis thought it was hysterical. He's like that. Etienne is mother's own—so serious. Left to himself, he'd be a full-blown radical, but Louis just likes to kick things over."

"Which club was it?" asked Rosalind.

Augustina shook her head. "I don't even remember. Grayson's? George's? Something like that."

"Graham's?" asked Rosalind carefully.

"Yes, that was it. Louis, fortunately or not, got tired of squiring me about and left me on my own while he played faro with some friends of his. I was watching the whist tables, and Salter began to talk to me. He said I looked confused and offered to explain the game to me.

"I told him I wasn't confused, I was trying to see if I could work out who was cheating. He was surprised."

"I imagine he would be." It was hardly a notion that a young debutante would have, much less admit to.

"It seems I was rather good at it," Augustina went on. "We picked out a number of the same people. After that, we strolled about the room, looking to tell the sharps from the flats. Those were Salter's terms. It was a good game, and we laughed—" Augustina's voice faltered. The smug light had left her and she looked young, and hesitant. "I'd never talked with a man like I did with him. He looked me in the eye. He didn't expect giggles and flirtation. He believed it was possible I had an intellect, and nerve. No one . . . no one ever treated me like I ought to be able to *do* things before.

"He asked me if I'd like to help him win a hand or two, and I said of course. We picked out a table where this one fellow was cheating, and Salter talked him into play. I pretended like I was drinking too much champagne and helped distract him. We won a great deal and the other fellow couldn't say anything, could he? If you're cheating, you can't complain when somebody cheats better than you.

"When it was time to go home, Salter slipped me half the winnings, and I gave some of that to Louis to keep him quiet. That was how it all started."

"Are you in love with him?" asked Rosalind.

"It isn't what I thought love was," said Augustina softly. "It's not hearts and flowers and stolen kisses. It's . . . we fit together, we work together and need each other. We . . ." She stopped. "He tells me I'm his anchor. That first night, he said he was amazed how I kept my head and didn't let him go too far. You may not believe this, but it was the most flattering compliment I'd ever been paid."

"I do believe it." Rosalind knew what it was not to fit into society's mold. A life on the edges was never easy, but at the same time, living within bounds could become stifling.

"Do you really?" Surprise colored Augustina's words. "Well, then you understand why I wanted to see him again. We worked out a scheme where we could be introduced in front of my family. And from that moment our relationship had two sides—the public courtship and the secret half, at the tables. I perfected the art of being both distraction and a lookout." Her smile was a sharp one. "When you're young and reasonably pretty, people are always going to underestimate you."

"And the fifty pounds comes from your winnings?"

"Salter opened us an account at a private bank."

"And you've continued to help him cheat?"

"It's all a cheat," Augustina snapped. "And before you blame Mr. Salter for corrupting my supposed innocence, I could have told you as much before I ever set foot in that gaming room."

Yes, I believe you could have, thought Rosalind. *I wonder how you came to learn so much so soon?*

"Miss Walford," she said. "You have been frank with me. Now I will return the courtesy. I have been gravely mistaken in the nature of your relationship with Mr. Salter. I compounded that mistake that I did not take time to get to know you for yourself. I am sorry.

"Your mother asked me to look into Mr. Salter's background. She was afraid he was a fortune hunter. I did discover that he was in debt, and that he had in the past been involved in a serious criminal conspiracy."

Augustina looked away. "The stock fraud. The one that started with the rumors about Napoleon's death."

That brought Rosalind up short. "You knew?"

"He told me about it. He told me everything about himself." Augustina smiled at Rosalind's surprise. "He wanted me to know what I was getting involved in."

"And his debts?"

"Why do you think he cheats at cards? So he can pay his debts. Unlike most of the dandies in the clubs." Her smile was tight. "You see, Miss Thorne? I am quite impervious to any blandishments on Salter's character. I know who I am . . . involved with."

"Then I must ask again, what do you want from me?" Rosalind spread her hands. "It does not seem I could offer you any help with Mr. Salter, or do you any harm with your mother."

Augustina's fingers knotted in her skirt again, and when she spoke, her voice was barely a whisper. "He's gone. I have not heard one word from him since the opera."

Rosalind blinked. "But it's only been two days . . ."

"He writes to me every day, Miss Thorne," Augustina snapped. "*Every* day. He knows I depend upon hearing from him. He would not leave me in suspense now, not when—" She looked away, her face flushed with anger, and with fear. "Not when he knows how worried I must be," she concluded firmly. "As to what I want, I want the answer to one question."

"What question?" Rosalind asked.

Now Augustina's face knotted itself as tightly as her hands in her skirts. "Did my family, my mother, do anything to ensure that Salter disappeared?"

CHAPTER 22

A Meditation on the Uneasy Nature of Courtship

The force of endeavour will do wonders towards acquiring the form and show of righteousness, by those who assume a virtue though they have it not.

Catherine Gore, *Sketches of English Character*

"Well, I think we can all admit that interview did not go as expected," said Alice.

They were in yet another hired cab on their way back to Little Russell Street. Alice and Rosalind shared one seat, while Amelia and her workbasket had the other to themselves. She was bent a little too diligently over one of Rosalind's cuffs, mending a worn spot on the edge. It was, however, impossible to miss the little glances she kept sneaking toward her employers, or, rather more specifically, toward Alice.

"No, it did not," agreed Rosalind. "And it's my fault."

"How?" demanded Alice.

"I took Mrs. Walford's word for what was happening in

the family, and I know better," she added. "I have a great deal of experience at how secrets grow between family members. I should have seen something was wrong."

Alice looked at Rosalind, her gaze holding remarkably steady despite the cab's jolting progress. "I imagine," she said finally, her voice as steady as her gaze. "It's hard to learn you do not possess omniscience."

The remark stung. "Am I being scolded?"

"A very little," said Alice. "But you must admit, Rosalind, you do sometimes seem to believe you should know more than any one person possibly could." She paused. "And you also might admit that you're still recovering from losing Devon this summer, and that's going to prey upon your attention."

Rosalind found she couldn't look at her friend any longer. Alice was right, although Rosalind hadn't actually lost Devon. She'd turned him down in favor of this life of hers, whatever name it might be called by. And then because she left Devon, Mrs. Kendricks left her, and this life and that choice was now all she had.

And Adam. Who was a choice as outrageous and uncertain as any other.

All these things had resulted in Rosalind throwing herself into her engagements and consultations. Since she'd returned to London, she'd answered more letters, accepted more requests than she ever had before.

In the depths of her heart, Rosalind knew it was fear that drove her. She was staring into a future that had no clarity, no safety, and no sheltering rules. She still had the protection of her birth and her gentility. She had her friendships, and her connections among the *haut ton*, but just now those seemed very fragile things to pin her future on.

So, she rushed from one engagement to another. She rushed to Mrs. Walford, and in her haste to resolve the situation, she had looked at Augustina only through the picture her mother painted. Over that, she'd laid a cloudy glaze of personal experience that came from sitting beside the wall at scores of social events and seeing hopeful girls dance themselves toward one single vision of the future.

Rosalind had assumed this was the future Augustina Walford was seeking. She had not taken the time to see that this individual young woman longed for something entirely different.

And now I may have ruined everything. Rosalind closed her eyes.

Alice gave out an impatient sigh. Cloth rustled as she shifted her position.

"Well, Amelia, as we must give Miss Thorne a moment to collect herself, did you learn anything interesting during our outing?"

There was a long pause. "I did meet the Misses Hodges," she said. "Very friendly, they were. Very glad for an extra hand for folding the linens, and they did talk a great deal."

Rosalind opened her eyes.

"Yes, I'm sure," said Alice. "What did they talk about? Did they say if anyone had been loitering outside the assembly rooms?"

Amelia remained bent over her mending, but she glanced up at Rosalind from under her eyelids. Rosalind nodded.

"There was nothing like that, but they did say their father is thinking to speak to Miss Thorne. They said that Mrs. Walford is driving them to distraction."

"How is that?" asked Rosalind.

"She's coming to them at all hours, setting up meetings with her charity committee. But why she can't meet with the committee in her own home, no one seems to know."

"I don't suppose they happened to overhear what gets discussed at these meetings?" asked Alice.

"No, they said that the committee was very particular

about having the door locked, and that the only reason their father's put up with it so far is they're paying extra for the privilege of keeping him up all hours, as they said he says." Amelia paused. "Did that help, miss?"

Rosalind could not help noticing it was Alice that she asked.

"Amelia"—Alice leaned forward and patted the girl's hand—"I owe you an apology."

In answer, Amelia drew herself up, very much putting on her dignity. "Yes, miss."

"Miss Thorne said you were an excellent and trustworthy young woman, but I did not entirely believe her. That was my mistake."

Amelia gave a small smile. "Well, to be fair, we didn't exactly know each other, did we?"

Alice smiled and Amelia blushed, and Rosalind realized that she was going to have to have a word or two alone with Alice, soon.

"Well, there we are, Rosalind," said Alice. "You wondered what Mrs. Walford was hiding! Secret meetings!"

"Of the Committee for the Relief of Widows and Orphans of the Soldiers and Sailors of the Holy Alliance," Rosalind reminded her. "No charity event can be managed without its committee. I've even been to a few of those meetings, you will recall. To present the plans for the ball."

"But in secret?" urged Alice. She'd caught the scent of a good story now and would not willingly let go.

"The late hours are unusual," Rosalind agreed. "But Mrs. Walford did tell me that she planned on holding the committee meetings at Upton's so the other members would be familiar with the rooms. She thought it would aid in planning the ball. Also, some of the gentlemen on the committee are simply not available during the day."

"Oh," Alice flopped back, deflated. "Well, there's still the question as to what's happened to Mr. Salter. I don't suppose the Misses Hodges noticed him skulking about?" she asked Amelia.

"They didn't say so, miss," Amelia told her.

Alice shook her head. "Too much to hope for. I suppose it's possible he's fled the country?" she added to Rosalind.

"Or at least gone into hiding," Rosalind mused. "A man who makes his living cheating at the tables is certain to have enemies, as does one who has debts and no means to pay. But if he was pinning hopes on Augustina and her fortune, why not send her a message?"

"Perhaps he tried. Perhaps it went astray."

"That's possible," said Rosalind. "But given that Salter and Augustina have been meeting secretly right under the family's nose for so long, they must have a fairly reliable system of communication. Mrs. Walford herself said she feared the Augustina was getting help from her brothers."

"It might be that learning about his debt was too much for Louis and Etienne, and they've started refusing to help our unusual pair of lovers."

"But Salter and Augustina shared a bank account," said Rosalind. "He could have left a message with the clerk. They haunted gambling clubs together, he could have left a message there. But he hasn't. Why not?"

"Could something have happened to him?"

"It's possible."

"Do you think she's right, then?" asked Alice. "That her family might have had something to do with it?"

"I think there is trouble in her family," said Rosalind. "I doubt as a child she harbored any ambition to be a gambler, or a gambler's assistant. There must be something in her life, her orbit, that fostered whatever her natural tendencies were in that direction."

"So you blame the family for the girl's indiscretions?"

"A girl may go to a gambling club on a lark, or a dare, but

it takes something more to make her want to become part of that world, or even believe it's possible for her to do so. Augustina is not a romantic. If anything, she's well on her way to becoming a cynic. That takes some hard experience."

"But from what she said, Salter coaxed her into going along with him."

"That was part of it, but not all of it. I have a feeling she's looking to escape from something. But what exactly is that? Is it the usual discontent of a young girl with a controlling mother? Was it simply bad luck that crossed her path with Salter, and he saw someone he could use?" Rosalind shook her head again.

"If they were truly committed to one another, an elopement would have been simpler," said Alice.

"It would," agreed Rosalind. "But then they might truly forfeit her inheritance, and Salter probably wasn't willing to take that risk."

"How much is she set to come into?"

"Three thousand a year." Mrs. Walford had told Rosalind that upon their first meeting, when she confessed she was afraid Horatio Salter was a fortune hunter.

"Mmm. Yes." Alice tapped her chin. "That's a lot to forego for a man with expensive tastes. So, you think that Salter and Augustina's original plan was to create the façade of a public courtship, get married, get the money, and then skip off to do as they please." She paused. "Sounds like Mrs. Walford's suspicions were correct in the essentials. She was just missing a few pertinent details."

"Yes," agreed Rosalind. "Except now Mr. Salter, who was so open with Miss Walford about who he is and what he does, has gone missing." Rosalind frowned. "I need to speak with Mr. Faulks. I need to find out to whom that promissory note he bought was originally given. It may be there was something about it that frightened our Mr. Salter."

"I think you'll need to speak to Mr. Harkness first," murmured Alice.

"Mr. Harkness?" echoed Rosalind. "Why?"

"Because he seems to be waiting on our doorstep."

Rosalind twisted around to see out the cab window. Alice was right. She had been so lost in their conversation and consideration that they had reached Little Russell Street without her even noticing. Mr. Harkness stood on their tiny stoop, blowing on his hands.

Usually when Rosalind saw Adam Harkness, her heart gave a particular flutter. Now, her heart thudded heavily, weighed down with sudden dread.

The horses came to a stop. Rosalind did not wait for the driver to come open the door. She let the window down immediately, worked the handle, and jumped down herself, careless of her hems and her half boots.

Mr. Harkness saw her and straightened. Rosalind raced up the steps, but he was already trotting down, and they met in the middle, face-to-face.

"Mr. Harkness! What is it?"

Mr. Harkness took off his hat. Rosalind's heart quailed. "I'm so sorry, Miss Thorne," he breathed.

"Is it Charlotte?" she asked.

"No, your father."

CHAPTER 23

A Cold and Final Message

Sudden violent deaths are of these kinds: 1: By the visitation of God. 2: By misfortune, where no other had a hand in it . . . 3. By his own hand . . . 4. By the hand of another man . . .

John Impey of the Inner Temple, *The Practice of the Office of Coroner*

Adam watched Rosalind take in his words. She swayed a little on her feet, but she did not speak. Only someone who knew her well could have seen the hints of distress in the way her hands clenched and how a very little color drained from her cheeks.

Alice Littlefield clambered out of the carriage, along with the new housemaid—what was her name?—Amelia. That was it. Both ran up the steps as well.

"Rosalind?" Miss Littlefield looked from her to Adam.

"It's Father," whispered Rosalind harshly. "He's dead."

"Oh, Rosalind." Alice put her hands on her friend's shoulders. "Oh, I'm so sorry."

Rosalind did not appear to acknowledge the gesture. "We should go inside."

She fumbled in her bag for her key, but the maid had already slipped past them and gotten the door open. The tiny foyer felt blessedly warm after Adam's long wait on the doorstep.

"Tea, at once, Amelia," said Alice. "No, best make it coffee. Never mind the fire, we'll take care of that."

"I'll do it," said Adam.

Rosalind lifted her eyes toward him. Those arresting eyes had always captivated him. Now they shimmered in the foyer's dim light, filled with tears that might never be shed.

He felt suddenly too large and too clumsy for this space, and he turned quickly away.

In the parlor, he set his hat on the mantel and immediately set about poking up the banked fire. Rosalind was careful with her coals, he knew, but he was lavish now. She would need all the warmth that could be had.

Stepping back from the rising flames, Adam ran his hand along his stubbled chin. He shouldn't have come here like this. His boots were caked in mud, he was unshaven, doubtless his eyes were red as if he'd been drinking. He'd been waiting for hours in the dank December weather. He could have gone to a pub or carriage house, or even back to Bow Street, but he did not want to miss her. There was every chance that news of the murder had reached the papers by now. He wanted her to learn it from him first.

This was the truth, but it covered another truth. Adam feared that if he let himself leave, he might also let himself find an excuse to keep from asking Rosalind the questions that he must.

The door opened. Adam's head jerked up. It was Alice Littlefield. She looked grave, and a little rumpled from the carriage ride. She closed the door behind her.

"Rosalind will be down in a minute. She needs to change."

She also probably needed time to collect herself. Adam felt his gaze drift to the closed door.

"Coffee will be here directly." said Alice, interrupting his thoughts as if she believed they could be leading somewhere dangerous. She was close to being right. "It will be terrible, but at least it will be hot. Won't you sit down, Mr. Harkness?"

"In one minute. There's a question I must ask you."

Alice froze in place. "What is it?"

"Was Ro . . . Miss Thorne home all last night? Did she go out at all?"

Alice's brow furrowed. For a moment, Adam thought she was going to start firing off questions of her own.

"Rosalind was home last night from dinnertime on," Alice said. "She never left the house. Amelia will say the same if you go ask her."

Adam nodded. "Good. Thank you."

Alice was looking hard at him. Adam could see the questions racing through her mind and he braced himself. In the end, though, she only asked one.

"Is Rosalind in danger?"

"Not from me," said Adam. *Yet.*

Alice nodded, reassured for now, at least. Further conversation was made impossible because the girl arrived bearing the massive silver coffee set. She placed it carefully on Alice's writing table. Alice was right. It was terrible coffee, although by no means the worst he'd had. It was indeed hot, and that made it more than welcome. There were some bread rolls as well and soft farm cheese. Adam split one open and wolfed it down gratefully. Alice fixed herself her own coffee and roll and avoided looking at him.

He heard footsteps and turned.

Rosalind entered the parlor, moving with deliberate calm. She was ashen and hollow-eyed, and carried herself with a dignity that would have done any queen proud.

"I'm sorry to have kept you waiting," she began, but her voice faltered. Alice went immediately to her side and took her arm to steer her toward the nearest chair, which happened to be the one at her writing desk, and sat her down. Neither Adam nor Alice attempted to speak. Adam's heart strained. She should not have to go through this. She had already suffered too much for her father's choices.

And now she will suffer again for his death.

"How did it happen?" Rosalind asked finally.

"It was murder." He spoke plainly. The only comfort he had to offer right now was his respect for her intelligence, and nerve. "He was found at Russell Fullerton's house. The coroner says he was stabbed. I'm so sorry," he added, feeling how ineffectual those words must be.

"Yes," Rosalind closed her eyes. "Yes."

Her hands trembled where they rested in her lap. Alice, on the other hand, glowered at him. He knew she was remembering how he'd asked about Rosalind's actions the night before.

Rosalind opened her eyes. Her hands were still. "Do you know who killed him?"

Adam dropped his gaze. The forged letter felt like a weight in his pocket. The questions he needed to ask only pressed it down more heavily. "Fullerton has been arrested."

"But was it him?" asked Rosalind, her words as sharp as Alice Littlefield's gaze.

"Circumstances tell heavily against him," said Adam. "Fullerton has a story of his own, of course, but he is lying about at least part of it, and he tried to conceal Sir Reginald's true identity from the patrol captain who found him."

"But you're not certain he did it," said Rosalind, and the disappointment in her eyes cut deeply.

"Not yet," Adam admitted.

The last of the color drained from Rosalind's face. Adam had to look away. He found himself staring at the coffee service and Alice's writing table. That table hadn't been there the last time he'd been here. Rosalind had written to him that Alice had moved in after her brother's marriage, and described in detail the ridiculous travails of adding another piece of furniture to this already crowded room. He had that letter, and all the others, in a box in his room.

"You will let me know if there's anything . . . anything you need of me," said Rosalind.

But Adam watched Alice, which was only fair, because she was watching him. No. That wasn't right. Her gaze flickered from him, to Rosalind, and back again.

Something was wrong. He could feel it. There was something going on between Alice and Rosalind that they were not saying.

Adam felt a corner of his heart crumble. He steeled himself and faced Rosalind again.

"I wanted to talk with your sister," he said. "But she doesn't seem to be at home. Do you know where she is?"

"She visited me a few days ago, as you know. We have not spoken since."

Rosalind did not lift her gaze as she spoke, and Adam wondered about that. More than once, he had watched Rosalind choose her words with special care, so that she could hold on to her secrets without actually telling a falsehood. She was doing that now.

Oh, Rosalind, why now?

Adam bowed. "I will leave you now. We will have to talk more, of course, but it does not need to be at once. Write to Bow Street as soon as you are ready. I expect"—Adam's gaze slipped toward Alice—"that there will be a crowd gathering as soon as word of this reaches the papers. I'll make sure a couple of constables are stationed at your door."

Rosalind also stood. She moved to open the door for him. Adam collected his hat.

"Thank you, Mr. Harkness," she said. Her voice was still

too soft. It was as if she could not draw enough air into her lungs to speak properly. "I don't . . . I didn't . . ."

But Adam bowed again, silently acknowledging her struggle, and the distance that must remain between them. For now.

He walked out the door before his resolve could waiver and he told her everything he feared. Because Rosalind was loyal to her sister, and he did not want to force her to have to choose between them.

Unless, he already had.

CHAPTER 24

When the World Turns Upside Down

There is one comfort in talking to you. One knows you mean what you say.

Catherine Gore, *The Banker's Wife*

Once Mr. Harkness left, Rosalind thought she would experience that dizzying rush of weakness that came with such shock. At the very least, she thought the tears burning behind her eyes would be released. But there was nothing, only a kind of gray numbness, as if both mind and body were at a loss as to what how to respond to this news.

Sir Reginald Thorne—*Father*—was dead. Not only dead, but murdered. Stabbed, Mr. Harkness had said. In darkness, while he sat in Fullerton's home, enjoying his poisoned hospitality.

The fact of her father had shaped Rosalind's entire life. When she was a girl, the household revolved around his moods and his needs. Her mother's first care had always been to lift him up in the elevated society he craved. His success was Mother's pride and her favorite ornament. As a girl, Rosalind had loved her father unconditionally, because she hadn't known what else to do. As an adult, her circumstances were dictated by his disgrace, and by the knowledge that he waited somewhere out of sight.

And now, he was gone. Wiped away.

Murdered. In Fullerton's house, under Fullerton's charge. While Charlotte was missing, and after Fullerton had threatened her and the life she had built for herself. Again.

"Rosalind?" Alice's concerned voice cut through the fog. Rosalind realized that she hadn't moved since the door closed behind Mr. Harkness.

"I'm all right," she said automatically. "I am."

"How could you possibly be all right?" demanded Alice.

"Because I have to be." Rosalind made herself turn and face her friend. "Alice, Mr. Harkness was right. This will be reaching the papers soon. I'll need . . . we'll need George's help. If the *Chronicle* takes the lead, the other papers will follow in terms of tone. . . ."

"I'll send a note round to him at once," said Alice. "I can draft an article and have it ready when he arrives. The Major will make room for it in the next edition."

"Thank you."

"We'd better let Sanderson Faulks know, too. He'll want to help, if there's anything to be done."

"Yes, you're right," Rosalind agreed.

Then, gently, Alice said, "As soon as I write George, I'll go try again to see what I can learn about Charlotte's whereabouts. That is, if you still want me to."

Yes. Charlotte. Rosalind crossed to her desk and quickly leafed through the stack of letters that had come with the afternoon post. Nothing looked to be in her sister's hand.

The fog inside Rosalind was lifting now, and some semblance of feeling seeped back into her blood. Worry, for instance, and sharp exasperation. And tangled, unwanted anger.

"Rosalind?" asked Alice carefully. "I noticed that when

Mr. Harkness said he wanted to talk to her, you didn't tell him Charlotte was missing."

"No, I didn't." Rosalind sat down in her desk chair. Her hands knotted tightly together.

"You don't seriously think Charlotte had anything to do with this?" asked Alice.

"I don't want to think it. I should not think it." Rosalind felt her hands tighten. "And it hardly matters what I think. There will be an inquest, and likely a trial. If Charlotte is called to court and cannot answer the questions put to her . . . Fullerton may yet escape. After all, he is still a gentleman, and she is a courtesan, and she held her father in close confinement for so many years . . ."

Rosalind found she could not finish. Under other circumstances, she might have been more dispassionate, but Adam's uncertainty troubled her almost as much as Charlotte's absence.

Alice sighed. "Good Lord, this mess keeps getting deeper." She stopped. "I'm sorry, Rosalind. That was a dreadful thing to say, when you just found out . . ."

Rosalind cut her off. "It is the truth, and I'm afraid we haven't yet heard the worst of it."

Because along with having to consider that Charlotte could be falsely accused, Rosalind had to consider the possibility that Charlotte might be correctly accused. Her sister had so much to lose just now, she might have been driven to act from desperation.

No. I don't believe it. I won't believe it. How could she have done this thing? She didn't know where Father was any more than I did.

Did she?

If Fullerton had already been in contact with her, she might. If she had agreed to look the other way while Fullerton took Father away. If . . .

Rosalind stared at the tidy stacks of books and papers on her desk. Had it been any other acquaintance, Rosalind would have applied to mutual friends to find out if they had any news. But despite their blood relationship, Rosalind and Charlotte were separated by an ocean of social conventions. If they had acquaintances in common, Rosalind had no idea who they were.

Which is also my fault. I did not want to know. I did not have the courage, or the honesty, to want to tie us together like that.

"We have to find her." It took Rosalind a moment to realize she had spoken the words out loud.

"We will," said Alice.

"You know Mr. Harkness asked me where you were last night," said Alice.

"I'd be disappointed if he didn't," murmured Rosalind. As soon as she said it, she knew it was the truth.

Alice was silent for a long moment. "Rosalind," she said at last. "Have you considered the fact that Horatio Salter is also missing?"

Rosalind frowned. "You don't believe Charlotte is somehow connected to Salter?"

"That is possible, but no, that's not what I meant. Earlier, however, you suggested Salter might be connected to Russell Fullerton."

Rosalind's head lifted. "Yes, that is possible. Fullerton and Salter are both members of Graham's Club, after all." She paused. "And from what Augustina told us, so is Louis Walford."

"Now that is a truly interesting coincidence," said Alice.

Before she could get any further, a knock sounded on the parlor door. Amelia entered immediately afterward.

"If you please, miss." Her cheeks were flushed, and her eyes were bright. Rosalind had not been crying, but Amelia had. Rosalind hadn't even bothered to look to see whether Amelia had been listening at the door when Adam told her what happened. Perhaps she hadn't. Perhaps Adam had spoken to the housemaid on his way out. It was the sort of thing he'd think of.

"There's a lady here for you." Amelia handed Rosalind the card.

Rosalind read the name and tried not to wilt. "It's Mrs. Walford."

CHAPTER 25

An Unexpected Caller

They will observe us, and perhaps think we are plotting something.

Maria Edgeworth, *Manoevering*

"Amelia, tell her Miss Thorne is not at home," said Alice promptly.

"No," said Rosalind. "That won't do. I need to see her."

"But surely whatever she has to say can wait, especially now."

A wave of weariness washed over Rosalind, and she was tempted to agree. But she shook this off.

"I wish it could. But if I refuse to see her today, I doubt I shall ever speak with her again. I have already embarrassed her publicly, and then I turn her away from my door?" Rosalind bowed her head. "After what Augustina told us, I feel I am under obligation for my carelessness. Besides," she added as Alice opened her mouth to protest, "given the family's connections to Salter, and to Graham's Club, one or more of the Walfords might well be involved with Fullerton. That means they might also be tied to the circumstances that have ended in my father's death. If I want to know the truth of what happened, I cannot now afford to lose my connection to the Walfords."

Alice threw up both hands. "Oh, very well. I suppose you're right. Again. Amelia, show Mrs. Walford in."

Amelia curtsied and did she was told. Alice put her hand on the coffeepot to ascertain if it was still warm.

"Perhaps you would rather . . ." Rosalind began.

"I'd rather stay right here, thank you very much." There was no contradicting Alice when she used that particular tone.

Nor, in this case, was there any time. Mrs. Walford sailed into the room. She had not allowed Amelia to take her coat, her muff, or her bonnet. Her face was thunderous, and Rosalind could in no way blame her.

"I came to find out the cause of your most unreasonable neglect of me," Mrs. Walford announced.

Which confirmed to Rosalind that Augustina must have intercepted her letter to Mrs. Walford. It was a simple enough matter in a large and busy household, especially if one had already been slipping extra sweeteners to the servants, which she probably had in order to facilitate her secret excursions with Mr. Salter.

"Miss Thorne, we had an agreement that you would conduct your inquiries discreetly and *promptly*," Mrs. Walford reminded her sternly. "But since then, not only have I been subjected to an embarrassing personal scene, but where I would have expected you to provide some kind of explanation I instead receive nothing but silence!"

It was only then that she noticed Alice sitting quietly at her table. Mrs. Walford's flow of outrage cut off abruptly.

"Mrs. Walford, my friend, Miss Alice Littlefield. Miss Littlefield, Mrs. Walford. Miss Littlefield writes for the *London Chronicle*," Rosalind went on. "She has been assisting me in drafting notices that will help direct the tone of the newspaper commentary on certain matters, including yours."

"Well, I am pleased to know you are doing *something*," said Mrs. Walford. "I will have you know, I had two days of dealing with Augustina's outrage and temper, without any of the support or mitigation that you promised. I am most grievously disappointed!"

"Mrs. Walford, I am sorry," said Rosalind. "But I have just received some grave personal news—"

Mrs. Walford interrupted. "The excuses of your personal life, Miss Thorne, have ceased to interest me. It is your responsibility—"

"Miss Thorne's father has been killed," said Alice.

Mrs. Walford froze, her mouth half-open, her blue eyes starting out of their sockets.

"Your father!" she cried. And again. "Your father!"

"Yes," said Rosalind, striving to match Alice's clear tones. "He was murdered last night at the home of an acquaintance. I have only just received that news."

Mrs. Walford closed her mouth like a trap, and she and Rosalind stared at each other. "What acquaintance?"

It was a strange question, perhaps brought on by the shock. *Or perhaps not.* "A Mr. Russell Fullerton," said Rosalind.

Mrs. Walford's face tightened. Rosalind watched her as she struggled to keep control over herself. She remembered saying to Alice how there might be some connection between Mrs. Walford, who had a great deal of money, and Mr. Fullerton, who made a career of taking money from women. Was it possible Fullerton's web reached up to Manchester? Or perhaps something had happened since the Walfords had come to London?

What if Mrs. Walford's curiosity about Salter's background was about more than his attachment to Augustina?

"I am very sorry for your loss, Miss Thorne," said Mrs. Walford finally. "This is . . . tragically unexpected."

"Thank you," said Rosalind, because there was nothing else she could say.

"I will leave you. I—" Mrs. Walford stopped. "Yes, I am very sorry."

Rosalind bowed her head. "I am sorry I was not able to complete our arrangement, but you should know I did discover something. I hope that you will hear me out."

"What might this 'something' be?" asked the widow impatiently.

"That you were correct," Rosalind told her. "Miss Walford is very much involved with Mr. Salter. They are much closer than I would have originally believed, but I am not sure it is the bonds of what one would consider a traditional romance."

"I do not understand you."

"You said you were concerned that Mr. Salter had ensnared your sons in his fraudulent schemes. I believe it is in fact your daughter who has been ensnared."

"Yes, by courting her for her fortune." Mrs. Walford spoke in that blunt, stubborn way of someone who could not make sense of this new thing they heard.

"No, rather by enticing her into some adventure."

Rosalind felt the weight of Alice's gaze on her, but she did not spare a glance at her friend. She needed to keep her attention on Mrs. Walford. Tired as she was, bewildered and angry as she was, Rosalind did not know when she might have another chance to try to draw Mrs. Walford out. She could not let this one slip past.

"I do not understand you, Miss Thorne." Mrs. Walford's words sounded suspiciously close to a plea. "You told me Augustina's heart was not engaged. You expressed certainty on the subject."

"I was wrong," said Rosalind. "But she has formed a real attachment. Whether it is simply the daring lark of a bored girl, or whether she has been lured and trapped in some way, I cannot tell, nor do I know if the attachment is real on his side."

"But why would she enter into his schemes? How *could* she?"

"You could answer that question better than I can."

"I assure you, Miss Thorne, I have no idea," Mrs. Walford protested.

"Then you must ask your daughter."

Rosalind waited for more bluster or denial, or at least more questions, but Mrs. Walford maintained her silence for a long, strained moment.

"I see," she said finally. "Thank you, Miss Thorne. That is . . . it is not what I wanted to hear, but it is something I need to know." She lifted her chin. "Now, I'm sure you wish me gone. Again, my condolences on your loss."

Rosalind nodded, and the widow whisked herself around to let herself out without even waiting for Amelia.

Alice collapsed into her chair. Rosalind drifted over to the window. Outside, Mrs. Walford was waiting for her driver to lower the carriage step. She was looking back toward the house. Rosalind wished she could see around the edge of the woman's bonnet. She very much wanted to know what Mrs. Walford's expression was.

Mrs. Walford had seemed truly shocked by the news that Augustina had formed a—call it a friendship for lack of any better word—with Mr. Salter. But why would she be? She was the one who feared elopement. Rosalind could not help thinking the cause of her shock lay elsewhere.

She had seemed equally shocked to learn that Sir Reginald had been acquainted with Russell Fullerton.

Alice had come up from behind her. "Come away from there, Rosalind."

But Rosalind didn't move. Mrs. Walford's carriage was pulling away, but a young boy in dark coat, flat cap, and knit muffler was running up the street, dodging the puddles. He hopped up the steps and pounded on the door with one red fist.

"What now?" murmured Rosalind.

"I'm afraid to find out." Alice grabbed up her reticule. Amelia entered the room a moment later. Alice took the note and gave Amelia a coin for the boy.

"It's for you." She handed the note to Rosalind. "Do you recognize that hand?"

The only direction on the outside was Rosalind's name, and that was written in a firm, broad stroke.

"Is it from Charlotte?" asked Alice.

"No." Rosalind flipped the paper over. It had been badly sealed with candle wax, which had been pressed down with a signet she didn't recognize, either. The paper was dirty and ever slightly crumpled, possibly from traveling in the ragged messenger's pocket. "At least I don't think so."

She broke the seal and unfolded the paper. The note was brief and imperious. Rosalind read it once, and then again, and once more, because she could not believe what she saw.

Alice craned her neck to read over Rosalind's shoulder. She gasped, and she swore. Rosalind very much wanted to do the same.

> *Miss Thorne,*
> *You will excuse the informality of this missive. I must request that you meet with me at my current place of habitation, that is, Clerkenwell Prison. I have a question of vital interest to myself, if to no one else, to discuss with you. I beg you do not delay, or the hangman may cheat you of your one chance to see me utterly at your mercy.*
> *Yrs.,*
> *Russell Fullerton*

CHAPTER 26

The Stage Has Been Set

. . . his system of cold-blooded self-command
afforded him singular advantages over the
offender.

Catherine Gore, *The Banker's Wife*

When Adam left Rosalind's house, his first impulse was to head straight back to Fullerton's and do whatever proved necessary to pry some truth loose from the cadaverous manservant Sparkes. What stopped him was the knowledge that any misstep—deliberate or accidental—would have consequences, and he could not afford them.

Neither can Rosalind.

Instead, Adam directed his footsteps back toward Bow Street. He shouldered his way through the crowd of complainants, witnesses, and constables who surrounded Stafford and his fellow clerks, all of whom were trying to take statements, issue orders, and clear away the idlers and the curious.

The relative quiet of the ward room and the patrol room was like a breath of fresh air, even if it was all strongly scented with the combined miasma from tobacco and old boots.

Tauton was waiting for him.

"There you are!" he cried as Adam hung his hat and coat on the pegs by the door. "I've something for you." Tauton pushed a paper packet across the table toward him.

Curious, Adam unfolded the packet. Inside waited five pieces of charred paper. Two were no bigger than Adam's thumb. The other three, though, they were fully as large as his palm. Clearly, Tauton had had a profitable morning with the ash pile.

"How'd you get these so fast?"

"Called in at the bakers up the way." Tauton nodded vaguely toward the doorway. "Borrowed the great sieve they use for sifting the flour, and the baker's boy to ply it. You owe me a crown for all that, by the way."

Adam reached into his pocket for his purse. He flipped the coin toward Tauton, all without taking his eyes off the fragments.

The two smallest were illegible except for a few individual letters. *Useless.* The larger ones, though, they were interesting. Adam drew up a chair to sit, carefully, so as not to make a draft that would scatter the fragile scraps.

The one closest to him was clearly a bit of a drawing, possible even a plan for . . . something. There were lines, both dashed and solid, and arrows, and some numbers. *Measurements?*

The second fragment was a list. With one gentle finger, he turned it so he could read it more clearly.

Hon. Car . . .

Mr. Fe . . .

Mrs. Sher . . .

"Names?" asked Tauton.

"So it seems," agreed Adam.

"A guest list?"

"A list of debtors?" countered Tauton.

"Or creditors."

The third scrap was difficult to make out. Adam leaned closer. There was a crooked line, a series of tentlike markings, an arrow . . .

"A map!" Adam looked up at Tauton. "That's a coastline, there." He traced air above the bold line with his finger.

"Odd little assortment," remarked Tauton.

Adam leaned back. "Not what I'd expect such a man to be holding." *Or burning.* "He dealt in letters, and other people's debts."

"And other people's secrets," Tauton reminded him. "Perhaps these papers were not his own."

"It's very possible. But why was it so urgent to destroy them?" He folded the packet closed around fragments.

"I don't suppose there's any chance he'd tell the truth if you showed him them?"

Adam chuckled ruefully. "I wouldn't want to rely on it."

Both men fell silent. Adam stared down at the packet. He thought of Fullerton with a dead man at his feet, locking the door to gain time. Not to hide the corpse or the weapon, but to toss incriminating papers into his fire. And yet, in the midst of this frantic activity, he left a letter lying squarely in the center of his writing desk.

Why not burn that as well?

Did Fullerton not notice it? Had it been acquired while he was out? But from where? It had not come either in the post or by hand. There was no seal on it. It hadn't even been folded. It was as if it had been written at that elaborate marble-topped desk.

And perhaps it had.

The dead man was a forger after all. He could well have been creating some material to gain a hold over Charlotte Thorne, or Rosalind, for himself or his new friend.

Adam felt his guts twist with distaste. What sort of man would smear his daughter with such obscenity? How could it even be imagined?

I owe Rosalind an apology, he thought grimly. When he'd returned her father's other forgeries to her, he'd believed Sir Reginald could not be as bad as she feared. How could he be? Adam did believe some other crime might be unearthed. Yet, he also believed if Sir Reginald escaped the law, the man could still be made to see reason, eventually, even if it required a threat or two, perhaps reinforced with a little blackmail brought to bear from a source other than his daughters.

But with such a slander in his pocket, he wasn't so sure anymore.

"What are you thinking, Harkness?" asked Tauton.

Nothing I'm ready for you to know about. Adam shook his head.

"I'm thinking Mr. Fullerton is either a careful strategist or the biggest fool I've ever come across," he said.

Tauton hiked his brows. "How so?"

"He tried to lie to us about who the dead man was. There's some sign he even tried to remove his signet ring. But he left a letter lying out on the desk that clearly points to the man's true identity." Even as he spoke, Adam remembered Captain Goutier's remarks about the state of the room—how tidy it was, even with the lamp spilled out on the floor.

It all felt off and yet oddly familiar. He'd noticed it at the time. Adam frowned at his thoughts.

Adam's brother-in-law, Freddy, was a sailor. Those times when he was in port, Fred and his mates sometimes picked up extra work in the theaters. Sailors were valued as hands for bringing the massive bits of scenery in and out. After all, they were not only used to complex, heavy labor but expert with all manner of ropes and knots. It transpired that Fred had developed a love for the theater and talked about it incessantly, much to his wife's amusement.

All at once, Adam realized why he was thinking of Fred now. "It's a scene," he said. "Just like out of a play. Fullerton laid out the hints and clues he wanted us to see." He stopped. "He even said it. He knew I'd be called in."

Tauton stared at him, clearly trying to make sense of this outburst. At last, he pursed his lips and gave a low whistle.

"Clever. But suppose you're right. What did he mean to do?"

Present the possibility that Rosalind and her sister might be dragged through the mud. Probably he thought I'd hide what I found in order to protect her. Maybe that I'd try to scuttle the investigation so her name would be kept out of the affair.

"He wanted to keep our attention on the dead man," said Adam. "He wanted us asking who this might have been and what did he do to get himself killed. If our attention was forced in that direction, we might forget to look too closely at Fullerton and wonder what he was doing that might have caused his guest to die."

Tauton cocked his head thoughtfully toward Adam. "That could be. It fits what you've told me so far. But you mentioned a letter. Can I see it?"

"I'd rather keep it close, until I know more." *Until I know for sure I'm right about this.* "But I will say it brings Rosalind Thorne and her sister straight into the center of things."

"Ah." Tauton nodded. "That would throw a cloud around the matter. But you know that his nibs"—he jerked his chin toward the door that led to John Townsend's private office—"will insist on reading it all for himself."

Adam grimaced. "Where is he?"

"Prince Regent's having a supper party tonight at Carlton House. Plunging early into the Christmastide. Townsend's off supervising the security arrangements."

"That buys us at least a few hours, then." Adam carefully folded the singed scraps back into their packet. "Perhaps until tomorrow morning."

"What are you going to do with this wealth of hours?"

"There's another man in this scheme." Adam fished in the table drawer for a stub of lead pencil and used it to label the little packet of scraps. "One Horatio Salter." He took the packet over to the battered wooden filing cabinet and tucked it into one of the folders with his name on it.

"Salter, is it?" Tauton scratched his chin. "Seems I know that name from somewhere."

"Well, he might have doings with our Mr. Fullerton, and he's gone missing. I know Fullerton won't talk to me. But this fellow might."

When Rosalind made the connection between the two, Adam had called it a thin chain. And so it was, but it was also all they had.

CHAPTER 27

The Haunts of Men About Town

Likewise it is to be inquired who were culpable,
either of the act or of the force . . .

John Impey of the Inner Temple, *The Practice of the Office
of Coroner*

Graham's Club was a place Adam passed on a regular
basis. He'd even guarded its doors on occasion. Any
place where there could be a clot of wealthy individuals
coming and going from their carriages was sure to attract
pickpockets and cutpurses. Special gangs of constables were
frequently recruited and organized under the charge of a
Bow Street officer to help keep the thefts down.

This, however, was the first time he'd ever been inside, and
he had to work to keep himself from staring about in amaze-
ment.

London was home to many grand and gaudy buildings,
but few boasted a staircase flanked by two gigantic bronze
statues of nude goddesses holding up fans of cards. The number and brightness of the chandeliers and new gaslight
torchieres rivaled any he had seen in the King's Theater or at

the opera. It was the middle of the day, a time that counted as early morning by the standards of the *haut ton*, but the sounds of voices, laughter, and the occasional shout of triumph drifted down from the warren of gaming rooms at the top of the stairs.

Adam thought of Fullerton's luxuriant home and decided this place looked exactly like the sort of haunt he would favor.

He'd expected his entrance to be challenged. In his plain coat and worn boots, he hardly looked the part of a member of such a place. He had barely set a foot on the plush red carpet when that challenge arrived. A towering, broad-shouldered, and garishly liveried footman bore down on him.

"May I help you, sir?" he inquired frostily.

Adam looked up into the man's sour face. "Hullo, Holloway. How have you been?"

That sour expression bled away, along with the color in the man's cheeks as Davey "the Lark" Holloway recognized who had just walked through his door.

"Hullo, Mr. Harkness," he croaked. "I, erm, that is, did you want something?"

"Not from you," Adam assured him. "But I need to talk to the manager."

"I thought that might be you, Mr. Harkness," drawled a lazy voice behind him.

Adam turned. Sanderson Faulks strolled across the grand expanse of the foyer and favored him with an elaborate bow. Adam had never seen Faulks dressed less than perfectly. Today, he wore immaculate buff breeches, a neatly tailored forest-green coat, and a fancifully knotted cravat.

"Mr. Faulks." Adam returned his bow. "I did not realize you were a member here."

"Yes, well." Faulks cast a sardonic eye over the statues and the gilded stairway. "It is not perhaps one of my favorite haunts, but I had business here today. As I gather do you. It's all right, Holloway," Faulks added, waving his walking stick toward the footman, a gesture meant to shoo him gently away. "I'll take charge of Mr. Harkness."

Holloway's relief was undisguised. "Yes, sir. Thank you, sir." He bowed and hastened away.

"Old acquaintance?" inquired Faulks.

"We've had words once or twice," replied Adam. "Nothing that should be allowed to endanger his position."

"Oh, I would never think to mention it. Now, sir, where can I escort you?"

"I had come to see the manager, but as you are here, I think I might as well speak with you. If you're willing."

Faulks paused and lowered his voice. "May I take it this is to do with a lady of our mutual acquaintance."

Adam nodded.

"I am entirely at your service, sir. Let us repair to a quieter location."

Faulks led Adam up the marble stairs and past the cavernous gaming room, to a room only half as large, this one dedicated to the business of eating and drinking. Despite his declaration that this was not one of his preferred clubs, Faulks was clearly well known here. All the patrons seated with their chops and their bottles of red wine seemed to have a nod or a bow for him. Faulks acknowledged the greetings with a weary wave of his neatly gloved hand.

They reached a small table under the mullioned windows. Faulks dropped into one chair in a great show of exhaustion. A waiter bustled over at once.

"Will you join me for a chop, Mr. Harkness?" he asked as he pulled his gloves off.

Adam tried to remember when he'd last eaten, and failed. *Mother would clout me on the ear.*

"Thank you."

"For two," said Faulks to the waiter. "And the potatoes and the wine sauce, and one of my reserved bottles of madiera from the cellar." He caught Adam looking at him, and he shrugged. "Just because one doesn't come often, it does not mean one should not be comfortable. Besides, you'd be amazed at the stuff they try to pass off in such places." He tossed his gloves aside. "Now, Mr. Harkness, how can I help?"

"Have you heard from Miss Thorne yet today?"

"I have not, but then I left home early. Well, early for me," he added. "Is something wrong?"

"Her father has been killed."

"God save us," breathed Faulks. "And you've told Miss Thorne? Of course, you would have. How did she take it?"

"Hard," said Adam. "But Miss Littlefield is with her."

"Invaluable Alice," Faulks murmured, and for the first time since Adam had met the man, Faulks looked genuinely ill at ease. "She'll look after Rosalind properly, because depend on it, Rosalind won't look after herself. I must go to her. I—" He stopped. "Forgive me, Mr. Harkness. This is a shock. My family was friends with hers for many years. We all but grew up together. In fact, once—" Sanderson didn't finish the sentence, he only shook his head. "At one time, I thought I should like to grow up to be just like Sir Reginald."

Adam looked steadily at him. Faulks laughed, just a little.

"I see what you're thinking, but do not mistake a shared taste for good tailoring for any similarity in men's character. What I do, I do honestly. I earn my monies, and I pay my debts. Still, this is sad news, and I am sorry for it. Do you know who did this abominable thing?"

"That's the answer we're looking for," said Adam. "But Sir Reginald was found in Russell Fullerton's study."

"Was he, begad? You surprise me. Fullerton is many things, but I never would have taken him for a murderer." He cocked his head toward Adam. "Or was it someone else?"

"As I say, that's what we're trying to find out. I'm here to learn what I can about Fullerton's doings, and to try to track down Horatio Salter."

"Well, on that our paths align. As for Fullerton . . ." Faulks paused and looked about the room. "I believe I see someone who might be useful in that endeavor. May I invite him over?"

"Please do."

Faulks rose languorously and strolled across to a table by the fire, where a grizzled, portly man in stovepipe trousers, a wine-colored velvet jacket, and a silver-patterned waistcoat was nursing his glass of port. He had a head of bushy gray hair, with whiskers and brows to match. After the exchange of a few words, the man got to his feet and followed Faulks back to their table.

"Mr. Harkness, allow me to present Mr. Charles Leggett, a highly respected subject of that kingdom known as the London Exchange. Mr. Leggett, Mr. Adam Harkness, principal officer of the acclaimed Bow Street police station." Introductions completed, Faulks signaled for the waiter to bring another chair and the men all settled back down.

"Pleased to make your acquaintance, Mr. Harkness. I've heard your name from John Townsend. He speaks very highly of you."

"Thank you, sir."

"Faulks says you're asking about Russell Fullerton?"

"I'm looking for anyone who might know about his recent . . . business dealings."

Leggett arched his shaggy gray brows. "I wish you luck, sir. Russell Fullerton kept his business to himself. If there was a gentleman more closemouthed, he'd have to be the blood relative of an oyster. And those who do know something will not be eager to share it with a member of your profession."

"Fullerton's in jail now, if that's of any help."

"Jail?" Leggett's pale-blue eyes fairly popped out of his head. "What for?"

"He killed a man." *Possibly.*

"Fullerton? Killed a man?"

Adam didn't say anything. Leggett rubbed his brow and tugged at his whiskers. He looked at Faulks for confirmation and received the barest of nods. At last, he leaned back, folded his hands across his stomach, and started to chuckle.

"Well, well! Fullerton, caught at last! I wouldn't have believed it. Should have stuck to being a foul blackmailer." He smoothed his whiskers down thoughtfully. "What is it you want to know, Mr. Harkness?"

"As I said, I'm trying to find out about his current business."

"Yes, yes," Leggett muttered. "You're sure he's in jail?"

"I saw him into the cell myself."

"Well, there's been rumblings that he was calling in some old loans." He paused again. "A rather large number of old loans. Caused great concern among some people; several had to scramble to raise capital. Fullerton did not like excuses at the best of times."

"And this was sudden?"

"Right out of the blue," said Leggett. "If it had been any other man, I'd've said he had some sort of note due himself and he needed to raise the funds. But if there was one thing Fullerton did, it was pay his bills." Adam didn't miss the fact that the man was already talking about Fullerton in the past tense, and he seemed to be relishing it. "That is, he did when he couldn't get other people to pay them."

"Did Fullerton know a man named Horatio Salter?"

"You mistake me," said Leggett. "I was not Fullerton's confident. I don't think he had any. He had people he owned, and who did as he said."

"But Salter is a member here?"

"Oh yes, the young nuisance. No profession of his own. Plays hard and deep. Gotten himself called out a few times, too. I wouldn't sit down with the man, or trust him with my sister, that's for certain."

A gambler and a card sharp, then. "But you know of nothing linking the two of them?"

Leggett blew out a long sigh. "Now, let me think. Oh, wait, yes"—he snapped his fingers—"I remember. It was Burnsby telling me over a game of cribbage. Good game. Good man, Burnsby, but no strategy about him. Plays like his hat's on fire, and can't get rid of—" Leggett cleared his throat. "Excuse me. Anyway. Burnsby said that Salter was asking questions about Fullerton. Wanted an introduction. I remember what he said, he said, *Can you imagine? Like wanting an introduction to your hangman.*"

"You're certain about that?" asked Adam. "It was Salter looking to meet Fullerton? Not the other way around?"

"As sure as I can be. Not much in the old upstairs, poor Burnsby, and as I said, no strategy about him, but he wouldn't be mistaken about that. Too extraordinary. Usually people are looking to get away from Fullerton, not get closer."

Adam wasn't prepared to agree it was extraordinary, but it was a surprise. Or perhaps not. Fullerton's main business was blackmail, and everyone knew it.

Perhaps Salter had something to sell.

"Do you remember when this was?" asked Adam.

Leggett scratched his whiskers and tugged. "Ah. Yes, I remember. Tail end of the Season, it was. Mrs. Leggett was under full sail to get us moved out to the country for the shooting. My boy's game, not mine, so I was busy getting myself out of the way. Spent rather more time here than usual. Yes, that was it. Of use to you, is it?"

"Possibly," said Adam. "I do thank you for your willingness to help."

The waiter had returned, with assistants, bearing trays and covered dishes.

"And here's your luncheon." Leggett pushed himself to his feet. "I'll leave you gentlemen to it. Faulks, we'll talk soon." He bowed. Faulks nodded. "Oh, and, Mr. Harkness, I'm sure should you need it, we can find you a good number of gentlemen prepared to swear that they'd seen Fullerton."

"Where?"

Leggett grinned, showing a row of dark, crooked teeth. "Wherever you like."

CHAPTER 28

Relative Positions

Nothing like truth, ever came directly from the
mother: there were always whisperings and
mysteries . . .

Maria Edgeworth, *Manoevering*

"Has Mother lost her mind?" Etienne slammed the billiard room doors open.

Startled, Louis jerked his arm. The tip of his cue glanced off the cue ball and skittered across the table's red felt.

Louis rolled his eyes. He'd retreated back here in the hope of a little distraction. Billiards wasn't a purely exciting game, like faro, but its physical intricacies gave him a chance to focus on something besides all the disasters, and near disasters, of the past few days.

"Did you hear me?" demanded Etienne.

"Of course I heard you." Louis bent over the table again, realigning his spoiled shot. "I just don't know what you're talking about." He tried to relax his wrists and focus on the billiard balls. There was an invisible line between them, and his cue, and his elbow, and if he bridged his fingers just so . . .

Etienne snatched the cue ball off the felt.

"She's bringing that Thorne woman back into the house!" Etienne brandished the ivory ball at Louis. "She actually went to see her yesterday, and she's writing to her this minute!"

"What of it?" Louis snatched the cue ball back. "The woman is helping Mother carry on with the charity ball. We should be thanking her."

He set the ball on the felt and tried to settle himself back into position for the shot.

"But how can she!" cried Etienne. "She's only going to stir up trouble! I would have thought that that ridiculous business at the opera would have been a perfect excuse to dismiss her."

Louis sighed. Obviously, Etienne had no intention of letting him get back to his game. He straightened up, which was when he also noticed that the doors were still open.

Oh, for God's sake. He brushed past his younger brother and slid the doors shut.

"There's only a few days until the event. Probably Mother decided it would look odd to dismiss the woman at this late date."

"But why would she care about that now?"

"Why are you asking me?" Louis picked up the chalk and freshened his cue. "Why not ask her?"

Etienne folded his arms and looked away. Louis sighed again. He also slapped his brother's shoulder. "You need to get a grip on yourself, Etienne. Nothing has happened, nothing will happen. Our plans are still moving forward." Louis's gaze strayed back to the table. *If I stand there, and angle the cue just so . . .*

"I don't know why I even bother," snapped Etienne. "You don't care anything at all about the cause. You never did."

"All right!" Louis cut him off. "If you're determined to have this out, let's do it properly." He met his brother's blue eyes, so very much like his own. Despite the three years between them, people sometimes took them for twins. "I don't care about the cause. But just because I don't care about politics and causes and mother's promises doesn't mean I don't care about this family, or you, or even our idiotic little sister."

Etienne stuck his chin out belligerently. Louis just shook his head. "Listen, Etienne, I'm just an observer in our little family drama. If you want to know what Mother's doing, ask Mother. If you want someone to rail at, you should try 'Stina. If she'd let on about the Thorne woman sooner, we might have had time to come up with a new plan."

"An observer?" cried Etienne. "Is that what you call it? When you were the one who brought Salter into this family in the first place."

"That wasn't me," Louis snapped. "That was 'Stina."

"You encouraged her. You went along with her. With both of them!"

Louis didn't answer him.

Etienne threw up his hands. "If you don't care about the cause, fine. Be just another lazy aristo, if that's what suits. But you might care about the fact that thanks to you, 'Stina's in over her head."

"What are you talking about?"

"I'm talking about the fact that despite the fact Salter's done a runner, our little sister is still carrying a torch for him."

"Again, what of it?"

"What does she actually know? What is she going to do next?"

"For God's sake!" Louis slammed his cue down on the billiards table. "I keep telling you, ask her!"

"Ask her what?" said a woman's voice behind them.

Both brothers spun around. The doors were open again. Their mother, Valentina Walford, stood on the threshold. Louis suddenly felt like he was six and had been caught stealing apples from the pantry. Anger at himself, and at her, surged through him.

"Mother," said Etienne. "We didn't . . ."

Mother closed the doors and made a great show of locking them. "If you want to communicate secrets, Etienne, you shouldn't shout," she said as she turned around. "What is going on in here?"

"Etienne is having an attack of nerves," said Louis.

"What on earth for?"

Etienne drew his shoulders back. "Why are you planning to bring that Thorne woman back?" He sounded petulant, and judging from the color in his cheeks, he knew it. Louis sympathized with him. At the same time, he was glad he was not the only one who still felt like a child when he was trying to face down their mother.

Her indulgent smile did not help. "You're worried about Rosalind Thorne? You should have come to me directly, Etienne."

"That's what I've been telling him," said Louis.

"Well, I'm glad you're both here, because that is the subject I wanted to talk to you about." There was a cluster of wingback chairs in front of the hearth. Mother settled gracefully into one. "Sit down, both of you." Etienne did as he was told. Louis eyed the door and considered bolting, but only for a moment. With a sigh, he did as he was told.

What else is there to do while we live in this house?

"It seems this once the evening papers are correct." Mother said. "The man who was killed at Russell Fullerton's house was indeed Miss Thorne's father, Sir Reginald Thorne."

The brothers exchanged a long glance.

"But the good news for us," she went on, "is that Russell Fullerton has been arrested for the deed and is sure to face the magistrates within the next few days."

Her voice was completely steady, detached even. Really, if she hadn't twisted their lives so much, Louis could find her iron nerve truly admirable.

Louis didn't want to think about all the times he'd thought

about just walking away. All the times he told himself he should make his own way in the world, as his father had done. Somehow, though, he'd never been able to make the break, at least not alone.

Maybe that's how this all really got started. The knowledge that if he was to get out of here, he needed the others to help him.

Louis rubbed his eyes.

"Is Fullerton guilty?" Etienne asked carefully.

"He certainly appears guilty." There was no mistaking the satisfaction in Mother's tone. "The papers are dropping some very potent hints as to his unsavory reputation. Not that the name of Sir Reginald Thorne is precisely covered in glory, either. The important thing is that the coroner's attention is directed toward him, and so is Bow Street's."

"There," said Louis to Etienne. He tried to sound hearty, but his voice trembled. "Told you there was nothing to worry about."

"All right, all right," his brother growled. "There's nothing to worry about. Poor milksop Etienne is fretting over nothing, again. But that doesn't explain why you are writing to the Thorne woman!"

"Because, Etienne," said Mother firmly. "We have only a matter of days left to us, and we need the charity ball to happen."

Louis tried to gather together his thoughts and his nerve. "Mother, Etienne may have a point. What if your Miss Thorne smells a rat? What if she decides to start asking questions about the charity, and the board?"

Personally, he didn't think Miss Thorne would, not with her father's murder to occupy her attention and feeling. *Poor woman*, he added, silently. He might not like her, but she probably didn't deserve this. Losing your father was never easy, he knew. At the same time, she could not be considered entirely harmless. After all, the woman had deliberately made herself into a sort of professional nuisance. Who knew what else such a creature might do?

"Miss Thorne will be thoroughly occupied," said Mother. "In fact, the reason I determined to bring her back was so we can be sure she is kept busy on matters that are advantageous to us. Salter may be gone, but we need to know where to and what he's doing now. I intend to ask her to help us in that capacity."

"But why her?" demanded Etienne. "Why not hire a runner? Or a thieftaker? *Anybody?*"

Mother's eyes widened in surprise. "Why, Etienne. Anyone would think you were afraid of a slip of a disgraced gentlewoman."

Etienne laughed grimly. "Mother, if there is one thing I've learned from being your son, *and* 'Stina's brother, it is that a determined woman is not to be taken lightly. Miss Thorne's father was murdered. Don't you think she's going to want to understand the exact circumstances?"

"Miss Thorne will know the circumstances, just as the rest of the world will," said Mother firmly. "They will all know that Mr. Fullerton was a blaggard and a scoundrel and he murdered his guest. In the meantime, we will continue with plans for the charity ball, and Miss Thorne will exercise her powers and contact her friends to help us find Mr. Salter, because I, of course, am worried that he might still try to contact Augustina."

"That he might," admitted Louis.

"He might never have stopped contacting Augustina," said Etienne.

This time Mother's surprise was genuine. "Do you know something, Etienne?"

"I know my sister." His mouth bent into a thin smile. "She's not happy and she's up to something."

"The pair of you should leave 'Stina alone," muttered Louis.

"I'm sorry, Louis," said Mother sternly. "I didn't hear you."

"Augustina made a bad decision, didn't she?" *We did.* "She got tricked, but so did the both of you." *And I helped, damn me for being too clever for anybody's good.* "You might show her a little sympathy instead of suspecting her of . . . something nefarious."

"Yes," said Etienne blandly. "Because what on earth would poor, silly little 'Stina do that was actually, what was your word, *nefarious?*"

"That's enough from both of you," snapped Mother. "Need I remind you that if you'd done your work properly, we wouldn't have to be worrying where Salter is at all?"

"It wasn't . . ." began Etienne

"We *thought* . . ." said Louis at the same time.

"Enough!" snapped Mrs. Walford. "There is plenty of blame to go around. We must all accept our share. I, at least, am working to correct my fault. Etienne, if you are so concerned about what Miss Thorne may or may not discover, then I suggest you leave off hectoring your brother, and me, and be the one to find Salter so we can determine if he is in fact plotting more mischief."

"Perhaps I will," said Etienne. *He means it,* thought Louis, a little surprised. A chill ran up his spine. When Etienne's temper got roused, what little good sense he had tended to get swamped.

My God, what a lovely, happy family we are.

"Are you really determined to go through with this?" Louis asked their mother. "So much has already gone wrong, we're putting the whole family at risk."

He'd hoped the appeal to family would at least make her hesitate. He was wrong.

"The cause is more important," she said. "Our promises are more important. I thought you both understood that."

"We do, Mother. But think," Louis urged. "What can Salter possibly do now?"

"Aside from ruin your sister?" inquired Mother mildly. "He can make it seem that the cause is a farce, and that we can be cheated with impunity. It must not be permitted."

Louis muttered under his breath.

"I did not hear you, Louis," said Mother, in the exact same tone she'd been using since before they were breeched.

Louis sat back in his chair. He looked to Etienne and then to his mother and made up his mind.

"I said, is Salter showing that the cause can be cheated, or that you can?"

"You would do well to remember, Louis, that as a member of this family, our troubles are yours."

"Mother, you may believe me when I say that I am intensely aware of that fact," replied Louis. "The only question left is what can any of us do about it?"

CHAPTER 29

To Venture into the Depths

Less glaring demonstrations of the same vice, the silent egotisms of personal vanity, intellectual pride, domestic self-seclusion, sordid calculation, and diverse others, glide through the world undetected, or arrayed in the mask and domino of virtue.

Catherine Gore, *The Banker's Wife*

Rosalind fully expected her friends to be upset by her decision to visit the New Prison. But even Alice, this once, had been genuinely shocked.

"You can't, Rosalind. This is madness. Even for you. Even for *me*."

Sanderson Faulks had appeared on the verge of raising his voice. "My dear Miss Thorne, I find myself almost ready to wish we had married, so that I would have the power to absolutely forbid you to do this thing."

Mr. Harkness, however, did not waste breath on admonishments. "I'm coming with you," he said.

As Rosalind moved to protest, Mr. Harkness cut her off, something he never did.

"I will wait outside so he will speak more freely, but I will be there." He lowered his voice, his face as grim and serious as she had ever seen it. "Fullerton has threatened your destruction. He may still be trying to carry that out. I will be there."

To this, Rosalind had no answer.

The place where Fullerton was being held was officially called Clerkenwell Prison. However, it was commonly known as the "New Prison," having been rebuilt after the original structure burnt down in the Gordon riots. Despite its new construction, it was as solid and forbidding as any medieval fortress. Rosalind found herself grateful for Adam's presence as he handed her down from the carriage.

He hammered on the turnkey's door, and when the wizened little man slid back the little shutter, he handed through his written orders. The turnkey squinted at him, then shrugged and opened the door.

Adam held out his arm.

"I believe this is the first time I've taken your arm, Mr. Harkness," Rosalind murmured as they walked beneath the long, dark archway.

"I believe you're right," he answered softly. "How strangely appropriate."

Rosalind felt the urge to smile, but it died immediately. The guard was plying one of his great iron keys on yet another closed door, and they were inside the prison.

They followed the turnkey through a sort of tunnel. To their left, a series of arches opened onto the bare prison yard, where men clustered. Rough shouts and laughter cut the dank, frigid air. To the right was the stone wall, with its stout, barred doors.

The jailor stopped in front of one of the doors and worked the heavy lock. He grabbed the lantern off the hook on the wall and walked into the darkness. It took all of Rosalind's nerve to follow.

Outside, it was broad daylight. In here, it was midnight, and as cold as it had been in the open air. The smell was overpowering. Rosalind extracted her handkerchief from her sleeve and pressed it against her nose. She struggled not to shrink back against Mr. Harkness as they were led up the slick, narrow stone stairs. The smell seemed to cling to the damp stones. She could feel it sliding against her skin. Rosalind, who believed herself to be hardened and practical in every way, shivered at the thought of coming into contact with those walls.

At the top of the stairs waited a corridor lined by more of the blank doors, all barred and fastened with iron locks. The only light was the turnkey's lantern. Voices drifted up from that pungent darkness. There were no words, just shouts, and groans, as if the place were peopled by anguished ghosts.

"If Fullerton seems inclined to talk, be sure to ask him about Horatio Salter," said Adam.

He means to remind me what we're here for, thought Rosalind, and she was grateful. "Have you learned something?"

"Possibly," he replied. "I'll tell you once we're out of here."

The turnkey had stopped. He handed Mr. Harkness the lantern while he took a fresh ring of keys off the iron hook on the wall and undid the iron-banded door.

Mr. Harkness let go of her arm and stepped back.

"I'll be right here," he reminded her.

"He will not do me any harm while he wants something from me," Rosalind said, hoping to reassure herself as well as him.

Mr. Harkness regarded her with his serious blue eyes. "Nonetheless."

The turnkey wrestled the door open. " 'Nuther o' yer lady friends, Fullerton," he bawled.

Rosalind turned, lifted her chin, and made herself sail into the prison cell as if entering a ballroom.

Compared with the corridor outside, the chamber was positively civilized. There was a fire in the grate and clean linen on the bed. The high slits of windows were barred but also glazed to provide some protection from the weather. The table held a basket of bread, cheese, and hothouse grapes, as well as a bottle of wine.

Rosalind had known, in a distant and abstract way, that a prisoner in any of the jails could purchase extra comforts and better food. Mr. Fullerton had evidently decided to avail himself of this privilege.

The man himself sat at a battered central table. As she entered, he stood and bowed with all his customary elegance.

"Miss Thorne. I must admit, I am surprised. I did not expect you to come."

Superficially, Fullerton was dressed as she had last seen him—in an immaculately cut coat and trousers. Now, however, he was without ornament. There was no chain on his waistcoat and no glint of gold or silver about him. His chin was unshaved and his hair pushed roughly back. For the first time, she saw a trace of fear in his pale, placid eyes.

"Will you sit?" He gestured toward one of the wooden chairs that had been drawn up to the table.

"No, thank you," Rosalind replied.

Fullerton shrugged and sat himself. "Should I bother to offer you a glass of wine? I have no tea and the vintage is passable."

"No, thank you."

He shrugged again and gulped the wine. Whether this was to show her he did not care or because he truly needed the fortification the wine provided, Rosalind could not tell. Her mind felt pressed in a vice made of anger and disgust, and yet she knew she must control herself at all costs. This man still lived and breathed. He still had communication with the world outside. That meant he was still dangerous to her and to those around her.

"I did not kill your father," he said abruptly.

Rosalind made no answer. Fullerton lowered his glass. His pale eyes narrowed at her.

"Now, Miss Thorne, you will do me a favor and attempt to think rationally. Why would I kill him? I had not yet gotten what I wanted from him. This may be demonstrated by the fact that you are still walking about London and being received in polite society. At least, I presume you are being received. By our good countess, perhaps?"

Rosalind lifted her chin and returned him a steady gaze she had perfected for use against drunk and ill-mannered fellows in many fine ballrooms.

Fullerton poured himself another glass of wine. He held it up to the light that filtered in through the barred window. "Thus far, I have avoided committing an actual crime," he said to her, and to the wine. "I find being accused of one distasteful."

"No crimes?" murmured Rosalind.

"None. It is not a crime to use what one learns from obtaining private information to one's own advantage. Or to loan money privately. These are the things I do. Sanderson Faulks does the same, and he is your intimate friend." He drawled the word *intimate*.

Rosalind turned and raised her hand to knock on the cell door.

"Damnit! I apologize! I apologize!"

Rosalind faced him again.

"What do you want from me, Mr. Fullerton?"

"I want you to exert your powers on my behalf, Miss Thorne. I want you to find out who really did kill your father."

CHAPTER 30

A Confidential Proposal

But if the inquiry be of what may turn out to be a business at the assizes, as murder, &c ... be particularly careful to take down the evidence of the fact and circumstances, as that no evidence may be wanted to elucidate the inquiry.

John Impey of the Inner Temple, *The Practice of the Office of Coroner*

For one of the few times in her life, Rosalind was struck absolutely speechless. Fullerton regarded her over the rim of his wineglass. His expression was strange, a mix of satisfaction and desperation. There was something else in it too—something she could not name but that made her skin crawl like the cold of the prison corridors.

"Surely you can afford ..." Rosalind began. Fullerton didn't let her finish.

"I can afford a great deal. I can, for instance, afford to make sure you will never again be in financial difficulties. Which I would, by the way, in return for your assistance in this."

"Why me?"

"Because I find I'm pressed for time," he drawled. "The inquest is scheduled for the day after tomorrow. Unless new evidence is discovered, or a new witness found, I have no doubt that I will be bound over for trial. Depending on the docket, that grand event may come up as early as the next day."

He was correct. Trials happened in the order that the cases arrived on the magistrate's bench. Each one could take as little as a half hour or as long as three, so there was no telling how many might be got through in a day. As a result, there was very little chance that any advance notice might be given to a prisoner. There would simply come some random time when Fullerton would be taken from his cell and ushered to court.

"So, as you can see, the machinery of the law does not leave me much time to locate a competent hand to help in my present difficulties."

Rosalind shrugged with an indifference that was only partly feigned. "If you are innocent, surely you can simply stand before the magistrate and explain yourself."

"Perhaps I could," said Fullerton. "However, not only are appearances against me, but several of the magistrates before whom I might be obliged to plead are not well disposed toward me personally. Rather, I should say, their wives and daughters are not. Therefore, even if I could present a compelling argument for my innocence, I cannot be sure of a fair hearing." His tone turned bitter. He swirled his wine in his glass and drank.

"You seem to forget, Mr. Fullerton, I also am not well disposed to you personally," said Rosalind. "You have repeatedly threatened my complete destruction, and that of my sister. You chose to try to use my father against me, and because of your actions, he is dead. Whether you held the knife or not, you are responsible. Why should I concern myself with your troubles?"

"Because, woman, I did not do it! And the one who did is still out there! Is he to be allowed to go free because you want revenge?"

Rosalind did not answer him. Instead, she met his eyes and held them for a long time. He returned her gaze with the cool arrogance that was so much a part of his bearing, but only for the first moment. Rosalind made herself see him clearly— his stubbled cheek, his dirtied hands and soiled breeches. One stocking had a tear. His shoes were scuffed, and the buckles were missing. It was cold here, despite the fire, and she could see the gooseflesh prickling his throat.

And he knew she saw it all, and she saw the traces of shame flicker behind his pale eyes.

"Tell me what happened to you that night. The entire story," she added.

Fullerton leaned back. He looked pleased that she was deciding to be so reasonable. Rosalind kept her face studiously neutral.

"I'd had to leave the house on business . . ." he began.

"What business?" she asked.

"My own."

Rosalind waited.

Fullerton reached for the wine bottle and poured himself another glass. *Are you having second thoughts?* she wondered.

"I went to meet with my banker to discuss a transfer of funds," he said, finally. "After that, I dined at Walsh's Chophouse with business associates. Messers. Kemp, Grandidier, and Chilcott," he added before she had to ask. "We discussed matters of mutual interest. After that I went to Graham's. I spoke with some other associates and wrote some letters in my rooms. After that, I went to collect a payment for a set of letters from Lady Fitzhugh."

"It must have been late by that time."

"It was part of the arrangement." His grin was feral. "Do

you require more details on the nature of her payment, Miss Thorne? I could provide them."

Rosalind returned him a look of cold contempt. He shrugged. "She got what she wanted from the exchange, and so did I. But as you may imagine, I cannot hold out any reasonable hope that she would go into court and swear to the fact that we were together."

"I imagine not," said Rosalind.

"It was late when I left her, and it was later by the time I got home. A carriage overturn and a public squabble between some worthless young hotheads delayed my return. When I finally got home and alighted from my carriage, two men burst out of my front door and barreled down the steps. One of them collided straight into me. We grappled for a moment, and he shouted blue murder."

Fullerton's eyes narrowed, his voice thickened, hoarse with more than bad wine and anger.

"I ran into the house, and into my study. Your father lay bleeding all over my carpet. which was, by the way, on fire where the lamp had been knocked over. I smothered the fire and turned to him, and got a great deal of blood on me in the process. But he was already dead, and the mob was at my door. In fact, they were through it. I locked myself in the study to keep from being torn apart. There I stayed until the watch was finally roused to action. There." He spread his hands. "That is the whole story."

It was not, but Rosalind was not ready to press him on that.

"You felt comfortable leaving my father to himself for an entire day?"

Fullerton waved this away. "My man Sparkes was with him, and Sparkes was under orders to provide him with all the wine he requested. I fully expected him to spend the day drinking himself into a stupor. Indeed, I have no reason to believe he did not."

This was plausible enough. "What was the nature of the understanding between you?"

"That I would help Sir Reginald return to his rightful position in society, and to expose the ungrateful nature of his two thankless daughters."

"And what was he to give you in return?"

"The ability to expose the ungrateful nature of his two thankless daughters."

Fullerton's pale eyes searched her face, watching for her discomfort, her anger, her broken heart. He would not find them. She had been scrutinized by far worse than he.

"What do you know of a Mr. Horatio Salter?" she asked.

Fullerton's brows arched. "Who?"

Rosalind regarded him silently.

"I promise you, Miss Thorne, I know no one of that name."

"I have it on good authority you do."

The anger that flashed across his face was so extreme that for a moment, Rosalind thought he meant to strike her. She did not let herself cringe, but she did tense, ready to throw herself sideways and scream for Mr. Harkness.

"What authority?" demanded Fullerton.

Rosalind said nothing.

"Oh, come now, Miss Thorne." He set his glass down. The anger was gone, replaced with a smile that was beguiling, even coaxing. For a moment, Rosalind saw the man as he appeared when he was trying to draw out some inexperienced young wife. He was cheerful and gentle. His pale eyes even showed some bit of understanding mirth. "Is this all to be one way? I have answered your questions. It's only fair you answer mine."

Rosalind said nothing.

"Come, come, surely I have a right to know who is accusing me?"

Rosalind turned her back and walked to the door. She raised her hand to knock.

"All right! All right! Come back." His sigh rattled deep in his throat, and that beguiling charm vanished as easily as it had appeared. "I do know Salter. At least, I know of him. We are both members at Graham's. He's a proud little scoundrel who thinks very well of himself and has some talent for faro and other such games. He said he was by way of coming into some quantity of funds shortly, and he wanted my advice on how they might be most discreetly and securely housed."

"When was this?"

Fullerton shrugged. "I don't recall. Two months ago? Three? He stood me to a drink. We talked. He went away." Fullerton paused. "But did I not spy him with you at the opera?"

Rosalind did not see the need to answer this, either.

"What would you offer me?" she asked. "If I was able to find what you need?"

"Ah!" Fullerton grinned, a satisfied, snake-like smile. "Now we come down to it. Five thousand pounds, Miss Thorne. Not a penny less."

Five thousand pounds. She could live well on that for the rest of her life. With such a sum she could purchase the lease on her house, keep several servants and even a carriage.

"I do not accept your money," she said to him. "But I will see if there is any information to be found. I will need your keys, both to your house and the room at your club."

"Now why would you need that?" He sneered, but his tone slipped past Rosalind, making no ripple on the surface of her calm.

"Because, Mr. Fullerton, if I am to assume that you are this once telling me the truth—"

"Would I have called you here to lie to you?"

"If you thought you had something to gain from it, most certainly," she replied. "But if you are not lying, then there are three possibilities to be considered. First, that my father died by random act. A burglar or some such."

"Unlikely," muttered Fullerton.

"Second, that some action of his own caused such shock or offense, and that the party decided murder was the only option."

Fullerton gestured impatiently. Rosalind frowned at him and was treated to the sight of Russell Fullerton looking momentarily guilty.

"The third is that someone wanted to give the impression that you killed him."

Fullerton glanced toward the door but said nothing.

"If that is the case, I could ask for a complete list of all the persons you have blackmailed, threatened, bribed, swindled—"

"You make your point," Fullerton snapped.

"Or otherwise defrauded," Rosalind concluded. "Or I could simply go through your remaining papers, which would be much more expeditious."

Now it was Fullerton who fell silent.

"I feel I should point out, Mr. Fullerton, your continued existence does not actually matter to me," said Rosalind. "If I wish to find out who killed my father, I can do so just as easily after you are hanged."

And then I will have both my answer and no longer need to worry about what you might do to me and mine next. She met his gaze.

"They will not admit you at the club," Fullerton growled. "No women are allowed."

"I will manage."

Fullerton quirked one brow, that satisfied smile playing across his face again. "And what would your ladies say if they . . . no, no. I spoke from habit, Miss Thorne, nothing more. But, no, you will not have my keys. You see, I do not trust you that much."

"Then I bid you good day, Mr. Fullerton." Rosalind turned her back and walked to the door.

"This again? You begin to bore me, Miss Thorne. I've offered you five thousand. You will have to learn—"

She pounded against the door with her gloved palm. "Jailor!"

"Wait!" cried Mr. Fullerton.

Outside, she heard the clink of metal against metal.

Fullerton cursed, and behind her Rosalind heard the sound of metal clattering against stone. Now she did turn and saw a ring of keys lying on the floor where Fullerton had tossed it.

Keeping her eyes fixed on his, Rosalind stooped to retrieve them and tuck them into her bag.

"Is there someone to whom I should apply if I find anything?" she asked.

"My solicitor is Wilson Rathbone of the Inner Temple. You may send to him at any time. He will know to watch for your correspondence."

"Wilson Rathbone of the Inner Temple," she repeated. "Very well." She faced the door.

"Miss Thorne?"

She turned again.

"I am guilty of a great many things. I do not regret them. The world is peopled by fools. If they can be taken advantage of, they deserve what they get. But I . . . I do not wish to die for the one thing I did not do."

Rosalind had no idea how to answer him and did not even try. She simply turned away and waited for the door to open.

Her heart hammered as she heard the scrape of the lock turning. Her thoughts, though, felt smooth, deep, and surprisingly simple.

She could leave him there. She could walk away and, in so doing, lay so many of her troubles to rest for good. Father was dead and soon Fullerton would be, too. He was a vile creature who used the weaknesses of others to enrich and to please himself. He preyed on women particularly. He would destroy her if he could. He had confessed it. He had threatened Alice, and through her George and Hannah.

He deserved to hang. There was no question of it. She could bring this about. She could still discover who had killed her father, still save herself and Charlotte and see justice done. She could just make sure this all came a little too late to benefit Russell Fullerton.

It was, and would be, entirely her choice.

CHAPTER 31

The Awful Breadth of Possibility

It is incumbent upon the prisoner to make out to the satisfaction of the court and jury; the latter of whom are to decide whether the circumstances alleged are proved to have actually existed . . .

John Impey of the Inner Temple, *The Practice of the Office of Coroner*

Despite the reassurance of having Mr. Harkness beside her, Rosalind scarcely felt able to draw breath as they were led back down the close, cold, echoing corridors and let back out into the street.

"There's a stable just around the corner," he told her. "Hatton is waiting there with the carriage." He offered her his arm once more, and she took it gratefully. Even here, amid the familiar traffic of humans and horses, the damp stench of the prison seemed to trail along behind them.

Perhaps it was not the stench, but the memory of what had passed inside the prison walls. Rosalind was not sure which had disturbed her more—the prison itself, her confrontation with Fullerton, or the cold realization that she truly did hold his life in her hand.

"I was only able to hear some of what was said," Mr. Harkness remarked. "What was it Fullerton wanted from you?"

"He wanted to protest his innocence," she said. "And to ask for my help."

"Your *help*?"

"As incredible as it may seem. He asked me to find who really did kill my father, and offered me five thousand pounds for it."

Adam said nothing immediately. They dodged the urchins, the beggars, and the pushcart men who occupied this shad-owed section of street under the prison's walls. Finally, they reached the corner of the grim wall and of the street. The liv-ery stable waited, solid and homely on the other side. Their driver must have been watching from the window, because he came out at once, touched the brim of his hat in salute to Mr. Harkness, and set about the business of harnessing the horses.

"What did Fullerton tell you happened that night?"

Rosalind repeated Fullerton's tale—how he went out on business, spent the day in the company of friends, and then the night in the company of a lady; how he came home only to have two men burst out of his house and raise the cry of murder. As she spoke, Mr. Harkness's familiar stillness de-scended over him, that curious, energetic silence that he said came from his time with the horse patrol, waiting for the highwaymen.

He said nothing at all until she was finished.

"That matches with the story he told Captain Goutier and me," said Mr. Harkness. "Do you believe him?"

Do I? "I do not want to. But it is possible."

"Why?"

"Because, as he himself pointed out, he was not finished with my father yet. The whole point of taking him up, if it may be called that, was to destroy me. That work is unfinished." Her eyes narrowed, remembering Fullerton's face as he spoke. "And . . . the way he told it, it had the feeling of a man recalling a memory. He is a skilled liar, but my sense was he was speaking at least some of the truth." She paused. "Besides, if he did commit the crime, would he not choose to spend his night in the company of someone willing to answer for him? As the business stands, he was with a lady who even he admits would have every reason to lie. As a plan of defense, it is at the least, exceedingly careless."

The carriage was ready. Mr. Harkness handed her in and helped her with the rug.

"Shall I take you home?" he asked.

"I think we should go at once to Fullerton's residence. He's given me his keys." She pulled the ring out of her reticule. "There may be something more to be found there."

Adam grinned. "And I want another word with that fellow Sparkes." He gave instructions to the driver, climbed in, and shut the door. The driver touched up the horses and the carriage started forward.

There was the usual negotiating of legs and rugs and selves that came from traveling in an enclosed carriage. The conveyance belonged to the Bow Street station and such was small, spare, and hard used. Still, Rosalind was grateful for the woolen rug and for not having to negotiate the winter streets on foot.

Mr. Harkness was looking out the window. His good humor of a moment before had faded.

"Is it possible Fullerton was lying?" he asked abruptly.

"About what in particular?"

"About his reasons for leaving your father alone that day."

Rosalind forced her reluctant mind to think. Now, of all times, she could not afford to have her wits desert her.

"Has this to do with something Fullerton said to you?"

"Not exactly." Mr. Harkness took a deep breath and

seemed to reach a decision. "It is more to do with a letter we found."

"What letter?"

"It was on the desk in the room where Fullerton and the corpse were found. It was written in what appeared to be a woman's hand, and detailed a salacious encounter with a young paramour." He paused. "It was addressed to you, and the signature was your sister's."

Rosalind's throat closed. "It could not have been," she said, and she was surprised her voice stayed so even. "Charlotte would never be so indiscreet."

"No," agreed Mr. Harkness. "I suspect it was your father's work. Given what you learned from Fullerton, I believe Sir Reginald was left alone to compose that letter, or one like it, to provide food for a scandal involving you and Miss Charlotte."

Now it was Rosalind's turn to look out the window. The nature of the streets was already changing, with vans and carriages replacing the pushcarts and wagons. The pedestrians were better dressed here, the stoops and doorways better kept.

"Was it in my hand?"

"No, I would have recognized that."

Her cold thoughts warmed just a trifle at this. "So, Charlotte's. Which would make sense. It would be hers he was most familiar with. And the letter was completed?"

"And signed. Fullerton had left it on the desk, despite the fact that he was taking considerable trouble to burn some other papers when he was found."

A point Fullerton had neglected to mention when he was recounting his activities. What other points did he leave out of that story?

"What is it you believe?" Rosalind asked.

The carriage jolted across a large cobble, rocking badly.

"Perhaps Sir Reginald had begun to make demands of his own," said Mr. Harkness. "They may have quarreled, and Fullerton may have lost his temper, or simply decided that Sir Reginald was more trouble than he was worth, now that he had the letter in hand. He killed Sir Reginald, and when he realized what he had done, tried to set the stage to make sure that as much attention as possible was thrown on your family."

"But if he wanted me to become suspected, why bring me here and ask me to help prove his innocence?"

"To force you to consider the letter, and the fact of your sister. To tear the two of you apart and increase the possibility of your relationship to a courtesan becoming public."

"He must have realized that I know my father was a forger, and that I would soon understand that he wrote the letter."

"And who would be most likely to kill him for creating a letter compromising Charlotte?"

Rosalind sucked in a sharp breath. *Charlotte. Charlotte who has not been heard from for two days already.*

If Fullerton did not do this thing, then she had to consider who did, and she could not rule Charlotte out.

Rosalind's heart constricted.

There are other possibilities, Rosalind reminded herself firmly. *There is Horatio Salter, there are all the Walfords in their turn. Fullerton has more enemies than the Tower has ravens. Any one of them could have done this thing.*

"You said he was found covered in blood," she mused out loud. "Surely, when a man has killed someone, the first thing he would do is wash himself. He would not allow himself to be caught quite literally red-handed."

"That bothers me as well," said Adam. "It's why I particularly want to talk to Sparkes, without his master present."

"Do you have any idea what sort of papers Fullerton was burning?"

"It seems to have been a fairly random assortment," said Adam. "We found a piece of a list of names, and a bit of what might have been a plan or blueprint, and another bit that looked like a map . . ."

Rosalind straightened. "A *map*?"

"Yes, there was not enough left to make out what exactly it was for."

A map, a list of names, a plan . . . Rosalind pressed her gloved fingertips against her mouth.

"What is it?"

"I . . . I'm almost afraid to say," she admitted. "It is . . . very farfetched."

"Even for you?"

Rosalind felt a tiny smile form. "Unfortunately, yes. I recently had some conversation with . . . a certain highly placed lady of my acquaintance and she . . . she suspected that Fullerton might be in the pay of Bonapartist spies." She paused and snuck a glance around the edge of her bonnet. "When you said there was a map and a plan, it made me think of that."

Mr. Harkness did not laugh, for which Rosalind was grateful.

"This lady has reason to know what she's talking about?" asked Mr. Harkness.

"Yes."

"I do not ask this lightly. I need her name."

"Countess Dorothea Lieven."

"I see." He fell silent again. Rosalind waited, but it was difficult. She wanted to know what he was thinking.

"So, Fullerton's two mysterious men might have been . . . agents? Provocateurs?"

"Perhaps." Rosalind's fingers twisted together. "But that raises another question. How would being involved with some group of Bonapartists require Fullerton to throw disgrace on me and Charlotte?"

"Unless we discover something new amongst his papers, the point of convergence would seem to be Horatio Salter."

"Who has not been seen since before Father was killed," said Rosalind.

Mr. Harkness nodded. "What did Fullerton tell you about Salter?"

"He said Salter came to him about some money. He implied it was gambling winnings, or something even less savory, that Salter needed to store securely and anonymously. Fullerton said he gave Salter some advice, and that Salter went away."

Mr. Harkness considered this. "I suppose it's possible. The man I spoke with at Graham's yesterday said Salter had been asking about Fullerton. He'd wanted to be introduced, it seems." He paused again. "As soon as we are finished at Fullerton's house, I will need to give this news to John Townsend."

"But shouldn't you wait until there's more proof?" asked Rosalind. "Mr. Townsend has not indicated any great patience with my . . . speculations." In fact, her previous encounters with the leading officer at Bow Street had been barely cordial, and he had even gone so far as to actively interfere with her work. He certainly would not approve of her involvement in matters he considered his personal provenance.

"I understand, but we cannot wait too long. The possibility of Bonapartists being active in London moves us into different territory."

They had crossed into the precincts of Mayfair now. Compared with the streets they had so recently left, these gleamed, even under the slush. The houses that lined the broad avenue were all new and freshly painted. The stoops were swept and scrubbed. Everything spoke of stability and prosperity.

Rosalind looked at it all and frowned. Then she drew in a deep breath. "There is something else I need to tell you."

"What is it?"

"I should have told you before. I was . . . I was hoping to keep her out of this. There were, there are reasons—" Rosalind shook her head. "I have been unable to contact Charlotte for the past several days. I haven't even been able to find her to tell her our father is dead."

"I'm sorry," breathed Mr. Harkness.

"Alice is trying to discover who Charlotte's new protector is, in case she's with him. But I haven't been able to understand why she'd leave without any word, right after she told me that Father had escaped her. I'm afraid," she admitted. "I shouldn't be. I have no reason to be. Not really. And yet—"

"And yet how could you not be?" said Mr. Harkness. "Murder has been done, there's some scheme being spun out. We know blackmail was going to be attempted, and your sister has gone without a word. You would not be human were you not afraid."

Gratitude flooded her. Rosalind turned her gaze to the peaceful street outside. She was glad for her felt-lined bonnet. She did not want Mr. Harkness to see her face at this moment.

There was something she had to say. Now. Before she lost her nerve, again.

"I've missed you."

"I missed you," he answered softly.

"I can't think why," she whispered. "I do nothing but bring you trouble. I . . . you've been injured helping me, not once, but twice." She'd quite literally had his blood on her hands. She could still see it sometimes when she closed her eyes. "I don't mind running my own risks, but you . . ."

"I am an officer of the courts and the law," he answered calmly. "It's my duty to run risks."

"It was not duty that had you protecting my house, or my carriage." *Or me.*

"But it was." She heard the smile in his voice and could

not resist turning her head to see him. "Because you in your way were seeking to uphold what is right."

Rosalind felt herself smile, and blush. "You make me sound like Joan of Arc."

"I don't mistake you for anyone but Rosalind Thorne."

Her heart seemed to be beating at the base of her throat. A lifetime's training warned her to keep still and informed her in great detail the dangers of showing any hint of all that she felt.

And she pushed them all to one side and reached out her hand to cover his.

He stared down, startled at last. Rosalind's heart beat once, hard. But then, Mr. Harkness—Adam—laid his free hand over their joined ones.

The driver called out to the horses, and the carriage rocked to a halt. Adam pressed her hand briefly, and they let go. Rosalind dropped her gaze, willing her cheeks to cease their burning.

Adam opened the carriage door and climbed out.

"Mr. Harkness!"

A thin young man came pelting up the stairs from behind the area railing of the nearest house.

"Thank God, sir!" The young man skidded to a halt in front of Adam. "I sent to the station for you, but it seems hours ago, and I didn't know what . . ."

"Slow down, Perkins," said Adam. "What's happened?"

"It's the manservant Sparkes, sir. He's been killed."

CHAPTER 32

The Advantages of Knowing Where to Look

WHY *are the English—the grave English—the intellectual English—the moral English—the greatest gossips in the world?*

Catherine Gore, *Sketches of English Character*

"Alice, my dear!" exclaimed the actress lounging beneath her silken coverlets. "Come give me a kiss." Elizabeth Crichton—Toast of the London Stage, Dame of the Dulcet Tones, Lady of the Ivory Hands, and possessor of a number of other similarly overwrought sobriquets—had always treated being "at home" a little differently. As soon as Alice arrived, the maid showed her straight into Elizabeth's boudoir. Although it was midafternoon, Alice thought it likely Elizabeth hadn't set one foot out of bed yet. Although, as always, her elegant auburn hair was suspiciously tidy, and her face decidedly freshly washed.

"Oh, and shut those drapes, will you?" Elizabeth made a great show of throwing her arm across her eyes. "Marguerite will insist on opening them no matter how much I suffer."

"Marguerite is a smart woman," answered Alice. "If you don't get at least little sun, you'll whither." Despite this assessment, she did twitch the velvet curtains closed. She also gave Elizabeth a peck on the cheek.

"I am night blooming, like the jasmine. I shall thrive, never you fear. Oh, and some water, there's a pet." She held out one slender white hand. Elizabeth's career on the London stage centered around the public's fascination with those dainty hands. Alice herself had been compelled to write paragraphs about them, which they had both laughed over later.

Alice sighed and poured the water, as instructed. Elizabeth was a good friend, but she was entirely a diva, and as such she required humoring. To an extent.

She held the glass up, out of her friend's reach.

"Sit up, Elizabeth," Alice said. "I need to talk properly with you."

Elizabeth pulled a face, but she did push herself upright. "What is it? I've no news for you, I'm afraid. December is the dreariest month, and even if it wasn't, I've seen no one. I've been in rehearsals for the past three weeks. We're to do *She Stoops to Conquer.* The new man, he's very good, but oh! Such a slave driver! I've a mind to walk away."

"You could faint at his feet," Alice suggested. "You're very good at that."

"You know I never faint unless I'm being paid for it." She gestured impatiently for the water, and Alice relented.

"Anyway, it's not news I'm after." Alice plopped down onto the chair at the bedside. "At least, not new news. I'm looking to find out about a demimondaine. A newish girl, English, but had been abroad in Paris for some years. She goes by the name of Cynthia Sharps."

"Oh yes." Elizabeth downed a large gulp of water. "Our paths have crossed a few times. Very clever girl. Striking rather than beautiful, but she has that easy charm that men so enjoy. She'll do well for herself, if she keeps her head."

"I've heard that she may have done well already."

"Oh?" Elizabeth arched her delicately, and carefully, shaped brows. "Perhaps I should be the one quizzing you."

"Do you happen to know who her current protector is?"

"Mmm . . . let me think." Elizabeth took another swallow of water. "Not someone in the first circles, I know that much. Now, did I see them . . . oh! Yes. That's right. She brought him backstage to meet me at the Drury Lane, right at the start of the season. We were doing *A Midsummer Night's Dream*, I was Titania. Now, in truth, I should have been cast as . . ."

Now it was Alice's turn to pull a face.

". . . And you gave me such a lovely compliment in your column, too, I recall," Elizabeth finished neatly, and with a dazzling smile. "The man's name is Merrick Black. I remember teasing him about how positively villainous it sounded. He took it in good part."

"Merrick Black." Alice extracted her notebook and pencil from her reticule and made a note. Elizabeth's eyes narrowed suspiciously.

"Alice, what is this?"

Alice ignored her. "What was he like?"

Elizabeth held out her glass peremptorily, and Alice refilled it.

"He's not quite as old as the hills, but he will be soon. He's back from his time in India, where he made the obligatory pile of money and is now determined to enjoy all the fine things English life has to offer, including young Cynthia."

Alice scribbled this down in her practiced shorthand. "You wouldn't know where lives? Or which club he belongs to?"

But Elizabeth had evidently had enough. "Why are you asking me?" she said, her tone now as suspicious as her gaze. "Why not ask Cynthia?"

"Do you know where she is?"

"Why should I?"

"No reason, just a hope."

"Alice," said Elizabeth sternly. "You've gone quite serious. Is something wrong?"

"It might be," Alice admitted.

"And you let me lie here and be frivolous!" Elizabeth threw back the covers and slid out of the bed. "Marguerite!" she bellowed, her voice suddenly low and carrying. The maid appeared at once. "I am getting dressed. I'll be with you in just a minute, Alice."

It wasn't a minute.

However, compared to some Alice knew, it really was only a short time before Elizabeth sailed out of her boudoir dressed in a green woolen walking costume trimmed with rich rose velvet.

The languishing dame of the boudoir had quite vanished. Elizabeth strode straight past Alice and seated herself at her clean, broad desk.

"Now, I'm going to give you a letter." She pulled out a fresh sheet of foolscap and uncapped the inkwell. "You are to take this to Verity Sainthill. I'll write down the direction for you. I'd go along, but I have to be at rehearsal."

"Verity Sainthill. I know that name," said Alice. "Wasn't she caught in a theater fire some years ago?"

"Yes, poor thing. She's in complete retirement now, but she still knows everything about everyone. This will let her know to help you." She signed the letter with a flourish, then sanded, sealed, and folded it to hand to Alice.

"I knew I could count on you, Bet-Bet." Alice used her old pet name. She also tucked the letter into her reticule.

Elizabeth regarded her with a mischievous gleam in her large, liquid eyes. "And when your business is done, you'll be back to tell me all about it?"

"Of course I will." Alice kissed her friend on the cheek.

"Good luck with your new tyrant. I'm sure you'll have him eating out of your hand in no time."

"Good luck to you as well, my dear." Elizabeth patted her cheek fondly and paused. "This doesn't by chance have something to do with your notorious Miss Thorne, does it? I believe I may have read something about her in the papers . . . ?"

But Alice just gave her a wink over her shoulder and slipped out of the room.

The stout, stern parlor maid who answered the door at the modest Kensington flat informed Alice that Miss Sainthill was not at home to strangers. Alice brandished Elizabeth's letter, which got her as far as the foot of stairs. The maid took the letter upstairs, presumably to her mistress. However, after the case clock indicated a full quarter of an hour had passed, Alice began to wonder if it hadn't been consigned to the fire instead.

She idly contemplated charging up the stairs like a pirate boarding a ship, brandishing her pen before her.

Then she smiled at that and wondered if there was a place for it in her novel. Then, she admonished herself for idle frivolity when she was on a serious errand.

Then, thankfully, the stern maid came halfway down the stairs and, without enthusiasm, informed Alice she was to "come up, if you please, but be warned, my mistress is not to be agitated or disturbed in any way."

Alice meekly promised to behave, followed the maid up the rest of the stairs, and waited while she was announced. At last, the gatekeeper stood aside and allowed Alice to walk into the shadowy chamber.

The door shut firmly behind her, and Alice stood blinking in the dim light.

"Miss Littlefield," said a low, harsh voice. "How delightful. Do come in."

"Thank you for agreeing to see me, Miss Sainthill." Alice stepped forward carefully, blinking again to help her eyes adjust. The thick curtains were drawn tight. Only two lamps burned low, and those were on the opposite side of the room from the Grecian lounge where Miss Sainthill lay.

"I'm always glad to meet a friend of our Elizabeth's. Dear girl." The chuckle was very like a cough. "Do sit, please." A round-backed chair had been drawn up toward the sofa, but not too near. Alice realized the placement was such that Miss Stainthill could see her guest without having to so much as turn her head.

Alice sat. She folded her hands, fixed a polite expression on her face, and turned her attention fully to her hostess.

The shadows made it difficult for Alice to see, but also made it more difficult not to stare to try to capture the details of her. Her head was wrapped in a loose turban. The end trailed down across her throat in imitation of a younger woman's long hair. This affectation only partly hid the scars that ran up Verity Sainthill's slender neck and across her jaw. The one hand Alice could see was covered with rough, puckered skin. The other, Miss Sainthill kept underneath her embroidered coverlet.

Alice remembered the news accounts of the fire. It was said this woman had been lucky to escape with her life. She also noticed how a tray of medicine bottles stood on the sideboard, where a tea set might usually be placed.

"Is Elizabeth here frequently?" Alice asked curiously.

"Many of the actresses come to visit," said Miss Sainthill. "I know, it's surprising, is it not? But somehow, I've become a sort of a good-luck charm."

Alice, who knew a great many theater people, found she could believe it. Here was living proof of all it was possible to survive. Verity Sainthill might be wounded, but she still radiated dignity and humor. It was a powerful combination.

"Because of that, you will find I am very well informed

about my old world, which is no doubt why Elizabeth sent you here." There was a knowing smile in the harsh voice. "Her letter tells me you are in need of some information about the demimonde. Who is it you want to know about?"

"I'm looking for a man named Merrick Black. He's been . . . with Cynthia Sharps of late."

"Oh yes. Mr. Black. He's new to our circles, you'll find, but very fond of the theater. Fortunately, Cynthia knows to treat him with a light touch, and he loves that she knows everybody. She'll do well, that girl," Miss Sainthill said, echoing Elizabeth's sentiments.

"I was hoping to speak with him," Alice said. "Do you know where I can find him?"

Miss Sainthill was silent for a minute. Alice heard an odd, ragged rushing noise and realized it was the sound of the actress's breathing.

"Now, I know you're a friend of Elizabeth's," said Miss Sainthill finally. "But I must ask—you're not planning to make trouble, are you?"

"I certainly don't intend to," answered Alice. "But there's been a family emergency, and if Cynthia doesn't come to address it at once, trouble may find her regardless."

Elizabeth fell silent again, and although Alice could see only a suggestion of her ravaged face in the shadows, she felt that she was being regarded keenly. She also felt the sudden urge to sit up straighter.

"I believe you," said Miss Sainthill finally. "Even though I have a sneaking suspicion that you are the A.E. Littlefield behind 'Society Notes.'"

Alice did not bother to demur. "I promise I'm not going after gossip. In fact, I sincerely hope to prevent it."

"Very well. Black's buying an estate in Buckinghamshire, I hear, but that's not yet finalized. So you'll probably find him at home in Berkeley Square. I understand he has installed Cynthia there."

Alice hesitated. She did not want to ask the next question, but she could not neglect it. "Is he married?"

"If he is, no one in this country's heard of it."

Well, that's something anyway. "Thank you, Miss Sainthill." Alice tucked her notebook and pencil away. "I trust you'll not think me rude, but I must go at once."

"Go, go. In fact, if you stayed any longer we'd both be in danger of a good scolding from Ophelia." This, presumably, was the maid, rather than the doomed girl of the Shakespeare play. "I wish you luck on your errand, my dear."

"Thank you." Alice got to her feet. "I hope I may call again."

"You shall always find me at home," replied Miss Sainthill lightly. "Now, begone!" she said, and Alice heard the imperious tones of the actress she had been.

Alice went and hurried down the stairs, brushing straight past the startled maid. She needed to get herself a cab and quickly. Charlotte needed to be found. If Rosalind was to face another blow from her family, Alice was utterly determined to do what she could to soften it. And if that involved some blackmail of her own special variety, then so be it.

And if it transpired that Charlotte was guilty of some part in the death of Sir Reginald Thorne, Alice would make certain it was not Rosalind who had to send her away.

CHAPTER 33

In the House of Misfortune

*When one thrusts or stabs another, not then hav-
ing weapon drawn, or who hath not then first
stricken the party stabbing . . . shall not have the
benefit of clergy, though he did it not of malice
aforethought.*

John Impey of the Inner Temple, *The Practice of the Office
of Coroner*

"Wait here," said Adam to Rosalind. Without looking
back, he jumped out of the carriage and bolted
after Perkins.

"How did this happen?" he demanded when he caught up
with the constable. "There were supposed to be two of you!
You were to keep watch on the house, front and back!"

"We was, sir! On my honor!"

"Where's your partner, then?"

"Out chasing after you, sir," answered Perkins shortly.
"No one could find you this morning!"

Perkins took him down the area stairs and down through
the kitchen door. At first Adam thought this was simply reflex. Constables did not often enter a house by the front door.

But as soon as they entered the kitchen, he saw a woman in a black and white uniform sitting at the central work table, her face in her hands. Bags of swedes, onions, and other goods slumped on the work table, indicating that the woman had just come back from her marketing.

Adam went over to her and touched her shoulder. "Are you all right?"

She responded instantly by straightening her shoulders, lifting her head, trying to hide the fact that she'd been upset at all.

"Yes, sir," she croaked. She was an aging woman with silver streaks in her brown hair. Her body still strong after what must be years in service, but her hands were scarred and worn. "It's a shock, that's all."

"What's your name?" Adam asked.

"Mrs. Harding, sir. I'm cook here. I was . . . Mr. Sparkes told me I should keep coming in, until things with the master got sorted. He still needed his meals, and so on."

"Yes, of course." Adam nodded encouragingly. "And you found him."

She swallowed hard. "In his room, sir. He . . . it was his habit to take a short rest in the afternoon when the master was away. I'd just gone to take him his tea . . ." She stopped and pressed her calloused hand over her mouth.

Adam touched her shoulder. "It's all right. Where is his room?"

"Second floor, beside the master's."

"Thank you." He paused. "Did you by chance know his Christian name?"

"Turrell," she answered. "He said it was a family name. Only thing his family left him. He said that, too."

Adam nodded. "Perkins, maybe you can make Mrs. Harding a cup of tea?"

Perkins looked at him like he must be joking, but quickly saw he was not. "Yes, sir."

Adam left Perkins with Mrs. Harding and started the climb up the back stairs to the second floor. He emerged into a broad, carpeted corridor lined with all sorts of fine ornaments and paintings that Fullerton had gathered for himself. One dark door hung open. A tray had been dropped on the floor, the cup, saucer, and biscuits all scattered about. The teapot lay on its side, and dark liquid made a puddle across the threshold.

Adam stepped over it and into the room.

Fullerton had not begrudged his man some creature comforts. Sparkes's room was furnished with carpets and a fireplace and good curtains. A solid armchair stood beside the hearth, with a carved table beside that holding a book and a decanter.

The armchair was knocked backward. The corpse that had been Turrell Sparkes sprawled backward over top of it. Violent death had robbed the man of all his solemn dignity.

Like Sir Reginald, he'd been stabbed. The quantity of blood spilled out across the carpet and chair was enough to turn even Adam's stomach. Adam set this aside and bent down beside Sparkes.

The corpse was still warm, and the blood only just beginning to dry, so the murderer had not been gone long. Possibly they'd been watching the house, waiting for the cook to go out for her shopping so they could more easily steal in and take care of their work. A knife still protruded from Sparkes's rib cage, leaving no doubt as to how he'd died.

Adam stood, wiping his hands needlessly on his breeches. Anger tightened his jaw, but he set that aside, too. He turned, looking at the plain, private room. Sparkes had clearly been a man of neat habits. Nothing was out of place, the brass-framed bed was fully made up.

No struggle. Taken by surprise. Probably sitting in the chair when the murderer arrived. Jumped up when his at-

tacker burst in, and was stabbed straight through. He might not even had had a chance to scream.

He scanned the thin carpet, but there were no footmarks. The murderer had gotten out as quickly as he'd come in and had left no blood trail in his wake. No drawer had been left open, and nothing except the chair was knocked over or disarranged. There'd been no search, then, nor any attempt at robbery, at least not in here.

If Sparkes had been downstairs, Adam might have been tempted to believe he'd surprised someone who had come to rob the house. But that was not the case. Whoever had entered this place had come here with the express intent to kill Sparkes.

Removing the knife from Sparkes's chest was a grim but necessary task. As before, it was a plain, well-used tool. The grip was worn smooth. The blade beneath the gore had the marks of having been resharpened several times.

Adam wrapped it up thoroughly in his handkerchief and, grimacing slightly at the necessity, stowed the weapon in his coat pocket. Closing the door behind him, Adam descended the main stairs to the elegant foyer. The first thing he saw was that the door to the book room was open. He caught a glimpse of a black skirt and pale gray coat at the threshold.

Rosalind had not waited in the carriage after all.

It took all his discipline to ignore this and go instead to the backstairs door and down into the kitchen. He put his bloody hands into his pockets and kept them there.

Perkins was sitting with Mrs. Harding. Between the two of them, they had managed to brew up a pot of tea and each now held a mug. Mrs. Harding looked much more composed than she had when he left her and Perkins.

She got to her feet. "If you're done with Mr. Sparkes, sir, I'd like to see him made decent." She smoothed her apron. "He wasn't a bad man. Strict, maybe. But then the master

liked things just so and came down like fury whenever aught
was out of place."

"Yes, of course," said Adam. "Perkins can help you."
Perkins did not look particularly excited about this, but he
didn't object. "We will need him taken to the coroner. I'll
have to send for a cart." He paused. "Do you know if he had
family?"

"He did not, sir," said Mrs. Harding. "No life at all outside this house." Her face twisted up, showing plainly what
she thought of that.

"Did anyone come to the door today? Any tradesmen?
Any messengers?"

"Not that I know of. We had a mess of them newspaper
writing sorts earlier, all hanging about making nuisances of
themselves with the neighbors. Your young constables,
though, they chased them off sharpish. And, of course, I can't
say what happened while I was out doing my marketing."

"Thank you, Mrs. Harding."

"Yes, sir," she said. Then, "Do I . . . Will I have to stay
here at all?"

"No, you can go home as soon as you've seen to Mr.
Sparkes, if that's what you want, but let Perkins know your
address. You'll be needed to give evidence at the inquest."

"Yes, sir." Adam understood by Mrs. Harding's tone and
her expression that she did not mean to stay in this house a
minute longer than necessary.

He couldn't blame her at all.

"All right, Perkins," he said. "You've got a job ahead
of you."

"Yes, sir," Perkins muttered. He touched his forehead
without enthusiasm and followed Mrs. Harding up the backstairs. Adam winced in sympathy. This was a very bad day
for the young man. They'd talk later. Just now, however, he
had some urgent matters to attend to.

The kitchen sink had a pump, which gave him a chance to wash his gory hands clean. That done, he started opening the drawers, searching for the knives. On the third try, he found what he was looking for. The working cutlery was all slotted neatly into their places—butcher knives, carving blades, paring knives, and cleavers. He pulled the knife that had killed Sparkes out of his pocket and unfolded his now thoroughly stained handkerchief so he could compare it with these others.

The handles were a match for style and coloring, and the blades of a similar shape. Adam stowed the weapon away again and shut the drawer.

The man, if it was a man, watches the house for his chance. He creeps in when the constables are occupied with clearing the sidewalk. He uses the side door, or one from the back garden. He hides in the house, perhaps even in one of the rooms down here, and waits his chance. When Mrs. Harding leaves to go to her marketing, he helps himself to a knife, does what he came for, and leaves.

Very neat, very cool, and very determined.

If that was what had happened, the only conceivable reason for Sparkes's death was that someone was afraid he might decide to talk about the other murder that occurred in this house. Someone had decided not to risk that.

Lost in these unpleasant thoughts, Adam climbed the stairs to the foyer. The door to Fullerton's book room was still open, and Rosalind was still inside.

She stood at the desk, her fingertips resting lightly on the marble top. She still wore her bonnet, so he could see nothing of her face. But he did not need to, he realized. He knew what her expression would be—solemn, clear-eyed, with only the slightest furrow to her brow to betray her anger.

The carpet was gone. The lamp was back in its place. The fireplace had been cleaned and fresh coals laid. All was ready in anticipation of Fullerton's return.

"What did you find?" Rosalind asked him. He'd made no noise when he entered, but she'd known he was there anyway. Adam's heart thudded oddly.

"Sparkes, Fullerton's manservant, is dead," he answered. "Stabbed."

"Like my father?"

"It was at least as swiftly done, but I think there was only one blow this time. I suspect the murderer was watching the house for their chance, and perhaps even hid inside for a while."

She nodded, absently, he thought. "I imagine it was to silence him."

"I know of no other reason. The newspapers reported that the only person in the house when Sir Reginald died was a manservant who offered no useful information. The murderer most likely decided to make that fact permanent."

She was silent for a long time. She was thinking of her sister—wondering if Charlotte was capable of being involved in these deaths, angry at herself for wondering, and equally angry for wishing she could ignore the possibility. He was as sure of all this as he was of his own name. When had that happened? He'd spent only a handful of hours in this woman's company, and yet he understood her more completely than he ever had any other person.

She turned to face him, her face determined. The furrow on her brow deepened, a telltale sign of the distress she wanted to hide.

"What did Sparkes tell you he'd seen?"

"He said he saw nothing. That he was up in his room. Sir Reginald had told him he could go to bed." Adam paused. "In fact, Sir Reginald had said that those were Fullerton's orders."

Rosalind looked to the desk again. There had been some attempt to clean the ink, but the porous marble had drunk too much of it. The stain was now a part of the stone.

"I don't imagine Sparkes gave you any idea who my father might have been waiting for?"

Adam drew back, startled. "How do you know he was waiting for someone?"

Rosalind's smile was thin. "My father was a selfish man. He believed that his needs should be well catered to at all times. The only reason for him to send away a servant was that there was something he did not want seen."

"Or heard." Adam nodded. "Yes, that makes sense. So it may be that Sir Reginald was expecting someone—"

"Someone he did not want Fullerton to know about. He would have known that Sparkes was his employer's spy."

Because the only reason Fullerton would leave him alone was if he believed he was well guarded.

"Therefore, he did what he could to get Sparkes out of the way," Rosalind went on. "While he waited here for his guest."

"Who then killed him. That was why there was no real struggle. Sir Reginald was off his guard."

"Yes," said Rosalind. "Unless . . ." She paused and crossed to the door. She turned swiftly, her skirts swirling about her ankles. She stared at the chair, one gloved hand in the threshold. Adam followed her gaze with his own. He saw the chair, the desk, the lamp, and the shadows of a windowless room.

And he knew.

"Unless it was a mistake?" he said. "The room is dim. Sir Reginald is hunched at the table. The assailant or assailants enter quietly. They see a gray-haired man in Fullerton's clothes, in Fullerton's study, writing at Fullerton's desk. They are already agitated because of the thought of murder. They stab him in the back, through the slats of the chair, and do not realize they have the wrong man until he falls at their feet."

"The two men." Rosalind inhaled sharply. "Assuming they were men."

"What do you mean?"

"Fullerton enjoys ensnaring women. The two who were seen leaving this house could easily be two of his female victims, dressed as men."

"It's possible. The only description we have of them is that they both wore great coats, which would fully conceal the person underneath."

"Especially if they were muffled against the cold," agreed Rosalind. "And assuming they existed at all."

"I hate to have to admit it, but they may have," Adam admitted. "Especially if Fullerton had somehow gotten himself mixed up with Bonapartist spies."

Rosalind said nothing for a long moment, and when she did her voice was low and harsh. "Or my father did." She paused again. And finally, "Or my sister."

CHAPTER 34

An Unscheduled Visit

In London, people are judged by the surface.

Catherine Gore, *The Debutante*

Even to Alice's jaded eye, the neighborhood of Berkeley Square was breathtaking. Stately homes, including the magnificent Lansdowne House, surrounded the lovely square. The winter park with its silver trees and snow-covered statuary took on an appealing and fanciful appearance.

For the consideration of a few pennies, the man shoveling muck in the street pointed out the correct turning to take her to Merrick Black's house. He assured her she'd know it by the red door and the new brass lamp beside it.

Her informant's description proved highly accurate. Mr. Black's home was a grand, but not a great, house. Clearly, it was entirely new, with everything in the latest style.

The light was already fading, and lamps shone brightly in the windows, as well as beside the red door.

Alice, in a gesture to both economy and optimism, paid off her cab rather than choosing to keep the driver waiting. Drawing her shoulders back, she marched up the steps and rang the bell.

A footman in red and buff livery answered. As soon as the door opened, Alice strode boldly forward. Startled, the man fell back and just like that, she was inside. It was amazing what you could do if you simply refused to be stopped.

"I have a message for the lady of the house." Alice held out the note she'd composed when she started out the day. The problem, she realized on the way, was she was not entirely sure what name Charlotte was using with her new protector and/or fiancé. She might be Charlotte Thorne, or Cynthia Sharps, or someone else altogether. "And you may give her this as well." She brought out her visiting card.

"It is the dinner hour," said the footman. "My master and mistress are not—"

"This is an extremely urgent matter." Alice pulled her gloves off. "I am prepared to wait for as long as necessary to speak with her, so you should probably just get on with it."

The footman was a stout fellow and looked likely to become belligerent. Alice returned her most implacable regard. He relented first, as most people did. With a frown to let her know she was very much in disgrace, he headed up the tightly curved staircase. Alice strolled about the foyer, admiring the tasteful art, the hothouse flowers in the graceful Chinese vase, and the branching chandelier.

The sound of footsteps on the stairs jerked Alice around. Charlotte hurried down the curving stairs, her half-fastened scarlet dressing gown flying out behind her.

"Alice? What is it? Is it Rosalind? Is she all right?"

"Yes, she's quite well," Alice answered. "Or she was when I left this morning."

Charlotte halted on the last stair. "Then what it is?"

"You're joking."

"Why would I be joking?"

Alice stared at her. Charlotte's eyes were wide, and she couldn't see any hint of concealment in her expression.

"I think we'd better go up to your rooms," she said finally. "I do have some news."

Charlotte frowned, looking very like Rosalind when she was at her most displeased. "If you insist."

"I'm afraid I do."

Charlotte rolled her eyes, clearly imploring someone above for patience with importunate lady writers. "All right. Come along, then."

Alice did.

Charlotte's suite waited at the top of the stairs. It was cleanly furnished—bright, airy, and comfortable. Charlotte always did have good taste. Her time in Paris, and Mr. Black's fortune, had combined to refine it.

Alice closed the door and turned the key in the lock.

"Now—" began Charlotte, but Alice didn't let her get any further.

"Where on earth have you been!" she demanded. "Honestly, Charlotte, you show up on our doorstep, tell Rosalind your father's been *kidnapped* and that you need her help, then you vanish entirely! Do you have any idea what you've put her through?"

Charlotte drew herself up in an attitude of lofty indignation Alice remembered from when they were girls. "If you're done scolding?"

"No," replied Alice bluntly. "In fact, I've just gotten started."

"Well, perhaps you can take a moment to remember that I was in *Bath*."

Alice shut her jaw closed so abruptly her teeth clicked. "You were not," she said, but this was from sheer surprise and she regretted the words as soon as they were out.

"What do you mean?" shot back Charlotte. "I went back to interview the servants again and make arrangements about the house. I made the decision after I saw you, and I wrote to Rosalind about it."

Alice's mouth opened, but nothing came out. She closed it and tried again. "Rosalind never got any such letter."

"She must have," said Charlotte, but her expression shifted, becoming uneasy. "Perhaps she forgot to tell you."

"No, she did not get the letter."

"Then it must have gone astray." Charlotte pressed her fingers to her mouth. "Oh! Poor Rosalind. I'm so sorry, Alice. I'll write a note at once for you to take back to her." She whisked around and hurried to her cherrywood writing desk.

Are you telling the truth? Alice watched Charlotte closely as she pulled out paper and a silver pen. It was true that letters did go astray, sometimes. Even important ones. But it was also true that sometimes they were never written in the first place.

Admittedly, Alice had never really gotten on with Rosalind's sister, even before she ran off with Sir Reginald. Charlotte had always seemed too clever by half, and too ready to run down anyone of their social circle who did not quite make it up to standard. Alice now understood this snobbery came from a combination of fear and her father's influence. As the oldest daughter, Charlotte had a kind of pressure on her that Rosalind escaped, at least while the household was still intact. And Alice certainly wasn't one to find fault with a woman for doing what necessity dictated.

And yet . . .

"When did you get back?" Alice asked.

"Just today," Charlotte answered smoothly as she unstoppered her inkwell and peered inside to see it had been filled.

"And you haven't seen the papers?"

Charlotte put the ink down and turned to face Alice. "I had other things to do than sit and read *The Times*. Alice, stop this. What's happened?"

Alice sighed sharply. She prided herself on her ability to

read people of all sorts, but Charlotte was beyond her. "And you promise me you were really in Bath?"

"Alice . . ." Charlotte began in a warning tone.

"Your father is dead."

Charlotte gazed at her blankly for a moment. Then, slowly, her lovely face screwed itself up tight.

"D-dead?" she stammered.

Alice nodded. "He was murdered in Russell Fullerton's house. Three nights ago now."

Charlotte clasped her hands and looked away. "Oh, good Lord," she breathed. "Oh no. No."

"Rosalind has been trying to find you ever since."

"Of course she has," breathed Charlotte. She pressed her hand against her mouth and her eyes. Alice, on reflex, pulled a handkerchief from her sleeve and handed it to Charlotte.

Charlotte accepted without demur and dabbed at her eyes.

"Rosalind must be frantic." She paused. "Is anyone else looking for me?"

"Not yet," replied Alice flatly. "Should they be?"

Charlotte's head snapped around. "Are you suggesting I had something to do with my father's death?"

"I don't know," replied Alice calmly. "Did you?"

Charlotte's face went deathly pale and her fist knotted around the handkerchief. Alice expected her to begin shouting. But her voice stayed low and even.

"You'd better go now."

"Not until you promise me you'll come to see Rosalind. She's in a horrible position."

"Rosalind cannot be in any danger," said Charlotte. "Her paramour is a runner."

"Which says you don't really know anything about Mr. Harkness. He'd arrest her in a heartbeat if he thought she was guilty."

That statement seemed to genuinely shake her. Alice frowned inwardly.

"He can't love her much, then," Charlotte murmured.

"Oh, to the ends of the earth, if I'm any judge. He'd do it, anyway. He's that sort. I expect that's why she loves him back."

Charlotte rubbed her temple, as if she felt a headache beginning. "Oh, that little . . . I never understood her."

Just then, the doorknob rattled. It was followed by a knock, and clearly one Charlotte recognized.

"Please, don't say anything." Charlotte flung down the handkerchief and hurried across the room to turn the key. Her expression changed entirely as she did. Between one heartbeat and the next, she became as cheerful and bright as a girl on an afternoon drive.

"Merrick!" She took the man by the hand and drew him into the room. "I'm so sorry, my dear. I had a sudden visitor."

"So Norrington said." The man blinked myopically at Alice.

"Mr. Merrick Black, Miss Alice Littlefield. She's an old friend of my family, most particularly my sister."

"Is she indeed?" He made a neat bow toward Alice.

Merrick Black was a little brown man with large brown eyes, raw-boned hands, and a stubble of white hair around his scalp. Sun and wind had cut deep lines around his mouth and watery eyes. He was not anything Alice would describe as handsome, but neither was he ugly, and for all his eyes appeared weak, there was a spark of real intelligence in them.

"Very glad to meet you, Miss Littlefield." Mr. Black wiped his hands together nervously, and his smile was strained, but at least he was trying to be courteous. Clearly, the idea that his paramour had a family of her own was still new.

But not a complete surprise. She has told him something.

"How do you do, Mr. Black?" Alice made her curtesy. "I understand you're recently returned from India."

"That's right, that's right. Back for good and all, and ready to finally set down roots, you might say." He looked to Charlotte—Cynthia—and his whole face lit up, like he'd never seen anything so lovely as this woman. "Friend of my Cynthia's sister, is it? Well, well, we'll have to be knowing you both better in the future. All well with her, I hope?"

Alice decided this was not the time for specifics. "There's been a bit of bad news. Cynthia will be able to tell you more," she said. "I am so sorry to have disturbed you both at this hour. I only had to deliver my message."

"Well!" Merrick clapped his hands together. "I'm glad you have. We're dining *en famille* tonight. She should join us, shouldn't she, Cynthia?"

"Oh no, I'm sorry," said Alice promptly. "I've an engagement, but thank you very much for your kind offer."

"Ah, well. Another time, then. Yes, I'll just leave you ladies to it. Miss Littlefield." He bowed again. He took Charlotte—Cynthia's—hand and pressed it gently. "I'll be waiting in the library, my dear. I'll tell Cook to hold the dinner."

"Thank you, my dear." Charlotte smiled again, and the man blushed. It made him look younger and possibly a tiny bit more handsome.

Alice found she could easily believe this man being delighted at the prospect of a child, and cherishing its mother.

It seems you and Rosalind have both chosen men who are just what they seem to be. All of Charlotte's levity, and a good bit of her color, faded as soon as she pocketed the door key. "I'll write that letter now." She brushed past Alice without looking at her. "I'll come to the house tomorrow."

"Better not," said Alice. "We're under siege from the press."

"You can't do anything about that?"

"Unfortunately, when it comes to a story about the murder of a baronet, my fellow scribblers are rather determined. Tell her you'll meet her at Clements's Circulating Library. Mr. Clements is a friend of hers."

"Yes, all right. Thank you." Charlotte dipped her pen in

the ink and began writing swiftly. "It will have to be in the morning. Merrick and I have some business with his solicitors in the afternoon." She signed the letter with a flourish.

"Ten o'clock, then," said Alice. Charlotte gave her a grim look. Alice ignored her. "And do make sure you're there. I'd really rather not have to lead those scribblers back to your doorstep."

"I almost believe you're serious." Charlotte sanded and sealed her note.

Alice made no reply. She just took the finished letter and tucked it into her bag. "I do wonder, though, why you didn't write again when you heard nothing from Rosalind."

Charlotte bowed her head. "Because I was distracted. Before I left . . . I . . . I decided to take Rosalind's advice."

"What do you mean?"

"I told Merrick the truth about our family, about Father. All of it. We quarreled, and when I left, I wasn't sure if he'd want me back. So I rushed through the business and hurried home and . . . well, we are reconciled as you see."

Alice caught Charlotte's gaze and held it. Memory clouded Charlotte's gaze, memory and fear. She might really have done it. Just as she said.

"Tell Rosalind I'm sorry," said Charlotte. "Tell her whatever happened, it was not my doing."

"I'll tell her everything you've said," said Alice. "We'll look for you tomorrow."

"I'll be there."

"And I'm afraid I'll have to ask you to call me a cab."

"Oh, never mind that. I've my own equipage, and my driver will take you where you need to go." She crossed to the bell rope and pulled it firmly.

"Thank you," said Alice. "Oh, Charlotte. For what it's worth, you were right to tell your fiancé the truth. I hope it goes smoothly from here."

Charlotte's smile was fleeting. "Thank you, Alice."

Alice allowed herself to be shown out of Charlotte's apartment. She thanked the footman, who placed the step for her, and then the driver, who closed the carriage door. Once secured inside the leather and velvet enclosure, she gratefully drew the thick driving robe up around her waist.

As the carriage rattled and jounced through the streets, Alice looked out the window at the lighted vehicles passing on either side, on their way out to whatever dinners and what entertainments December had to offer. She thought about Charlotte, and her elegant house and her Mr. Black, who was trying so very hard and who looked at her like he'd never seen anything so precious.

She also thought about how Charlotte had looked her in the eye and lied to her. There had been no letter. Perhaps there had not even been a trip to Bath. That lie had been delivered smoothly and skillfully, and with complete faith that Miss Alice Littlefield would accept her words at face value.

But why? What are you hiding?

And how on earth am I to tell Rosalind?

CHAPTER 35

The Consequences of Personal Problems

My heart's not like an aloe . . . that wants a hundred years to bring it into bloom.

Catherine Gore, *The Banker's Wife*

The early December darkness was settling in by the time Rosalind returned to Little Russell Street. Mr. Harkness had sent her on alone because he wanted to supervise the transport of Sparkes's body to the morgue. He had also sent one of the constables back to Bow Street to request more men to keep guard of the house against curiosity seekers and the inevitable newspaper men, and so needed to wait for their arrival.

A constable still waited by her gate. He exchanged greetings with the driver and helped Rosalind out onto the walk.

The foyer was dim and empty when Rosalind opened the door. She'd only just begun to tug at her bonnet ribbon when Amelia came racing up the passageway, her face flushed, and her hands covered in flour.

She saw Rosalind, and her face fell into a distinct expression of disappointment. She rallied quickly, however, and wiped her hands on the sturdy kitchen apron before coming forward to help with Rosalind's coat.

"I'm sorry, miss," she said. "I was only just now putting the pie in. Have you by any chance had some word from Miss Littlefield?

Oh dear. "She has not returned, then?"

"No, miss. Not a word from her. I . . . you don't suppose anything's wrong, do you?" she asked. "Only, with there being a murder and constables at the door and all . . ." She let the sentence trail off.

I really must talk with Alice. "I'm not at all worried about Alice," said Rosalind firmly. "In fact, I'd be much more worried about anyone who tried to get the better of her. Now, tell me, has the post come? And then you should probably get back to dinner preparations. I'm sure Miss Littlefield will be famished by the time she does get home. I know that I am."

"Yes, miss," said Amelia a little guiltily. "Should I bring in some bread and cheese?"

"That would be lovely, thank you."

Rosalind took herself into the parlor. The stack of letters was impressive. She sat down at her desk and began opening them. As she did, she was starkly reminded how very much she'd been neglecting her personal business.

Dearest Rosalind, read the first, from her friend Margaret Lowell.

> *I have only just now heard the news of your father's death. Oh, my dear, how horrible for you . . .*

And from Lady Jersey:

> *. . . so very distressing for you. I trust you will take every precaution against the gossips that will surely be*

swarming about. Of course, you may call upon me quite as your friend and you know I am silent as the grave . . .

Countess Lieven was a little more circumspect:

I am terribly sorry, and hope that this had nothing to do with our recent business. You may call on me at need.

There were plenty of other hands and seals she recognized—school friends, family friends. She had no doubt they all contained condolences, and gentle hints for news.

I should have been writing to them, not waiting for them to write to me. Rosalind looked at the heap of letters. Her old black dress felt suddenly too tight and too thin for the season. The room had grown cold despite the fire. Or perhaps it was just she who had gone cold. There was so much to do. Arrangements that should have been made days ago. But she hadn't even considered them. She hadn't wanted to. It was as if she couldn't bring herself to truly acknowledge her father's death until she knew why he died.

She sat there, staring stupidly at the unanswered letters. She wanted to cry. She needed to cry. It was perfectly all right. She was alone without even Alice to see, but the tears would not come. Not yet.

I need to know why, she told herself. *As soon as I know why . . . the rest will take care of itself.*

That might even be true.

A carriage rattled up to the door and stopped. Rosalind stared out the window and saw Alice climbing out of the new, enclosed, and obviously private vehicle. She jumped to her feet, and to conclusions.

She found Charlotte!

Rosalind ran into the foyer as the door opened. Alice, looking more than a little subdued, closed the door behind herself.

"Are you well, Alice?"

"Oh yes, perfectly, only a little tired."

"Amelia's bringing bread and cheese." Rosalind moved forward to help Alice with her coat and bonnet. "I take it you found Charlotte?"

"Yes, I'm afraid I did."

"Afraid?" said Rosalind.

"Let's go inside."

Rosalind followed Alice, her heart in her mouth. It was extremely unlike Alice to be so very serious, especially when she'd successfully completed a personal quest.

Alice settled at her writing table. "The good news is I found Charlotte's protector, and she was at his house. She spoke to me and wrote this for you." Alice pulled a note out of her reticule and handed it to Rosalind. "And she pledges her word to meet you at Mr. Clements's Circulating Library tomorrow at ten precisely."

Rosalind read the note and frowned. "Charlotte went to Bath? *That's* where she's been?"

"So she told me. That's the news that is less than good."

"What do you mean?"

"She was lying, Rosalind. I'm certain of it."

"I see." Rosalind did not question Alice's conclusion. Her instincts in these matters were honed as sharp as Rosalind's—sharper perhaps, because she added her experience as a newspaper woman to her experience in society.

Amelia shouldered her way into the parlor, carrying a tray with bread, soft cheese, and a very welcome pot of tea. Alice immediately began clearing a spot for it on her table, and Rosalind pretended to keep her attention on Charlotte's note and not to notice the little glances and grins that the maid was directing toward Alice.

Rosalind waited until Amelia had left to ask her next question.

"Do you have any guess as to why Charlotte lied?"

"Only the obvious. That she didn't want you, or me for that matter, to know what she was really up to."

"Yes." Rosalind turned away to lay Charlotte's note on her stack of correspondence to be answered. As she did, she idly noticed that the next letter on the pile of recently arrived post was from Mrs. Walford.

"What will you do?" asked Alice.

"I will hope very hard she keeps her promise to meet me tomorrow." Rosalind picked up the letter. "After that, I don't know."

"I'm sorry," said Alice softly.

Rosalind waved this away and poured herself a cup of tea. "What did she say about father?"

"She seemed genuinely surprised when I told her what happened. But she also seemed aware that it put her into awkward circumstances. She asked if anyone was looking for her, aside from you. I said not yet, but I expected they would be."

"Yes," Rosalind answered distractedly, thinking of the letter Mr. Harkness had found that looked to be in Charlotte's hand, but that father had probably written. *Probably.* "It's even more likely now."

Alice paused in the act of spreading the fresh farmhouse cheese onto the dark brown bread. "Why now?"

"There's been another murder," said Rosalind. "Fullerton's manservant is dead."

"Good Lord," breathed Alice. "How? When?"

"He was stabbed. Just today," Rosalind told her. "At Fullerton's house. Mr. Harkness believes that it was to keep him from giving further evidence about Father's death."

Alice put her slice of bread down. "Which means Fullerton either had to arrange for the death of his own servant, or . . ."

"Or it was someone else." Rosalind remembered standing in the book room where her father had died, wondering who he was waiting up for that he didn't want Fullerton's servant and spy to know about.

It doesn't mean that it was Charlotte he was waiting for. And even if he was waiting for her, it doesn't mean she ever went to see him, let alone that she . . .

Rosalind cut that thought off, or rather, she tried to. Because now she also had to contend with Alice's news that Charlotte had lied about where she'd been for the past three days.

In a desperate bid for some form of distraction, Rosalind broke the seal of Mrs. Walford's note, as if the act would help break the chain of unwanted thoughts forming inside her.

"What's that?" asked Alice.

"It's a note from Mrs. Walford." Rosalind scanned the neatly written lines. "She's asking me to call at the house tomorrow to talk about the charity ball."

"Oh, Rosalind, you can't still be thinking to go through with that?"

"What choice do I have?" Rosalind threw up her hands. "Another man is dead, and Fullerton is only one part of the tangle. Salter is connected to him, and so are the Walfords. I must talk with them again and find out if their presence runs deeper than just coincidence."

Alice took a big bite of bread and cheese and chewed belligerently, but she didn't actively argue.

"And yes, before you say it, I do have reason to believe that it's true," said Rosalind. "Given Salter's previous involvement with a major fraud, I had thought that Fullerton was using Salter. But Mr. Harkness says that it appears that Salter approached Fullerton, rather than the other way around."

Alice paused in midchew. "Whatever for?" she mumbled around her mouthful. "Could Salter have wanted a loan?"

"Or perhaps he had something to sell."

"Something about the Walfords, for instance?" suggested Alice.

"Yes." Rosalind paused again. "He certainly seems to have been at pains to insinuate himself into the family. He establishes himself with Louis, and then with Augustina. He decides it's not enough to seduce her in the usual way, he has to draw her into this extraordinary partnership—" What did Salter really think when Augustina turned out to be so eager to join him as a sharp in the card room? Was he startled? Could he not believe his luck? Augustina spoke of a deep camaraderie between them. Was that real, or had Salter deceived her?

"But you started to find out too much, and then when the Walfords saw Fullerton at the opera they knew something was in the wind?"

"Yes. Louis might very well know Fullerton on sight, from Graham's. And Salter certainly would have." She paused. "Do you know, as he was talking with Sanderson, Salter became deeply disconcerted. I thought it was something to do with the note, but it could have been because he'd spotted Fullerton."

"Rosalind." Alice tore her piece of bread in two and then set both halves back down again. "If that's what happened . . . There are two Walford brothers . . ."

"And Fullerton says two men ran out of his house," Rosalind finished for her. "Yes, I've been thinking of that as well. But it could just as well have been Salter and Augustina."

Alice swallowed. "You can't mean it. Fullerton said men."

"Two figures. In the dark, in great coats. Who can say for certain what sort of person was under there?"

"I see what you mean," murmured Alice. "But that would mean Augustina was lying from beginning to end when she spoke to you at Upton's."

"Yes," agreed Rosalind. "It's not impossible. She began by

sending for me under false circumstances, after all. Her real purpose might have been to gain the upper hand over me. If I'd accepted her money, she could always threaten to tell her mother or someone else who could spread the news of my duplicity."

"If that's the case, I'm not at all sure you should be going to the Walfords alone." Alice popped a piece of bread into her mouth.

Rosalind hesitated. "I don't intend to," she said. "I plan on taking Amelia with me."

Alice straightened up abruptly, and her face turned a rather extraordinary color. For a moment Rosalind was afraid she was choking.

"Whatever for?" Alice demanded. She covered her mouth and blushed more deeply.

"On the chance that she may recognize one of the Walford brothers as the 'gent' who was trying to get information out of her."

"Are you sure that's a good idea, Rosalind?" said Alice. "After Fullerton's servant was killed to make sure he didn't give evidence?"

"If her gent was involved in killing Sparkes, she's already in danger and will be safer with me than left home alone."

"I suppose," said Alice, but she was clearly uneasy. Which might have been perfectly comprehensible concern for any vulnerable person placed in a position of potential danger.

Or it might be something else.

Rosalind sighed and glanced toward the parlor door. There was no sign or sound of their maid. Yet.

"Alice," she said. "You will be . . . careful with Amelia?"

Alice lifted her chin. "I'm sure I don't know what you're talking about."

Rosalind ignored this. "And you'll let me know if we should find her another place?"

Alice looked away, her cheeks fading from their previous scarlet into an entirely uncharacteristic shade of pink. "There's nothing for you to worry about."

"Yet?" suggested Rosalind.

"All right, yet," said Alice. "I admit, before I was trying to determine if she was, if we were of a complementary type. One likes to know. One wants to be able to . . . well, help. You know how things can be difficult, and awkward. But she's a surprising young woman and—" Alice stopped and then started again. "She's asked me to teach her to read."

Rosalind's brows arched. "Did you say yes?"

"I did. I promise it won't interfere with her housekeeping. It might even improve it. We can start with some cookery books. I've had a look at the pie she was making for dinner, Rosalind, and—" Alice saw the look Rosalind was giving her. "And yes, I will let you know if we need to find her another place."

"And I promise I'll take care of Amelia while we are out tomorrow," said Rosalind.

Alice returned a surprisingly stern glare. "Just promise you'll take care of yourself, Rosalind. I do not like this tangle of yours."

"We've been in worse places," said Rosalind lightly.

"No, we really haven't," replied Alice. "This one has become quite personal."

Rosalind wanted to argue, but it was all she could do to try to suppress the sharp shiver that ran up her spine.

CHAPTER 36

Removed from the Scene

*A man generally esteemed and respected—a man
eminently qualified to figure to advantage on a
tombstone.*

Catherine Gore, *The Banker's Wife*

By the time Adam returned to Bow Street, the night patrol
was streaming out the station doors to form up in their
various groupings under Captain Goutier's direction. Goutier
waved in acknowledgment as Adam trudged up the steps. He
waved back. He was tired. He wanted a drink and his supper.
He wanted to sit in the parlor and listen to his family chat-
tering about the news of their days.

He wanted to see Rosalind and give her some good news.

He wanted answers about this damned mess with Fullerton.

Sam Tauton was the only one still in the patrol room when
Adam got there. The grizzled officer had a copy of the *Hue
& Cry* open in front of him and was running one blunt finger
down the columns of descriptions of stolen or recovered
property, his lips moving soundlessly as he read.

"Hullo, Harkness," he said without glancing up. "Hear you've had some more excitement out in Mayfair."

"Fullerton's servant is dead." He threw himself into the chair across from Tauton. "And in broad daylight, while we had men guarding the house."

Tauton pursed his lips and gave a low whistle. "That won't please his nibs." He nodded towards Townsend's office.

"Don't I know it." Adam sighed. "Is he there?"

"He will be. He's going over some lists of assignments with Stafford." Stafford was the station's chief clerk. "What's your thinking? Starts to look like Fullerton can't have done the deed. We certainly know where he was today."

"Unless he had an accomplice," said Adam. "That one I was talking to you about before. Horatio Salter."

"Horatio Salter?" boomed a new voice. "Who wants to know about him?"

John Townsend strode into the patrol room.

Townsend was a stout, vigorous man about twenty years older than Adam. Despite the winter weather, he still wore a broad-brimmed white hat more suited to the garden than the street. The hat had been a gift to Townsend from the Prince of Wales, and he was seldom seen without it.

"Salter's name has come up in conjunction to the murder today in Mayfair, sir," Adam told him.

"Has it begad?" Townsend froze on the threshold of his office. "You's better come in and tell me about it, Harkness."

"Of course." Adam got to his feet. Tauton gave him a seated bow and a raised brow.

Townsend's office was well furnished, especially in comparison to the business-like patrol room. Clocks and china knickknacks and snuff boxes—all gifts from grateful members of the *haut ton*—decorated every surface. Townsend took off his white hat and hung it carefully on the carved stand beside his desk.

"Now," he said as he settled behind his desk and gestured Adam to a chair. "What has Horatio Salter to do with your Mayfair business?"

Adam didn't answer at once. John Townsend had little use for Rosalind Thorne. He admitted her to be clever, but he did not care for any civilian, especially a female, to be offering their opinions, let alone their assistance, to the police station he ruled. That Rosalind had any number of aristocratic connections gave her some credit with Townsend. The man was an unabashed social climber. He cherished his relationship with the Prince Regent, and the fact that he was frequently given charge of the prince's watch and purse when His Royal Highness was spending an evening at the gaming tables.

This provided some good news from Adam's perspective, as it meant Townsend could be counted on to take the murder of a baronet very seriously. The bad news was that it also meant he was ready to blame the crime on the person who matched his idea of who would commit such a crime, rather than the person who actually did it.

"We know Salter has connections to Fullerton," said Harkness. "They are members of the same club, and Salter campaigned for an introduction to him. We know that Fullerton is a blackmailer and a moneylender, and it's possible that they may have had recent dealings with each other. It is my understanding that Salter's perviously been involved in serious fraud—"

"Oh, that's true enough. Took him up myself. Slippery as a live eel, though. Had to let him go in the end," Townsend added sourly. "He had his story and stuck to it. Swore he'd had his information from another gentleman he'd met in passing, and that as far as he had known it was all true. Didn't find out until later he was helping spread a lie. Fairly threw

himself on the mercy of the court, pleading youth and igno-
rance and I don't know what else. The fact that he was a
skinny youth with his beard barely beginning to sprout helped."
Townsend made a wry face.

"Has he been heard from since?"

"Not a word. I warned him off at the time. Might have
given him a thing or two to think about when I did." Townsend chuckled as if remembering a child's gift. Adam looked
away for a moment.

"Harkness, I've questioned Captain Gautier about what
he found at the house," Townsend went on. "His report is
clear. There seems no reason to doubt Fullerton was Sir Reginald's murderer. He all but had the knife in his hand."

"Yes, sir, but I'd like to be able to provide the magistrates
with positive proof, if it's to be had. As far as we know,
Fullerton had no reason to kill his guest. What drove him to
such a step?"

Townsend shrugged. "A quarrel perhaps? Over money, or
women? We know Fullerton was a scalawag, even if he did
keep himself outside the law's reach. Such a man needs little
excuse to turn to violence."

A jury might even agree with that. While Adam had faith
in the common sense of his fellow Englishmen, he also knew
they were ready to believe that a man who committed one
sort of crime would be just as ready to commit another.

"But then who was it murdered Sparkes? He must have
been killed to keep him quiet."

"You said it yourself. Fullerton is a man with highly unsavory dealings. The jailers at Clerkenwell confirm he's had visitors of all sorts since he's been there. I expect we will
discover that he paid some ruffian of his acquaintance to
stop the man's mouth."

Adam remembered how Sparkes had behaved when Harkness first spoke with him—the way he had looked to Fuller-

ton before he answered any question. Then there was what Fullerton had told Rosalind, that he'd left Sir Reginald alone, trusting Sparkes to watch him and keep him safe.

Was it possible Fullerton had become convinced this man would betray him?

How?

"Fullerton claims that when he got home that night two men rushed out of his house screaming blue murder."

"Have you been able to discover these men?"

"No, sir, not yet, but the fact of Sparkes's murder suggests they might exist."

"Might," Townsend emphasized. "I cannot allow you to sow doubts in a jury's mind over a paltry 'might' and the account of a man who is known—indeed, well known—to be a liar and scandalmonger. In fact"—Townsend leaned back with a satisfied smile—"I've had several letters from prominent persons congratulating us on finally bringing the scoundrel to heel."

Adam's heart plummeted.

"I am quite satisfied. We have Fullerton. You arrested him yourself, a fact for which you are to be commended." Townsend folded his hands across his paunch. "It was his house where the murders occurred, and he who was found, covered in blood, standing over the dead man. If he can account for all of this in court, let him do so. If all he can offer is phantoms and fairy stories, then he must suffer the consequences."

Adam's jaw clenched. He'd hoped that Salter's name, and his connection with a serious and prestigious case, would pique Townsend's interest and his sense of importance. But Townsend valued results and convenience even more than his own pride. The second murder, with Bow Street at the sight, would raise howls in the press. Townsend wanted a quick end to the case.

And the thing that would get his attention—the possibility

of Bonapartists active in London itself—was too tentative at this point. Even if Adam told Townsend all he knew about the Walford family, and Countess Lieven's hints to Rosalind, it would not be enough, especially if he had to bring Rosalind's name into it. She was quite right. Townsend did not trust or appreciate her gifts.

"It would still help the case if we could question Salter," Adam tried. "He may talk even if Fullerton won't. If he can give us a fuller picture of Fullerton's doings, it will help convince the jury of Fullerton's essential nature. He is a gentleman," he added. "The jurors will be reluctant to believe he could kill a guest without a strong demonstration of his lack of character."

Townsend hesitated.

"I'll only need a couple of days to track Salter." I hope. "If I can bring the magistrates a more complete picture of Fullerton's activities, we'll be in a stronger position with respect to the jury."

But Townsend shook his head. "No, I'm sorry. If Sir David or one of our esteemed magistrates requests we bring more information, Bow Street of course will assist to the furthest extent of our abilities."

Adam bowed his head in acquiescence. Inside, he was relieved. Here was a path he could follow. He could talk with Sir David, ask him to speak to Mr.—

"You, however," Townsend went on, "will be busy elsewhere."

Adam's head snapped up. "I'm sorry?"

"Yes, it seems you've become something of a victim of your own success."

"I don't understand." His brow furrowed.

"As I'm sure you know, His Royal Highness, the Prince Regent, is planning on hosting several different Christmas celebrations at Carlton House. I was there myself just yesterday, discussing matters of security with the house guard, and was favored with an audience with His Royal Highness. I was offering up a few names to join the security detail and he mentioned you."

The Prince Regent mentioned me? Harkness had to work to keep his jaw closed.

"I've tried to tell you, Harkness, you need not only to understand that you are a rising star of Bow Street, you need to *act* like it. It seems His Royal Highness has begun to hear report of you in certain quarters. From Lady Melbourne, for one, before she passed, and from Lady Jersey as well, and, it seems, even from the Countess Lieven. In addition, the newspapers have begun to link your name with several . . . dramatic investigations. Suitably impressed, His Royal Highness has specifically requested that you join in the security arrangements at Carlton House." Townsend leveled a quelling gaze at him. "I expect you to be quite sensible of the honor being shone to you by this."

"Yes, of course, I am," said Adam quickly. "And under any other circumstances, I would naturally accept the assignment immediately—"

Townsend stared at him as if he'd suddenly begun to speak French. "There cannot possibly be alternate circumstances. The Prince Regent has *asked* for you."

"I understand that, sir. But we have this matter of two murders in the same household. Sir David asked—"

"That matter will be more than adequately investigated by one of our fellow officers. Sir David will be disappointed, but I will explain the matter to him." Townsend paused. "Unless you are worried about someone else being disappointed? Someone intimately connected to this business?"

Adam struggled to keep his voice level. "If you are referring to Miss Thorne, sir—"

Townsend didn't let him get any further. He leaned forward. "I want to be very clear, Mr. Harkness. You do not have a choice in this matter. First thing tomorrow morning, you will come with me, and the other members of our detail, to Carlton House. There, you will take up your new duties, and you will dedicate your much-lauded skills to them for the next three days. If I find reason to believe that you have given this duty less than your full attention, you will no longer consider yourself an officer here. Have I been plain enough, sir?"

Adam did not believe himself to be a man of active imagination. For a moment, however, he very clearly saw himself rising to his feet, walking out of this office, out of the patrol room, out of the ward room, and out of the receiving hall, right into the street. All without pausing, or looking back.

And then?

What then?

What would his family do without the support of his wages, not to mention the rewards and the fees his work earned.

Without his resources as a Bow Street officer, how would he help Rosalind?

Three days, he told himself. *Three days only.*

But Fullerton's trial could happen anytime during those three days.

"What of Mr. Salter?" Adam asked.

"You will inform the officer who takes over the inquiry of your assessment. If he sees fit to pursue Salter, you may be sure I will recommend it." Townsend got to his feet, which compelled Adam to do the same. "You have done your duty there, Harkness. I expect you to proceed to your new assignment."

"The inquest for Russell Fullerton is tomorrow," Adam reminded him. "My testimony will be required."

Townsend clearly did not care to be reminded of that. "You seem to consider yourself the indispensable man in this effort," he murmured. Adam's jaw clenched again. "Should you be called, you will be given leave, of course. In the meantime, I will send a letter to Sir David and ask whether he will accept a written affidavit bolstering Captain Goutier's testimony, which I'm sure will be quite thorough. Unless you have concerns on that score?" He raised his bushy gray brows at Adam.

"No, sir," he said.

"Good. Then we'll see you here tomorrow morning at eight o'clock, in your best, if you please. And you may close the door on your way out."

CHAPTER 37

Secrets Between Sisters

*It grieves me much to spoil the romance, to
destroy the effect of a tale, which might in future
serve for the foundation of some novel . . .*

Maria Edgeworth, *Manoevering*

The hitch in Alice's arrangements with Charlotte was that
Mr. Clements's library did not open until noon. Not
wishing to risk another round of letters that might go astray,
Rosalind waited outside, grateful for her stout half boots,
and the fact that it was not raining.

Waiting did, unfortunately, give her more time to reflect
on the letter the runner from Bow Street had brought her this
morning.

> . . . *I have been left without choice in the matter. I am
> spending the next three days dedicated to the protection
> of the Prince Regent and his guests.*
> *I told Townsend about Salter's association with
> Fullerton, but it was not enough to change his mind. He
> did admit to me he believed Salter guilty of earlier bad*

conduct, although he was never able to prove it. I am concerned that some of his aristocratic connections have suggested that the world would be better off without Fullerton in it.

Unfortunately, this is not something I can prove.

I know you will proceed in your own fashion. I can only urge you to be extra vigilant. I do not like the shape of this thing. Sparkes's murder worries me. Townsend's refusal to look for possibilities beyond Fullerton worries me more.

Write to me to let me know how you get on, and if there is anything that I can do. You have more than one friend here who would be glad to help as soon as you ask.

Ever Your Servant,
Adam

It was a deeply personal finish to an otherwise grim and disappointing letter, and Rosalind's breath hitched when she saw it. She could not help remembering the touch of his hand and the feel of his strong arm beneath hers.

Mooning over a signature. Rosalind sighed sharply. *I will start giggling next. Really. At such a time, and at my age. What am I come to?*

The bells had begun tolling ten o'clock. Rosalind looked up and down the quiet street. *Where are you, Charlotte?* she thought, already worried.

But the worry did not last long this time. A shiny carriage came rattling down the street, drawn by a pair of matched chestnut bay horses and attended by a driver and an outrider both in livery. It drew up beside Rosalind and stopped. The occupant let the window down and leaned out.

"What is this?" cried Charlotte. "Rosalind Thorne standing about in the public street?" Then she saw that the shutters were still up on the library windows. "Ah."

A whole host of emotions welled up inside Rosalind at the sight of her sister, sitting casual, comfortable, and well-coiffed inside her carriage, as if nothing at all was wrong. With the grim strength of long practice, she swallowed them all.

One day, I will scream, she promised herself. *One day, the whole world will hear it.*

"It's all right," Rosalind murmured. "The weather is not bad. We can walk a bit."

"Don't be ridiculous." Charlotte reached through the window and worked the door handle. "Get in. We'll go to my house."

"Your house may be watched." Despite the best efforts of the Bow Street constables, Rosalind had to sneak out her own back door and through the garden to avoid being seen by the newspaper men this morning.

But Charlotte just laughed. "If my house were watched, my footman would have discovered it well before now and chased the bounder off. It's part of his job."

Knowing something of the efficiency of Charlotte's household, Rosalind relented and climbed into the carriage.

"Did Alice give you my note?" asked Charlotte as soon as Rosalind's rug was arranged and the carriage had pulled into the traffic.

"She did," said Rosalind. She had hoped for more time to gather her thoughts before the subject would have to be broached. "I wish you'd told me you planned to return to Bath."

"I did write, but—"

Rosalind interrupted. "You see, Mrs. Kendricks is living in Bath, with her sister. I could have told her you would be there."

"As lovely as it would have been to see her again, there was nothing I could not manage for myself."

"She walks by the house regularly," said Rosalind. "Since she moved out there."

"Well, now she can save herself the trouble," said Charlotte, just a little too quickly.

"Yes, I suppose." Rosalind turned to look out the window and waited for Charlotte to say something else.

She did not. Rosalind's heart sank lower.

Fortunately, Charlotte's driver was skilled and efficient, and the traffic had not yet reached its height for the morning, so the silent drive was also a relatively short one.

"Tell Cook to send up whatever's hot," Charlotte instructed the maid, Jane, as she helped them off with their coats and bonnets. Like Rosalind, Charlotte had dressed in mourning black. Her clothes were of a more recent vintage than Rosalind's own, which were left from when her mother had died.

"Oh, and a pot of coffee as well, Jane," Charlotte added. "I hope that's all right," she said to Rosalind as they started up the stairs. "I developed a taste for coffee in Paris and never really returned to tea."

Rosalind expected Charlotte to take her to the salon on the first floor, where she'd been before. But instead, her sister led her to the second floor and into a sunny suite of rooms. A pair of French doors opened onto a tiny balcony that overlooked the rooftops. A few sorry winter sparrows huddled on the neighboring slates.

This was, Rosalind realized, the place in the house Charlotte reserved for herself. It was clean and comfortable, but quite plain. Her sister's "taste" had all been exercised on her receiving rooms downstairs. Up here, the emphasis was on utility and comfort. Curiosity dampened her worry and her anger, and Rosalind gave herself permission to roam about, taking in the details of this private room. There was a shelf full of books and another of bound magazines. A warm fire crackled in the hearth. The furnishings were all stout, with very few frills.

But what Rosalind noticed most particularly was the easel beside the window bearing a charcoal sketch of a winter landscape.

"You kept up with your drawing," she remarked.

"Yes." Charlotte took one of the chairs by the fire. "My one regret about Paris was that I didn't have more time for lessons. What about you?"

Rosalind shook her head. "No, there was no money for such things after . . . well, after. Besides, I was never as good as you."

There were a few paintings on the walls—lovely, richly colored scenes that Rosalind's rather spotty arts education suggested to her were probably of the Amsterdam school.

But there was one other sketch hanging with them. This one was done in bright pastels. It showed a couple waltzing.

It was Rosalind, as she was shortly after her debut, and the man who held her was clearly Devon Winterbourne, now Duke of Casselmaine. The man she had turned away from only a few months ago. They had been rendered clearly in simple, graceful lines. But what was truly surprising was the expression Charlotte had given this younger Rosalind. It was not a young girl's fulsome delight. There was uncertainty in younger Rosalind's expression, maybe even a little fear.

How did she know? I didn't even know then.

Rosalind turned quickly away from the drawing to find Charlotte watching her closely.

"What will you do with this house once you are married?" asked Rosalind quickly. She crossed to take the other chair by the fire.

"Mr. Black has agreed it should remain in my name," said Charlotte. "I intend to lease it out and put the monies in trust for the child. That way, if anything . . . happens, they will not be left without means."

"A sensible plan," murmured Rosalind. "Can I ask, when did Mr. Black propose to you?"

"The first time was some months ago."

"Why did you wait so long to accept him?"

"There was no child then, and I thought he might change his mind." Charlotte shrugged, affecting her practiced carelessness, but this time it fell just a little flat. "Men do when they propose to their mistresses. And, of course, there was Father."

Of course. Rosalind nodded. "Why ever did you go away with him?"

It was the question she'd wanted to ask for years, and now that she finally faced her sister in private she could no longer hold it back.

"Because he asked me," replied Charlotte simply. Rosalind thought she might leave it there, but then, she went on, softly. "He told me he had enemies who were attempting to ruin him. He said I was the only one he could trust, the only one who truly loved and cared for him. He played upon my pride, and my affection. I had visions of some glamorous life in the shadows. I would take care of him while he worked with his powerful friends. Eventually, he would achieve the triumphant public vindication that he always swore was just a matter of time. Even when we were crossing the Channel in the dead of night to escape his creditors. Even when, night after night, what I saw was him spending his time, and what money we had, in the casinos and the theaters." She spoke softly to her hands. "I let myself believe him. I *made* myself believe him, for as long as I could."

"I'm sorry," said Rosalind. And she found that she truly was.

"It was my own fault," muttered Charlotte.

"No, he lied to you. You loved him as a daughter should, and he made use of that."

Charlotte lifted her gaze. There were tears in her bright eyes, and Rosalind felt her throat close.

"Do you know, for years, after I began my career, I imagined what it would be like if we met again," Charlotte said quietly. "I imagined you spitting at my feet, or slamming the door in my face, or some such." She smiled. "I suppose I have never lost my penchant for the dramatic."

"I missed you, Charlotte. Every day."

"And I missed you, Rosalind."

Rosalind held out her hand; a moment later, she was enfolded by her sister's embrace for the first time since they were children. Rosalind held her close, her heart full to bursting, and wished the moment might never end.

But, of course, it must. There was far too much to do. They must let go, retreat back to their separate chairs, smile and gather themselves.

Besides, at that moment the maid and the footman arrived bearing dishes and a tablecloth, which they arranged on the oval table by the French doors.

Charlotte's cook had provided a ragout of winter vegetables, fresh brown bread rolls, and stewed preserved apricots in a light custard. Everything was excellent and Rosalind said so.

"Cook is from Paris," Charlotte told her. "Everyone wants one of their male chefs, but I'd take Madame Dumont over any of them." As if to demonstrate her sincerity, Charlotte took a long swallow of the very strong coffee.

"I never asked you about your life in Paris." Rosalind broke apart one of the hot, fragrant rolls. "What it was like?"

Charlotte leaned back and turned her head, staring out the French doors. All the sparrows had fluttered away, and there was nothing left on the slates but tiny heaps of sooty snow.

"It was very glamorous," she said finally. "We had a grand flat in the Faubourg Saint-Germain, and we dined out every night. Just as he promised. I was his hostess, and everyone praised me for my cleverness, my wit, and all my other charms. I was dazzled. When we weren't visiting, or at the opera, we were in the casinos.

"It was a long time—oh, a year at least—before the money troubles all began again." She spoke lightly, but Rosalind could hear the strain in her voice. "Of course, according to Father, it was somebody else's fault, and if he couldn't find a scapegoat, he could always blame the cards. Slowly"—Charlotte paused and her mouth twisted into a self-deprecatory smile— "very slowly, I began to realize that the stories were just that. Stories he told himself to keep from being afraid, to keep other people from realizing he had nothing at all, and finally to keep me from leaving him to go back home.

"Not that there was any home to go back to. I'd heard that mother was dead by then."

Rosalind blinked, tears prickling unexpectedly.

"Father cried, for a bit, when he heard. Swanned about in mourning until he got bored with it." She smoothed down her own stark black skirts. "But if he stayed away from the casinos and the parties, we would not have any money at all, and the French are much less forgiving of English debt than English tradesmen are. So, we were obliged to go back to work."

"Work?" echoed Rosalind.

Charlotte nodded. "That was how I was thought of by then. The parties and the gambling and the spinning stories to borrow the money, this was how we got our living, as surely as if we'd been hat-makers or bricklayers. He started writing begging letters again. Or rather, I started writing them, because my French was better."

And so he saw your writing a great deal. Rosalind knotted her fingers together.

Charlotte addressed herself to her ragout again. "I realized something else at the time. I was being used. Men like a pretty woman. I made a nice distraction, and my company was a lure for the men. His friends."

Like Augustina for Salter. Rosalind thought. *Oh, Augustina.*

"There were nights, when things went badly, that he would blame me. I had looked tired, I hadn't smiled enough." She waved her hand. "Well, by then I knew what was going to happen to me. No home to go to, no dowery, my father falling deeper into dissipation and no skill of my own except being charming.

"My one resolve was that if the choice must be made, it would be my choice, and I would make it for my reasons. So that was what I did. He was a delight." Her smile at the memory was a genuinely happy one, and Rosalind felt an entirely expected wave of relief. Charlotte had made her own life and had been happy. She could be happy again.

If only other choices, and other circumstances, did not get in the way.

"We had such fun," Charlotte went on. "I met some astonishing people. There were salons and concerts and I began to live for myself and enjoy it."

"And yet you continued to keep our father," said Rosalind.

"Yes, I couldn't seem to make myself leave him, as much as I wanted to some days. It was not easy. We fought, especially when I went out without him. But we kept the flat, and the bills were paid, and we muddled along, or I thought we did."

Rosalind dragged her spoon through her dish of fruit and custard. "Why did you come back to England?" she asked.

"Homesickness, mostly," said Charlotte. "A bit of pride. And of course, the fall of Bonaparte and the occupying army and everyone jostling each other for position and trying to work out what's going to happen, and the Bourbons and their Ultra White faction deciding to settle some very old, very nasty scores. It just seemed safer."

Which was all perfectly reasonable, and Rosalind believed her. *But she's not saying everything.*

Rosalind sighed and folded her napkin. "Charlotte, I have a difficult and rather strange question."

Charlotte arched her brows.

"Did father—was father—ever politically entangled in Paris?"

Charlotte laughed. It was a long, full laugh that left her breathless. She put her hand on her stomach as she wheezed. "Father! Oh dear. He could adapt to any company, but he abhorred politics and ridiculed politicians. It was one of his party tricks. He could do the most astounding imitations."

"And you?" asked Rosalind quietly.

"Rosalind," said Charlotte sternly. "You're after something. What is it?"

"Do you know the Countess Lieven?"

"No. Do you?"

"As it happens, I do."

"Goodness," murmured Charlotte. "What circles you move in."

"She wants to meet you."

Charlotte's air of gently mockery vanished at once. "Whatever for?"

"She believes you, or Father, might have connections to the Bonapartist supporters in London."

Rosalind thought Charlotte would laugh again, but her face fell. Indeed, her expression quickly passed surprise and showed a flicker of fear. "She thinks I'm a spy of some sort?"

"I don't know, exactly, but she wants to talk to you. I told her I would ask."

"Why would you do such a thing?" Charlotte demanded. "You have no business making promises for me, no matter how grand your company."

Rosalind tried not to wince or to wonder what about this made Charlotte suddenly angry.

"I didn't promise you'd do anything. I promised I would ask, and I did it because I am under obligation to her for a favor she did me, and because I may need her help again if I am to discover what really happened to Father."

Charlotte looked genuinely surprised. "What do you mean? Fullerton murdered father."

"He says he did not."

"Of course he does."

"He asked me to find out who did."

Charlotte stared at her, shock erasing all her cultivated sophistication.

"Rosalind," said Charlotte slowly. "Please, tell me you did not agree to this madness."

Rosalind remained silent.

"Have you lost your mind?" asked Charlotte icily.

"Not yet," replied Rosalind.

"The man killed our father!"

"I don't know that."

"Does that matter?" Charlotte threw out of her hands. "He's a foul blackmailer! Let him hang and good riddance to him!"

"Yes, I've thought of that," said Rosalind. She had. As she stood in the cell with him, as she walked beside the turnkey down the dark stone corridor, as she'd laid awake in her bed staring at the ceiling. "And I've decided I won't be rid of him dishonestly."

Charlotte's face had gone taut. She stared angrily at the remains of their meal, and for a moment, Rosalind felt certain she was going to sweep the dishes to the floor.

"What does it matter how he is gone, just so long as he *is* gone?"

"It matters to me," answered Rosalind, and as soon as she said it, she felt how very much it was true.

Charlotte got to her feet. She paced to the fire and stood there, twisting her hands.

"You understand he will not be grateful. He will not be merciful to you, neither will he change his ways."

"I know that."

"And you'd still do his bidding?"

"It is not his bidding, Charlotte. It is vital we find out who really killed Father."

"He did!" she cried.

"Think, Charlotte. The killer is still out there. They have killed a second man to silence him—"

"What!" Charlotte staggered and grabbed the mantel to keep her balance.

"I'm sorry." Rosalind hurried to her sister. "I'd forgotten you would not know. Fullerton's manservant is dead as well. He was the only other person in the house that night. Whoever did this may strike at me next, or you."

"Or they may have finished their work in getting rid of a monster! They should be applauded, not hounded by a . . ."

Rosalind drew herself and waited for Charlotte's assessment of her.

"Rosalind." Charlotte seized her hand and pressed it hard. "You can't do this. Let it be. Let *us* be."

At what cost? Rosalind bit her lip.

"Charlotte. I do not want to ask this, but now I must. Did you kill Father?"

CHAPTER 38

Accusations

A woman who is known to play the fool is always suspected of playing the devil.

Maria Edgeworth, *Belinda*

"*What?*" cried Charlotte.

"Did you kill him?" repeated Rosalind, marveling a little at her own grim calm. "You could have. You had reason to, and there are signs that he was waiting for some visitor when he died. It could have been you."

Charlotte's face went paper white.

"There was a letter written in your hand on the desk in the room where he died," Rosalind continued. "It's viciously incriminating. He could have been intending to blackmail you, or just helping Fullerton to do so. You did not meet me as planned. I had not heard from you for nearly three days, and your servants could not say where you were."

"I told you! I returned to Bath. It was you yourself who put the thought in my head. I wanted to make certain none of the servants had been bribed, and to—"

"You could be lying." *You are lying.* "What will you do if Fullerton decides to accuse you?" Rosalind went on. "If he gets desperate, he might do it. What if there's a trial, and you are called before the magistrates?" *Or I am?* "What story will you tell? Would your fiancé be willing, or even able, to swear in court that you were with him the entire time we failed to find you?" She paused and let this sink into her sister's thoughts. "And now that Fullerton's servant is dead, it might be thought you returned to kill him so that he would not be able to name you. After all, Fullerton could not have done it. He's in jail."

Charlotte turned her face away. Rosalind knew she was being brutal. She would ask forgiveness later.

"Unless we discover who really did this thing, we both remain in danger."

Because that was the other thread to this tangle, one that Rosalind had not wanted to see clearly. It was farfetched, but so was everything else that had happened. That this was the master plan. That Fullerton had staged the scene, had allowed his own arrest, specifically to incriminate Charlotte, and her.

But why then call me to him? She frowned at her own thoughts. *To hedge his bets,* she answered herself. *If I will not be caught one way, I will be caught the other, and Charlotte with me.*

Charlotte wanted to argue. Rosalind could see it in the way she held herself. It was the fact of Sparkes's death that silenced her. Without that, she might have been able to say that Rosalind's fears were exaggerated.

Charlotte could still say that it must have been Fullerton who organized his servant's death. If Fullerton were guilty, he would have a great deal to fear if Sparkes decided to speak before the magistrates.

Rosalind and Charlotte had both lived with some form of danger and uncertainty for much of their lives. They knew what it meant and how if felt. Would Charlotte choose to wade deeper into that?

She hung her head, and Rosalind had her answer.

"What are you going to do?" asked Charlotte.

Rosalind glanced at the clock. "I am going to call on a Mrs. Walford. She and her family are connected to Fullerton through a man named Horatio Salter, especially her daughter, Augustina, and her son Louis." As she spoke these names, Rosalind watched for Charlotte's reaction, but Charlotte's expression remained entirely indifferent. "I believe the Walfords and Salter may be caught up in the events that led Fullerton to take up our father in the first place."

"Are you certain of that?"

"Not yet," Rosalind admitted. "But I will be soon."

"Because this is what you do."

"Yes."

Charlotte fell back in her chair, making a show of weariness. Except, Rosalind realized as she looked into her sister's eyes, it was not entirely a show. "Whoever these Walfords are, I do not expect they will thank you for exposing them in this way."

"No."

"I don't understand you," breathed Charlotte.

"I don't understand you, either. Not entirely. But here we are anyway."

Rosalind waited. *What will you do, Charlotte?* Rosalind felt her heart drumming against her ribs, hope and fear driving her pulse.

What Charlotte did was draw her shoulders back. "Very well." She waved toward Rosalind, a practiced, insouciant gesture. "If it will help matters, arrange the meeting with your countess. I will attend."

"Thank you, Charlotte."

"I just hope you will be careful. I do not like the fact that Fullerton's actually asked you to prove his innocence."

"Neither do I, but as I said—"

"Here we are. Yes." Charlotte's face tightened again. Rosalind felt her own jaw clench in answer. Charlotte was trying to decide whether she would speak.

Please, Rosalind begged silently. *Whatever it is, tell me. Please.*

"I did go to Bath," said Charlotte finally. "I spoke to my servants there. They denied any possibility of bribery, and I am ready to believe them. I paid the rent on the house for another month. You can check with the landlord, or have Mrs. Kendricks do it. You see, at the time, I thought I'd be bringing Father back."

Rosalind hoped Charlotte didn't hear her let out the breath she'd been holding. "Why didn't you let me know your plans?"

"Because I needed to think," Charlotte said, wearily. "And because I did not know for certain if I really was going to come back to London, and because I was angry with you."

This last surprised her. "What had I—"

"You pointed out that I had to tell Merrick about Father, about our family and our past. My past. You were right, and I did not want you to be, because I did not know if I had the strength to follow it through."

Rosalind lowered herself into the chair opposite her sister, so they would be at eye level with each other. "Did you tell him?"

"As it happens, I did." Charlotte's mouth curled into a tiny smile. "I realized that if I brought all the family lies into my marriage, they would never leave. They'd be my child's constant companions, whether they ever found out the specifics or not." She paused, and her hand shook where it lay on the chair arm. "We argued for hours. We took turns breaking down in tears. I was so afraid he was going to send me away. I was so angry with you. But in the end, he told me he understood. He forgave me and I forgave him all the things he'd said. We'd been reconciled for less than a day when Alice found me." She lifted her eyes. "I had no idea what was happening to you, or that Father had died. I swear I did not. I hadn't seen a paper since I left London, nor had I looked at my letters."

But because of what she'd seen at Fullerton's house, there was one more question that still had to be asked.

"Did he write to you? Or ask you to visit him?"

Charlotte frowned, startled. "How did you know?"

"I believe the night he died, Father was waiting for someone. I thought it might be you."

Charlotte looked away, and Rosalind's heart plummeted. *She's going to lie.*

But after a long moment's hesitation, it seemed that Charlotte changed her mind. "Yes, he did ask me to come to him, although it was more of an order than a request."

"Did you go?"

"No," said Charlotte. "I did not. The letter was sent to my house and arrived while I was in Bath. By the time I got it, he was already dead." She paused. "Do you believe me?"

It was odd to hear her ask this now. She hadn't before. Rosalind had the distinct feeling what she actually meant was, *Do you trust me?*

Do I trust her? After all she has done, and all I have done. Do I?

After all those years of separation, all those years while Charlotte stood by their father, with only one letter to break the silence between them.

Do I trust her?

Rosalind looked around the plain, neat, private room. She looked at the sketch, of her waltzing with Devon, and the question Charlotte had put in that other Rosalind's eyes.

Do I?

She thought about how Charlotte could have lied, but chose not to.

Rosalind made her decision.

"Let this be my answer. Are you at liberty tomorrow night, Charlotte? Because I am very much going to need your help."

CHAPTER 39

All the Hidden Meanings

*What object can your mother have but your
good?*

Maria Edgeworth, *Manoevering*

Rosalind's errand to call upon the Walfords was made
faster and much easier as a result of Charlotte loaning
Rosalind her carriage and driver.

"It is no bother," Charlotte had said. "You will simply
bring it back to me when we meet tonight for our rendez-
vous."

So, Rosalind rode in comfort back to Little Russell Street
to collect Amelia, whom she found in the parlor with Alice,
laboriously copying a line of letters. With her maid, a very
full book satchel, and her fresh hopes mixed with a few fresh
fears, Rosalind returned to the Walfords.

Mrs. Walford was in her morning room. The footman
showed Rosalind in with Amelia following silently behind.
The widow sat at her work table by the windows, poring
over stacks of papers.

"Good day, Mrs. Walford." Rosalind made her curtsy. "I
trust you do not object to my maid. I thought it possible

there might be errands to run." Before Mrs. Walford could answer, Rosalind gestured to Amelia. The girl stepped smartly forward with Rosalind's satchel and then retired immediately and properly to the chimney corner.

"Yes, of course," replied Mrs. Walford. She looked strained, Rosalind thought. There were dark circles under her eyes, and her skin had drawn itself tightly across her cheekbones.

"Thank you for coming, Miss Thorne," she went on. "I apologize again for the necessity of it. I have sent for tea. Will you sit?" She gestured to a second chair at the table.

Rosalind sat. Mrs. Walford at once began stacking her papers up and returning them to their folios. They looked to be ledger sheets and supply lists. From where she sat, Rosalind could not read the cramped handwriting clearly.

To do with the manufactory? She knew from previous conversation with Mrs. Walford that the business was held in trust for her sons to inherit, but she herself had a supervisory role in running the mills. Probably, there was a board of trustees somewhere who would sign off on her decisions and oversee expenditures. The law might allow a widow more independence than a wife, but complete freedom was still frowned upon.

Rosalind wondered how Louis and Etienne felt about being kept waiting. Neither one had struck her as being particularly patient.

Very like their sister in that regard.

"Have you learned anything more about your father's . . . tragedy?" asked Mrs. Walford.

"Not yet," said Rosalind.

"Had he been acquainted with his host for very long?"

"I do not know. My father and I were not on speaking terms." *Why this interest?* she wondered.

"Oh, I see. It is a horrid thing when family members forget what they owe to one another." Rosalind inclined her head in general agreement with this. "I saw . . . it was in the papers that there was a second murder in the same house. You must have been very shocked to hear of it."

"Very," agreed Rosalind. *What is this about?*

"I do not suppose . . ." Mrs. Walford hesitated. "I do not suppose that with your various connections you have heard any more about that?"

Rosalind looked at her drawn and serious expression and saw again the signs that Mrs. Walford had not been sleeping. She thought about Salter's disappearance and about Fullerton's two mysterious men.

Before, when Rosalind had considered the possibility that the Walfords were involved in the events surrounding her father's death, it had always seemed farfetched. Now, however, Rosalind found herself wondering if that possibility was really out of the question.

"I'm sorry to say that I have not heard anything new," Rosalind told her. "Beyond the fact that the officers do believe that the two incidents are tied together."

"Of course," said Mrs. Walford. "That would be the natural conclusion."

"Yes, it would," agreed Rosalind.

She was spared from having to make further remarks by the footman arriving at the door with the tea tray. Amelia promptly relieved him of it and carried it to the tea table and set about arranging the things.

Mrs. Walford took herself over to the sofa. There, she sat down and began the quiet ritual of checking the pot, pouring out the tea, and fixing a cup for Rosalind. She knew Rosalind's tastes from their previous meetings and did not need to ask before adding a slice of lemon to the cup.

Rosalind took her place on the settee. She watched the older woman, with no concern that she might be caught staring. Mrs. Walford paid her no attention. She was keeping all her focus on her own hands, as if she was afraid what might happen if her concentration slipped.

Something is very wrong.

Rosalind accepted her tea and drank the obligatory swallow before she set the cup down. She took a deep breath. What she was about to say was a risk, but if she did not speak, it would seem strange.

"Mrs. Walford, I recognize that my personal circumstances have interfered with your plans for the charity ball. Rather than further inconvenience you, I am prepared to step aside. I have brought my notebooks and a list of names you should contact directly regarding the final arrangements. I have written to Mr. and Mrs. Hodges at the assembly rooms, and you may be assured they are fully informed as to the current state of preparations. You may rely on them both entirely. They will help ensure that your event is a success."

A small smile of understanding stole across Mrs. Walford's face. "And thus I am very neatly admonished for doubting you, and I daresay for my rudeness. I apologize, Miss Thorne. I did not ask you here to indulge in vulgar curiosity, I promise." Mrs. Walford laid a hand over her stack of folios. "Miss Thorne, this event is very important to me. The cause it represents is dear to me, as it was to my late husband. The sacrifice made by the widows and orphans of those who died in the recent wars must not go unrecognized," she added firmly. "And yes, I will be honest with you, I hope the success of this ball will help open doors for me, and for my children, especially Augustina. I want you to help me finish what we have begun. In truth, I need you."

"I am sure you can do whatever you set your mind to."

"I can't keep Horatio Salter away from my daughter," she said flatly.

Rosalind started. "You have seen him?"

"No, but . . . my maid intercepted this." She drew a tightly folded note from her sleeve and handed it to Rosalind. Rosalind unfolded the paper and read:

Salter:
I have to see you. Our regular place tomorrow night.
I'm frantic with worry.
   A.

Rosalind looked from the page to Mrs. Walford. The widow watched her intently.

"It sounds to me more as if Augustina has not heard from Salter," said Rosalind.

"It may be, but what if she is still in contact with him, even now? What if they are planning to elope?"

"Even now?" echoed Rosalind.

Mrs. Walford looked away and bit her lip. "Even now that his character has been made clear. Even now that he chose to vanish rather than explain himself."

Rosalind ran her thumb over the note and tried not to frown. There was something hollow in Mrs. Walford's words. She was worried, but not about what she'd said, at least not entirely.

What is it you know? Rosalind wondered toward her hostess.

"What has Miss Walford said about Mr. Salter since she last saw him?" Rosalind asked.

"Nothing that could put my mind at rest," Mrs. Walford told her. "She is suspicious of what happened at the opera. She veers from believing that promissory note your friend produced to be fraudulent to declaring she does not care if Salter has debts. Indeed, she seems to believe anything and everything except that Salter is a schemer."

Rosalind met Mrs. Walford's gaze and saw both worry and accusation. A dozen questions flickered through her mind, but one stood out from the sudden tide.

"Why are you speaking with me about this? I have already failed you in regards to Mr. Salter and Miss Walford. A runner or other such inquiry agent would serve your ends better than I could," said Rosalind.

"It is a matter of expediency," said Mrs. Walford. "I want him found quickly."

It struck Rosalind that Fullerton had said something similar to her.

And Fullerton wishes to use me for his own ends. What are your ends, Mrs. Walford?

"I cannot bring some variety of thieftaker into the house and have him stomping about asking rude questions, drinking away his fee, and fobbing off my impatience with platitudes. I admit I have misgivings, and that I hesitated before returning to you." Rosalind felt certain this much at least was the truth. "But I am convinced you are best placed to act, because you have already made many of the necessary connections to Mr. Salter's acquaintance to inquire more closely into his whereabouts." Mrs. Walford paused. "And I believe you are more motivated than any private agent might be."

She spoke with sincerity, and she was of course correct on several levels. Rosalind was indeed motivated to discover the truth of what was happening, and for more reasons than Mrs. Walford could possibly know. But this conversation was only raising more questions in Rosalind's mind.

It was time to try a different tack.

"I can see all this has been very difficult for you," she said quietly.

Mrs. Walford looked a little startled. "Yes, it would be for anyone, but you see, I had promised my husband when he lay dying that Augustina would be married safely and well. It was all he wanted for her."

Rosalind nodded in sympathy but said nothing.

Mrs. Walford was smiling at some memory. "He was a good man. There are so very few like him. He felt that money was a tool. It should be used to make a better world. He wanted to build, wanted to grow beyond what he was. Not just to be rich for the sake of riches." She twisted her fingers together. "He was the one who saved me from being just another featherhead in a nice dress. He filled our lives with *purpose*." She paused. "And he wanted me and our children to remember what his dreams were for."

From memory, Rosalind heard Augustina's voice. *He tells me I'm his anchor. That first night, he said he was amazed how I kept my head and didn't let him go too far.*

So that was where the young woman had gotten her ideas of partnership from. She had seen it at work in her own home and longed for something similar. Then, she got tossed into the London marriage market, with its priorities of rank, looks, and fortune. Because her mother had promised she should marry well and safely.

No wonder she was disappointed.

"Given this situation with Mr. Salter, and its implications for Miss Walford's future," said Rosalind, "perhaps it would be better for you to cancel the charity ball."

"How?" demanded Mrs. Walford immediately. "The ball is almost upon us. Cancellation is impossible."

This was the response Rosalind had expected, but she pressed forward anyway. "Surely, given the seriousness of the situation, your attention should be with your daughter and your family." *Given your repeated declaration of your fears. Given that you have brought me back and pronounced yourself desperate.*

Given that you want Augustina married not just well but safely.

Given that Augustina deserves some chance to explain to you what she wants.

"You rebuke me, again, Miss Thorne, and you are right to do so," said Mrs. Walford. "But you do not, you cannot, understand how much I have poured into this. My standing with the board, my standing with . . . society itself hinges on this event. What use will I be to my children if I am made a laughingstock now?"

There was something about this whole conversation that did not make sense. For half of it, Mrs. Walford was in agonies about her children, especially her daughter; for the other half, she was ready to dismiss that same daughter for the sake of her ball and the standing she hoped it would bring her.

That daughter who was perfectly willing to use her brothers to achieve her own ends. She had said as much to Rosalind.

That daughter who had her own funds and her own secret life. Rosalind rubbed the note in her fingertips again.

I perfected the art of being both distraction and a lookout, Augustina had said. And Charlotte, later, had nearly echoed those words.

I made a nice distraction, and my company was a lure for the men.

Both young women, using and being used. Both negotiating partnerships they thought were based on a genuine love and affection, but were really based on a need for money.

Charlotte had learned better, and turned away. What would Augustina do?

What is she doing?

"Have you told Miss Walford you are going forward with the ball?" she asked. "Or your sons?"

Mrs. Walford drew back, confused by the question. "I have, as a matter of fact."

"And they made no objections? They voiced no concerns?" She paused. "Or encouragements?"

"They understand fully that our reputation as a family hangs on our success with this event. Why would you ask?"

"I am trying to understand the current mood of the household," she said, which had the virtue of being close to the truth.

Before she could expand on this, however, the footman knocked again at the door. He entered and bowed.

"Ma'am," he said. "I must inform you that—" He hesitated.

"What is it?" snapped Mrs. Walford.

"Ma'am, it's Mr. Salter. He is downstairs and wishes to see you."

CHAPTER 40

Returns and Recriminations

*He would have started with horror at the idea of
disturbing the peace of a family; but in her family,
he said, there was no peace to disturb . . .*

Maria Edgeworth, *Belinda*

Mrs. Walford was still struggling to her feet when Horatio Salter strode into the room.

"Mrs. Walford." He went to her at once and bowed deeply. "Ma'am, I must offer my sincerest apologies, and I only hope—" As he straightened, he saw Rosalind. "Ah. It seems I am too late." He nodded toward Rosalind, and she nodded back, briefly.

Wherever he had been, Salter did not look as if he had suffered any sort of hardship. His dress was neat and precise. His hair had been combed into fashionable curls, and his cravat was perfectly tied.

The glimmer in his eye as he looked at Rosalind was entirely self-satisfied. Rosalind felt a prickle of warning race down her spine.

"Mr. Salter," said Mrs. Walford, forcing Salter's attention

back to her. "I must say, I am most surprised to see you here."

"I'm sure you are. And I admit, I considered staying away for even longer. That was cowardly of me."

"What is it you want?" the widow asked icily.

"I want a chance to explain. You have heard some stories about me recently." He spoke this much directly to Rosalind. "It is not your fault, Mrs. Walford. It's mine. I should have spoken to you in confidence as soon as I began courting Augustina. But I was afraid to lose your good will, and now I must pay the price for my cowardice. I can only ask you to listen to me and to not judge until you've heard everything."

His face and voice as he spoke seemed entirely guileless. Rosalind knew a moment's cold doubt. She already knew she had been careless in her approach to this business. She had been mistaken about Augustina's actions, and her nature. Was it possible she had been mistaken about Salter's as well?

Amelia sneezed.

All startled, they turned their heads. Amelia stood in her corner, apparently mortified, her hand pressed against her nose. She snatched her handkerchief out of her sleeve and hid her face and, presumably, her blush.

Salter's eyes narrowed, just slightly. Rosalind's throat constricted.

Mrs. Walford and Salter had already looked away, attempting to forget this sudden interruption. Rosalind was the only one who saw Amelia peek over the edge of her handkerchief and nod her head toward Horatio Salter.

Rosalind's breath stopped.

Salter? She stared silently at the maid. Amelia read the question in her eyes and nodded again.

Rosalind faced her hostess and the others again. She hoped if they noticed any change in her color they would put it down to her being startled and a trifle embarrassed.

So, it was Salter who had watched her house and tried to suborn her servant. Rosalind studied the man. But what for? Had Fullerton warned him about her? Or was he acting on his own?

"Very well, Mr. Salter," Mrs. Walford was saying. "I believe you were going to tell us where you have been."

Whatever he was going to tell them would have to wait yet longer. He barely had time to open his mouth when the door flew open and Augustina burst into the room.

"Salter!" she shouted.

In an instant, Salter was on his feet. Augustina ran forward but pulled up short, just out of arm's reach. She stood staring up at him as if she were starving. Rosalind knew for certain if there had been no one to see, she would have been in his arms, and he would have held her close. That need shone as brightly in his eyes as it did in hers.

As it was, he simply bowed, holding himself stiff and correct.

"Miss Walford," he murmured. "I am very glad to see you."

Augustina drew herself up, dignified, correct, and coldly furious. Rosalind watched the girl summon the rigid control that propriety demanded, and felt a deep sympathy.

"I'm sorry to have burst in like that," she said. "But I had just been given to understand you had arrived. As you may understand, I have been anxious to hear from you."

Mrs. Walford was frowning. She clearly did not like this display, less because of the improprieties Salter and Augustina barely held in check, but because of the unspoken affection that vibrated between the two of them.

"Well, since you're here, Augustina, you may as well stay," said Mrs. Walford with frosty resignation. "Mr. Salter was going to explain to us where he has been for the past few days. At least, that is what he says," she added sternly. "Will you sit, Mr. Salter?"

"Thank you." Mr. Salter hitched up his stovepipe trousers

and sat in the round-backed chair by the hearth. Augustina lowered herself onto the settee beside Rosalind. No one moved to offer him any tea.

"I will start with what happened at the opera." He rested his elbows on his knees, hands folded. "That man, Faulks, who addressed me—he was deceived, I'm afraid." Salter glanced toward Rosalind as he said it. Rosalind returned a blank expression. "The note he purchased was an old one. I had discharged the debt some time ago, and I thought the paper had been destroyed. It should have been. Unfortunately, it seems I trusted the wrong man. What I've been doing the last few days is trying to convince him to speak the truth and save both of us from . . . any sort of public declaration or legal action." Salter reached into his coat pocket and pulled out a letter. "Here is the letter he's given me, detailing the matter, and his mistake. He undertakes to write to Mr. Faulks and explain the whole of the matter."

He held the letter out for Mrs. Walford. She eyed him with open suspicion as she broke the seal and read.

"He does say that the note is one of several he sold, and that it should have been destroyed rather than exchanged. He offers a full apology," said Mrs. Walford. "It is signed by a Mr. Hamish Greer."

"I knew it!" cried Augustina. "I knew some explanation would be found."

Then why did you come to me with your bribe and your suspicions? Augustina had believed her family might have caused Salter to vanish or flee. Any ordinary girl with a pair of protective brothers might think something similar, but Augustina was not any ordinary girl.

There was something more to her fears. Rosalind was certain of it.

"I am sorry I did not write to you sooner," said Salter. "But I wanted to make sure the affair was entirely settled before I ventured an explanation. And once I had . . . I couldn't wait for the post. I had to come myself." He let his gaze drift toward Augustina.

"Well!" Mrs. Walford turned toward Rosalind. "What do you make of all this, Miss Thorne?"

Rosalind remained silent. She remembered Augustina's story of how she and Salter had learned to work the gaming rooms. She remembered the studied insouciance in Fullerton's manner when she mentioned Salter's name, and her own certainty that he was dissembling.

She also thought about her years of friendship with Sanderson Faulks. Sanderson had never once let her down when she needed him. He would not be so careless as to acquire an old or discharged note, whatever that letter might say.

Rosalind found herself wondering who Mr. Greer was, and how Salter had convinced him to write his apology.

"If you are satisfied, Mrs. Walford, that must be the last word. But," Rosalind added, "there is another matter."

The look Augustina and Salter exchanged was so swift, Rosalind might have missed it if she hadn't been watching them closely.

"What else could there be?" protested Augustina. There was urgency in her voice and her expression, which was natural. But to Rosalind it also felt like a plea.

Stop now, she seemed to say. *Don't go too far.*

It was addressed to Salter, and he knew it.

"Augustina," said Salter. "Please, don't. It was bound to come out. We both knew that."

Trust me, his tone said.

You were ready for this, Rosalind thought. Of course he was. He would have been foolish not to be. But if he was ready, why wasn't Augustina?

"Well, I'm sure I don't know what you are talking about," announced Mrs. Walford.

"But you should, ma'am," said Salter. "Miss Thorne will have told you about my previous encounter with the courts, and the Bow Street runners." He passed one neat hand over his brow. "I was seventeen when it happened. I was idling about the coffee shops as a young man will, and there was a great deal of agitation and excitement. Somebody was saying that Napoleon was dead. There was a general clamor, but I didn't join in." He paused, as if searching for words. "I had . . . call it some respect for the emperor. I am a loyal subject of the Crown, and yet, his declarations on the rights of man, the freedoms we should all enjoy, that the best should not be ruled by the worst because of an accident of birth—" He swallowed. Mrs. Walford's hand strayed to her collar and tugged. "I thought those ideas were admirable, as were his attempts to govern by them. I could not join in the celebration of the death of such a man. So, I left. I didn't know my behavior meant I'd be singled out."

Mrs. Walford tugged at her collar again and at her lace cuff.

"Later, after it became known that the news was all a lie and part of a grand scheme to defraud the stock market, I was shaken awake in the middle of the night by a squadron from Bow Street. They were led by a Mr. John Townsend. They dragged me in and questioned me. It seems some of my fellows at The Cocoa Tree had resented my quiet and decided to name me as one of the men who had started spreading the rumors.

"I tried to explain to Townsend, but he wouldn't listen. It was . . . difficult." Salter winced. Augustina pressed her hand over her mouth. Mrs. Walford sat back. She looked frankly skeptical, but she was listening. "Townsend wanted me to give him names of my imagined confederates. He insisted that I had been paid to spread the rumors that had done so much damage. When I was hauled up in front of the magistrates, I truly thought I was done for. But perhaps it was because I was so young, or perhaps because I was able to honestly plead that I knew nothing at all, and Townsend had to concede I told him nothing, nor could the men who named me be found . . . I was declared innocent and let go.

"And that, ma'am, is the whole of my story. I swear to you."

"And you decided you should keep this a secret?" cried Mrs. Walford.

"He didn't," said Augustina promptly. "He told me."

Her mother glared at her. "And you kept it to yourself?"

"Of course I did," her daughter answered. "I knew what you'd think. You'd never make any allowances for him having been just a boy at the time. I was afraid, Mother. I already loved him so much . . ." Augustina turned her face away, blinking hard as if to hold back tears.

"Augustina," breathed Salter. "It is not her fault," he declared stoutly to Mrs. Walford. "I asked her to keep the matter in confidence . . ."

"No, Salter," said Augustina. "I won't let you. It was my doing, Mama. Salter wanted to tell you, but I convinced him to wait. I wanted us publicly engaged before we ventured the truth."

"Then Miss Thorne got hold of the story," said Salter. "And I knew I had to come forward. But as she is here, I must presume you have already heard the worst. I only ask you to judge fairly, ma'am. Would I have come back at all if what I say now is a lie? Surely it would have been easier, and safer, for me to simply vanish."

Augustina was holding herself so stiffly she was almost vibrating with the effort. Salter, on the other hand, was completely relaxed into his role. His tone, his whole manner, urged Mrs. Walford to listen to what he said, and to trust in him.

But Augustina did not trust him. She was frightened about something, and Rosalind wondered about it. Especially since she was playing along with what was, among other things, an attempt to discredit Rosalind.

Augustina had said that Salter saw her as his anchor. He

was the one who was prone to lose his head. She was the one who kept him from going too far and, perhaps, from saying too much.

Is that what you're afraid of now?

She remembered the way Augustina burst into the room, and the shock in her voice and manner.

Have you two even had a chance to speak since you met me at Upton's?

What if they hadn't? Then, Salter wouldn't know that Augustina had lost her nerve, or that her fear had driven her to tell Rosalind at least something of the truth about the pair of them.

And while Salter might be aware, he was prone to overconfidence, just now he was fully enjoying his own performance. That made him unpredictable. Rosalind had witnessed this phenomenon more than once. It was a common failing among overconfident suitors, natural boasters, and men like her father.

"While I am very pleased to hear you may be exonerated from that earlier mistake," said Rosalind, "that was not what I was going to ask about."

"Oh?" Salter raised one inquiring brow.

"I wanted to ask about your connections to Russell Fullerton."

"Ah. Yes," Salter murmured. "I can understand why that subject would interest you. May I offer my sincere condolences for the loss of your father, Miss Thorne?"

Rosalind nodded once. Out of the corner of her eye, she watched Augustina. The girl had her hands clasped together in her lap, and the knuckles had turned white.

But it wasn't only Augustina. Mrs. Walford too sat rigid and still, her entire attention focused on Salter. Rosalind had the feeling she could have smashed the teapot to the floor and not gotten a reaction out of either one of them, so intent they were on what Salter might have to say.

"I must own that my association with Mr. Fullerton is not something I am proud of," said Salter.

"Salter," said Augustina. "There is no need for you to do this."

He glanced at her, smiling fondly. "Let us make a clean breast of it. Then there will be no more surprises." Now he spoke directly to Rosalind. "And Miss Thorne will be able to expend her energies on helping your mother's charity ball be a success, rather than chasing rumors."

He meant, of course, to shame her.

"Fullerton and I both belong to Graham's Club, Mrs. Walford," Salter went on. "He had heard of my association with your family. Possibly through Louis, although I can't imagine—" He paused and shook his head. "At any rate, he drew me aside one evening and tried to tell me, in confidence, that perhaps I did not want to risk my reputation in association with . . . such persons."

Mrs. Walford went absolutely white. "And what did you say to him?"

"Salter," began Augustina again. "You cannot have paid attention to what such a man said."

"Of course not. I told him to go to—that is, I told him I would not attend to a single word of this nonsense. But then, he mentioned that the late Mr. Walford—that there were certain questions of a political nature. It was all lies, of course," Salter added quickly. "And I knew that. I, of all men, know perfectly well how easy it is for a rumor to get out of hand. Indeed, I wonder if Fullerton thought my previous encounter with Bow Street might leave me more susceptible to believing such stories."

Mrs. Walford said nothing at all. Augustina's gaze darted from Salter to her mother, and back again.

"But then he told me he had proofs. Letters." Salter bowed his head. "He offered to sell them to me."

"Salter," breathed Augustina.

"You don't need to worry about them anymore," said Salter. "The matter is taken care of. These supposed letters are destroyed." He looked directly at Mrs. Walford. "There is no danger whatsoever of your family's name being subject to any further rumor."

Why are you doing this now? Why in front of me? Rosalind thought toward Salter. *Because you want me to hear you have a story ready, you want it to be seen that you have Mrs. Walford in your grip.*

"If that is true, Mr. Salter," said Mrs. Walford, "it would seem I owe you a debt of gratitude."

Salter returned a seated bow. "Nothing is owed, ma'am. I regard your family very much as my own." He let his eyes slip toward Augustina. "I could not permit such a pall to be cast over their reputations." Then, his tone turned hearty. "Especially not with your grand ball so close. I hope very much, Mrs. Walford, that you will not object to my requesting the honor of escorting Augustina?"

Augustina was also looking at her mother, but not as a girl would look upon the achievement of her hopes. It was clear what Salter was doing. He meant to checkmate Mrs. Walford, as well as Rosalind. If the widow believed his story, she would be firmly under obligation to him, and also under his power. Because if Salter had proof that the former Mr. Walford was involved in radical politics, or worse, he could let it "slip out" if he chose to.

It was an underhanded scheme, but it was also a sound one. What did Augustina think of such open blackmail? Rosalind wondered.

The girl did not look pleased. Indeed, to Rosalind, she looked terrified.

"Well." Mrs. Walford smoothed her skirts. "If it is what Augustina wants."

She turned to her daughter, and Rosalind saw an awkward and unfamiliar hint of pleading in her expression.

Salter turned, beaming to Augustina. His expression said, *Look how well I have managed.*

But Augustina did not see it that way. She wasn't even looking at him anymore. She looked to her hands in her lap, and Rosalind had the sudden idea she was trying not to cry.

Perhaps because she had enough family feeling that she did not want to gain her suitor's acceptance in a way that would cost her mother her pride.

Or perhaps she had realized how easily Salter's story could be interpreted as a reason for him to commit murder.

CHAPTER 41

A Chance Encounter

*And such as be founden, and be not culpable,
shall be attached until the coming of the justices,
and their names shall be written in the coroner's
rolls.*

John Impey of the Inner Temple, *The Practice of the Office
of Coroner*

Adam had taken on any number of unsavory duties in his time. He'd stood up all night waiting for poachers, lay down in shallow bogs waiting for highwaymen, and waded into unruly crowds trying to prevent brawls over cards from turning lethal. But none of them could match the sheer misery of patrolling the streets of London in mid-December.

Townsend insisted that Adam was wanted at Carlton House for his particular skills and sharp instincts. When Adam arrived, however, he was given a horse and a patrol of four men, and tasked with the job of walking around the royal residence, from Cleveland Row, to Marlborough Road, to the Mall and back up through the alley behind the stable yards, in order to ensure they all remained free of "suspicious or unsavory" personages.

As a precaution, Adam couldn't fault it. These grand residences tended to have a surprising number of gates and little doors tucked away in the shadows so that the servants could more easily come and go, and not all of them stayed locked as they should. The walls were stout, but a determined man could scale most of them. Adam put two of his patrolmen to the test, and they both managed to climb the wall nearest the stables and drop into the Carlton House gardens in less than two minutes. Not a soul raised the alarm.

He was going to have to request more men, and possibly an allotment of rum to help keep them warm. Adam eyed the gray sky sourly. It was going to be a long night.

It had already been a long day. He'd been up early to be at the station house, as ordered, and from there had marched with the other handpicked patrolmen to Carlton House. Townsend had ridden before them in his carriage. Adam had just had time to get himself signed in with the chief of the house's regular guard and hear his assignment before he had to be signed out again so that he could make his way back to the Bow Street court in time for the inquest into the death of Sir Reginald Thorne.

The inquiry unfolded much as Adam had expected. Sir David presided over an orderly court. The jurors viewed the body, looked over the wounds, and heard them explained. Captain Goutier described how the body had been found, and how Fullerton had been found in the same room covered in blood, and how Turrell Sparkes, now also deceased, had been unable to provide any useful additional information.

Fullerton, shaved, combed, and contemptuous, stood before the coroner. He gave his testimony as if he could not believe he was actually having to explain these things yet again. He said that Sir Reginald was a business associate staying with him for a few days. He said that he'd been out on business all day. He'd come home late and been nearly knocked down by the two men who rushed from his house. Sir Reginald was already dying, if not dead, when Fullerton found him.

Adam noted how Fullerton's gaze roamed the courtroom, searching for something, or someone, he could not find.

Adam took the oath, and the stand, and agreed that the story Fullerton told him now matched well with what he'd said on the night. He confirmed that Captain Goutier had told him that Fullerton was covered in blood when the patrol first found him. He emphasized what Fullerton had tried to gloss over, that Fullerton had chosen to spend his time burning papers while his "business acquaintance" lay dead at his feet. He added that Sir Reginald was known to be an invalid and supposed to be recovering in Bath, which made the assertion that he was a business associate difficult to understand.

Sir David questioned him about the search for the two men, and Adam admitted that no sign of any such persons had been found, neither had any of the neighbors when questioned been able to report they had seen them.

The jury debated the issue for fifteen minutes altogether and returned a verdict of "murder by person or persons unknown," with the recommendation that Russell Fullerton, currently in custody, be bound over for trial in the magistrate's court.

In all, the proceedings took less than two hours from start to finish, and that included the time it took for the jurors to be paid for their service and depart in a body over to The Brown Bear for a pint of beer.

"I'm sorry, Harkness," Sir David had said as the men walked out of the court afterward. "I know you've got your doubts about Fullerton's guilt, but without another plausible story to fit the circumstances . . ."

"I know," said Adam. "How long have we got before the trial, do you think?"

Sir David shook his head. "I'll see if I can find out, but you know as well as I do that the speed of the docket can hinge on anything from whether all the witnesses are sober to what the chief magistrate ate for lunch."

Adam chuckled, but without real warmth. "Well, we must hope, I suppose, that some person in this disaster has been careless."

"I wish you luck." Sir David shook Adam's hand. "How does Miss Thorne?"

"That, sir," piped up a cheerful woman's voice, "is ever the question."

Adam swung around. Behind him stood Alice Littlefield. She carried a notebook and pencil in her gloved hands, indicating that her visit to the inquest had been in at least some measure in her official capacity as a writer for the *London Chronicle*.

"Are you acquainted with Miss Thorne, Miss . . . ?" said Sir David.

"Sir David Royce, may I introduce Miss Alice Littlefield, of the *London Chronicle*," said Adam quickly. When it suited, Alice, like her brother, might fail to mention that anything she heard might end up in the columns of that particular publication.

"Ah." Sir David made a polite bow. "I fear you must excuse me then, I have an appointment."

He strode briskly away. Alice favored Adam with a sour glare. "That was unnecessary."

"Sir David is a friend," said Adam as he started walking up the street.

"So am I." Alice fell into step beside him. "Oh well." She tucked her book and pencil into her reticule. "It's not as if I don't have plenty for the article. The Major will be quite pleased. A gruesome murder is always good for sales. I could only wish it wasn't Rosalind's father."

"Miss Thorne did not come with you?" said Adam.

"No, she had other business elsewhere. Please don't think she's trying to avoid you personally," Alice added.

"I don't. I expect she judged there was nothing useful she could do here."

"Yes, exactly, and why dwell longer on the messy and unpleasant facts of Sir Reginald when she can be busy solving a problem instead?"

Adam looked down at her from the corner of his eye.

"Yes, I'm a little put out with her," said Alice bluntly. She hiked up her hems to negotiate a slush-filled pothole. "I'm afraid you'll find that as intelligent as she is, Rosalind sometimes works a little too hard to make reason fit over emotion."

"I had noticed something of the kind."

"Yes, I expect you had. Well, shall I tender her your regards? She was very disappointed when she heard about your change of assignment."

"As was I. And yes. And as I expect you'll give her all the details of the inquest, tell her I will write soon."

"Naturally. Good luck to you, Mr. Harkness."

Adam had bowed and let her go. It wasn't easy. What he really wanted was to grab her and demand to know how Rosalind had looked, what she was doing, how she fared, and was everything quiet at the house. Townsend didn't seem to have missed the two constables Adam still had delegated to keep watch over Little Russell Street, but he would soon.

Rosalind's personal deadline for resolving this tangle might be the date of Fullerton's trial, but Adam was determined to have it unravelled before Townsend forced him to reassign the men.

So while he rode the monotonous route around the walls of Carlton House, half of Adam's mind was occupied sorting through what was known about the death of Sir Reginald Thorne and Turrell Sparkes.

Which is next to nothing, he thought irritably.

The horse felt the way his body tensed and snorted a warning. Adam clicked his tongue reassuringly and forced himself to relax. That wasn't easy, either. He'd seldom felt so useless.

They turned the final corner onto the Mall.

"All right, men," he called out, mostly to distract himself. "Almost there. Get yourselves a minute in the guard house to thaw out, and then it's back at it."

The acknowledgments were more grumbles than anything else, but Adam couldn't find it in him to reprimand them, especially not as the snow was beginning to fall more thickly now.

They reached the main gates at the same time as a new, gilt-trimmed enclosed carriage with the Prince Regent's crest emblazoned on the door. Adam reined in his horse to let the vehicle go by. Consequently, he had a good view of the lady inside, before she managed to draw her veil down to hide her face.

Adam blinked and then kicked his cranky horse in the ribs to urge the beast to follow the carriage.

They crossed the broad yard and rounded the corner of the west side of the house. It came to a halt beside one of the many side doors of the royal residence. Adam jumped down from his own horse at the same moment that the groom placed the step. The carriage door opened for a woman dressed in an elaborate black velvet cape. If it had not been for his clear glimpse earlier, he never would have known who was concealed beneath those yards of fabric.

But he did know. It was Charlotte Thorne.

Charlotte Thorne, who had come to her sister in distress and then vanished. Charlotte Thorne, who had as good a reason as anyone to wish her father dead and Fullerton compromised.

Charlotte Thorne climbing out of the Prince Regent's carriage while a footman held the house door open for her.

"Miss Sharps," he said, using her pseudonym.

She drew up short. For a moment, he thought she might refuse to acknowledge him.

"Mr. Harkness," she said at last. It was hard to make out her expression under her veil, but her voice was as frosty as the wind blowing over the wall. "This is most unexpected."

"I'm sure it is. You have business here?"

"So it appears."

Adam lowered his voice. "Does Rosalind know you are here?"

"That, sir, is none of your concern."

"I'm afraid it may be. Your whereabouts have become Bow Street business of late."

Charlotte made a low, strangled noise in her throat. "I am afraid I do not have time for this. I am expected."

"I need to speak with you, Miss Sharps," Adam insisted.

"Well, perhaps you should take the matter up with my host," she snapped. Then, she turned and sailed into Carlton House.

The footman closed the door behind her and left Adam standing.

CHAPTER 42

Last-Minute Details

A strange house, where one can't get at the simplest truth without a world of difficulty.

Maria Edgeworth, *Manoevering*

"Do you believe it, Miss Thorne?" asked Amelia. "What Mr. Salter said?"

They were once again in Charlotte's snug carriage, being driven back to Little Russell Street. After their conversation with Mr. Salter, Mrs. Walford had declared she was too exhausted and amazed to continue, and asked Rosalind to meet her at Upton's the next day. Rosalind, unable to think of an excuse to stay—at least not one that she could offer in front of Mrs. Walford, Augustina, and Salter together—had no choice but to comply.

"I think I believe part of it," Rosalind told Amelia. "The problem is, I can't make up my mind about which part."

"I must say, Miss Augustina didn't look any too pleased, even after all the trouble he says he went through for the sake of her family."

"And after all the trouble she went through to point me towards her brothers." Rosalind looked out the window. The weather had turned gray again, and the clouds pressed down low over the rooftops. There would be more snow soon. "I wonder if she expected him to come back at all."

"I don't understand."

"When Miss Walford met us at Upton's, she carefully and firmly pointed me towards her brothers as the troublemakers in this matter. She wanted to know if they had anything to do with Salter's disappearance. Now, Salter comes back, openly, and her shock is real. So is her surprise that he has a story to explain away every single thing I'd so far discovered."

"And there's that note," said Amelia. "The one her mother gave you."

"Yes, that too." Rosalind laid her hand over her reticule. "Which makes me wonder why he did not let her know that he was planning to come back to her. Augustina described a genuine partnership between them. A less than respectable one, but a partnership all the same. If they had a regular method of communication, why would he not let her know?"

And why involve the maid? Augustina's usual methods for circumventing her mother involved her brothers.

Of course, if she truly believed her brothers were involved in keeping Salter away from the house, she might be less eager to involve them in her private machinations.

"I wonder if anyone in this family is talking to each other at all," said Rosalind, half-bewildered, half-exasperated. "It seems that they all have their own schemes, and each one is dependent on the actions of the others. At the same time, they've become so used to not being able to trust one another, they cannot break the habit of keeping their own secrets."

Amelia shivered. "Secrets quick become habit. That's a fact."

"Yes," agreed Rosalind softly. "Yes, it is." But even as she spoke, the words touched off a spark in her mind. "Amelia, you said you heard from the Misses Hodges that their father was being driven mad by all the requests from Mrs. Walford's committee. You said they were hiring extra men. Do you know what it was those men were for?"

Amelia frowned and hesitated. Then she shook her head. "If they knew, miss, they didn't say."

Rosalind nodded. She also stretched up awkwardly and rapped hard on the carriage ceiling.

"Yes, miss?" called the driver through the trap.

"A change of plans. Take us to Upton's Assembly Rooms."

"Aye, miss," he replied, unperturbed, and Rosalind dropped back onto her bench.

"Upton's, Miss Thorne?" said Amelia. "Now?"

"Yes, now," replied Rosalind. "I need to start finding out exactly what Mrs. Walford is keeping from me, and Upton's may be my best chance."

"Miss Thorne! I did not expect to see you." Mr. Hodges stood up to bow as the porter showed Rosalind and Amelia into his office. The assembly room manager was a balding man with shaggy brows and wore a pair of pince-nez spectacles perched on his high-arched nose. "I heard about your father. My sincerest condolences."

"Thank you, Mr. Hodges," replied Rosalind. "And I honestly did not expect to be here at this hour, but I've just left Mrs. Walford . . ."

"Ah, yes, Mrs. Walford." Mr. Hodges tucked his thumbs into his waistcoat pockets. "I don't know where you found this one, Miss Thorne."

"I understand she's been difficult, and I know you have risen to the occasion."

"I hope I have, and I have to say, I hope it's worth it. If this was the Season—well, never you mind. That's just me grousing is all. How can I assist you?"

Rosalind held up her notebook. "If you could just walk

me through the rooms so that I can check off the progress with the decorations, and the furniture arrangements . . ."

He looked at her mourning attire, his brows knitted in consternation. They both knew she should not be even leaving the house yet. For a moment, Rosalind thought he would make some remark. Thankfully, he seemed to think the better of it, and just said, "But of course. If you'll come with me."

Rosalind followed Mr. Hodges up the stairs and through each of the rooms. Workmen thronged through the space, hanging bunting and silk in the charity colors of red and blue. In the card room, the muslin covers had been stripped from all of the tables, and red and blue ribbons tied the curtains back and made rosettes to decorate the walls. Rosalind held her book open as she walked, diligently, if somewhat impatiently, checking off each of the points she had listed.

If the event was to go forward, this was not the time to neglect the details.

The tables were in place in the long dining room. Rosalind queried as to when the flowers were expected to be delivered and about the number of cooks and staff to be brought in to oversee the service. Had the wine been delivered yet? How many more cases had yet to arrive? These were points that they had been over before, but Mr. Hodges answered her questions patiently.

"Everything looks quite in order, Mr. Upton, as I knew it would be," said Rosalind as they left the bustling card room. "Now as to the extra men . . ."

"Yes, I had Mrs. Walford quizzing me about that just yesterday. I imagine you'll want to make sure of the strong room as well?"

"Yes," said Rosalind at once, consulting her book as if that item were written there. "Exactly."

Mr. Hodges took Rosalind down the plain, but clean, service stairs. They passed a number of women in laundress uniforms hurrying up with yet more linens, herded by Mr.

Hodges's oldest daughter. Once they reached the passageway for the first floor, he paused.

"Just let me fetch a light." He ducked into the nearest of the workrooms and returned with a lit candle. "If you don't mind . . . ?"

Rosalind took the candle from him so his hands were free to sort through the ring of keys on his belt. Uncomfortable memories of the turnkey and Clerkenwell jail rose, but she batted them back. At length they came to a solid, windowless door, banded with iron and painted black. Mr. Upton worked the lock and stood aside to let Rosalind go first.

It was a plain workroom, with a table at its center. Shelves lined the walls. There were no windows or other doors.

"Good as a bank this." Mr. Hodges rapped hard on the door. "The boxes will be safe as houses. Naught but the one key, and I'll be keeping that with me." He shook his head. "Was the lady ever robbed, Miss Thorne?"

"Not to my knowledge."

Mr. Hodges pursed his lips. "Well, maybe she doesn't trust our London ways. I must have gone over this with her a dozen times."

"It is her first experience with such a public event," murmured Rosalind. "It is perhaps natural that she should experience some thrill of the nerves."

"Thrill of the nerves." Mr. Hodges chuckled. "Ever the diplomat you are, Miss Thorne. Well, inexperienced she certainly is. I tried to tell her that no matter how fine this auction of hers is, there won't be more than a few hundred pounds sterling changing hands at the ball itself. All the rest will be in promises and notes. Any bank drafts will be written the day after."

"But she didn't listen?"

"She did not." Mr. Hodges sighed. "She seems to think there'll be a deal of cash, and that it must be kept not only under lock and key but guard as well."

"Yes. Well." Rosalind held the candle up higher and turned in place, as if examining the windowless room. "I thank you for your time, Mr. Hodges, and your trouble. I'll be back with Mrs. Walford again tomorrow, but I'll do what I can to reassure her that everything really is in order."

"She ought to know herself by now. Sorry, Miss Thorne, grousing again. I just don't like it when I feel like my work's being treated as second-rate, is all."

"It's perfectly all right, Mr. Hodges," murmured Rosalind. "I feel much the same."

CHAPTER 43

The Importance of Orderly Recordkeeping

*And should this letter be brought to light, she
must be irremediably convicted of the basest
duplicity.*

Maria Edgeworth, *Manoevering*

Rosalind and Amelia arrived home to an empty house. Alice, Rosalind knew, had gone to the inquest and this evening planned to visit her brother, George, and his wife.

"He's made a whole series of entirely unreasonable threats about what he'll do if I don't come and catch him up on everything that's happened," Alice had said. "I shouldn't give in, but I don't want him to turn into a grump for Hannah."

She had hoped to hear about the inquest, and if Alice had spoken with Mr. Harkness and did he have any message for her, but her trip to Upton's had kept her too late.

But perhaps it was just as well. Rosalind's mind felt distracted enough as it was. She did not need extra thoughts of Adam Harkness cluttering it any further.

She told herself this two or three more times, just to make sure she believed it.

"Should I make some tea, miss?" Amelia asked, as she

helped Rosalind off with her bonnet. "I'm afraid at this point, there won't be anything but cold pie to go with it."

"That will do nicely," said Rosalind. She did not truly want a cold pie, especially the pie Amelia had made yesterday, but it was her own fault for keeping her maid away from home so long.

"Be sure to invite Charlotte's driver in and make sure he has his tea as well," said Rosalind. "Let him know I'll be needing the carriage tonight." Tired as she was, her day was a long way from over.

"Yes, miss." Amelia folded Rosalind's coat over her arm.

"Oh, and, Amelia, that was well done, back at the Walfords."

"Thank you, miss," replied Amelia primly, but there was a cheeky light in her eye. "I'm glad I could give satisfaction."

In the parlor, Rosalind poked up the fire and drew her woolen shawl around her shoulders. She sat down at her desk and riffled through her carefully ordered stacks of correspondence.

It was odd, she reflected. The past few days had as much to do with letters as they did with deceptions. Sometimes they were one in the same.

Rosalind pulled out the note Augustina had sent to lure Rosalind to Upton's and signed with her mother's name. This, she smoothed open on the blotter.

Then she opened her reticule and brought out the other note Mrs. Walford had given her just today—the one Mrs. Walford said was written by Augustina and that she intercepted from Augustina's maid. She laid it beside the first letter.

Then, to be certain of what she was seeing, Rosalind also brought out one of the many letters that had passed between her and Mrs. Walford during the past few months.

Rosalind looked from one letter to the next. There was no question. The brief note attributed to Augustina that seemed to beg Mr. Salter for some reply had been written by Mrs. Walford. The sharp tips given to her letters *e* and *s* were unmistakable, as was the elaborate curl in the crossing of her *t*'s.

The letter summoning Rosalind to Upton's was in quite another hand—that one most likely *had* been written by Augustina.

Augustina worries about what her mother is doing, and her mother worries about what Augustina is doing, and both of them fear what may have happened to Mr. Salter. And both of them want to use me to solve their problems. As, it appears, does Mr. Russell Fullerton.

But they don't want the truth. They just want the problems to go away.

Rosalind pressed her fingers against her eyes. Strain and confusion had set her head to aching. *Augustina wants me to worry about her brothers. Fullerton wants me to worry about my sister. My sister wants me to worry about Fullerton. Mrs. Walford wants me to worry about Salter.*

Which is interesting because Salter wants me to worry about him, too, and that's why he was so willing to talk about such private matters in front of me. He wanted me to know he had an explanation to counter anything I might say. And that he, too, had power over Mrs. Walford.

But Mrs. Walford lied to me. Rosalind touched the note that Mrs. Walford had said was from Augustina. *She did not believe I would help her find Salter without this. Why is that?* She bit her lip as the answer came. *Because she came to me as the worried mother, and so must continue with that disguise. Which means she is trying to hide something.*

But there was another possibility, and it had been there from the beginning. There was just so much clutter, accusation, and deception, Rosalind had not been able to see it clearly.

Rosalind had assumed that it was Fullerton and Salter who had fallen in among the Bonapartists. But Salter said Fullerton had information about the late Mr. Walford. He said Mr. Walford had been involved in radical politics.

Mrs. Walford had loved her husband. Mrs. Walford, despite all the chaos and scandal that circled around her family, insisted on going forward with her charity ball. The cause was that important to her, she said, and to her late husband. Despite her declarations of worry about her daughter, despite her fears of elopement, the cause and the charity ball remained more important.

All of which raised the question, What was Mrs. Walford really doing?

Rosalind reached up to the shelf of books above her desk.

The life of any London hostess was mapped out in her personal ledgers. A hostess would have a visiting book to record callers and cards received. There would be a dinner book to preserve menus, seating arrangements, and guest lists, not to mention account books for expenditures and receipts. If she was truly diligent, there would be an additional book for correspondence, as well as a day book or journal.

Rosalind kept her own set of books. Her visiting book had changed in character from her youth. Now it contained the names of as many milliners, porters, and shopkeepers as it did society matrons and their assorted daughters. Her correspondence book overflowed.

But it was her dinner book that she opened now.

Rosalind's dinner book was not a record of her own dinners but of other people's. Some of the information it contained she gleaned from friends whose letters she copied into the pages. But there were also plenty of newspaper clippings. The grandest hostesses of the *haut ton* had their entertainments duly described and recorded by writers like Alice, and, naturally, the guest lists were published along with all the other details. A record of London dinners could provide an excellent road map of who was currently welcome in which houses.

Rosalind flipped her pages over to *H*, and to Holland House.

Lady Holland had been at the opera on that so-eventful opening night. Mrs. Walford had gone to speak to her.

Augustina said that the only people they knew in London were mother's political and émigré friends.

Lady Holland was highly political. Lord Holland was an outspoken partisan who did not scruple to make speeches and write letters declaring that imprisoning Napoleon on St. Helena was a blot on the national honor.

And yet, Mrs. Walford had declared they knew no one in London, and when she needed someone to look into Salter's background, or to assist her daughter in society, she had not gone to Lady Holland but to a stranger.

Rosalind turned the pages and ran her fingers down printed lists, looking for accounts of the dinners at Holland House. Those guest lists were full of active members of the both houses of Parliament and also showed a decided preference for members of London's extensive French émigré community.

She saw no mention of the Walfords.

She did, however, find several names that were entirely familiar. Rosalind left the dinner book open on her desk and reached for the satchel she'd taken to the Walfords. She extracted a notebook and flipped it open to the guest list for the charity ball.

She took up her pencil, underlined what she found, and marked the pages with slips of paper as well.

Because every last member on the charity board, except for Mrs. Walford and her son Etienne, had dined at Holland House at least once this season.

Rosalind sat back and stared at the books, and the letters.

She thought about the countess, and she thought about her father, and Salter, and Fullerton.

She thought about Fullerton and the papers he had been burning, and the scraps that Mr. Harkness had retrieved.

She pushed the books and letters aside in an uncharacteristically tidy heap and pulled out a fresh sheet of paper, took a quill out of the stand. She bent over the page and began to write.

She had barely signed her name when the parlor door opened, bringing with it a blast of cold air from the foyer.

"Oh, thank goodness!" Alice hurried over to the fire and held out her hands. "I'm half-frozen."

"Alice!" cried Rosalind. "I thought you were having dinner with George and Hannah."

"I was, but Hannah's under the weather, poor thing. Although I've got my suspicions as to what the cause might be."

"Meaning?" Rosalind folded the note she'd been working on.

"Meaning I might soon become a crotchety maiden aunt." Alice's dark eyes sparkled merrily. "Don't say anything to George. I'm not sure Hannah's even told him yet. So. What happened with the Walfords today? That is where you went today?"

"To the Walfords, and to Upton's," Rosalind told her.

"Upton's?" said Alice. "What did you want there?"

"To find out what Mrs. Walford has been doing when I'm not about."

"And did you?" Alice left the hearth and dropped into her own chair.

"Some of it." Rosalind leaned toward her friend. "Alice, you know that we've been trying to work out how and why Fullerton and Salter came to be involved with Bonapartists?"

"Yes."

"I'm not sure that they are. But Mrs. Walford definitely is."

Alice stared. "You'd better start from the beginning."

"You can see for yourself."

Rosalind opened the books on her desk and showed Alice the list of board members for Mrs. Walford's charity, and how well it matched up with the guest lists for the dinners at Holland House.

"Good Lord," murmured Alice. "But what can it mean?"

"I think Mrs. Walford's widows and orphans charity is a blind. I think she means to give the money she raises to some Bonapartist cause."

"You're joking."

"I'm not. Mr. Hodges says she's been pestering him about the security of his strong room. He tells me she expects there to be a great deal of cash stored in the strong room. What if the plan is something like this? After the ball, Mrs. Walford is going to have the ticket money, plus whatever money is raised at the auction, transferred to some agent?"

"Good Lord, Rosalind, how many plots are we dealing with? I am beginning to lose count. There's Fullerton and your father, and Fullerton and Salter, and now Mrs. Walford and all the young Walfords—"

"Assuming they're working together on this thing."

"And Salter and Augustina in it for themselves." Alice threw up her hands. "I give up!"

Rosalind looked at the letters and the lists. "They must be connected," she said. "We just haven't seen how yet."

"Does that include your father's murder?" asked Alice. "You did remember the inquest was today?"

"Yes. Father's murder, and Mr. Sparkes, as well. Because if father was not killed, Sparkes would not have been, either."

"Fullerton has been bound over for trial," said Alice.

"I felt sure that he would be."

"You're not going to talk about it, are you?"

"No," said Rosalind flatly. "I haven't the time."

"Why not?"

"Because I want this settled, Alice. I am tired of wading through this morass of confusion, and I am especially tired of the feeling that I am being used, by Fullerton, by Father, rest him, by Mrs. Walford *and* all the Walford siblings, not to mention Mr. Salter, and yes, by her grace the Countess Lieven."

Alice cocked a thoughtful brow toward her. "So what are you going to do?"

"First, I am going to make sure this letter gets to Mr. Harkness." Rosalind held up the note. "Then, I'm going to find out if Fullerton left anything useful behind him before he was arrested."

"You're going back to his flat?" asked Alice.

"On the contrary. I'm going to break into his rooms at Graham's Club."

CHAPTER 44

A Meeting of Like-Minded Fellows

A covenant also, contained in a deed to do a direct act, or to omit one, is another species of express contracts . . .

John Impey of the Inner Temple, *The Common Pleader*

It was a cold wait until the Walford sons emerged from the nest. Salter cursed when he saw the two of them together. He'd hoped to corner Louis alone.

Evidently Madame Walford decided her eldest son wanted watching.

Salter had, of course, been turned out of doors immediately after the Thorne woman left, without any chance to speak to Augustina. Not that it mattered. They would be together tonight. *And every night after this.*

But first they must make sure of her brothers.

Normally, he'd leave them to 'Stina. She had, after all, been managing them since they were all in leading strings. But it was highly likely that she was going to be under her mother's eye until late tonight. So, that left him on watch in the cold.

Well, what cannot be cured must be endured. He blew on

his hands and ducked out of the doorway where he'd been hiding himself. Etienne—who despite appearances could be the quicker of the two—turned abruptly, yanking on his older brother's sleeve as he did.

Salter pasted a broad grin on his face and opened both hands as if in greeting.

"Gentlemen!" he cried. "We should talk, don't you agree?"

"God above, Salter!" cried Louis. "You've got a lot of balls coming back here now!"

"I agree. But I've also been standing in this foul cold for I-don't-know-how-long waiting for you both to come out. Come, I'll stand you both to a drink." He gestured up the street, in the direction of a public house.

The brothers eyed each other.

"Don't do it," said Etienne.

"We need to know what he's up to," said Louis.

"As if he'd tell us," Etienne muttered, again proving that he really was the smarter of the pair.

"Go along if you want to," said Louis.

"I'd rather he was with us," said Salter. "You'll only have to tell him everything later anyway. I know you lot can't keep secrets between yourselves."

"And if I won't go?" asked Etienne.

Salter shrugged. "Go tell your mother your brother's in bad company then, see if she thanks you for it."

Etienne glared at him. Louis shoved his brother's shoulder. "Come on, Etienne. What harm?"

Etienne muttered something under his breath but gave way. Salter grinned and gestured for the two of them to walk on ahead.

The pub was filled with carters and gardeners, shop-keepers and grocers, all the sorts whose livelihood came from supplying the prosperous houses that lined these streets. The arrival of three gentlemen caused a silence to fall, but as they took the table in the far corner and did nothing more extraordinary than collect three glasses of hot toddy from the landlord, they were soon ignored.

"So what were you doing back at the house," asked Louis, blowing hard on his toddy.

"Smoothing things over with your mother." Salter sipped his drink cautiously. He didn't know the house, or the strength of the drinks. He needed a clear head for this. "I'm only sorry it took so long. But things, as you know, have become a little complicated."

Etienne, for his part, ignored his drink altogether. He just leaned back in the chair and stretched out one long leg. "Do you know what, Salter? I rather admire your gall."

"Etienne, don't be an ass," muttered Louis.

"No, I do," said Etienne. "Very few men of your sort are actually ready to put themselves in real danger for money, and yet"—he lifted his steaming glass and eyed Salter over the rim—"here you are."

"Am I in danger?" inquired Salter mildly. "From whom? Not you two?" He paused. Etienne was doing his best to look threatening, and it was all Salter could do not to break into a laugh. "You'd better talk to your mother before you do anything. She might have new orders for you."

Etienne flushed and made to get to his feet. Louis put a hand on his brother's arm. "Steady on. He's only trying to get a rise out of us."

Salter smiled. "I do apologize, of course."

Etienne subsided, reluctantly.

"You said you wanted to talk," said Louis. "What about?"

"Our plans, of course." Salter took another sip of the toddy and made himself swallow. The stuff had been sweetened and cooked to the point it was more like drinking tar than liquor.

"We have no plans," said Etienne flatly. "Not anymore."

"I'm afraid that's simply not true, Etienne," Salter told him. "We are going ahead, as we discussed."

Louis took this news with admirable calm, but a distinct tightening around his jaw. Etienne's blue eyes started out of their sockets. "Louis, you're not listening to this."

"Louis doesn't have a choice," said Salter. "And frankly, neither do you."

Etienne leaned over the table. For a minute, Salter thought the boy was going to grab his sleeve, but he just whispered harshly. "You're only alive because we changed our minds. You should think about that."

Salter leaned toward him so they were all but nose-to-nose. "I'm alive," he said, enunciating each word clearly, so as not to be mistaken, "because you both misjudged me and the situation." He sat back. "You should be thinking about what you're going to be telling your mother, by the by. She was not at all pleased to see me, and will certainly be wanting a word with you."

"You need to stop mentioning our mother," growled Etienne. To emphasize the point, he curled his right hand into a tight fist.

Salter ignored this. "You need to stop telling me what I should and should not say." He took another swallow of the truly awful rum. "Now, I've got no quarrel with you, or with what happened." He rested one elbow over the back of his chair, feigning a casual pose. At the same time, he measured the distance between himself and the young hothead, ready to fall sideways and out of reach if he needed to. One hand toyed with his glass. A splash of that stuff in the face would slow Etienne down nicely, if it came to it. "That night, you were sent to get rid of me, I accept that. If Augustina was my part of my family, I wouldn't have been pleased to have me breach the gate, either. But it's what happened afterwards that you need to deal with immediately."

"What do you mean?"

"I'm sure you've already thought of some story to explain your whereabouts for when Sir Reginald Thorne died. But you need to remember that I can contradict that, if I have to. I'm sure that Bow Street would be very interested to hear you went from threatening me to try to threaten Mr. Fullerton."

Etienne turned scarlet, but Louis just contemplated him coolly. "And what would Augustina say to learning you sold out another man to try to save your own hide?"

"I'm perfectly sure of Augustina's loyalty. Are you, Louis?"

"You've already told her, haven't you?" said Etienne. "You must have, to keep her with you."

"Actually, I haven't. She's already been forced to choose between me and you, and I'd rather not make it any harder on her if I don't have to." He leaned forward. "Come now, I'm willing to let bygones be bygones. What do you say, Louis? You need the money as much as we do. There's no reason at all why we shouldn't just go ahead with things."

Louis was thinking. His bright eyes darted back and forth, showing all his internal calculations clearly.

Come on, come on. I need this money. So do you. Come on.

Salter saw the exact moment Louis made his decision. A heartbeat later, he turned to his brother.

"Etienne?" said Louis.

Etienne folded his arms. "No," he said. "I want no part of it."

"But we had an agreement—"

Etienne cut him off. "I was wrong to make it. I won't repeat my mistake." He got to his feet and tossed off the rest of his toddy with one go. "And before either one of you get any ideas." He set the glass back down and got to his feet. "Remember that if I'm found dead and Mother has to go into mourning, there won't be any charity ball, and all your work will have been for nothing."

Etienne jammed his hat on his head and walked out.

Louis stared as Etienne stalked out of the pub. He cursed, jumped to his feet, and slid out from behind the table. "Wait here," he said to Salter. "I'll get him."

He didn't bother to look back, just ran out into the darkening night. The streets were full, and he had to fight his way through the crowd of men and women jostling with one another on their way home. The crowds also meant it took longer than it should have to spot Etienne's gray coat and shining hat among the forest of others.

Louis shoved and elbowed his way forward until he caught his brother by the shoulder and spun him around.

"Etienne!"

Etienne shook him off. "Get off me!" growled Etienne.

"No," said Louis. "Etienne, you have to talk to me."

"Why?"

"Because I'm your brother."

"And I'm yours, and you just sided with that . . . creature." Etienne pointed over his shoulder toward the pub.

"I know. I know." Louis held up both hands, gesturing for Etienne to calm down, even though he knew it wouldn't work. But he had to do something. Etienne could ruin everything right now, and he would if he got mad enough. "If there was any other way, I would never have done it."

"Any other way to do what, Louis?" Etienne demanded. "What are you actually doing?"

"The same thing Augustina is," Louis answered. "I'm doing whatever I have to to get myself out of this mess that our mother has created." *Our mother, our father, and you, my brother.* "I understand you when you say you can't be a part of this anymore. I really do. Because I feel the same way."

"Then stop listening to Salter and come home!" Etienne seized his arm. "If we both talk to Mother, she'll listen."

Louis covered his brother's hand where it held his sleeve. "What then? We'll all be trapped, just like before. The only thing to do is move forward."

Etienne abruptly let go of Louis's arm, and Louis tensed, ready for the blow he was sure was coming. But Etienne just waved dismissively. "Which just happens to be what you want to do. How convenient."

"Then tell me what else to do."

"You could try honoring our parents' sacrifice instead of mocking it."

"Sacrifice?" Louis barked out a laugh. "What sacrifice? They've spent money. Money that should be coming to you and me, by the way. And 'Stina. It's not like they've really risked anything."

"I'm not sure His Majesty's agents would agree with you."

Idiot! Louis swore, glanced around, grabbed his brother's arm, and dragged him closer to the wall of the green grocers.

"If that's the way you feel, why did you agree to go along in the first place?" demanded Louis in a harsh whisper. Etienne didn't answer. "Ah. I see." Louis nodded. "To get rid of me."

Etienne drew himself up, trying to muster some dignity. Louis was only just able to stop himself from rolling his eyes. Etienne always did this when he was caught out in a moral contradiction, and it never worked. "I am not proud of myself."

"No, I imagine not," drawled Louis. "I'm sure it dimmed that shining light of honor you carry inside yourself. But it's all right with me if that's what you want. Easier all around. We'll do the work, and all you have to do is hold fast to your wish to have Mother to yourself. After tomorrow night, you

won't have to worry about me or Augustina anymore. Whatever you and Mother want to do, there'll be no stopping you.
Seen in that light, we're doing you quite the favor."

Etienne looked away, as if he could see some answer float-
ing on the wind above the people's heads.

"You do realize Salter probably killed this Sir Reginald,"
he said.

Louis waited until a gaggle of clerks and shop girls had
passed by.

"I do know," Louis breathed as loudly as he dared. "All
the better for him to get out of the country, *quietly.*"

"And you'd let 'Stina go off with a murderer?"

Louis looked his brother right in the eye. "What makes
you think I'm going to let her?"

Etienne narrowed his eyes. Louis made himself keep his
gaze steady. *Believe me, believe me, believe me,* he prayed
silently. *Just a little longer, and then it won't matter anymore
which of us did what.*

All at once, Etienne's shoulders sagged, and Louis had his
answer.

"So you won't say anything to Mother?"

"Yes, all right," muttered Etienne.

"That's all you have to do, Etienne," Louis was saying.
"And as soon as we're gone, you can tell her whatever you
want."

Etienne's lips flickered into a thin, sharp smile. "Oh, I will,
believe me."

CHAPTER 45

Masquerade

*He was connected with a set of selfish young men
of fashion, whose opinions stood him instead of
law, equity, and morality . . .*

Maria Edgeworth, *The Dun*

The one time Rosalind had entered inside the exclusive precincts of Graham's Club, she had also been in disguise. That, however, had been the night of the Cyprian's Ball, when women were openly welcomed in the club. She'd been able to slip in through the front door.

She'd expected a bit more trouble this time, but only because she had not counted on Charlotte's familiarity with the club, and its staff.

Charlotte ordered her driver to take them around to the back of the club, and instructed him to let them off at the corner. Moving with perfect confidence in the dark and narrow street, she approached the club and the doorman.

"Good evening, Patrick," she purred. "What a dreadful cold night for you."

"Ah, I've had worse, Miss Sharps," he replied. "Now, I hope you're not after me to let you in here, are you?"

"Would I ask you to risk your job for me?" Charlotte laughed. "I just thought you might like a drink. On a night like this, you certainly deserve one." She held up a pair of coins and then pressed them into the porter's palm. "For all your kindness to me."

The porter snickered and pocketed the coins. He also turned his back and strolled up the street a little ways, just as if he was stretching his legs. Charlotte nipped through the low back door, with Rosalind right behind her.

They found themselves in a dark and confined space with a plain wooden stairway rising to the left. The only light was a bare glimmer from some window overhead. The place smelled of dust, refuse, and old onions.

"I hope you know where we're to go," breathed Charlotte. "I've never had the privilege of visiting Mr. Fullerton's rooms."

"Fourth floor," said Rosalind. "Room eight."

Gathering up her hems, Charlotte started climbing the stairs. Again, Rosalind followed, bemused and nervous. Charlotte had been quiet on the ride here. Her only remark was how effectively the white cuffs and collar that Amelia had stitched turned Rosalind's mourning dress turned it into a maid's uniform, especially with the addition of a white mob cap.

Now, following behind her, Rosalind wondered if she'd made a mistake in trusting her sister. Charlotte stood on the cusp of a new life. She had so much to gain and so much to lose. She had already lied, and those lies still hung in the air between them. Rosalind had chosen to set them aside, but they were still there.

Do you trust me? Charlotte's question echoed in Rosalind's mind.

She had thought that by asking for help, and bringing Charlotte here, she could prove to them both that her trust in her sister was real. But Rosalind found her doubts would not be banished simply because it was what she wanted.

They reached the third landing. Rosalind was struggling to breathe quietly. Charlotte paused and drew off her rich, wine-red velvet cloak and handed it to Rosalind. Like Rosalind, she had abandoned mourning for the night. Rosalind smoothed the cloak over her arms and assumed a maid's posture—back and shoulders straight, eyes modestly cast downward. It wasn't so different from how she'd been taught to stand when getting ready for her debut. Charlotte cast an appraising eye over her, and then reached out and straightened her cap slightly.

She opened the door and glided through. Rosalind, despite her doubts, followed behind.

After the darkness of the stairway, the light in the corridor felt dazzling. Graham's had been famously fitted for gaslight, and the sconces blazed on both sides of a corridor hung with gilt framed mirrors and numerous paintings of horses, dogs, and smiling women.

They had not gone ten steps before a footman in the club's livery turned into the hallway, carrying a silver tray. Rosalind's heart froze, but Charlotte just seized her hand and giggled with a showy, girlish air, and ran past the startled servant, pausing just long enough to wink at him.

Rosalind waited for the shout for them to stop, but none came.

"Here it is," said Charlotte. "Eight. Where's the key?"

Rosalind, fumbling slightly because of the cape, pulled the key from her coat pocket. She passed it to Charlotte, who unlocked the door so they could both duck inside.

Darkness filled the room. The only light came from the corridor behind them, but there were candles in the stand by the door. Rosalind took one up and held it to the flame in the nearest gas sconce to light, and then used that to light the others.

Charlotte locked the door. Both paused for a moment,

breathing and listening, and looking about themselves in the flickering light.

"Well," murmured Charlotte. "No one's ever going to accuse the man of good taste."

Fullerton's rooms were a study in gilt, silk, and marble. Lavish paintings decorated the walls. The bed was hung with rich velvet curtains and tied with gold cords.

Rosalind thought of Fullerton in his prison cell and decided she should turn away from that. The emotions it raised did her no credit at all.

"We must hurry." She laid Charlotte's cape on the bed. "The footman . . ."

"Will assume we're, or rather I'm, here for an assignation with a member and won't say anything," said Charlotte calmly. "Do we know what we're looking for?"

"Letters, papers, notes, bank drafts." Rosalind tugged on the drawer of the bedside table. "Anything that might indicate what his recent business was."

The drawer was locked, but Rosalind was ready for that. She'd already noticed that Fullerton's key ring did not include any smaller keys such as would fit the lock on a desk or table. She dug in her coat pocket and came up with a letter opener.

"I'm surprised your runner has not already been here," remarked Charlotte. She opened the huge, carved wardrobe and began pulling out the drawers and peering through the hanging clothing.

"He's a principal officer, and he's been assigned to new duties," said Rosalind shortly as she slid her letter opener into the crack above the drawer.

"So you haven't spoken to him?"

"I've written him. I hope to see him tomorrow. Why do you ask?"

Charlotte shook her head. "I don't think he likes me."

"He worries about me," said Rosalind. The drawer gave a satisfying click and slid open.

"I worry about you." Charlotte stared at the open drawer. "Although, perhaps not for the right reasons."

The drawer held several porcelain snuff boxes, a woman's brooch in the shape of a flower, and a necklace of garnets. No letters nor memorandum books.

Charlotte in the meantime was digging under the pillows and the mattress. "Be sure to check behind the paintings," she said. "Many gentlemen keep a secret cupboard in the wall or under the floor boards."

"Don't forget to look under the bed," said Rosalind. "People will keep doing the obvious thing."

"I should think a man like Fullerton . . ." She stopped. "No, you're right. There's a trunk here. Help me."

It was a low, flat, leather box, bound and studded with brass. It was also abominably heavy, and it took both of them to drag it out.

"What does he have in here? Cast iron?" muttered Charlotte.

Rosalind knelt down and tried the lid. It was locked, of course.

"Here, let me." Charlotte knelt beside her and pulled two pearl-headed pins from her hair. A long, golden curl fell across her neck.

Rosalind scooted to one side. Charlotte bent down close to the lock and stuck both pins inside. Her eyes narrowed down to a squint of concentration as she flicked the top pin up and down, bit by bit working it deeper into the lock. Rosalind's heart hammered against her ribs, almost drowning out the soft clicks of Charlotte's pins against the delicate, hidden mechanism.

"And you worried about me and my letter opener," murmured Rosalind.

"Yes, well, you're supposed to be the respectable one."

Watching was difficult. Rosalind's attention flickered from the door, to her sister, and back again. An unwanted spasm of nerves shuddered through her. Charlotte was taking too long. Charlotte could not possibly do this. Where could she have learned it? Rosalind wanted to ask, and she wanted to urge Charlotte to hurry. She wanted to snatch those ridiculous pins from her hands.

Then came a last click, louder than the others. Charlotte sat back on her heels. Rosalind stared at her for a moment.

"You never told me you could do that."

"There's a great deal I haven't told you yet." Charlotte tucked her pins back into her hair. "And I suspect there's a great deal you haven't told me."

Rosalind ignored that pointed retort. She snapped the latches on the trunk. Charlotte brought the candelabra close while Rosalind lifted the lid.

Inside lay piles of neatly folded clothing—stacks of shirts, stockings, breeches, and boots. Charlotte grimaced, disappointed.

But why so heavy?

Rosalind bit her lip and dug through the old clothing, down to the bottom of the trunk, until her hands touched metal.

A strong box.

No, two.

No, three.

She grabbed the first one to lift and nearly dropped it.

"Good Lord, what's he keeping in here?" she breathed. "Charlotte . . ."

Charlotte handed her the candelabra and pulled her pins out again. This time she took longer. Rosalind looked to the door, and the clock, and bit her lip. There was no reason for anyone to come here, that they knew of, but then, how much did they know about Fullerton's friends, and his enemies?

"Got it," whispered Charlotte triumphantly. She lifted the box lid. Rosalind raised the candles and stared.

The candlelight fell on stacks of gold coins. Sovereigns and guineas. Piles of them, filling the box.

All three boxes.

And she knew.

"He was going to run," she murmured. "Mr. Harkness told me he'd been calling in his debts." She lifted one gold coin. "He was packed and ready to leave."

"Perhaps as a precaution?" suggested Charlotte. "In case something went wrong?"

"But what?"

Charlotte had no time to answer.

The doorknob rattled.

CHAPTER 46

A Real Risk of Discovery

*Though little accustomed to hold his opinion
against the arguments or the wishes of the rich and
fair, he, upon this occasion stood his ground . . .*

Maria Edgeworth, *Manoevering*

Rosalind stared at her sister. There was only a heartbeat to react and they both moved. Like mistress and maid in a Drury Lane farce, they shut the trunk, shoved it under the bed. Charlotte dove under the bed. Rosalind blew out the candles and dove after her.

The door opened a heartbeat later. Rosalind heard the soft shuffle of feet on the carpet, moving with exaggerated care. A pair of men's buckled dress pumps came into view, outlined in a circle of golden lamplight. Rosalind rolled her eyes and strained with all her might, but she could see no higher than the gentleman's calves clad in anonymous white stockings.

The man stopped in the middle of the room and turned. The circle of light on the carpet grew slowly, so he must have raised the lamp. Rosalind held her breath. Beside her, Charlotte bit her lip.

He must have seen what he wanted. He crossed the room, moving more quickly now. There was a rustling noise and a thud.

His heels faced the bed. Rosalind gathered her nerve and made a decision. Carefully, she scooted herself forward.

Charlotte clamped her hand on Rosalind's wrist. Rosalind froze. The shoes turned, just a little, but then turned back. The rustling continued.

Rosalind scooted forward again. Half her mind tried to concoct an excuse in case she was caught. Half her mind tried to guess how close to the edge of the sheltering bed she dared get.

There was another thud and a click. Rosalind risked another half inch.

And had to swallow her gasp of surprise.

The man was Horatio Salter. He stood at the far wall. One of Fullerton's cherished nudes had been taken from its place.

A hidden cupboard. Charlotte was right.

Salter was working at the keyhole with something that looked like a piece of elaborately bent wire.

Of course. He would not have any hairpins. Rosalind felt a desperate urge to giggle.

She could just hear the soft exhalation of his curses. Then there was another click, and the panel opened. Salter looked around. Rosalind dropped her face to the floor so the light would not catch the gleam of her eyes.

When she dared to look again, Salter was up to his elbows in the cubby, bringing out papers by the fistful. From this awkward angle, she thought they might be bundles of letters, but they could as well have been legal papers or bonds. Some he stuffed into his pockets, others he jammed back into the cubby.

There was another click. Salter swung toward the door.

The door opened. Rosalind clenched her jaw.

A woman, or at least a woman's pink skirts, swung into the room. The owner shoved the door shut.

Whoever she was, Salter was expecting her.

"It's not here," he hissed. "You promised it would be here."

"I thought it would."

Augustina. Rosalind bit the inside of her cheek to keep back her gasp of surprise.

Augustina moved into Rosalind's field of vision. She wore a filmy gown with yards of tulle and net. Silk ribbons and brilliantines shimmered in the lamp light.

"Fullerton's led us a dance," she said, disappointed. Not angry.

"You said you were sure!"

"I was! And I was wrong. How many times have you been wrong about a sure thing?" She put both hands on her hips and glared at him.

Salter hung his head. "Yes, yes, all right. I'm sorry. But I told you, it doesn't matter. We don't need Fullerton's money. Not now."

Augustina hesitated. "Salter, let's just go. The carriage is waiting. We can start for Dover tonight."

"Without money?" shot back Salter. "The bank won't be open until nine in the morning, and even then we've only a few hundred—"

"We can make money! It's what we do!"

"But not enough." He took her hand gently and kissed it. "'Stina, you're the one who said you wanted to get as far away as possible." He hesitated. "It's only one more night."

"One more night for everything to go wrong! Or for Mother to discover our plans!"

"Your mother doesn't worry me," said Salter.

"She should," said Augustina. "She should frighten you to death."

"We've *already* handled her. She thinks I've saved her

blessed schemes. The only thing left that worries me is Miss Thorne."

Rosalind stiffened. Charlotte shot her a sideways glance.

"Oh," said Augustina. "You don't have to worry about her."

"But if she gets it into her head to make mischief at the ball . . ."

"She won't be at the ball."

"Of course she will," said Salter.

"I tell you she won't. Her father's just died. She's in deep mourning. She can't make any public appearances."

"Well then! There really is nothing to worry about," said Salter. "It's all arranged. Tomorrow night, we disappear."

'Stina's silence said she did not believe him. Maybe she wanted to, but she couldn't. At least not yet. She turned, looking about the room. Rosalind imagined her sharp and secret mind cataloguing the profusion of ornaments and art.

"Perhaps he's hidden it somewhere else," said Augustina.

"Where?" asked Salter. "'Stina, I said . . ."

But Augustina wasn't listening. "Have you looked under the b—" Rosalind shrank back reflexively. Augustina moved, and Rosalind lost sight of everything but her hems.

"Salter," breathed Augustina. Her hems swished as she turned. And Rosalind knew. She was holding up Charlotte's cloak, which Rosalind had left on the bed.

Salter must have made some gesture, because Augustina ran. The door opened and closed.

"Who's here?" Salter croaked. "Come out, damn it."

Rosalind got ready to move, but Charlotte beat her to it.

"Only if you promise not to laugh," she sang out.

Rosalind stared at her, mouth agape. Charlotte ignored her.

"I promise to ring your neck!" growled Salter.

"Oh dear." Charlotte laughed. "And I thought this club was only open to gentlemen!"

"What the devil . . ."

Charlotte thrust both hands out from under the bed. "You'll have to help me."

Rosalind cringed backward. Salter grabbed both of Charlotte's wrists and pulled her out from under the bed and onto her feet. She laughed delightedly.

"And such a handsome rescuer, too!"

Salter stepped away. "What on earth are you doing here?"

"Isn't it obvious?" Charlotte asked. She turned on her tip toes and sashayed around him. At least, Rosalind assumed it was a sashay. Her hems floated in with great animation. "I was hoping to surprise Mr. Fullerton. A bit like Cleopatra wrapping herself in the carpet, only I had no carpet and . . . oh dear." She pressed her hand to her forehead. "It's so very warm in here." She staggered back and put her hand on Salter's chest. "Would you open a window? I'm quite well, but the champagne, you understand." She giggled again.

"Oh God!" He thrust her backward. She stumbled, whooped, giggled, and plumped herself down on the edge of the bed. Now, her full skirts blocked Rosalind's view of what was happening.

They also blocked all possible view of Rosalind.

"Listen to me." Rosalind thought Salter leaned close to her sister. "You cannot say one word about what you've seen today."

"Seen?" Charlotte's voice was confused and bleary. "What on earth could I have seen from under there?" Salter didn't answer, and Charlotte went on. "Besides, it would spoil such a luscious secret."

Still no answer.

Charlotte sighed deeply. "I will admit I was disappointed that Fullerton did not come to keep me company, but now I see something I like so much better." Charlotte's skirts shifted, and the bed creaked. "Shall we be friends, you and I, sir? It's been such a terribly dull evening, hasn't it? You must be especially bored since your other lady has so inconsiderately abandoned you." She giggled again, and the bed creaked again, and Rosalind felt her cheeks burning like fire.

"Whore," he said through grated teeth.

"But such a very fine one," breathed Charlotte. "And I assure you, I can prove what I say, especially with such a grand, handsome gentleman."

Salter grunted. The bed bounced. Charlotte laughed. Rosalind dipped her head again, wondering what on earth she would do if this did not end soon. But then, blessedly, she saw Salter's shoes hurry across the carpet. The door opened. The door closed.

Rosalind stayed where she was. So did Charlotte.

"I think it's safe now."

Rosalind crawled out from under the bed. Charlotte stood up and looked sadly down at her sparkling dress, now streaked with dust and grime. "This was quite new an hour ago."

"Thank you, Charlotte. If he'd seen me, he would have recognized me."

"I rather thought so. Who were those two?"

"Horatio Salter and Augustina Walford," Rosalind told her.

Salter and Augustina looking for Fullerton's money boxes to flee the country. At least, that was what Augustina wanted to do.

Salter, very clearly, had other plans.

CHAPTER 47

Familial Affections

*She had such an opinion of her mother's address,
such a sublime superstitious dread that her
mother would, by some inscrutable means, work
out her own purposes, that she felt as if she could
not escape from these secret machinations.*

Maria Edgeworth, *Manoevering*

"Did you find it?"

Augustina hung her head. She'd seen the light coming from under her mother's door. She should have doubled back and come up the main stairs, but she was tired and cold, and there was an ache inside her that all Salter's confidence had not been able to erase. So, she was careless and tried to sneak past, and now she was caught.

She turned. Mother stood in her doorway, a candle in hand.

"Find what?" Augustina asked, trying to muster at least a little insouciance.

"Whatever it is you went out after."

"I don't—"

But Mother cut her off. "Augustina, stop. I recognize, too

late I'm sure, that I've been acting like a fool. I hope we can put an end to that now."

"Is your foolishness now my responsibility?" inquired Augustina tartly.

"I didn't say that. I . . . it is freezing in this corridor. Come in and sit down."

It was freezing, and Augustina's satin and tulle dress was too light for winter. She'd worn it because it had never been seen in Graham's before and would help her go unrecognized.

The fire in Mother's hearth had been allowed to burn down to the coals. Despite this, the lingering warmth was truly welcome. Augustina drew a chair up close and held her hands out.

Mother was watching her. Augustina could feel it against her skin, even though she kept her own gaze on the glowing coals.

"Were you with Salter?" she asked.

Augustina didn't flinch and didn't answer. *You'll have to try harder than that, Mother dear.*

Mother sighed and sat down on her sofa. "I understand you feel I've invaded your privacy by bringing Miss Thorne into the matter, but what was I to do? There was nowhere else I could go to ask—"

"Miss Thorne?" Augustina snorted, mostly for the pleasure of seeing Mother wince. "You think this is just because I'm angry about Miss Thorne?"

"No," said Mother. "I know it is not."

"Well, that's something I suppose," said Augustina to the dying fire.

"Augustina, look at me."

Reluctantly Augustina did as she was told. Her mother's eyes were very large and had always been praised for their expressiveness. Now, they just looked tired.

"How much do you know?" she asked.

"About what?" replied Augustina with bitter frivolity. "Needlework? Music? Modern languages?"

"The charity ball," Mother answered. "Our work in London, and elsewhere."

"Rather more than you want me to, I should imagine," she replied. She rubbed her eyes. The smoke and heat were beginning to sting.

Or maybe it was something else.

Mother sighed and leaned back, as if she was the one who was too tired to bear it anymore. "I was afraid you had discovered us."

Augustina's temper snapped. "Were you?" she sneered. "May I ask why? You trusted Louis, you trusted Etienne. Why didn't you trust me?"

"I did trust you," Mother said. "I do."

"How am I supposed to believe that?" Augustina shot to her feet, the combination of anger and fear giving her sudden energy. "When during all these years you never told me anything!"

Mother looked away. "I promised your father," she whispered.

"What are you talking about?"

"When your father was dying he made me promise that you would be kept safely out of . . . whatever we must do. He was afraid that our workings might—bring about the end of the family, and it gnawed at him. So, he wanted one of you to go on and marry, and have children. It was decided it should be you. The name would fall away, but no matter. If we were taken up, it would have anyway. But the bloodline, that would continue through you."

"And you decided this on my behalf?"

"I did promise. He was dying, Augustina. He was my husband."

"You didn't once think to tell me?" whispered Augustina.

"I could not." Mother's voice was hollow. "That would have broken my promise."

Augustina stared at her. A thousand memories flickered through her mind, like the waves of heat across the coals. All she had done. All she had caused to be done. The endless searching and sneaking, the laughter and the anger. All because the one thing she did know was that she was shut out and alone, that her brothers—selfish Louis, foolish, idealistic Etienne—would always be held in greater esteem.

No one recognized her worth, no one understood her to be capable until she found Salter.

That was what she had always believed, and now she heard this, and it was somehow worse. Because perhaps Mother had seen all she was, and all the help she could be to the family and their precious, damned cause, and had ignored it, anyway.

"It was wrong," said her mother. "I should not have promised, and he should not have made me." She lifted those expressive eyes, and Augustina saw the tears shimmering in them. "I am sorry, Augustina. Please, I beg you, if you believe nothing else, believe that."

Augustina always wondered what it felt like when a person's heart broke. Now she knew. It sent a tremor of cold through the body. It split nerve and resolve in two. Augustina felt a tear trickling down her cheek but could not muster the will to wipe it away.

"I believe you," she said.

Mother stood. Augustina opened her arms, and her mother fell into her embrace. They stood like that for a long time, and for a handful of moments, Augustina let herself be as she was when she was a little girl, and her mother's arms were the best and safest place in the whole world.

But slowly, Mother let go. She tipped Augustina's face up

and pulled a handkerchief out of her sleeve to wipe away the tear that her daughter had ignored.

"There," she said. "Augustina. If there's anything you want to tell me, I'll listen. The promise I made your father, it's broken now. It doesn't matter anymore."

Augustina stepped back. She looked at her mother, tall and magnificent and determined, and loved her and believed her.

"No," she said. "There's nothing."

CHAPTER 48

Revelations over Breakfast

We joined forces, and nothing could stand against us.

Maria Edgeworth, *Belinda*

"Am I right in guessing I'm not the only one who didn't get any sleep last night?" said Adam as he stepped into Rosalind's little foyer.

Rosalind let Adam in herself. He was unshaven and his face was ruddy from cold. He stripped off his gloves and immediately took off his hat to run a hand through his hair.

He was not normally so self-conscious, and for reasons she did not entirely understand, it made Rosalind smile.

"Yes. By the time I got home, it seemed easier to just stay up. Please, come in." She let him hang up his things on the pegs by the door and then took him into the parlor. "There are fresh crumpets, purchased from a man Amelia assures me bakes the best in the market. There's coffee as well."

"Thank you."

Rosalind sat down and knew a moment's unaccountable nervousness.

"We are friends, Mr. Harkness, are we not?"

He raised both brows. "I should hope that we are."

"Good. Then you will not judge me for this." She speared half a crumpet onto a toasting fork and held it over the fire. "I'm afraid that besides some sweets and a pudding or two, this is the extent of my cooking skills."

He was eyeing her with a kind of bemused tolerance. Rosalind felt herself beginning to blush, and worse, she lacked the fortitude to fight it back down. When Charlotte had dropped her off at her door last night, she had come in to find Amelia and Alice both asleep in parlor chairs and the fire burnt down to a single glowing coal. She'd shaken the women awake and sent them each, stumbling and bleary-eyed, to bed.

But she had not followed. She'd used far too much fuel to bring the fire back to life, and sat up the rest of the night, watching her blaze. The hours crept on, and everything she had seen and feared and come to believe tumbled through her mind.

She'd combed her books and records, comparing letters and bills from Mrs. Walford's event to other records she'd kept in her journals of past dinners and routs she'd assisted with.

By the time December's feeble dawn allowed one tentative sunbeam through the drapes, Rosalind was tired, she was frightened, and yet, she also felt she had reclaimed something—a form of confidence that had been badly shaken in the past few days.

She felt certain she had the threads of this problem in hand. All that remained was to find the way to lay them out straight.

She needed help, and wonder of wonders, help was there. Again.

Always.

Rosalind looked up and met Adam's eyes.

Adam had not stopped watching her, not for a moment. But that bemusement she'd seen before was gone. She saw that in this moment, in her crowded parlor, over this impromptu and improper breakfast, he was asking the same question Charlotte had.

Do you trust me?

They both should have known the answer to that by now. But given her own reticence, she did not in any way blame him for needing to ask again. Instead, Rosalind let him look, and she let him see. Adam smiled, that unfair, beautiful crooked smile, and this time Rosalind did not look away.

Slowly, the smile faded, replaced by a quiet solemnity. Rosalind nodded once. The trust between them might be building, but it did not replace the need for questions, and answers.

"Have you heard from your sister yet?" he asked.

Yes. We have to talk about Charlotte. Now.

"Yes, I have." Rosalind turned the fork a little. "In fact, I spent most of last night in her company."

"You did?"

When she'd written to ask Adam to come here this morning, she hadn't told him about her plan for last night. The truth was, she had not been sure what would happen between her and Charlotte at Graham's, or what she would be able to tell him this morning.

I am going to have to apologize to them both for being a coward. I hope.

"I met her at about eleven, and she dropped me off here close onto two in the morning."

"May I ask . . ."

"She was helping me search Fullerton's rooms at Graham's."

Adam was silent at this. Rosalind expected that he'd grown used to her sudden declarations by now. At least, she hoped he had. She slid the slice of crumpet from her fork to a plate and held it out to him. He busied himself with spreading on a thick layer of butter and jam.

"I saw her yesterday as well," he said finally.

Rosalind started and almost dropped the other slice of crumpet she was trying to fix onto the toasting fork. "You did? Where?"

"Going into Carlton House."

A wave of relief washed over her. "Yes, that would fit. Thank goodness."

"You're ahead of me in this. Here. I'll take that." He plucked the fork out of her fingers and held it to the fire.

Rosalind sighed in mock outrage. "Neither you nor Alice seems to believe I can toast a crumpet."

He smiled. "I grew up with four brothers and sisters, some of whom were much younger. This was practically my vocation." As if to prove it, he picked up his own crumpet with his free hand and took a healthy bite without taking his eyes off the one he was currently toasting.

Rosalind resisted the urge to laugh at this display of domestic skill. She wrapped her hands around her coffee cup.

"I'd been wondering about Charlotte. I thought, perhaps, she'd accepted a commission from some agent to carry a message of some kind from Paris to London. Perhaps more than one."

"Because of what the Countess Lieven said to you?"

"Yes, and because last night I watched her pick not one but two locks, and play the coquette under circumstances that were best described as challenging. It made me think this was not the first time she'd searched a room or had gotten caught somewhere she should not be."

"You think your sister well placed to be a spy?"

"It was a possibility. And I was afraid it might be for the French. Or some segment of the French. But if you saw her at Carlton House, then perhaps the messages she carried, if she carried them, were for the Crown."

Adam slid the crumpet onto her plate, and Rosalind reached for the jam pot. "I'd feel better with proof."

"So would I, but at least there's hope."

"At least." Adam speared another slice of crumpet. "Did you find anything at Graham's?"

"I believe we did." Rosalind took a large bite of crumpet and was ready to allow that Adam's skills with a toasting fork were at least as good as Alice's. "We found a packed trunk that, among other things, held three strong boxes, at least one of which was filled with gold coins."

Adam watched the fire, and the fork, for a long moment. "So Fullerton was planning to flee the country. I had heard from another member of the club that he was calling in several large debts."

"Furthermore, Charlotte and I were not the only people who meant to search his rooms that night."

"Rosalind Thorne!" Alice's outraged shout cut through the room.

Alice threw open the parlor door and stood on the threshold, hands on hips. "Alone with a man and *crumpets!*"

Adam raised the fork. "Breakfast, Miss Littlefield?"

Alice lifted her chin and walked primly across the crowded room. She pulled her chair up nearer to the hearth and held out a plate to let Adam drop the freshly toasted crumpet onto it.

"You're just in time," said Adam. "Miss Thorne was telling me what she found at Graham's last night."

"You got in?" Alice cried. "Was Charlotte there? What did you see?"

Rosalind described the whole adventure, ignoring Alice's coughing fit when she described hiding under the bed. She also glossed over some of Charlotte's more blatant coquetry with Horatio Salter.

"Do you think Augustina and Salter were looking for the money?" asked Alice.

"I think it very likely."

"But why would they think he'd be keeping such a quantity of money in his rooms?" asked Adam. "No hiding place there would be as secure as a bank, witness the fact that between you you were able to defeat several of the locks in the room."

"As to that." Rosalind set her cup and plate aside. "Mr. Harkness, did you bring those scraps of paper you were telling me about?"

Adam laid the toasting fork on the hearth and pulled an envelope out of his jacket pocket.

"Alice—" Rosalind began.

Alice cleared a spot on her table by unceremoniously shoving aside a great mass of books and papers. Adam opened the envelope and carefully laid down three scraps of singed paper—the one containing the partial list of names, the one that looked to be some sort of drawing, and the one that could have been a piece of a map.

Rosalind opened her own desk and brought out the letters from Augustina and Mrs. Walford. She laid the letters on the table above Adam's scraps. They all crowded round. Alice helpfully pushed the drapes open farther to allow in more of the watery winter daylight.

It was Alice who saw the similarities first.

"This one." Alice tapped the letter nearest her. "It's the same hand as this list." She touched the largest of the scraps. "See there? The *E* is almost a single line rather than a loop."

"I'd agree," said Adam.

"Yes," said Rosalind. "I suspected as much. This"—she touched the fragment of guest list—"was written by Augustina."

"Why? What for?"

Rosalind felt a tight smile form. "To try to dupe Russell Fullerton."

CHAPTER 49

Conclusions over Coffee Cups

They shall also inquire of all accessories before
the fact . . .

John Impey of the Inner Temple, *The Practice of the Office
of Coroner*

"Augustina Walford was trying to dupe Russell Fuller-ton?" exclaimed Alice. "What on earth would make her think she could do such a thing?"

"Who on earth?" Rosalind corrected her. "And it was Horatio Salter, of course. We've been—at least, I've been—looking at this situation backwards. I assumed that Fullerton had somehow heard that the Walfords had a fortune that might be easily stolen and had coerced Salter into helping with the scheme."

"But it was Salter who approached Fullerton," said Adam.

"Yes, and both Fullerton and Salter subsequently lied about their relationship. Fullerton said Salter wanted advice about money. Salter said Fullerton was planning on black-mailing Mrs. Walford about her husband's radical politics." Rosalind paused and felt her eyes narrow, trying to see the memory. "Mrs. Walford was shaken by that story. She hadn't expected it."

"Wait," said Alice. "Are you saying the Walfords really are secret Bonapartists?"

"Was this Augustina blackmailed by Fullerton?" asked Adam. "To get hold of some secret of her mother's?"

"Not quite," said Rosalind. "I didn't understand it until last night, and I wasn't sure until I saw this." She touched the largest of the singed scraps. "You see, Augustina told me she'd met Salter at Graham's. She'd been taken there by her brother Louis as a lark. They formed an unexpected bond. Augustina was lonely. She felt frustrated and confined. Salter was someone she felt she could confide in, and she did.

"Augustina knew about her family's involvement with radicals and Bonapartists. She told Salter, and Salter sensed an opportunity for gain. Perhaps even enough to allow them to elope together without having to wait for Augustina to come of age.

"He approached Fullerton and suggested he had access to some highly compromising information. Fullerton would have known, or found out, Salter's connection with an earlier scheme that had been so large it had nearly brought down the stock markets. So, he would believe Salter was capable of acquiring secret information that he was willing to sell."

"But surely he'd also know it might be a fuddle," said Alice. "After all, that other scheme was all based on a lie."

"Except the Walfords really were involved in radical politics," Rosalind reminded her. "And Augustina really was by now a fixture around the gaming clubs. Fullerton would find it easy to believe a girl like that would be desperate for money."

"Because that was his business—extracting money and favors from women who gambled too deeply," murmured Adam. "He saw what he expected to see."

"Exactly. So, between them, Salter and Augustina created

a set of plans." She touched the second singed paper, the one that appeared to be a map. "Perhaps they were even based on papers Augustina discovered in her mother's keeping. They offered to sell these to Russell Fullerton."

"I thought Salter loved her," said Alice. "These are deep waters to drag someone you love into."

Rosalind felt her brows knit together. "Salter is a schemer, a gambler, and someone who enjoys the thrill of a successful bet." An image of her father at the card tables flashed through Rosalind's mind. She set it aside. "I believe he does care for her, and they both believe she curbs his worst impulses."

"Oh, I've seen that one," said Alice. "My parents were like that, but it doesn't work. If the thing goes wrong, he just gets to blame her for it. Or worse, she blames herself." Alice took an abrupt swallow of coffee.

Rosalind bowed her head in acknowledgment of this. "If they'd left at once, it might have been a good sign that their partnership was real. But Salter is more interested in the theft now, and in the money, than he is in keeping himself and Augustina safe."

"So what went wrong?" Alice tipped her coffee cup again and took a long swallow. "I'm assuming something did."

"Fullerton decided that he would revert to type. After receiving the plans, he withheld the final payment and threatened to blackmail the pair of them, and perhaps Augustina's family, in the bargain."

"Just as Salter said he did," murmured Adam.

Rosalind nodded. "Lies work best when laced with the truth."

"So, Salter and Augustina duped Fullerton, and then Fullerton turned around and duped them," said Alice. "Very neat."

"But that makes no sense," said Adam. "A man like Fullerton would only make such a move if he believed there was a chance for a large profit. You say Augustina was not yet of age. She did not have her own money, and there's no indication that Salter was a rich man. What did he hope to gain?"

Before Rosalind could answer, they all heard a knocking on the outer door.

"That will be Sanderson Faulks," said Rosalind. "I asked him to join us here. I very much believe we will need his help before the end of this business."

"You got Sanderson out of bed before noon?" Alice stared at her, frankly amazed. "I never would have believed it."

Like Alice, Amelia was now awake and she answered the door. A moment later, Mr. Faulks strolled into the parlor and bowed to them all.

"I see I am not the only one to boldly venture out so early at our Miss Thorne's command."

Rosalind sighed patiently. "Come in, Mr. Faulks, and have a cup of coffee." She poured out for him and added the smallest splash of fresh cream from the jug.

Mr. Faulks accepted the cup and inhaled the fragrant steam. He also eyed Rosalind in mock concern.

"I made it, so you needn't worry," she told him.

He drank and closed his eyes in deep appreciation. "Perfection. Thank you, Miss Thorne." He looked about for a chair, but finding none, moved to stand by the window.

"Did you speak with Mr. Greer?" asked Rosalind.

"I certainly tried," said Mr. Faulks. "But Mr. Greer seems to have decamped from London entirely, and left his landlady no information about where he had gone or, indeed, when he was expected to return."

"Who is Mr. Greer?" asked Adam.

"A thoroughly unpleasant little man with more money than scruples," answered Mr. Faulks. "He makes most of that money through buying and selling other men's debts. I recently had occasion to purchase some notes of hand from him that had been originally written by our fascinating and questionable Mr. Horatio Salter."

"And Salter attempted to deny the debt by telling Mrs. Walford that he had paid them off a long time ago," said Rosalind. "And he produced a letter supposedly from him affirming that fact."

"Which seems unlikely to be genuine, as Mr. Greer has suddenly become unavailable to give any further information," said Alice. She rubbed her forehead. "Rosalind, this business of yours is in danger of giving me a megrim."

"Believe me, Alice, I understand." Rosalind sat down in her desk chair. "I can't remember when I've had less sleep."

"So." Alice took another drink of coffee. "Salter and Augustina try to fob these probably fake plans to rescue Napoleon off onto Fullerton. Fullerton turns around and settles into his usual blackmailing ways. Mr. Harkness is right. He'd only do that if he thought there was profit to be made."

"And there was. Salter let the fact slip when he let me hear that Mrs. Walford really was involved with radical politics, and possibly worse."

Sanderson raised his eloquent brows. "Dear me. Have we strayed at last into politics?"

"Purely by accident, I promise you," said Rosalind. "But it seems Mrs. Walford came to London with a specific purpose, and it had little to do with getting her daughter married. At some point, she or her husband had quietly become connected with the Holland House set, and they meant to contribute a large sum to the conspirators and their attempt to free Napoleon from exile."

Her small audience stared at one another, and at her.

"Yes, I know," said Rosalind. "I would have believed it to be ridiculous. I might still, if Countess Lieven had not confirmed the existence of such schemes."

"Well, thank you very much," said Alice tartly.

"I'm sorry," said Rosalind "But you know the Major is not above printing rumor to sell papers."

"He's not, but you might have shown a bit more faith in George."

"I will apologize to George when this is over," Rosalind assured her. "Mrs. Walford's intention is to pass the money off to the conspirators at her charity ball. The money will be kept in the strong room at Upton's and handed to the relevant persons at the end of the evening."

Adam shook his head. "It seems plausible, in general. But why concoct such an elaborate scheme to allow the money to change hands? There's too much that could go wrong."

"Certainly it would have been much simpler to give some instructions to her bankers," said Mr. Faulks.

Rosalind and Alice looked at each other. Alice rolled her eyes.

"Mrs. Walford is a wealthy widow, yes," said Rosalind. "But much of the money she holds is actually in trust for her children. She probably has a widow's portion that's fully in her control, but the rest—that will be overseen by a board of trustees and probably several male guardians, until her sons come to their own at twenty-five. Those men will have the power to review, and override, large expenditures."

"So, the problem becomes how to get hold of a large quantity of her money without arousing the trustees' suspicions?" said Adam.

"Yes. Mrs. Walford's solution was to invent a charity, one with a pious and patriotic aim that cannot be argued with. She brings in other persons—men and women both—to create a board and give it an air of respectability. They all just happen to be from the Holland House set. With their help, she creates a large and expensive event. Then, she pads all the bills and probably invents other costs out of thin air." Rosalind paused and took a swallow of her own cooling coffee. "I spent some time last night comparing costs for the Walford's event with similar expenses from the same purveyors. Hers are distinctly larger, and without good reason."

"So, the bank advances the money, she pays the tradesmen what she owes and keeps the rest," said Adam. "As Miss Littlefield says, very neat."

"And the night of the ball, that money will all be at Upton's in the strong room. Probably what was meant to happen next was that the money would be entrusted to members of the board, who would undertake to deliver it to the appropriate parties."

"And that's what Fullerton was after? That money?" asked Alice.

"I think so, yes," said Rosalind.

"But how did he expect to get to it?" asked Adam. "And what has this to do with your father's murder?"

"I don't know," admitted Rosalind. "What I do know is that Mrs. Walford became suspicious of Mr. Salter at some point and reached out to me. Salter must have mentioned my presence to Fullerton, and Fullerton took up Father in order to curtail any inquiries I might make."

"Which tells us Fullerton believed the money could be gotten," said Adam. "Otherwise he wouldn't have bothered to bring your father into it."

"Yes," agreed Rosalind. "And from what I heard last night, Salter still believes it can be gotten. I believe that at some point, he and Augustina had planned to steal the money from Upton's strong room during the ball."

"How would they break in? And get past the extra guards Mrs. Walford was hiring?" asked Alice.

But Adam just shook his head. "They wouldn't have to break in. Miss Walford simply tells the man in charge she has instructions from her mother to start transferring the money."

"Or she might have one of her brothers with her to bolster the story," said Rosalind. "Louis, for instance, is on the charity board. If he tells Mr. Hodges that his mother had given instructions that it's time to move the boxes, who is going to question him?"

"A risky maneuver," remarked Mr. Faulks. "What if they were to be seen?"

"By whom?" asked Rosalind. "Everyone will be upstairs at the ball. If they are careful of the timing, they will go during the height of the dancing. They won't be missed before the auction, possibly not even before the supper. Even then, it will take time to realize what is really wrong."

Adam considered this. "As a plan, it's incomplete. I can tell you that two persons are not enough to make off with any truly significant amount of coinage, especially when one is a young girl. It takes a certain amount of brute strength to carry away gold and silver."

"It's also quite a risk for them to run simply to hand the money to Fullerton," added Mr. Faulks.

"Unless they decided that Fullerton should be killed, and killed Sir Reginald by mistake," said Adam.

Alice tapped her fingertips on the edge of her coffee cup. "In which case, Augustina and Salter get to keep all the money in lieu of Augustina's portion, and they are away with the fairies. It's genius, in its way." She paused. "And even better, Mrs. Walford won't be able to say a word. How can she complain of the theft without it being discovered that money was to help in this mad scheme to pay for boats and men to rescue Bonaparte?"

"But did Salter kill Sir Reginald?" asked Adam quietly. "If it happened that Sir Reginald died because of a mistake, it is less likely to be Salter's doing, since Salter knew Fullerton the best of any of the would-be thieves."

"Let's not forget that Mrs. Walford may have gotten wind of Fullerton's plotting," said Rosalind. "He might have written her directly and said he had those plans in hand and would use them. She could have gone herself to kill him."

"Or sent her sons," said Mr. Faulks quietly.

"That's possible," said Rosalind. "Etienne at least would have done it. He is starved for approval, and he is the one of them who believes in his parents' cause."

"So, it is possible Fullerton told the truth about the two men he saw," pointed out Adam.

"So, the Walford sons go to Fullerton's house," said Adam. "They kill Sir Reginald, perhaps without even realizing their mistake, and run out, bumping into Fullerton on the way. Fullerton rushes in, realizes that to be caught with a set of treasonous plans and a dead man is very dangerous indeed, so he sets about burning the papers as quickly as he can."

"Normally, I wouldn't hang anything on the possibility of Russell Fullerton telling the truth," remarked Mr. Faulks, "but that has the ring of genuine plausibility about it."

Rosalind stared at the scraps of paper and the forged letters in front of her. She was missing something, and she knew it. Something someone had just said, something that needed to be turned around so it could be seen better.

But one thing was already very clear.

"If Adam is right, and Salter and Augustina together aren't enough to steal that much money, what if one or more of the brothers is going to help? They all take the risk, all divide the spoils, and all scatter to the four winds."

"So, one way or another it is on us to stop this mischief at the Walford charity ball," said Sanderson. "Or am I mistaken as to why you have summoned us all here at this truly uncivilized hour?"

Rosalind felt herself smiling at her friend. "You are not mistaken, Sanderson. It's past time we came up with our own plan." She hesitated and looked toward Adam. "Unless . . . ?"

Adam was also smiling, but there was no humor in his expression. "I must leave to join my patrol. I will talk to Townsend, you may be sure. He may listen, he may not. So, it would be as well to have another plan ready." He drained his coffee cup.

Rosalind stood. "I will walk you out."

Adam bowed to Alice and Sanderson, who both made themselves busy with the coffee things.

Rosalind followed Adam into the foyer and waited while he donned his hat and coat.

"I'm sorry to be asking yet more of you," she whispered to him. "I had hoped this would all be over much sooner and then we—" She stopped. The words felt pathetic to her. A little girl's complaint of loss and confusion. Not that she had truly believed she would ever make some grand declaration of love. *But it should be more than this*, she thought, and was surprised at her own peevishness.

But when she looked up, Adam was smiling—that crooked, unfair, dazzling smile that had caught her heart from the first day.

"There's time, Rosalind," he whispered. "And as long as we have that, I have faith we will work things out."

Rosalind glanced at the parlor door and at the hallway to the kitchen. Then, feeling greatly daring, she reached up and laid her hand against his cheek. The curve of his jaw fit neatly into the hollow of her palm. The stubble pricked her skin, but some part of her unnamed and barely suspected enjoyed that sensation, the way she enjoyed his warmth, the hitch of his breath. She laid her hand against his throat and felt the pulse there, and then against his chest, where his heart beat as fast as her own.

"Will you kiss me?" she asked him.

"Gladly."

The kiss was a soft, yet confident, gesture. He had wanted this for a long time, just as she had. And he did not want to make a mess of it. Just like her.

So he was slow, warm, savoring. Discovering. He had kissed other women, she knew that, but as she had kissed other men, she could hardly fault this. She liked the touch of him, the unique scent and warmth of him. The way she could feel him smile and the jolt of pure gladness that shot through her when he did. The natural way in which he opened for her, and the way she responded in kind.

The slow, blooming realization that she could spend a very long time enjoying all the sensations that came with this man's kiss.

It was Adam who broke the kiss. "We should not trust too much longer to Miss Littlefield's patience," he whispered. "I will send word as quickly as I can. And whatever happens tonight, be careful." He drew his fingertips across her cheeks, before he turned and strode out the door, leaving Rosalind giddy and breathless.

Enough. Rosalind drew herself up. *He is right. There is time, or there will be. Because first, there is a great deal to do.*

And she must begin by visiting the vicar's wife.

CHAPTER 50

The Last Throw

Half my theory proved just; that is saying a great deal for any theory.

Maria Edgeworth, *Belinda*

At first, Rosalind's attendance at St. Margaret's, a modest church three blocks from her home, was a matter of maintaining appearances. As a single woman with her own establishment, it was important that she present a thoroughly respectable aspect for the neighborhood. Close as her street was to Covent Garden and Drury Lane, she could be easily mistaken for something other than she was. Regular attendance at church helped cement appearances.

St. Margaret's vicar, the Rev. Mr. Button, was a mild man whose (usually short) sermons centered around the importance of kindness and charity. It was his wife, however, who confirmed for Rosalind that this was an appropriate church for her. Mrs. Button also believed in charity, mercy, and good works, but she carried them out with the kind of firm decisiveness one might expect from a commander in the field.

After Rosalind's second Sunday at St. Margaret's, Mrs. Button cornered her after services. "Miss Thorne, I'll thank you to come to tea this afternoon. I've a girl who is in need of employment. She's a good girl, though there's many would not see so at once. They say you know everybody in London. You surely will know who needs a smart, teachable girl. We shall expect you at three."

And she sailed off. Rosalind, breathless, did not dare refuse.

The girl turned out to be a young Black woman named Naomi, who had fled a Barbados plantation with her mother. Her mother's health had broken under the strain, and Naomi was desperate for work. She had been a cook on the plantation, and Rosalind was able find her a place with Mrs. Whittaker, a friend of her godmother's who had just lost a kitchen maid to a hasty marriage.

St. Margaret's became Rosalind's church, and Rosalind made a point of cultivating Mrs. Button's friendship. She had the feeling it might be useful one day.

She'd been right. As soon as she told Mrs. Button that her father had died, she was sat down with a cup of tea, while Mrs. Button proceeded to make the arrangements, and the decisions—as to the coffin, the flowers, the candles, the timing of the service, the purchase of plot in the churchyard, the relative advisability of having another current dress dyed for mourning, or purchasing secondhand. The only thing Mrs. Button did not have to arrange was the funeral notice for the papers. Alice had already promised to take care of that.

Rosalind felt some guilt at this abdication of responsibility, but primarily she felt relief that for once someone else knew all the things that should be done. Her mind was so overloaded with concerns about what must happen this evening that there was no room left to make these final choices on her father's behalf.

Thankfully, Charlotte had been able to answer the urgent note she sent round by hand, and had arrived barely five minutes after Rosalind did. She now sat in one of Mrs. Button's exceedingly uncomfortable chairs, drank the weak tea, and murmured, "Yes, if you think it best," and "I'm sure you're right," at appropriate intervals.

Distracted as she was, Rosalind did not miss the searching glances her sister cast at her. At first, it was silent acknowledgment of the irony of the situation. It was the first time in years that the two of them openly acknowledged their relationship, and it was because of their father's funeral. But it didn't take long for Rosalind to see that Charlotte was worried about more than what might be a suitable contribution to the church and whether the black crepe for the decorations could be gotten ready in time.

At last, the tea was finished and Rosalind and Charlotte were sent on their way with very clear and very firm instructions about when to return.

Charlotte lowered her veil before they stepped out into the street, effectively concealing her expression from Rosalind's scrutiny.

"Are all vicars' wives like that?" asked Charlotte as they stopped beside her carriage. "I don't think I've never met one before."

"She's a rather extreme example of the type," Rosalind admitted.

"I suppose I'll have to get used to them. They tell me such women are a feature of a respectable life." She shook her head at this. "Can I drop you somewhere?"

"No," said Rosalind. "I'll walk, but, Charlotte, I need your help."

"What again? Please tell me this will not involve ruining another dress." Her words were light, but Rosalind heard the strain underneath them. She could not see clearly through her sister's veil, but she knew Charlotte wanted to be gone.

"I hope not," said Rosalind. "But it will involve your connections at Carlton House."

"Ah." Charlotte smoothed the cuff of her black kid glove. "So, your Mr. Harkness told you I was seen."

"He did."

"Rosalind, this . . . connection is not one on which I dare presume. If I misstep, there could be real trouble."

"I know, but I need you to try. There's no one else I can turn to this time."

She looked away and sighed. "Very well. One last time. What is it you need?"

"Mr. Harkness!" bawled the footman. "Your presence is required!"

Adam reined his horse up short and stared at the man. His little patrol had just completed yet another circuit of Carlton House. The Prince Regent had another soirée planned for this evening, and for the one after that. Adam had not been so impatient for Christmas's arrival since he was a boy.

He was exhausted. He was angry. He was tired of being cold and bored and kept at this monotonous duty when Rosalind was planning how to uncover a theft and a murder. He was ready to storm Clerkenwell Prison and wring Fullerton's neck for placing them both in this position.

"Mr. Harkness!" called the footman again.

The man stood in the doorway of Carlton House, one of six doors in this side of the house, Adam knew, because he'd counted them. He was in the full scarlet and gold livery, wearing a caped coat against the weather, which was at least as bad as yesterday.

"By whom?" Adam demanded.

"If you will come with me, sir?" said the footman.

Adam frowned and bit back a sharp reply. His temper had grown increasingly ungovernable as the cold, miserable day wore on. Not only was the weather bad, but his men were both bored and tired, having to take up their rounds again after a night of short rest. Worst of all, his mind could not settle. His thoughts kept racing ahead to tonight, and what would he do if he could gain Townsend's permission to go to Rosalind's assistance.

And what he would do if he couldn't.

Because no matter what Townsend said, he was not leaving her alone.

But to go to her aid, he might just have to take leave of Bow Street for good.

Adam swung himself off his horse and handed the reins to the groom. "Go get yourselves warm, lads," he said to his men.

Then he followed the footman into the house. Water dripped from his great coat. He did remember to remove his hat.

The palatial corridor wrapped him in the glow of gilding, lamplight, and warmth. It occurred to Adam that this shining glamor was the effect Fullerton was trying to create in his home. Fullerton, however, had neither the space, the fortune, nor the staff to manage it properly, so all he had been able to create was a poor imitation of these elegant surroundings.

The footman stopped in front of a pair of doors, knocked once, and drew them open.

"Mr. Adam Harkness," he announced, and stood aside.

Adam stepped into the room. It was as broad, grand, and gilded as the corridor had been, with a painted ceiling, two crystal chandeliers, and a whole series of arched windows overlooking the snowy gardens. John Townsend stood in front of a rose marble fireplace, his hands behind his back. He glowered at Adam as he entered. There were other men there, too—footmen in their wigs and scarlet livery, servants and clerks with their books and pens, and a group of men in black coats and trousers who could have been anything from doctors to clergymen to schoolmasters.

But the person who commanded his attention immediately lounged in a carved chair by the windows. He was a portly man sporting a perfectly kept wig, a shockingly patterned waistcoat, and a brilliant blue jacket. He had small but sharp eyes, and a rather long nose, and it took Adam more time than it should have to realize who this person was.

As soon as he did, he bowed deeply and stayed there.

"Your Royal Highness," he murmured.

"Mr. Harkness," said the Prince of Wales. "I am told we need to talk about your recent activities. And, it seems, some of the company you've been keeping."

When at last the time came to depart for the evening's event, Rosalind was able to reflect that one advantage of including Sanderson Faulks in their venture was his dedication to comfort.

From the outside, Sanderson's carriage could not be told from any of a dozen others arriving out front of Upton's Assembly Rooms. But the seat was broad enough for Rosalind and Alice to sit without having to draw their skirts close. The cabin was lined with velvet and padded satin and amply supplied not only with rugs but with foot warmers and muffs.

The day had proved unspeakably long. After Adam left them, Rosalind, Alice, and Sanderson had talked for hours. Amelia had come and gone, bringing many pots of tea and plates of biscuits in stony silence. The girl was furious that she was not allowed to "be in at the finish," as she put it.

"Augustina knows you're Rosalind's maid," Alice reminded her. "If you're seen, she'll grow suspicious."

"No one looks at servants!" Amelia shot back. "And they'll be seeing all of you, won't they?"

"Salter will look at you," said Rosalind. "And he will recognize you and he might make trouble."

What neither Rosalind nor Alice pointed out was what

that "trouble" might include. Whoever had killed Sir Reginald and Sparkes was going to be at the assembly tonight, and they had already demonstrated how much they would do if threatened.

She had heard nothing from Charlotte since they parted at the vicarage.

She had heard nothing from Adam since he walked out her door that morning.

Which was not something she should think about. Remembering their kiss caused an unfortunate change in her complexion. The last thing she needed was for Alice or, worse, Sanderson to comment on this point.

Sanderson's driver steered them into the line of waiting carriages in front of Upton's. Every window in the assembly rooms was ablaze with lamplight. The walk and the street in front of the building were crowded with people jockeying to see the guests in their finest heading into the ball.

Rosalind gazed at the brightly lit building with a mix of envy and apprehension. She'd worked so hard to bring this thing about, and now she could not go inside to see how well she'd succeeded.

Somehow, that stung worse than the fact that Salter and Augustina were using her carefully planned event to rob Mrs. Walford blind.

Or that Mrs. Walford had used her skills to create such a glittering veil for her attempt at treason.

Which only goes to show how vanity robs one of all good sense. Rosalind shook her head.

"Don't worry, Rosalind." Alice patted her hand. "I'm sure it is all going marvelously."

Of course Alice knew what was bothering her.

"Just promise me you will look out for each other."

"Only if you promise you will look after yourself," replied Alice. "I don't like leaving you alone out here."

"There is no need to worry, Miss Littlefield," said Mr. Faulks, as easily as if they were simply talking about a dinner party. "My driver and the outriders are all under orders. She will be attended at all times. No one, however desperate, will be able to approach Miss Thorne this evening without their notice."

"Nonetheless," said Alice to Rosalind.

"I do promise," said Rosalind.

The plan was quite simple. While Alice and Mr. Faulks kept watch from inside the ball, Rosalind would circle the building in the carriage, keeping watch for the cart or carriage that would be needed to carry the money away. Most likely it would be brought around the back of the building to the small area closest to the strong room. Unfortunately, she would be unable to keep the carriage there without attracting suspicion. But as soon as she spied any activity, she would send one of Sanderson's outriders into the ball to fetch him and Alice.

"Well, we know that attendance is excellent," sighed Sanderson. "This line is not moving at all. I'm afraid if we are to get inside before midnight, Miss Littlefield, we shall have to walk."

"All right, Rosalind?" asked Alice.

"Yes, do go." She gave them both a smile. "Then I can fidget in peace. Remember, the carriage will be under the streetlamp on the hour, so you can send me word of what's going on inside."

"You may rely on us," said Sanderson smoothly. He rapped on the carriage ceiling with his stick. "We'll be getting out here, Rogers!"

"Good luck." Alice gave her quick peck on the cheek as she climbed out after Mr. Faulks.

"And you." Rosalind returned her smile and the squeeze of her hand.

Rosalind watched her friends make their way into the bright crowd until they were lost among the other backs and hats and bodies.

"Move us on, Rogers," she called to the driver.

"Aye, miss!" he called back.

Rosalind wrapped her arms around herself, huddled a little farther under her rug, and tried not to feel alone.

CHAPTER 51

Lowering Clouds

By what art these gentlemen raised money, I never troubled myself to inquire; it might have been the black art, for anything I know to the contrary.

Maria Edgeworth, *Belinda*

It was a bloody awful night. John Budgen slapped his hands together to try to get the blood flowing. Cold as a witch's tit and clouds blacker than the devil's bunghole. There'd be snow, too, and it'd be just his bloody luck he'd still be standing here when it came. Only good news was that froze as it was, this soddin' alley didn't stink all the way to high heaven.

Soddin' gentles and their soddin' ideas. Not one of 'em knew what work was. Didn't see none a' them standing out here in the dark with a cart. Probably try to stiff him out of his fee, too, just see if they didn't.

Serve them right if he doubled his askin' price. That'd show them, making an honest cove stand out here, risk the horse, risk the wagon, not to mention 'is skull if some damned—

"You there."

Budgen turned and found himself facing the biggest, blackest man he'd ever seen in his long London life, and that was saying something. For a minute, he was so surprised, he forgot to curse.

" 'Oo the 'ell?" he croaked at last.

"Bow Street." The man dropped a heavy hand onto Budgen's shoulder. "And the good news is, you've just been saved a night out in the cold."

Alice Littlefield had been to more balls of more varieties than even a truly dedicated person could shake a stick at, so she had a connoisseur's eye. Even allowing for the bias of friendship, she could see that Rosalind had truly outdone herself.

Upton's Assembly Rooms were hung with festive bunting in patriotic colors, with just enough Christmas green and gold to keep it all from feeling mawkish. An impressive crowd of the glittering, the great, and the merely good strolled between the rooms, admiring the decorations and the passing gowns and jewels. The musicians playing for an enthusiastic crowd of dancers were in time, and in tune, and the dancers themselves looked determined to enjoy the last of the town festivities before the *ton* removed itself to the countryside for Christmas.

Now that we were inside, Alice was able to properly see her escort. As usual, Mr. Faulks looked splendid. He wore white silk breeches and a sapphire-blue coat and a cravat of so many elaborate folds, Alice speculated his man surely must have been tying at least since he'd left their house that morning.

"You wound me, Miss Littlefield," he said. "I would never have such a slacker in my employ. This did not take above three hours."

Alice swatted him lightly with her silver lace fan. "We are being serious this evening, Mr. Faulks."

"Which would give the game away to anyone who knows me." He nodded to two passing gentlemen. "Have you spied our hostess yet?"

Alice craned her neck. "Yes, this way." She gave Sanderson's arm a tug.

"I think not," he said. "I should be sorry to neglect you in any way, but the last time the Walfords saw me, it was at the opera and I was trying to help chase away Mr. Salter. So, I think discretion is the better part just now."

"Oh yes. I'd forgotten about that. It seems so long ago now."

"An eternity." Sanderson was already scanning the ballroom. "I shall find myself some shadowed corner and keep an eye on the Walford sons, while you ferret out mother and daughter. I think I've already spied young Master Etienne, in fact." He kissed her hand. "Good luck. We will meet at the front stair in one hour."

"Don't be late this time," said Alice, but Sanderson was already gone.

Alone, Alice mustered her best public smile, snapped open her fan, and sailed through the crowds to the doorway where their hostess stood, welcoming her guests and beaming with pride. Augustina stood beside her mother, nodding her head and murmuring pleasantries.

Sanderson might wish to remain discreet, but Alice saw nothing wrong with disconcerting the Walfords. If they were nervous and prone to mistakes, so much the better.

". . . such a very important cause," a dowager in too much powder and too many frills was saying. "The families of our brave fighting men *must not* be allowed to suffer, especially at the Christmas season."

"Thank you so much." Mrs. Walford squeezed the other woman's hands. "I trust you'll remember that when our auction begins." She turned toward Alice with a vaguely welcoming smile before the other woman had to commit herself.

"Mrs. Walford?" Alice made her curtsy. "We have not been formally introduced, but I'm Alice Littlefield. We met at Miss Thorne's the other day."

She watched concern flicker behind Mrs. Walford's eyes as she remembered what day that must have been.

"Of course," she said smoothly. "How do you do, Miss Littlefield? Have you met my daughter, Augustina?"

The sound of her name pulled Augustina's attention down to Alice, and Alice saw her eyes widen.

"How very nice to meet you, Miss Littlefield," Augustina murmured.

"And you, Miss Walford. What a lovely event. The decorations are beautiful."

"Thank you, I do hope you will enjoy yourself."

"I'm certain I shall." She smiled and nodded vaguely and stepped away, so that she would not hold up the line of people waiting for Mrs. Walford's attention. A glance over her shoulder told her that Augustina was watching where she went.

Alice strolled into the reception room as if she meant to examine the items out on display that would later be auctioned off.

Four, three, two . . . she counted.

"Miss Littlefield."

She smiled and turned toward Augustina.

"Miss Walford."

"I had no idea you were joining us this evening."

"Strictly in a professional capacity, I assure you," said Alice easily.

"I don't understand . . ."

Alice leaned in close. "Don't tell anyone," she said in a

stage whisper. "But I am also A.E. Littlefield. I'm here to write about the event for the *London Chronicle*."

"Oh! Oh, I see. Well. Perhaps you'll deliver a message to Miss Thorne on our behalf, when you see her next."

"I'd be glad to," said Alice, but inside she felt distinctly wary.

Augustina's smile broadened, but when Alice looked into her eyes, they were still cold. "Please make sure she knows that the whole of this evening is her doing. Not one bit of this would have happened without her."

Before Alice could answer, Augustina glided off into the thickest part of the crowd.

The carriage turned the corner, easing into the shadows on the far side of the assembly rooms. The driver slowed the horses to a bare walk through the stretch of darkness. Rosalind pushed the curtains back and strained her eyes to the limit to try to see what might be happening in the little alleyway that branched off from the main street.

Motion caught her eye. She banged on the carriage ceiling. Rogers drew the reins up and brought the carriage to a halt.

Two men stood at the alley mouth. One was gesturing toward the high street.

She knew that confident motion, and she knew him.

"Adam!" she cried. Then she remembered to let the window glass down.

Adam, of course, saw the carriage and then he saw her. Glancing quickly in each direction, he ducked across the street. Rosalind opened the door so he could climb in. She also knocked on the ceiling to let Rogers know they should walk on.

"Hullo." He smiled as he settled on the seat across from her.

"I don't . . . I didn't . . . you didn't send any word!" Rosalind was aware she sounded like she was scolding, but she really couldn't help it.

"There was no time," he said. "It all happened late this afternoon and there was a fair amount to arrange."

"How did you convince Mr. Townsend to let you come?"

"I didn't," he said. "The Prince Regent did."

"The Prince Regent . . ." Rosalind pressed her hand against her mouth. "Oh, Charlotte . . ."

Adam raised both brows. "Charlotte?"

"When you told me you had seen her, I thought she might have the ear of someone who could influence Mr. Townsend. I had no idea who it would be." She sank back against the squabs, amazed.

"Well, we'll both thank her later." Adam leaned forward. "Tell me what you have going."

"Alice and Mr. Faulks are inside watching Salter and the Walfords. I'm to get reports every hour, and we've been circling the building waiting for matters to begin, but we've seen nothing. Including you." She glared at him in mock anger. "Until now, of course."

Adam bowed his head in acknowledgment.

"I've only Captain Goutier and two others with me," he told her. "It's a busy night. The constables who aren't needed at Carlton House are at the opera and the theater. It seems the whole city is having one last burst of revelry before the holiday. But the good news is, Goutier's spied out at least one of their wagons, and he's taken the driver's place."

"Excellent. We'd planned to let the robbery begin, if we could, and then raise the alarm."

Adam nodded seriously. "Well, you may consider the alarm to have been raised, and hopefully we will catch them all red-handed."

Louis Walford was watching the dancers in the bright ballroom. They were all plainly enjoying themselves, but all he could manage to feel was morose and boredom. Time had slowed to a crawl. He was beginning to wonder if the clocks would ever sound midnight, to signal the start of the auction and the supper, and the time for them to finally put their plan into motion.

Someone behind him cleared their throat.

"Mr. Walford? A word if I may?"

Louis turned to see Mr. Hodges, the assembly room's manager, standing discreetly beside the door.

His heart thumped and he took a minute to school his features into a calm mask before he approached the man.

"Nothing wrong I hope?" said Louis. "I'd just been thinking to come find you and let you know what an excellent job you've done."

"Thank you, sir," said Hodges. "I just thought you'd be glad to know we've got a couple of runners on the grounds now, so if you'd any worries—"

"Runners?" To Louis's shame, the word came out as a squeak. "Bow Street's here?"

"Yes, sir," said Hodges. "Now, the principal officer, Mr. Harkness, he's asked to keep it all quiet, the better to flush out any thieves who might have designs on the place, but as you'd been so worried about our security measures, I thought I'd tip you the nod, as it were. You should keep it to yourself, of course. Although," he added, "you might let your mother know. She was worried as well."

"Yes, of course." Louis swallowed. "I had no idea the runners were planning on being here."

"It'll be Miss Thorne's doing, depend on it," said Hodges. "There's nothing she can't arrange."

"Yes," murmured Louis. "Yes, I'm beginning to understand that."

I just hope it's not too late.

Now he had to find Salter.

*   *   *

"Salter."

The music and the noise of the dancer's feet almost drowned out the sound of his name, but Salter knew at once who was speaking. He would have known her voice in a crowd much larger and louder than this. Salter eased himself backward, fading toward the wall. Augustina was already there, sheltered from the view of much of the gathering by one of the room's bunting draped pillars.

She looked flushed. He'd only seen her truly nervous once or twice before, and never without cause.

"What is it?" he asked softly.

"Miss Thorne's set some of her people on us, Salter," Augustina answered. "There's a Miss Littlefield here, and I've just spotted Sanderson Faulks."

Salter pursed his lips in a soundless whistle. "Well, we knew that was a possibility, even if she couldn't be here herself."

"Yes, I know. I do. But I'm worried. Etienne's jumpy as a cat, and Mother's starting to notice."

"How is Louis?"

She shook her head. "Grim. Pacing. They're going to lose their nerve, Salter. Soon."

"And you?"

She smiled gamely. "Never."

"I know," he breathed. "Tell you what. I'll go take a turn through the rooms, just to make sure everything's all right. You go tell your brothers that's what I'm about. See if you can think of some small things to keep them occupied."

"Yes, all right. I'll drag one or the other of them out on the dance floor so we can talk."

"Good idea." He stretched his hand out, and she touched his fingertips to hers. "Almost done. Just three hours, my dearest, and then we fly."

"I wish we were already gone."

"Three more hours," he repeated, careful to suppress his annoyance. She needed to stop saying that. She needed her mind on where they were now. *He* needed her mind on where they were now. "Trust me that long."

He told himself it meant nothing that he had to say that. Of course she trusted him, as he trusted her. There was no doubt.

She brushed his hand again and slipped out from behind the pillar. He watched her navigating the edges of the dance floor, pausing to exchange greetings and pleasantries with the guests. So beautiful, so natural. With her beside him, there was nothing he could not do.

Now he just had to make sure they could stay together.

Salter tugged on his jacket to straighten it; put a polite, bored smile on his face; and strolled away in the opposite direction.

The carriage pulled to a stop beneath the flickering street-lamp just as the bells began to ring. With the skill of a born Londoner, Rosalind fastened on the sound of a single bell in the ragged cacophony and counted its steady tolling.

Eleven o'clock.

The carriage rocked as the driver and one of the outriders climbed down to check on the horses and probably to reassure them as well. It was not only the human beings who were having a long night.

The footwarmers had died about a half an hour ago, and the cold was beginning to creep into the carriage, but at least she was out of the wind. She hoped Sanderson was going to offer his men something extra for their duty tonight.

She rubbed her hands together and pushed the window curtains a bit farther. There were still knots of loiterers on the walk in front of the assembly rooms, but most people had sought shelter. Despite the lamplight coming from the windows, she couldn't make out any silhouette that looked like Alice or Mr. Faulks.

The bells had faded away. Rosalind told herself to be patient. All was right. They were not in this alone. She was not alone. All that was required of her was that she wait and keep alert.

And it was still too much.

Muttering some highly unladylike curses at the limited field of view offered by the window, she snapped the catches and let down the glass so she could stretch out and see farther up the walk. It was not something a polite woman did, of course, but she was hardly engaged in a polite activity.

It seemed that impropriety could have its reward. As she watched, she saw Adam emerge from one of the little areas that provided access to the assembly rooms' lower floors and cellars.

She reached out for the handle and opened the door, but he held up both hands.

"I only have a moment," he said. "I've spoken to Mr. Hodges and let him know we're here, and I found Mr. Faulks." He shook his head. "If ever he wants to give up . . . whatever it is he does . . . I'd be happy to take him on at Bow Street. I've never seen a man do such a job of shadowing in all my days."

Rosalind laughed. "I'll let him know. Are all our Walfords safe inside?"

"As of ten minutes ago. Miss Walford has been seen with Mr. Salter. Mr. Hodges says his men are reporting all is quiet down in the strong room."

"And the money was brought? As we expected?"

Adam nodded. "I had a word with one of the guards. He said they'd spent a good half hour loading in the boxes before the start of the ball."

"Did you let him know to be on the alert?"

"I'm waiting for signs of movement," he said. "I don't want to give them time to get jumpy. Those fellows are bully boys, not constables. They talk too much and get too nervous. At least one's half-drunk already. One or another might even get it into their heads that actually having to stop a thief is not what they signed up for and just walk away, and then we're a man down if there's a fight." He touched her hand where it rested on the windowsill. "How have things been out here?"

"Entirely quiet," said Rosalind. "I'm starting to wonder if I was mistaken about their plans."

"There's another hour until the auction, and the supper," Adam reminded her. "They won't move before that."

"What makes you so sure?"

"Greed. There should be another hundred pounds or so gathered in for what's on offer. They won't want to leave that behind."

"No, I expect not." She made a face. "I wish I was inside."

"I know. I could remind you that I feel better with an extra pair of eyes out here."

"Would you mean it?"

"Yes."

Rosalind smiled. "Very well, then, I shall remind myself of that once every quarter hour." She paused. "You should go."

He took up her hand and held it for one brief moment. Then, he turned and strode back the way he'd come. Rosalind waited a minute before she let the glass back up. Suddenly, she was not cold at all.

She did not see the man standing on the walk turn and hurry after Adam, his hat brim pulled low over his brow.

Louis finally found Salter coming up the narrow backstairs, slowly and thoughtfully. His expression was as if he was pondering some deep question of philosophy.

Louis's blood burned. If they hadn't been in public, he would have grabbed the man and planted a fist in his face to remind him how serious tonight's business was.

This was it. This was his chance to get away from Mother and her causes and her schemes. Away from Etienne and his posturing, away from a future of factories and figures and other people ordering him around. Deciding who needed to live and who needed to die, and expecting him to do the dirty work.

He hated the fact that he'd all but fed Augustina to this creature, but there'd been no other way. He was realistic enough to know he needed someone with Salter's nerve and experience to pull this off.

Louis dragged his mind back to the present and strode over to Salter, cutting him off before he could get to the auction room door.

"Where the hell have you been?" he demanded in a rough whisper.

It would have taken a much denser man to miss the urgency in his tone.

"What's the matter, Louis?" Salter folded his hands behind his back and ambled slowly away, letting Louis fall into step beside him. Louis kept his tone casual and remembered to nod to the guests as they drifted past.

"It seems our inestimable Miss Thorne has found a way to make trouble after all. I just heard from Hodges that she's brought Bow Street down on us."

Salter muttered under his breath. "So that's who she was with out there."

"What? She's *here*?"

"Yes, she's here, and so are her friends." He paused, and his eyes darted this way and that, looking at the faces, the windows, the doorways. "We need to start shifting things, now."

Louis blanched. "We can't . . ."

Salter chuckled knowingly, as if Louis had just told a lewd joke. Then he leaned in and whispered in his ear, "Louis, listen to me. We're caught. It's already happened. Our only hope is to move as quickly as possible and slip through the net before it's entirely closed. You go find Augustina, and tell her to get everything ready, and meet me at the area door. She'll know which one."

Frustration burned, but Louis knew he was right. "And what are you going to do?"

Salter drew back and returned a small, quiet smile. "Take care of Bow Street."

Sampson Goutier blew on his fingers and slapped his arms, trying to smack some warmth back into himself. *You owe me for this one, Harkness.* He cast an eye on the lowering clouds. After years in the navy, and then again a member of the river police, he'd thought himself immune to damp and cold. But tonight London was pulling out all her tricks—her drafts and her drips, and her slush sloughing off rooftops right down a man's collar.

And her snow. He eyed the clouds. *Don't forget all the bloody snow.*

He glanced down the alley in either direction. At one end, a footman in the wig and caped coat of the room's livery shifted uncomfortably from foot to foot. Sampson grinned. Poor Perkins. Well, they'd make it up to the lad somehow.

In the other direction, two idlers lounged against a wall, passing a jug between them. One of them, as if sensing Sampson's gaze on him, raised the jug in salute. Sampson nodded his reply.

The off horse whickered uneasily and stamped its foot.

"I know, I know." Sampson caught the horse's bridle and stroked its nose, bringing his face close so his warm breath blew on the horse's cold skin. "I'm not exactly having a grand time, either."

It was a bad night to keep the horses standing. The cold was going to be getting into their joints. *God knows it's getting into mine.*

Knowing he'd be out with a pair of cart animals that would be anything from overworked to bad-tempered, or both, Sampson had taken care to provide himself with some winter apples. He pulled one out of his pocket now, along with his pocketknife, and offered a half to the restless beast. The ragged horse nuzzled the treat and chomped.

"Soon." He told the animal as he rubbed its ears. "Hot mash for you, hot brandy for me, eh?"

A sound reached him, a light footstep against stone. Sampson whirled around, causing the horse to whinny in high-pitched annoyance.

But there was no one there.

Adam stalked through the cellars of the assembly rooms. The warren was brightly lit, with staff scurrying to and fro, getting ready for the supper. It looked like chaos, but there was order to the activity, and no sign, at least to Adam's eye, of it being disturbed by any untoward activity.

Yet. His jaw shifted. He needed to check the storeroom again. The back of his neck was prickling. Adam didn't believe in instinct, but he felt sure that something was happening.

He'd just pivoted on his heel, when he heard footsteps coming up the flagstone corridor behind him.

It was Mr. Hodges puffing up to him.

"Mr. Harkness! It's Miss Thorne!" the manager cried. "You're needed at once. She says come meet her and Miss Littlefield outside."

Not bothering to stop long enough to thank the man, Adam pushed past him and into the kitchen, then out the door and up the stairs into the darkness of the street. The cold hit him like a wall. He saw the carriage in the distance.

As he passed by one of the areas, Adam felt the shift in the air, but he was not fast enough. He heard the grunt, felt the breeze, began to pivot, but the blow took him in the small of the back, and the pain robbed him all ability to move.

The second blow came as a fresh burst of pain against his skull. Adam saw stars. Then he saw nothing at all.

CHAPTER 52

Execution

Necessity had no law.

Maria Edgeworth, *Belinda*

Alice was beginning to get worried. It had been a good quarter hour since she'd last spotted Augustina Walford.

Everything had been going well enough. She'd seen Miss Walford come out from behind her pillar, where she'd doubtlessly been stealing a moment with her Mr. Salter. She'd circled the ballroom calmly enough, talking to the guests and enduring some remarks from her mother.

"Why, Miss Littlefield!" cried a voice at her shoulder. "I didn't know you'd be here."

Alice had wanted to close her eyes and groan. But of course she couldn't. Instead, she put on her sunniest smile for the dowager, who hailed her from one of the little gilt chairs reserved for the chaperones.

"Lady DeRoverea! How lovely! I had no idea you were going to be here, either." Daniella DeRoverea was another of those ladies of fading fortune who kept their place in society largely by being a reliable and entertaining gossip, and as such, Alice was always glad of her acquaintance.

Almost always.

"Well, it's late in the year, needs must." Lady DeRoverea glanced about the room. "Even a few hours in this motley collection. Have you seen any news?"

"Not yet." Alice leaned in, close and confidential. "But I might, if I'm allowed to continue."

"Oh, you sly thing!" Lady DeRoverea pinched Alice's arm playfully. "You must come back and tell me all about it."

Alice had laughed and promised, and slipped past as quickly as she could.

But by then Augustina was gone, and try though she might, Alice hadn't seen her since. Sweat was beading around her hairline. Worry made it increasingly difficult to appear casual as she moved from room to room.

And it was almost time for her next meeting with Mr. Faulks. Alice tapped her fan against her wrist and headed for the auction room.

"Augustina!" Louis caught up with her at the bottom of the backstairs. "Where on earth . . ."

Augustina knew how she looked—rattled and out of breath. How else should she look? Everything was collapsing. Everything *had* collapsed, and for all their glorious, clever planning, not one of them had seen it happen.

"Louis. Thank goodness." She swiftly took her brother's arm and steered him into the ballroom. Thankfully the musicians had just struck up another country dance and the noise would cover all they said.

"I've just been down to the strong room," Louis was saying. "No one's . . ."

"Shut up!" she whispered hurriedly. "We're nicked!"

Louis stared at her. "What are you talking about?"

"Bow Street. They're here."

"I knew that!" he sneered. He actually had the nerve to

sneer. "Hodges let it slip. Salter says you're to get everything ready and meet him by the area door, and that you'd—"

Augustina cut him off. "It's no good. They already put one of their men in for our carter, and they're watching the alley front and back."

That, at least, was enough to make him pay real attention. "My God . . ."

"Yes," she agreed. "I'm going to warn Salter. Get Etienne and the two of you go to the card room. Get a table near the back door. One of us will come up that way and let you know the plan to get us out."

"You're not the one giving—"

"I am!" she snapped. "There's no time for argument. Go!"

Thankfully, Louis went. *That will keep them both well out of the way.*

"Augustina? I hope nothing's wrong?"

Mother was coming down the stairs, carefully, of course, so as not to tread on her elegant hems.

Augustina swallowed a scream. Of course it was Mother. She always managed to appear at just the worst moment. Augustina faced her and waved her fan. *Be airy, be sunny*, she ordered herself. *Pretend it's all such a good joke.*

"Oh, Etienne's just been hanging about the card room too much," Augustina said. "I sent Louis after him. They should be out here with the guests."

Mother's expression was impassive. You'd have had to know her very well to see the chill of worry in her blue eyes. "I just wanted to say you've been doing an excellent job this evening, 'Stina. I know this has not been easy for you."

Augustina laughed, a high, horrible titter. "Well, if there's one thing I know how to do, it's put on a show."

Mother grimaced. "And your Mr. Salter? Where is he?"

"Actually, I was just going to find him." This, finally, was the truth. "You'll excuse me?" She made to brush past her, but Mother stopped her with a word.

"Augustina?"

Augustina balanced on her toes, as if she meant to run. Perhaps she did. She made herself settle down on her heels and turn. "Yes?"

Mother moved closer. Augustina smelled musk roses, powder, and sweat. "You know the building is watched tonight."

Augustina's heart froze. *What do you know? What have you seen?*

"I had wondered," she breathed. "I thought it might be."

"Yes, a last gift from Miss Thorne it seems." She smiled briefly, keeping her attention more on the crowd than on Augustina. "You'll be on time for the auction?"

"Of course," said Augustina brightly. "I'll find Salter and we'll be there straightaway."

Mother reached out and took a lock of Augustina's hair between her fingers, tightening the curl as she used to when 'Stina was a little girl. "I hope . . . I very much hope . . . that you will find a way to be happy, 'Stina. That's all I've ever really wanted."

Augustina felt a lump in her throat. She could not make herself answer. She kissed her mother and gave her a brief hug before she hurried away.

Because Mother knew perfectly well something was wrong, and she was saying good-bye.

Alice was quite sure she'd never been so glad to see Sanderson Faulks as she was now. Dropping pretenses, she rushed over to where he stood at by the railing at the top of the stairs.

"We've lost Miss Walford," she told him. "It's my fault. I found her talking to her mother and then her mother got in my way and wanted to talk and I lost her again."

"I admit, I find that more than mildly concerning." Mr. Faulks was watching the stream of people heading toward the auction room. "Our Mr. Salter seems to have given me the slip as well. As has Louis Walford."

"Louis?" breathed Alice. "Surely not."

Mr. Faulks shrugged one shoulder. His eyes never stopped scanning the crowd. "We did say two was not going to be enough for this little game. Why not bring one or more brothers into it?"

"Especially if they were going to need to get out of town on their own accounts. Blast it," Alice muttered through clenched teeth. "Things must be moving. I'll go see if I can station myself somewhere en route to the strong room. You'd better go tell Rosalind, and find Mr. Harkness."

"Harkness first," said Sanderson. "He'll need to alert his men."

Alice nodded in agreement. "And I'll talk to Mr. Hodges on the way."

Sanderson touched her shoulder briefly. "Take care, Alice. If I fail to bring you home, I rather think that little maid of yours will have my guts for garters."

Sanderson bowed and breezed away.

It took forever for Augustina to work her way through the kitchen. She had to pretend to be merely checking to make sure everything was going smoothly, which meant she also had to listen to Mrs. Hodges extoll the excellence of each one of her staff. When Augustina finally escaped into the relative quiet of the warren of storage and cellar, her heart was hammering like she'd just run a hundred miles.

The workroom where she and Salter had agreed to meet in case of emergency was dark. A little bit of torchlight filtered through the head-high windows, but he'd lit no candle nor lamp.

So, at first Augustina thought the bundle at his feet was nothing but a heap of old clothes. It wasn't until her toes touched the boot soles that she realized it was a man.

Her heart stopped dead. The world swam and blurred and threatened to fade away altogether.

"What have you . . . what have you . . ." she choked.

"It's all right, he's just unconscious."

Augustina couldn't stop staring. She had gone ice-cold. She was shaking.

"You're sure? You're sure, Salter?"

"I promise." Salter wrapped his arms around her. "Come on, pull yourself together, dearest."

Yes, pull yourself together. Augustina squeezed her eyes shut.

"We have to get out of here," she breathed.

He sighed sharply. "'Stina, I *told* you. He's fine."

"But we're not." Her eyes flew open. "The alley's watched. Bow Street's put a runner on the cart. We're done for."

Salter stared at her. She watched him struggling to turn her words into something other than what they were—the end of everything.

He let her go and paced away, and then back. He ran both hands through his hair and looked down at the crumpled form at his feet.

The kick he aimed at the man's stomach was swift and savage. Augustina slapped both hands over her mouth to muffle her scream.

"Damnit, no!" Salter roared through clenched teeth. "I did not plan so hard for it all to come to nothing!"

Augustina caught him by both arms. "It's *over*, Salter. We lost. We need to go. I'll get a cab. We can be out of London in an hour and catch the stage to Dover from the Greensward Inn . . ."

"I said no! We'll go to the strong room, make some excuse, get the men—"

"Salter!" She shook him, hard. "It won't work!"

"It will! If you just . . ."

"I will not *just*!" she said, dropping her voice low. They

were in danger of being heard. "I am leaving, whether you come with me or not. I've already . . . we've already . . . we'll be caught, Salter, we'll be *hanged*. Please. I'm begging you. Save yourself. Save me."

He stared at her as if he did not recognize her. One heartbeat. Two. Three.

Eternity.

Salter let his breath out in one long, shuddering sigh. "Yes, all right. Get the cab, have them pull up outside. We'll bring him and dump him on the road somewhere once we're sure of our escape."

Now it was Augustina's turn to stare. "Why?"

"Because if Bow Street gives chase, we may need a bargaining chip."

They rounded the corner onto the high street yet again. Rosalind was becoming heartily sick of her patrol. She would rather have paced up and down the walk herself at this point. She could hardly have been colder. Well, perhaps she could. The wind nudged playfully at the side of the carriage and made the fresh falling snow swirl and sparkle in the torch light.

But the snow was not yet so thick that she didn't see the coatless man standing under the streetlight.

"*Stop!*" Rosalind beat her fist against the carriage ceiling. But the driver had already seen and was turning the horses to draw up beside the curbstone.

Rosalind let the glass down. Snowflakes swirled in, stinging her eyes and cheeks.

"Mr. Faulks!" she cried. "What is it?"

"Harkness is missing," Sanderson said breathlessly. "So is Salter."

Rosalind, struggling with skirts and coat, lunged for the door. "Where is Miss Walford?"

"Gone as well."

Rosalind stared up and down the street. Where could they be? What could have happened? Could Adam have been taken unawares? Her mind threatened to go blank.

What do I do? What do I do?

She saw the two women in turbans and plumes, the crowd of dandies arguing with one another, the man supporting his drunken companion into the cab, the old woman leaning on her young companion, gesturing to the harassed-looking gentleman . . .

Rosalind's head whipped around, instinct answering where eyesight had not.

The man with his drunken companion, coming up the area stairs. The sagging man's head turned, showing her just a flash of profile, a line of chin and shoulder in the shadows, but Rosalind could never be mistaken.

That was Adam Harkness staggering into the dark, and Horatio Salter who held him up. The approaching cab negotiated its way to an empty spot on the cobbles.

Rosalind yanked her bonnet off her head with one hand and ripped a pin from her hair with the other. Ignoring the stares, and the shouts, Rosalind ran.

She ran for dear life—her life, Adam's life. Her old boots slipped on ice, and she tumbled to the ground and bounced up again like an India rubber ball. She felt nothing. She just kept running.

She crashed into someone. She stumbled, righted herself, and ran.

The cab door opened. Hands reached out. Adam was waking up and beginning to struggle. The driver was climbing off the box, offering to help.

"Hurry!" shouted someone.

"She's gone mad!" shouted someone else.

She missed her step and her ankle turned. Pain jolted up her leg, and she nearly lost hold of her bonnet and pin.

Horatio Salter shoved Adam against the cab and turned to

face Rosalind with his hands out. Rosalind shoved her bonnet right into his face. Salter cursed and batted it away.

She jammed her hairpin into his hand.

Salter screamed and staggered.

"Here now!" The driver grabbed Rosalind's shoulders and hauled her backward.

"The watch! The watch!" cried Rosalind. "Murder!"

Now heads turned, glasses were raised. So were the lanterns and the torches of the drivers and outriders from the other carriages.

"What are you on about?" The cabman whirled Rosalind around.

"She's mad!" cried another voice. Augustina. In the cab.

"She's not." Adam pressed himself against the cab, fighting to stay on his feet.

"She's mad, and he's drunk," said Salter firmly, holding his bleeding hand. "Help us here, fellow."

The driver looked from Adam to Rosalind to Salter.

"There!" shrieked another voice. "Unhand her, you cad!"

Alice. Of course it was. Charging up the walk with Sanderson Faulks right behind.

Rosalind yanked herself out of the driver's hands and dodged sideways to Adam. She dragged him back away from the cab. He struggled and sagged, almost taking her down with him.

"She has a gun," he mumbled.

Rosalind jerked her head around, staring into the cab. Augustina crouched between the seats. She clutched a tiny gleaming pistol in her gloved hand and pointed it directly at Rosalind.

"Get up on the box, Salter," Augustina ordered.

Rosalind drew herself up. The world seemed suddenly still. She couldn't even feel her own heartbeat anymore.

"Which of us are you going to shoot, Augustina?" she asked calmly.

"Does it matter?"

"A little. But you should realize you have nowhere to go afterwards. Not like when you killed my father."

"What?" cried Alice. She and Sanderson had reached them. Rosalind had entirely forgotten they were following. She could not acknowledge them now. The only really important things in this moment were Augustina and that gun.

Salter was staring at Augustina.

"Salter, get up on the box!" Augustina cried. "We've got to get out of here!"

"Here, you are not taking my cab!" shouted the cabman.

The driver jumped forward, the gun swung around. Adam leaned in and lost his balance. Sanderson grabbed him. Alice grabbed Salter.

Rosalind dove headfirst into the cab—heedless of dignity and pain and safety—and grabbed Augustina's wrist. There was a shouting and screaming, and the girl squirmed, and the gun barrel flashed.

The shot rang out, a cloud of smoke. Rosalind screamed, at least she thought she did. She was quite deaf. She staggered backward, the useless gun in her hands. The heat of the barrel shot through her gloves a moment later, and she screamed again and dropped it.

There was commotion, she supposed, and shouting. But all she was aware of was Augustina, staring at her, her hands fallen helplessly at her sides.

Rosalind was breathing. Augustina was breathing. There was no blood—

"Somebody's paying for that!" shouted the cabman. "Out, you fool girl! Git out, I sez!"

—because the bullet had gone through the roof of the cab.

Alice grabbed Rosalind by the shoulders and turned her. She was saying something. Rosalind's ears rang. Alice waved her hand in front of Rosalind's face and then hugged her.

"All right. You're all right."

Salter yanked Augustina out of the cab and began dragging her down the street.

"Stop them," mumbled Rosalind.

"Hold this!" cried Sanderson. He shoved Adam toward the women.

Sanderson ran like a greyhound and grabbed Salter by his wounded arm before he'd gotten more than a few yards. Augustina screamed and lunged for him, but Sanderson dodged backward.

"Bow Street!" bellowed a new voice. "Bow Street!"

Captain Goutier, and Mr. Townsend, and the other runners were there now, coming down the steps, and up the walk, and even up the stairs from the basement. The crowd was shouting and jostling and cheering.

"Now then! Now then! Stand back! We're needing room here!" Captain Goutier waded through the crowd to meet Mr. Faulks and take Salter from his arms, so now Salter only had to deal with Augustina.

Rosalind turned. She felt light as a feather. She noticed Alice was crouched on the walk, heedless of her lovely dress, holding Mr. Harkness upright.

Slowly, carefully, Rosalind came and sat down beside them.

"Let her go!" Salter was shouting as he twisted uselessly in Captain Goutier's hands. "She has nothing to do with it!"

"She does," said Rosalind, but then she realized that no one would be able to understand her from down here. So, reluctantly, she climbed back onto her feet. It was far harder than it should have been.

She faced Augustina Walford, who Sanderson still held tight. There was no telling which of them was more disheveled. She noted how the snow clung to the other woman's hair and melted to make droplets like tears on her cheeks.

"How did you know?" Augustina asked.

"My father was waiting up for my sister when he died," she said. "He was drunk, so he didn't hear you when you crept in. Did you know who you killed? Or did you realize your mistake afterwards?" she asked. Augustina looked away. "You must have thought quickly when you saw you'd gotten the wrong man. You must have understood that Fullerton on the run because of a murder charge would be just as good as Fullerton dead. And so you stabbed him a second time, to make sure." Rosalind, in that distant place her mind seemed to have gone, felt something like admiration. "You knew exactly what you were doing when you spoke to me at Upton's. You wanted to point me to your brothers. The two men Fullerton said—" She stopped. "Why did he implicate two men?" Her brow furrowed.

"Because they were supposed to kill Salter," said Augustina. She was trying to straighten up and regain some of her own dignity. "Mother had realized he was up to something more than courting me. Your little bits of information allowed her to put the pieces together. So, she sent them to take care of him, and they went. They *went*," she repeated viciously. "But poor dears let themselves be talked out of it." She smiled fondly at Salter. "He was able to blame everything on Fullerton and said he had all the plans that we'd so carefully forged. He said if they wanted to keep the family safe, it was Fullerton they needed. So they decided to let Salter, their good friend, go and went after Fullerton instead."

"Augustina, please stop," said Salter.

"But you'd already done the work," said Rosalind.

"As always." Augustina sighed. She turned to her lover and took his hand. "I'm sorry," she breathed. "I am. But Fullerton never would have let us go. Not even after we paid him off. He would have come back."

She was right, of course. He would have, months, days, and years later, he would have kept on coming.

Rosalind realized she was beginning to tremble. Her reserves of strength, such as they were, were all beginning to fail.

"What in God's name is happening!" cried a woman's voice.

Mrs. Walford. Rosalind did not have the strength to turn around. It didn't matter.

"It's an arrest, ma'am," answered Captain Goutier. "Miss Augustina Walford, I am arresting you in the King's name on the charge of murder most foul and the breach of the King's Peace for the deaths of Sir Reginald Thorne and Mr. Turrell Sparkes . . ."

"What!" cried Mrs. Walford. "Stop this! My daughter has killed no one!"

"You stop, Mother," said Augustina. "Just stop. Go back to Louis and Etienne. I'm ready. I am." She turned to Captain Goutier. "Please, take me away from here."

The captain handed her to the constable. "Perkins, you take charge of her while I help Mr. Harkness."

Perkins took hold of both of Augustina's shoulders. The young woman let herself be led docilely away.

Mrs. Walford drew herself up. Rosalind, from that distant place she'd gone, watched curiously at the cold determination that came over her expression.

"She did not kill the man Sparkes," announced Mrs. Walford. "I did."

All the assembled crowd stared. Augustina wrenched herself around in Perkins's grip so she could stare, too.

Rosalind bowed her head.

"You knew," she said. "You knew it had been Augustina."

"There was no one else," said Mrs. Walford. "The boys . . . when I heard about their failure with Salter, I knew it could not be them. I killed him to silence him." She looked Augustina directly in the eyes. "To protect my daughter."

There was commotion. There were questions and shouting. Rosalind paid no attention to any of it. She just sank back down beside Adam and shivered. It was very cold. Except for where his skin touched hers. That was not cold at all.

"You saved me," he mumbled.

"I'd say it was about time, wouldn't you?" answered Rosalind.

Then, she leaned her head against his and let the world go away for a while.

CHAPTER 53

Laid at Last to Rest

*The great man murmured away his useless life,
ringing the golden bells of his gorgeous rattle with
as doleful a measure as though they were solem-
nizing a funeral.*

Catherine Gore, *The Banker's Wife*

It was not precisely a social rule that forbid women from attending the burial of a loved one. It was more a sign of
consideration. It would not do for anyone to become too
emotional during that particular ceremony; therefore, it was
thought advisable that anyone who might be prone to exces-
sive weeping, or—heaven forbid—fainting, should remain at
home.

Rosalind felt she had done quite enough fainting for a
while. It really was a cold, undignified activity.

The funeral had been arranged for the afternoon. Which
turned out to be just as well. It allowed Rosalind to be present for another—she supposed she should call it ceremony,
for lack of any better word.

Russell Fullerton had been released from prison this morning. Rosalind had been there, standing in the street outside

the prison, waiting for him. She'd told Alice she was walking by herself for a while, before the funeral.

That was mostly true.

Fullerton had had his finery returned to him—his silk coat, his chains, buckles, and pins, even his hat. He strolled out of the prison gate. The turnkey held his hand out, to shake Mr. Fullerton's or receive a tip, perhaps. Fullerton looked down his long nose at the man and walked away.

Of course, he saw her at once. She was not trying to hide. He sauntered across the street and bowed.

"Miss Thorne. I believe I am in your debt." Fullerton bowed. "Your reputation does not do you justice."

Rosalind nodded.

"I wish you would consider joining forces with me. You do realize that if the two of us worked together, all of London would be at our feet."

Rosalind thought of Augustina, pale and fainting in the constable's arms, with her partner staring after her.

"I think you will not be so anxious to take me into partnership when you hear what I have to say," she told Fullerton.

"Take care, Miss Thorne." He rested both hands on his walking stick. "I am kindly disposed toward you, but that may change. I will not be threatened, even now."

"Nor will I, Mr. Fullerton. Which is why I have sent the papers and letters that were retrieved from your strong box to Mr. John Townsend of the Bow Street police office."

"Papers?" Fullerton arched one brow.

"Certain documents and letters discovered in your rooms, some of which pertain to plans for the rescue of the emperor from St. Helena."

Fullerton had sensibly divided his spoils so that they could not all be taken from him at once. Unfortunately, as things turned out, it also meant he had not been able to destroy them all at once.

Fullerton gaped at her. "Those plans were false! You must know that!"

"Must I? Well, I shall write to Mr. Townsend as soon as I have the time. Also, the Countess Lieven, of course. She has been made aware of their existence. I believe her husband the ambassador and Lord Palmerston, who is a very good friend, have also taken an interest."

"You're lying," he growled.

Rosalind looked at him coolly.

"I should wring your neck."

Rosalind said nothing.

"I will have you in the end, Miss Thorne. You will not—"

"I suggest we end this conversation, Mr. Fullerton," said Rosalind firmly. "I'm sure you have a great deal to do. And when the day comes that you do complete your revenge against me, please be aware that the *London Chronicle* will publish a second large bundle of letters and papers, with advantages, detailing the extent of your predations against London's aristocracy, including your scheme for aiding the Bonapartists. I believe there may be a series written on the subject, and that certain publishers have already expressed an interest in putting out a bound version."

Fullerton stared at her, his face utterly blank. Then, much to Rosalind's surprise, he began to laugh. It was a long, loud, full-bodied laugh. He bowed as well, sweeping off his hat to her in the deepest, most complimentary fashion. Then, he had turned and walked away, swinging his cane freely until he had vanished into the London crowd.

Now, though, Rosalind stared at the open grave with its plain coffin lying at the bottom. The day was damp and confining with the clouds settled so low over the graveyard it felt like if she reached up, she'd graze them with her fingertips.

She was quite alone. Charlotte was late. Or not coming. Or something. During the service, Rosalind had sat in the church with Alice on one side of her and Adam on the other and tried not to resent it. No old friend from the past had come. No cousin, however distant.

Adam had taken her arm as they walked in procession behind the hearse, but he was at the bottom of the hill now, with the others. Even the vicar had gone. She was still here. The sextants were waiting to start their work, and she was waiting . . .

For what exactly?

"I rather imagine I am supposed to pray for the repose of your soul, and so forth," she said to the open grave. "Or at least that I should hope one day I am able to do so. I confess, though, now I find I am mostly disappointed. You see, Father, I had a great deal to tell you." She paused for a moment and then went on softly. "It was my intention to explain in great detail to you about how quickly Mother broke after you left. It was the bailiffs, and the dunning letters, and all the men we'd never met, who wouldn't believe that we didn't know where you were, or that you'd left us with no money at all.

"She never stopped believing in you, though, which I suppose should please you. To her last breath, she was certain you were coming back. There was no need to do anything but wait. She did not need to eat, or wash, or dress, and in the end, she did not need to breathe.

"But perhaps she can now explain those days better than I can.

"I meant to explain to you what it was to be left alone. To know I had a sister and a father, and to know that they cared nothing for me. That when my mother died, we did not even know how to tell them it had happened. That I was utterly dependent on strangers for my support. That I needed to make a living, and had not the least idea how, because all I had been raised to be was Sir Reginald's daughter.

"I meant to make you listen, just once, even for a single moment, I was going to make you understand, truly, wholly understand what you did to all of us.

"And now I will not even have that."

Rosalind reached into her reticule. She pulled out a bundle of letters tied in black ribbon and dropped them down. They landed on the coffin lid with a dull thud.

"Rosalind?"

It was Charlotte. Rosalind lifted her head and saw her sister standing at the foot of their father's grave. She was in black velvet, and her lace veil billowed in the wind. She looked fine and dramatic. Father would have loved it.

"I'm sorry I was late. I had . . . people to talk to."

"It's all right," said Rosalind. "I'm glad you're here, though. I wanted to thank you for your help."

Charlotte waved this away. "I only did what anyone would."

"Anyone who has some influence in the highest circles."

"Well, I hope you won't be counting on them again." Charlotte picked her way carefully to Rosalind's side. "As of now that is all finished. I pleaded my belly as it were, and have been granted permanent leave from my . . . duties."

Rosalind nodded. "That is probably for the best."

"You won't tell Alice?" said Charlotte quickly. "About my work as a messenger?"

"No, of course not. Charlotte . . . I believe I owe you an apology."

Charlotte gave one of her sparkling laughs. "I believe I shall accept." She laid her hand on Rosalind's arm. "Take care of yourself, Rosalind. And wish me luck."

"Of course I do."

Rosalind embraced her sister and relished the feeling of being held close, despite the wind and the cold. Then, Charlotte released her and straightened; assuming a jaunty air, she turned and sailed away.

Rosalind watched her until she had disappeared among the stones. Emotions poured through her, too many and too fast for her to be able to name them all. Perhaps she never would.

But she turned to go down the hill, threading her own path toward the gates.

And there stood Alice, and Sanderson, and even Amelia hovering in the background with an extra shawl.

And Adam. First and last, and always.

"Well," she said as she drew up to them. "Now we are all here. Let's go home."

AUTHOR'S NOTE

"Truth is stranger than fiction, but it is because Fiction is obliged to stick to possibilities; Truth isn't."

Mark Twain

I've done a lot of research for these stories. Most of it has been around general conditions that would exist in Rosalind's London—how society functioned, how Bow Street operated, how Almack's actually decided who was going to get into its exclusive assemblies. This time, though, I used some very specific, and very strange truths.

Yes, in fact, there were plans to rescue Napoleon from his imprisonment on St. Helena's. Some of them involved a hot air balloon. Some of them involved corsairs outfitted and crewed in Argentina. Napoleon's brother Louis did coordinate efforts from America. There was talk of Napoleon conquering Mexico and using the new empire as a base to reconquer Europe. The submarine was a late entry.

If you're interested in reading about the assorted conspiracies and the outcomes, I recommend *The Emperor's Last Campaign: A Napoleonic Empire in America* by Emilio Ocampo.

The story of the submarine appears in *Smithsonian Magazine*: https://www.smithsonianmag.com/history/the-secret-plot-to-rescue-napoleon-by-submarine-1194764/.

For a summary of the 1814 stock market swindle, you can see https://www.thehistorypress.co.uk/articles/napoleon-is-dead-the-great-stock-exchange-fraud-of-1814/.